STEVEN PETERSEN

The Eye of Odin

A Lightning Goddess Novel

To K, M, O, and E, the inspirations for Thyra. You're all stronger than you know.

Contents

Prologue	1
Chapter 1	10
Chapter 2	22
Chapter 3	34
Chapter 4	40
Chapter 5	52
Chapter 6	65
Chapter 7	76
Chapter 8	84
Chapter 9	91
Chapter 10	106
Chapter 11	119
Chapter 12	127
Chapter 13	134
Chapter 14	152
Chapter 15	163
Chapter 16	176
Chapter 17	195
Chapter 18	199
Chapter 19	209
Chapter 20	216
Chapter 21	233
Chapter 22	236
Chapter 23	254
Chapter 24	266

Chapter 25   268
Chapter 26   284
Chapter 27   292
Epilogue   302
The Lightning Goddess continues the fight! 312
Chapter 1   313
About the Author   318

Prologue

The ground shook as the battering ram struck. The heavy wood gates were close to caving in, and it was clear to the defenders that the battle would soon move inside the walls.

Thor, the god of thunder, looked around at the grim faces surrounding him. They all recognized the truth. They all knew what waited on the other side of those gates, and they knew that they would not be able to withstand the tide that was about to wash over them. Asgard, the home of the Aesir, would fall.

And it was their fault.

The battering ram struck the gates again with a thunderous crash, sending debris and splinters the size of stakes flying through the air. Three men were impaled by those stakes near the front of the lines, but the defenders simply pulled the dead aside and someone else took their place. There was no time for mourning. Not now.

The battering ram was pulled free from the splintered gates, and immediately a hail of arrows and spears came flying through the gap created by the ram. A few more of the defenders fell to the sudden onslaught, thinning their numbers even further, but shields were raised, and a quick volley of arrows from this side of the gate ended the attack.

But another one would come. And another after that. The gates would be battered open the next time the ram struck and then the real battle would begin. Thor did a quick count and realized that there were less than a hundred men and women left to defend the gates.

"We will repel them," a deep voice said at Thor's side. He turned and looked at Odin, the Allfather. Odin wore a grim, determined expression, but Thor could see past the mask to the fear beneath.

"Perhaps," Thor said. "But how many times can we do it? You saw their numbers. It is only a matter of time before they overrun us."

"They will cower before our power," Odin said firmly. "They are peasants. Once they see the gods they worship releasing their fury upon them, they will remember their place."

Thor was not convinced, but the time for arguing the point was past. He had tried dozens of times before, and Odin had refused to see the truth. Now, it was too late.

"The gates would have held if the gatekeeper had been here," Odin muttered. "He has betrayed us."

Thor almost snorted in derision and anger. "Only because he felt betrayed by us."

"He is a traitor to the Aesir!" Odin snapped. "If he ever returns to Asgard, I will kill him myself."

"He won't return," Thor said grimly. *Because there will be nothing left to return to.*

The battering ram swung in again, and this time the meager attempts at strengthening the gates were defeated. The gates crashed open with a resounding bang. For a brief moment, everything stood still. Thor had experienced the same thing in hundreds of battles before. He knew what came next.

The attacking horde came bursting through the torn gates and crashed into the front line of Asgard's defenders. The air was filled with arrows, spears, and the blood-chilling screams as men and women died.

Odin thrust his mighty spear at the attacking horde and a line of flame the color of the sun seared into the first ranks. He roared with the thrill of battle and charged into the fray. Thor was quick to unleash a lightning bolt from Mjolnir, but he did not share his father's euphoria. The outcome was already clear in his mind. He would do as much as he could to save the lives of his fellow defenders, but he had already come to a conclusion about what he needed to do.

He strode forward, lightning flashing into the ranks of the attacking horde and mingling with the magic of the other gods as they sought to hold back the tide. The line of defenders was holding for now, but their numbers were growing thinner with each passing moment. Recognizing this, Thor stayed back and waited for the first hole to appear. When it did, he struck fast and hard, charging forward and swinging his mighty hammer with enough force that it sent the first man hurtling backward into his comrades, knocking several to the ground. Thor sent a bolt of lightning into the ranks of the attackers, scattering them and granting the defenders enough time to close again.

He stepped back and called out over the din of battle, "Hold! Stand strong, defenders of Asgard!"

Down the line, Odin strode to the front, lancing fire into the attacking ranks. He stepped forward, and the defenders followed the Allfather. He pressed forward again, each step reclaiming vital ground. Thor saw what he was trying to do and rallied the defenders in front of him. If they could just push the attackers back to the gates where the enemy would be bottlenecked, they might stand a chance of holding them off.

"Protect the Allfather!" Thor roared. His rally cry was met with cries from the defenders in front of him as they surged forward.

Thor sent another blast of lightning out in front of him and began to move to join the line when something struck him in the chest and threw him backwards. He was airborne for what felt like an eternity before finally falling back to the earth. He rolled to his feet and looked for what had hit him. To his surprise, all of Asgard's defenders were down. Even Odin was on his knees, struggling to stand when a lone figure strode through the gates, a singed banner held in one hand, and a gleaming sword in the other. Even from a distance, Thor recognized the dark hair and pale eyes of Surtur.

"Is that all you have, Asgard?" Surtur yelled in challenge. He strode up to a downed defender and slammed the standard of his banner down savagely into the chest of the man. He looked around, fire in his eyes. "You are not gods! No more will we bow down to you! Asgard is ours!"

Thor watched as the tide of the attacking army began to surge forward again, sweeping around their leader. He saw Odin rise and charge Surtur, his spear leveled for a killing blow, but Surtur saw the attack coming and slapped the spear aside. No novice to battle, Odin accepted the parry and used the momentum to bring his spear sweeping across at neck height. Surtur ducked beneath the spear, and then had to jump back to avoid being gutted as Odin reversed the spear's momentum. In a flash, Surtur leapt forward, his sword searching for Odin's flesh. Spear and sword came together in quick succession and then the two combatants came apart.

Odin fell into a defensive posture, and began to retreat, clearly favoring his left leg. Even from where he stood, Thor could see the reason. A deep gash on Odin's thigh gushed blood, turning his pants red. Surtur raised his sword in the air, the steel dripping red with the Allfather's blood.

"He bleeds! The Allfather bleeds!"

The attacking horde responded by pushing even harder against Asgard's defenders. Thor sent a blast of lightning into the attackers, but he knew it wouldn't be enough. All it did was slow the tide briefly.

But it was long enough for him to meet the one-eyed gaze of Odin. The old man nodded to his son, and Thor's heart sank. He saw the resignation in his father's eyes as the Allfather finally recognized the dire truth. With a bellow, Odin thrust his spear forward, a line of fire lancing into Surtur's horde with devastating effect. Odin kept up the assault, his voice ringing out loudly in a roar of outrage and denial.

And then both his magic and his roar were silenced. The Allfather slowly sagged to the ground, a broadsword through his back. A badly burned, still smoking Surtur pulled his sword free of Odin's body and stood over the dead god. He bent down and lifted Odin's spear overhead.

"To the Hall of Odin!" Thor said to the defenders nearest him. "Go! The gates are lost. Defend the Hall!"

The half dozen men did as they were told and ran further into the city, leaving Thor alone. The rush of Surtur's men began again, and Thor let them come. He gathered his magic and let it swell inside him until he felt like he would burst. He waited, the storm raging inside, until the attacking horde was nearly on him and then unleashed his power in an angry torrent that turned the world blue-white.

He kept the onslaught going until his strength almost failed him. As much as he wanted to stand and fight until he had nothing left, he knew there was something more important he needed to do. Without looking at the damage he had inflicted, he turned on his heels and began to run as thunder rolled away in every direction. He passed the empty, gilded halls of the Aesir without looking. Their splendor was a stark reminder of why this day had come. The flames of Surtur's rage would turn it all to ash and the winds would carry the remains of their hubris away.

He reached the Hall of Odin, the screams of the pursuing army ringing in his ears and swept past what was left of Odin's personal guard. He continued into the very heart of the hall, into Odin's throne room, and slammed the doors behind him.

"What is happening?" a female voice asked in horror. "Where is the

Allfather?"

Thor turned around and faced his mother, Freya. Centuries of life had done nothing to dim her youth, but in that moment, Thor saw the toll those long years had incurred on her. She looked old and frail.

"Odin is dead," Thor said. He crossed the room and passed Freya. "They're all dead, or soon will be. Heimdall, Villi, Ve, Tyr, they've all fallen."

"What?" Freya shook her head. "How?"

"Surtur," Thor answered grimly. "His army will be here soon."

A testament to her strength, Freya didn't let any grief she might have felt show on her face as she followed Thor to the pedestal that stood beside Odin's throne.

"He cannot be allowed to have this," Thor said, looking into the blue flames ringing the Eye of Odin. It felt like a lifetime ago that he had first held the talisman Odin had obtained from Yggdrasil in exchange for his right eye. The Allfather had used the Eye to give power to those he chose and make them gods among men. If Surtur managed to get his hands on it, there was no telling what he would do or what he might be capable of.

"Then we won't let him have it," Freya said. "We stand together."

"And we will fall together." Thor shook his head. "I will not risk leaving the Eye open for the taking."

"What will you do?" Freya asked. "You cannot run and hide. As long as you live, Surtur will hunt you. There will be no safe place for you as long as you carry the Eye."

Freya was right. If Thor tried to steal away with the Eye Surtur would follow, and he wouldn't stop until he had both Thor and the Eye.

There was only one way to keep the Eye from Surtur's grasp.

"Then I will take away his reason for hunting me."

Freya shook her head. "I don't understand."

"He wants the Eye," Thor said. "I won't let him have it. It's too dangerous for any one man to have."

"What are you saying?"

Instead of answering, Thor began to draw on his magic, filling himself until he felt like he was going to be torn apart. He gripped Mjolnir in both hands and used it as a conduit to draw even more power. The hammer began to throb with power, lightning dancing around it in a dizzying display.

"Thor," Freya said, taking a tentative step back, clearly understanding what he meant to do. "You can't do this!"

"This is the only way," Thor said. "The Eye must be destroyed!"

He raised his hammer overhead and swung it with a mighty roar.

Time stood still as Mjolnir met the Eye of Odin, the magic of Thor's hammer and the magic of the orb mixing and then opposing each other. Thor channeled every bit of magic he could draw into the hammer, willing it to destroy the Eye. He felt the magic of the Eye swell in response as it attempted to defend itself.

Thor put every last bit of strength he had left into the blow, ignoring the searing pain that ran through his body. He felt the magic of the Eye waver slightly, and then crumble. Resistance gone, Mjolnir continued it's devastating arc, striking the orb and shattering it.

The destruction of the Eye created a vacuum that pulled Thor forward and then threw him backwards as the magic of the Eye exploded outward. He slid across the floor, finally coming to a stop against the doors of the throne room.

Freya was at his side almost immediately. "Thor!"

He waved her off and rose to his hands and knees. He looked at the pedestal and saw the shattered orb lying all around its base. He exhaled in relief.

"It's done."

"You could have killed yourself," Freya snapped. "The Eye gave you your magic—what made you think of trying to destroy it?"

"I did what needed to be done," Thor said. "It's destroyed."

Freya didn't look convinced, but she didn't refute his claim. Thor rose to his feet with some help from Freya and took measure of his injuries. Amid the searing physical pain, he felt a different, alarming sensation. Where there had been a vast well of power there was now emptiness. Fear tried to overwhelm him, but there was no time for such emotions. He could still help in the fight.

He retrieved Mjolnir and held it at the ready. He did his best to keep the shock he felt from showing on his face when his fears were confirmed. He failed. Concern flashed across his mother's face. "What's wrong?"

"I'm fine," Thor lied. He had destroyed the Eye, but it seemed he had paid the price. With the destruction of the Eye, he had been stripped of his magic.

The sound of battle rang through the hall. Freya's jaw clenched tight. "We cannot stay here. Asgard is lost."

"I will not run away," Thor said defiantly. "Let them come. I'll make a stand worthy of songs."

Freya's face tightened, revealing wrinkles around her eyes that Thor had never noticed before. Finally, she nodded. "Then we stand together."

As much as he wanted to argue, to tell his mother to escape while she could, he knew it was useless. Surtur would run down any surviving Aesir and kill them. Freya would only be delaying the inevitable.

Nodding to his mother, Thor gripped Mjolnir tight in one hand and pushed the throne room doors open. Surtur's army had breached the doors and the last few of Asgard's defenders were about to give way.

Summoning his will, he charged forward with a bellow and threw Mjolnir with all his might. Even without lightning shooting from its surface, the weapon was devastating as it plowed through the ranks of Surtur's army.

He followed right in its wake, extending his hand to recall his hammer. He felt the hammer respond and begin to return to him when a sharp pain from his belly caused him to falter. He stumbled to his knees, his hands reaching up and closing around the shaft of a spear protruding from just below his ribs.

Confusion filled him. He hadn't even seen it thrown. The heat of his blood left him as his life began to fade. He let his hands fall to his sides. He looked up just as Surtur's banner filled the doorway and the last of Asgard's defenders gave way. Surtur's horde thundered down on him, but surprisingly none paid him any attention as they passed. They knew a dead man when they saw one.

He couldn't help but feel that this wasn't how it was supposed to be. Centuries of life, and this was how it was going to end? Kneeling on the gilded floor of his father's hall, skewered like a pig? For some reason, it didn't make sense. This wasn't how he was supposed to die—powerless and alone while invaders destroyed his home. He should have done more to stop this day from coming. But he had failed.

What mattered, though, was that Surtur would never have the Eye of Odin. Thor may not have been able to stop Asgard from falling, but he hadn't failed completely. That last thought brought a small smile to his face as the god of thunder sagged forward and fell into death's embrace.

Chapter 1

Thyra Ariksen's heart pounded in her ears as she spun past the defender and snapped her lacrosse stick forward. Time seemed to slow down as her eyes tracked the ball on its course through the air. She could tell from the ball's path that the hapless Meridian goalie had no chance of stopping it.

Thyra pumped her fist and let out a triumphant yell as the ball snapped the back of the net. Her voice mixed with cheers from the eighty spectators as her teammates rushed to mob her.

"Ladies and gentlemen, we have a game on our hands!" a voice over the loudspeaker said. "With that score by Thyra Ariksen, Timberline High has tied the game at twelve with three minutes remaining in the second half of the State Girls' Lacrosse Championship."

Thyra was so pumped after scoring the goal that the announcer's butchering of her name didn't bother her the way it usually did. No matter how many times she told people it was pronounced 'teer-ah', they still said 'thigh-ra', like she was a chicken thigh on the loose.

The Timberline team hurried back to the middle of the field, taking note of the signal from their coach to have Thyra go to the center for the ball drop from the referee. Thyra approached the center of the field and dropped down to her hands and knees. Just across from her, a dark-haired girl in the blue and gold of Meridian High did the same. Thyra wasn't surprised to see that it was Maddie Tramwell, the leader of the Meridian team and Thyra's rival for lead scorer in both club and school seasons.

Maddie had been the premier lacrosse player in Idaho for years and had offers from several universities to play for them after she graduated in a few short weeks. Although she was older than Thyra, they had played against each other for the past two years, with Maddie always maintaining her spot as the best girls' lacrosse player.

Until this year, that is. At the end of the season, it was Maddie Tramwell with sixty-five goals scored and Thyra with seventy. The Meridian senior hadn't been pleased to have her title usurped by a sophomore, and their rivalry had turned even icier.

"You won't get another one," Maddie said around her mouth guard. "I'm gonna send you home crying."

"I'm surprised to see you at the circle," Thyra said. "I thought your coach liked to keep you wrapped in bubble wrap over along the sidelines."

Maddie sneered. "I'll remember you when I lift the Championship trophy next week."

Thyra bit down hard to keep from firing off the first thing that came to her. It had been a physical game, and her blood had been on low boil since the start of the second half. So far, she had managed to keep her temper in check. Letting it take control, this close to the end, would not do her or her team any good.

The referee came over and blew his whistle, dropping the ball to the ground. Thyra's eyes tracked it as it fell and she burst into motion the moment it hit the ground, her stick swiping across and knocking the ball out of the reach of her opponent. Thrya was on her feet in a flash and after the ball. She saw two of the Meridian defenders rushing to intercept the ball, but she beat them to it easily, scooping it up with her stick in a fluid motion. She lowered her shoulder and pushed past them into the open field.

Thyra's electric blue eyes scanned the field and caught sight of a black jersey streaking towards the goal to her right. Her teammate held up her stick as she entered an open space and Thyra passed the ball with a swift motion. Thyra pivoted and cut to the left behind a Meridian defender too busy watching the ball's progress to mark her. Remembering what her lacrosse coach always told the team, she kept moving without the ball and looked for space.

The Meridian defenders all began to sink toward their goal, cutting off the Timberline attack. Their attention was on the movement of the ball and they didn't notice the pocket that opened just to the right of the goal. Thyra saw the opening and hoped that the ball would find its way to her when she got there. Streaking to the left, she curled around behind the goal.

As if sensing Thyra's presence, her teammate rushed towards the goal, drawing the defenders towards her. Just before she ran into a knot of blue and gold, she faked a shot on goal, pivoted, and snapped her stick to the side. Thyra saw the ball streaking through the air and reached out with her stick. She felt the tug as the ball entered her stick's pocket, and spun on her heels, bringing her stick around in a blur.

The Meridian goalkeeper never had a chance to stop the ball as it zipped past her and into the back of the net.

Thyra leapt into the air and pumped her fist as the referee's whistle blew. She slid to her knees as her teammates rushed to mob her.

"Another lightning fast goal by Thyra Ariksen! That makes six, and the Timberline ladies have needed all of them tonight. With that, Timberline moves into the lead with two and a half minutes left to play."

Thyra could suddenly hear the sound of Coach Jones's voice yelling for his team to get back for the face-off. Thyra looked and saw the referee already moving back to the circle, ball in hand. Clearly, he was in no mood to let the clock tick down while the Timberline team celebrated. Thyra rushed back to the circle and got into position.

On cue, Maddie dropped into position across from her.

"No more," she hissed.

Thyra smiled cockily. "You said that last time."

The referee's whistle sounded as he dropped the ball between them. Thyra tried to swipe the ball to the side, but Maddie was ready this time and got her stick in the way. They came together, jostling for position and the ball. The Meridian girl suddenly shifted position giving Thyra an open path to the ball, but just as Thyra reached out with her stick, she felt a lancing pain run up her left arm, and she let go of her stick. Thyra waited for the whistle to blow in response to the illegal check but no whistle came. Too late, she realized that Maddie had used her body to block the ref from seeing the cheap shot.

By the time Thyra recovered, the Meridian team was already streaking down the field with the ball. Thyra hurried to give chase but was too late. She could only watch as the Meridian girls made three swift, precise passes before sending the tying score into the back of the net.

Coach Jones was yelling at the ref as Thyra walked back to the center of the field. Clearly, he had seen the cheap shot from where he stood, but the ref ignored him as he trotted back to the center of the field.

Thyra glanced up into the crowd—the bleachers were full of spectators tonight—and looked at the spot where her mom, Sharon, sat. As always, her mom was one of the loudest in the stands. Tall and athletic, Sharon Ariksen looked like she could easily run out onto the field and run circles around any of the girls. She made a motion to remind Thyra to breathe, and Thyra nodded her understanding.

"Thyra!" Coach Jones yelled, snapping her out of the daze she had fallen into. He held up his thumbs with a concerned look. "You good?"

Thyra nodded and gave him a quick thumbs-up before hustling back to the center and getting into position.

"The score is tied again, ladies and gentlemen, with less than two minutes to go in play. This looks like it will be a true battle for the ages, and it very well may come down to the very end."

Cheers from the crowd for both teams filled the air in response to the statement.

"Did I hurt you, cupcake?"

Thyra scowled as Maddie got down into position with a smile on her face.

"Don't call me that," Thyra said.

"Why not, cupcake?" Maddie sneered. "Does it hurt your feelings?"

Thyra's tenuous hold on her temper evaporated. This time, when the whistle blew, Thyra didn't watch the ball fall. Her eyes never left Maddie's face as she hurried to scoop up the ball. Thyra let the Meridian senior get to her feet uncontested and start running. She stuck close until she saw Maddie begin to make a pass. Thyra didn't let her finish the motion. She charged forward and put her shoulder squarely into Maddie's side.

At sixteen, Thyra was younger than most of the girls she played with, but years of gymnastics and months spent in a local CrossFit box had covered her five-foot ten frame with layers of hard muscle that few girls her age could match. She had a reputation for punishing opponents with her unique mix of speed, strength, and killer instinct. When she hit someone, they felt it. Maddie Tramwell was no different and ended up in a heap on the ground, gasping for breath.

Thyra stood over the prostrate form of the Meridian girl and sneered. "Did that hurt, marshmallow?"

The whistle blew as the ref came rushing in.

"Charging!" The ref called out. He reached into his pocket and pulled out a yellow card. "Two-minute penalty and both sides receive a final warning!"

Thyra couldn't believe it as she turned to the ref. "Two minutes?! That's the rest of the game. You might as well eject me!"

"Cool it, young lady," the ref said grimly.

"Cool it?" Thyra asked, her eyebrows rising. The referee was probably old enough to be her father, but that didn't matter as Thyra stepped up so that she was nose-to-nose with him. "If you weren't so blind you would have seen that cheap shot she gave me and she'd be the one who got the penalty. But, no! You're too busy counting down the seconds until you can go back to whatever hole in the wall you live in to actually do what you're being paid for!"

"Last chance," the ref said.

"Last chance for what?" Thyra snapped. "Open your eyes and ref the game."

"Should have kept your trap shut," the ref said. He stepped back and held up a red card. "You're ejected!"

Thyra's eyes went ablaze, but her teammates appeared between her and the ref before she could give the ref a real reason to eject her. She fought against the hold for a moment, but finally allowed them to push her away from ref.

Meanwhile, Coach Jones had gone apoplectic on the sideline. "Ejected? What for? That was a legal hit, ref! You've got to be kidding me. Where did you learn to call the game? The U10 league?"

"Cool it, coach, or it will get worse for your team" the ref warned. "Meridian starts with the ball."

Thyra's teammates ushered her to the sideline and off the field. She walked by Coach Jones but couldn't bring herself to meet his eyes.

"Bad timing, Thyra," he said as she passed. Those words stung deeper than any lecture he might have given her.

"That was a crap call, Thyra," one of her teammates said in an attempt to console her, but Thyra was too angry to respond.

She tore off her goggles and threw them onto the ground before

15

sinking down onto the bench, unable to look up and watch the rest of the game. She had done it again. She had let her temper get away from her and had let her team down right when they needed her most. This kind of temper tantrum might be forgivable in any other situation, but in the championship game? Thyra felt sick just thinking about it.

She heard the rumble of the loudspeaker but was too numb to register what was happening on the field. At some point, she became faintly aware of her teammates dropping onto the bench next to her with defeated expressions and tears in their eyes. That was all the confirmation she needed that her fears had come true. The sound of the final score came over the loudspeaker and rang in her ears.

"The Meridian girls are State Champions with a 14-13 win over the Timberline Wolves."

Thyra covered her face with her hands. She heard Coach Jones say something as her teammates slumped onto the bench beside her but was too numb to hear or care. She didn't know how long she sat there with her head in her hands, but she was aware of her teammates getting up and leaving one by one until she sat alone.

Finally, she felt someone put a hand on her shoulder and a familiar voice spoke softly. "Hey, Lightning Bolt."

Thyra looked up at her mom and saw the puffiness in her eyes.

"Let's go home," Sharon said softly. "We can grab a pizza on the way. Maybe you can convince me to get some ice cream, too. Eat our feelings until we're too sick to care. What do you say? I think a night like this calls for some Chocolate Brownie Thunder or Moose Tracks."

"I'm not hungry," Thyra said softly.

"We both know that's not true," Sharon said. "You're always hungry."

"Not tonight," Thyra said glumly.

Sharon sighed softly. "It was a bad ending to the game, Thyra. But it isn't anything that a pizza and ice cream-induced coma can't help soothe away."

Thyra wasn't so ready to forget the sting of the loss, but she felt her anger melting as she looked up at her mom.

"As long as you buy each of us a pint."

Sharon's megawatt smile split her face. "I think that can be arranged. Come on, Lightning Bolt."

Thyra retrieved her gear and stood up. Sharon wrapped an arm around her daughter and began to lead her towards the parking lot.

They were halfway to the car when her smile faded and she cleared her throat. Thyra cringed in expectation of the lecture she knew was coming.

"That was quite the hit you put on Maddie Tramwell,"

"She called me 'cupcake'," Thyra explained. "I couldn't let that slide."

"Yes, you could have," Sharon said. "We've talked about this, sweetheart. I love that you play hard, but that temper of yours gets you into trouble. You went head-hunting when you should have kept your cool."

Thyra let the rebuke sting for a moment. "Do you think Coach Jones will be mad for long?"

"I'm sure his face will return to its normal color by next season," Sharon answered. "Maybe you'll get away easy and he'll only make you carry all the equipment bags for half the club season. But I'd plan on spending some time on the bench this summer if I were you."

Thyra grimaced at the thought.

Her phone buzzed in her bag and she pulled it out. She saw she had a message from Rich, one of the boys' lacrosse players that she knew. She opened the message and saw a link with a few words written below it. *You're YouTube famous! This baby's going viral!*

Thyra tapped on the link and waited while the video loaded. She immediately wished she hadn't. She saw Maddie Tramwell running with the ball and then suddenly go airborne as a girl with a wrist-thick, blond braid bull-dozed into her. It sounded like a thunderclap and groans from the crowd were audible as they reacted. Thyra cringed as she watched herself stand over her downed rival. The video zoomed in on just as the referee came rushing into view. The video had a good look at her face for a brief moment just before she spun on the referee.

What she saw during that brief moment made her stomach sink—her eyes shone an unnatural electric blue!

"What's that?" Sharon asked.

Thyra watched the video again before turning the phone so that her mom could see. She pressed play and waited to the end, hoping that she had imagined the flash of light, but she saw it again. It was brief, but there was no mistaking it.

"Did you see that?" Thyra asked. "What was that at the end?"

"See what?" Sharon asked. She cringed and shook her head. "That hit looks worse from this angle."

"Not the hit," Thyra said. She rewound the video and froze it on her face. "That! Look at my eyes. That flash of light."

"What are you talking about?" Sharon said. "I don't see anything."

"My eyes!" Thyra said. "They're glowing! Do you see that?"

"Glowing?" Sharon laughed dismissively, although Thyra swore she saw a tightening around her mom's eyes. "Don't be silly. It's just the way the light hit them. Your eyes have always done that when the light hits them just right."

"Like that?" Thyra asked.

"It's something that's always been special about you," Sharon said.

"How come I've never noticed it before?" Thyra asked.

"It only happens when the light is right, and it's always just for an instant," Sharon explained. "You've never seen it because you're never looking in a mirror when it happens."

Thyra wasn't sure she believed her mom's explanation. "You don't think that looks weird?"

"No, it's just the way your eyes are," Sharon said. She shrugged.

"What else would it be?"

Thyra didn't have an answer for that. She stared at the still of the video. There was no doubt in her mind that her eyes were shining. No, not shining—glowing!

"You're tired, sweetheart," Sharon said. "It was just a trick of the light. Nothing to worry about."

Thyra grudgingly closed the video and slid her phone back into her bag. Her mom's explanation made some sense, and there were no rational alternatives. While it bothered her that she had never heard mention of this "special" characteristic, she realized that she might be exaggerating what she saw. She was tired and was coming off an adrenaline high and was probably just imagining things.

"You're probably right," Thyra relented. "It was just a trick of the lighting."

"Of course, I'm right," Sharon said. "Now, about that pizza and ice cream. How does an extra-large Hawaiian sound?"

Thyra rolled her eyes and sighed. "Pineapple doesn't belong on pizza, Mom."

Sharon gave her a shocked look. "Says who?"

"Everyone," Thyra said with a chuckle.

Sharon shook her head, pulling Thyra's head onto her shoulder and a sad expression crossing her face. "I'm so sorry I've failed you. To think, my child doesn't like pineapple on her pizza? Where did I go wrong?"

Thyra snorted but kept her head on her mom's shoulder. It felt good to have her close.

They were almost to the parking lot when Thyra felt an itch between her shoulder blades. She turned and looked back toward the field. A lone man stood at the end of the bleachers, his arms crossed over his chest as he watched Thyra and her mom. Even from a distance, Thyra could feel a strange, predatory energy coming from him that sent a shiver down her spine.

"Something wrong, sweetheart?" Sharon asked.

"There's a man watching us," Thyra said in a quiet voice as she faced forward again.

"A man?" Sharon turned around. "What man?"

"The one at the end of the bleachers," Thyra said. "He's got dark hair and a beard."

Sharon shook her head. "Honey, there's no one there."

Thyra spun around, her eyes going to the spot where she had seen him, but the man was gone.

"I swear I saw someone standing there," Thyra said. She looked at her mom and saw the concern there. "I'm being honest, Mom. I saw a man standing there watching us."

"I believe you," Sharon said. She glanced back toward the field and shrugged. "But whoever it was is gone now. Probably just a maintenance worker here to check on the field and turn off the lights."

"Maybe," Thyra said grudgingly. She shook her head. "Maybe I'm just seeing things."

Sharon smiled ruefully. "Glowing eyes and a strange man watching you from the stands? I think you're just tired. Let's get home. Pizza, ice cream, and a cheesy rom-com is exactly what you need."

Sharon linked her arm through Thyra's and led her to the car. Thyra threw her bag into the trunk and slid into the passenger seat with a sigh. As she did, she noticed that her mom lingered for a moment before getting into the car, her eyes scanning the field carefully. Her features tightened and the concern expression returned.

But then it disappeared. Sharon slid into the car, a smile on her face. She started the car and turned up the radio with a laugh.

"Pizza and ice cream coma here we come!"

Thyra smiled in appreciation of her mom's attempts at alleviating her distress over the loss of the game, but the smile was superficial.

She couldn't move on from the loss that quickly. Even worse, she couldn't forget the video and the glow she was sure she saw in her eyes.

As the car pulled away, Thyra glanced back at the field, hoping against hope that the man she thought she had seen wouldn't be there.

Her stomach sank. He was back, and the feeling of his eyes on her made Thyra's skin crawl. Thyra was about to say something to her mom when the strange man took a step into the shadows and disappeared.

Chapter 2

Thyra slipped through the door just as the bell rang. She hurried to the nearest open chair just as her English Literature teacher, Mr. Agi, put down the chalk he had been holding and turned around. As usual, he wore a mischievous smirk on his face as he adjusted his glasses and looked around the room.

"Take your seats!" he said. "The school year is quickly coming to an end and I need to make sure I haven't wasted another year of my life telling stories that no one cares about."

This was met with a few chuckles from the class. Mr. Agi smiled, mischief in his gray-blue eyes. "So, tell me, what have we spent the last ten weeks learning about?"

The questions were met with silence as his students all did their best to avoid making eye contact. Mr. Agi scratched at his gray beard while he waited for an answer.

"This will be something you're tested on," Mr. Agi said after a long silence. "So, don't think silence will be mistaken for ignorance. Spit it out, or I promise that the test I write will be double the torture and graded like a master's thesis!"

"The gods?" Anna Gonzalez, one of Thyra's teammates from the lacrosse team, offered weakly.

"Ah, someone brave enough to speak," Mr. Agi said. "Thank you, Ms. Gonzalez. Would you care to elaborate?"

"We've read the old myths about the Roman, Greek, and Norse gods," Anna said. "You showed us how those myths carried over into more modern stories."

Mr. Agi nodded. "Well, at least one of you was listening to my rambling. We've learned how many of the tales surrounding these gods were used as a means to explain the inexplicable—the origin of man, the creation of the world, the movement of the sun and moon, what have you. Some stories were the result of deeds performed by men and women. Stories that were elevated to the status of myth and legend after generations of being retold by gifted storytellers with a penchant for embellishment."

Thyra couldn't help but smile at Mr. Agi's description. English Literature was not a class many high school students looked forward to, but with the arrival of Bruce Agi to Timberline almost a year before, that had begun to change. He had a gift for spinning a tale, making it so vivid that his students could almost see it happening with their own eyes. His class was never boring.

Theories about his backstory ran wild through the student body, each one more outlandish than the last. Some swore that he was a hermit that had spent his youth traveling the world, living a minimalist lifestyle, all to collect stories from the people he met. Others thought he was an eccentric millionaire that lived in a mansion with a massive library full of rare books he'd spent years poring over. Whatever the truth was, one thing was agreed upon by anyone that spent time in his classroom—Mr. Agi was unlike any other teacher at Timberline.

"So, what are your thoughts?" Mr. Agi asked, crossing his arms over his chest. "What conclusions have you made about our most recent area of study—Norse mythology?"

"They had a problem with incest," came a snarky reply from the back of the room.

"A tragic flaw if there ever was one," Mr. Agi said with a nod. "But, not exactly the response I was looking for. What else?"

"Thor was a legit bad-A," Tony Reynolds said. "Dude ran around with a hammer, calling down lightning bolts, defeating giants, and had, like, a dozen different ladies on the side. No wonder the Vikings liked him so much!"

"Probably for the same reasons you like him so much, Mr. Reynolds," their teacher said with a crooked smile. Tony shrugged, a big smile on his face.

"So," Mr. Agi said, addressing the class as a whole, "thus far we think they were too friendly with their own family members, and we like that Thor had a hammer and was good with the ladies."

"Sounds about right," Tony piped in again.

"Well, I'm glad the past few weeks were so educational," Mr. Agi said. "If that is all you got out of it, I may as well begin packing my things. It's been a pleasure meeting you all, but I think I may need to find a different calling in life. A traveling encyclopedia salesman, perhaps. I might be more successful trying to take on Google single-handedly than I've been as a teacher."

This was met by laughter. A wry smirk crossed Mr. Agi's face as he went over to his sturdy wood desk and sat on the corner.

"Honestly, is there nothing else? Any other insights at all?" Silence reigned for several long seconds. Thyra shifted in her chair and the slight motion drew her teacher's attention. "Ms. Ariksen, what are your thoughts? If my etymology is correct, your name is a version of Tyr, the Norse god of war."

"Ha! That fits," Tony piped in. "I watched that hit she put on the girl from Meridian like a hundred times over the weekend! It was worthy of a spot on SportsCenter."

Several others hooted in agreement. Thyra rolled her eyes and did her best to ignore them.

"Okay class," Mr. Agi said with a rueful grin. "Let's give our YouTube celebrity a break. I think thirty thousand views over the weekend is enough shame for now. Let's hear what Thyra has to say. What are your thoughts on the gods of your ancestors?"

Thyra felt every eye in the room on her as she scrambled to form an answer. Her mother had told her stories about the Norse gods when she was younger. Tales so vivid that Thyra could have sworn her mom had experienced them herself. Those stories had been the highlight of her childhood.

"I don't know if I have an answer, Mr. Agi," Thyra said slowly. "My mom used to tell me some of these stories when I was little. She seemed to believe they were important, even if they were only stories."

"So, what does your gut tell you?" Mr. Agi asked.

Thyra shrugged. "I think that while the Norse gods are more myth than real, they might have been based off of the actions of real people. The stories have survived for centuries, so, I think that means they have value."

"So, the Mighty Thor might have been real?" Mr. Agi asked. "Loki, Odin, Freya, the giants, all of them, might have been based off of real people?"

His piercing eyes remained on Thyra until she nodded her head. Mr. Agi seemed pleased with the answer as he turned his attention to the rest of the class.

"What does the rest of the enlightened mob say? Does Ms. Ariksen have a sound opinion? Could the Norse gods have been real people whose feats were embellished through the ages by men? Could they have been men made gods?"

The class was silent for a time until Anna raised her hand slowly. Mr. Agi nodded to give her permission to speak.

"What do you think, Mr. Agi?"

"Turning the question back on the teacher, are we?" A roguish smile crossed his face. "Fair enough. I believe I told you when we started

25

this block of study that I too have Norse heritage. With that said, I find many of the stories about the Norse gods to be overly dramatized. Men needed a means to explain their lives, and so they created gods to give meaning to their actions. It's been the same all through history. The stories that seemed more plausible endured, which is why we still have organized religions such as Christianity, Judaism, Islam, Buddhism, and Hinduism. The stories that were not as plausible fell from favor, which is why there are very few who still believe in the polytheistic religions of the Romans, Greeks, and Norsemen anymore."

Mr. Agi paused and took a deep breath. "So, to answer the question in a more direct way—no, I do not think that the gods we read of ever existed. Not in the forms described, at least. I believe that many of these stories are the result of an excellent storyteller and strong drink, not true events."

"Why did we spend time reading it then?" Tony asked. His eyes lit up suddenly and a hopeful look crossed his face. "Does this mean that we won't be tested on any of this?"

"No, this material will still be testable," Mr. Agi said. There were a few pained groans, but he ignored them. "Why did I have you read these stories? The answer is simple, and we've already heard it—there are lessons to be learned. Odin hanging from the world tree, Yggdrasil, and then sacrificing an eye for wisdom teaches us that we often must sacrifice something in order to receive something greater in return. Thor's exploits inspired courage. Freya's magic gave hope to people who were looking for a miracle when science was still in its infancy. All of these stories give meaning to life and taught important lessons. That context is mirrored in much of modern literature."

Thyra felt a flash of pride as Mr. Agi spoke. This was her heritage, and it was nice to hear it being taken seriously, even if it was only a collection of stories.

"We've covered a lot of material, much of which the school board said held little value. They wanted me to spend the semester reading Charlotte Bronte and Jane Austen." Some of the boys let out pained groans. "Be careful, gentlemen. There are young ladies casting daggers at you with their eyes right now. Those stories have their place, and an important one at that. That being said, variety is important, and although wading through the stories from antiquity has been difficult at times, I hope that you have all gained a greater appreciation for the art of storytelling and the importance of recording these tales."

The door to the classroom opened suddenly and Coach Jones stepped into the room. Thyra felt her heart sink when his eyes fell on her.

"Coach Jones," Mr. Agi said. "What a surprise. What brings you to our midst today?"

"I need to speak with Thyra," Coach Jones said without looking away from Thyra.

"Can it wait?" Mr. Agi asked. "We're in the middle of a class discussion."

"No."

Mr. Agi's eyebrows rose at the curt answer. "I hope this isn't lacrosse business. I believe she has time in the gym later today. Surely, you can wait until then."

"This can't wait, Bruce," Coach Jones said, finally looking at the English teacher.

Mr. Agi sighed. "Well, then. I guess there is nothing that can be done. Hurry back, Ms. Ariksen."

Thyra stood slowly. She received a sympathetic look from Anna as she crossed the room and followed Coach Jones into the hallway. The walk to his office was spent in silence. Thyra didn't dare look up and spent the entire time staring at the floor. She began counting floor tiles in an attempt to stop thinking about what kind of punishment Coach Jones had in store for her.

Coach Jones stopped in front of the door and Thyra felt her throat tighten. It had been the longest and shortest walk of her life all at the same time.

"I'm sorry for losing my temper," she blurted out in a rush. "I know I let the team down."

Coach Jones turned toward her and blinked in confusion. His expression softened. "No wonder you looked so sick. That isn't why I pulled you from class, though. Yes, I admit I was disappointed in you for going head hunting, but what's done is done. I can't say that I wouldn't have done the same thing if I was in your shoes. That's not to say that it was the right thing to do, though. You getting ejected hurt us when we needed you most.

"But I have an entirely different reason for pulling you out of class. I have someone who wants to meet you," he paused and held up a finger, "but I want to give you a warning first. This guy is going to promise you things in an attempt to fill your head with grand ideas. Don't get swept away in the moment. There's something about this guy's story that I don't buy."

A dozen questions filled her, but before she had a chance to ask them Coach Jones pushed the door open. He held it for Thyra and then let it shut behind them. His office was actually a corner of the trainer's room where an old wood desk and a few metal chairs had been brought in for the coaches to use. While the head football coach had a nicer office, the other coaches were relegated here.

One of the metal chairs was occupied by a man wearing khakis and a dark polo. He stood when he heard them enter and turned around. Thyra stopped in place as a chill ran down her spine. It was the man from the other night!

"Thyra, meet Fenton Ririe," Coach Jones said as he moved to the desk and took a seat.

The man smiled behind his thick beard and extended a hand toward

Thyra. "Pleased to meet you, Thyra."

Thyra reached out and shook his hand carefully before sitting down in an empty metal chair. She slid the chair back as she sat to put as much distance as possible between herself and Fenton Ririe. If he noticed her discomfort, he didn't show it.

"Fenton is a recruiter," Coach Jones explained. "He's from a junior college in the Midwest that is actively recruiting female lacrosse players."

"That's right," Ririe said. "I represent Folkhaven College in Wisconsin. Have you ever heard of us?"

Thyra shook her head.

"That's no surprise," Ririe said with a shrug. "We are relatively new to the lacrosse scene, and word hasn't spread. But, the Folkhaven Wolves," he pointed to a wolf's head embroidered on his polo, "are the fastest growing women's lacrosse program in the nation. We've set a goal to be competitive on a national level within the next two years, and the only way to do that is to recruit the best talent."

"And somehow that brought him to us," Coach Jones said.

Ririe smiled ruefully. "That's right, although I must admit that I came to watch the Meridian team. Your name wasn't even on my radar before the game, but it was after your performance. You made quite an impression! After watching you, I knew I had to meet you in person and extend an offer to you to come play for Folkhaven."

"But, I'm only a sophomore," Thyra said, casting an uncertain look at Coach Jones.

"Coach Jones informed me of that," Ririe said without hesitation. "But, I'm happy to say that isn't an obstacle. You could enroll at Folkhaven this summer and start classes by the fall."

"How?" Thyra asked. "I still have two years of high school left."

"Simple," Ririe said with a confident smile. "All you have to do is pass the GED and then you can skip your junior and senior years

29

completely. We're seeing more and more young, bright, talented kids like you leave high school early in order to pursue higher education and increased opportunity to craft their skills. After watching you play, I can tell you that your skill is leaps above any competition you'll face here in Idaho. Why waste your time here when you could be playing for us and getting your name in front of the biggest lacrosse programs in the nation?"

Thyra felt her heart begin to race at the prospect of playing at the next level. It had been her dream to play for one of the best lacrosse programs since she started playing the game ten years ago. She had posters on her walls of players from the big lacrosse schools out East, and always imagined one day her face would be on one of those posters. Now, that opportunity seemed one step closer to becoming real.

"You think I'm good enough to play in college? Right now?"

The recruiter nodded. "I do. But I also see how much better you could become if you were allowed to play against a higher level of competition. You already outclass what is around you. How can you expect to get better if you don't face a higher level of play? You can do that with us at Folkhaven. In two years' time you could be playing for one of the premier lacrosse programs."

"But," Coach Jones interrupted, "what you're proposing is dependent on Thyra passing the GED."

"Something you assured me was well within her academic capabilities," Ririe said.

"I don't doubt that she could do it, but I'm not sure it's in her best interest," Coach Jones replied. "She'd be leaving her home and moving halfway across the country to go to a school no one has ever heard of to play on a team that has no proven track record to back up what you are saying. You say that two years spent on your college's team will get her name in front of big lacrosse programs, but I think the possibility of winning two state championships here could have the same effect."

"You're wrong," Ririe said in a tense voice. "You of all people should know that lacrosse is still small in the U.S. While it is growing, most of the big programs are on the East Coast, and that is where they do their recruiting. They do not allocate the resources to other areas, especially small markets like Idaho. That is where Folkhaven is different. We want the best players this country has to offer, and we are willing to put forth the effort to find them. And not only find them, but develop them into truly special talents."

Ririe turned to Thyra. "And you are one of those special talents. With the right training, I assure you that your potential is limitless."

There was something about the way Ririe said that last word that sent electricity through Thyra's entire body, but not in a good way. Although he still wore a friendly smile, his eyes had changed. She suddenly felt like a wounded deer being eyed by a hungry wolf.

"I think you are good enough to start on our team as early as next spring," Ririe continued. "From there, I think your talent and usefulness to Folkhaven will only increase. You must come to Folkhaven. It's the only place where your unique talents can be fully realized."

The predatory look in his eyes intensified. Thyra sat back and crossed her arms over her chest protectively.

"I think we've heard enough," Coach Jones said, clearly sensing Thyra's unease. "I'm not even sure why I agreed to this, but I shouldn't have."

Ririe turned on Coach Jones. "You agreed to this because I am short on time and needed to speak with Thyra immediately."

Coach Jones shook his head. "I shouldn't have. An unofficial visit without a parent present is highly inappropriate. If you want to recruit Thyra, you'll need to set up an official visit with her mother present. Although, at this point, I would advise Thyra not to take another visit from you or anyone from your school."

"That would be a mistake on your part," Ririe said in a voice that made Thyra's hair stand on end.

"The mistake was ever allowing you to speak with Thyra," Coach Jones said. "We're done here. Thyra, I will walk you back to class."

Glad for the excuse to leave, Thyra began to stand. Before she could reach her feet, though, Ririe reached out and her by the wrist in an iron grip.

"You must come to Folkhaven," Ririe said, his voice lowering to a growl. "Your potential is being wasted here. Only we can help you become what you were meant to be!"

Coach Jones was between them in a flash and broke his grip. "That's enough! I don't know what kind of program you're running, but I will not stand for the use of intimidation tactics or physical force." He looked over his shoulder at Thyra. "Go back to class. I will make sure Mr. Ririe is escorted off of campus and sent on his way."

Ririe stood up and faced Coach Jones. At six foot three, Coach Jones was not a small man, but as Ririe rose to his full height he seemed to dwarf the lacrosse coach. Thyra couldn't explain it, but she was sure that Ririe hadn't been that big before.

She didn't stick around to wonder about the sudden change. Glad to be away from the recruiter's presence, she bolted out of the training room and hurried down the hall just shy of breaking into a run.

Not ready to return to class and the questioning looks of her classmates, she continued right past Mr. Agi's classroom and headed for the girl's bathroom. Doing a quick check to make sure she was alone, she shut herself inside one of the stalls and sat down.

Her heart racing, she reached for her phone and quickly dialed her mom's number. She listened as it rang over and over without being answered. She waited for her mom's voicemail to come up but was surprised when the line suddenly went dead. She tried her mom's phone again, but the call was dropped after the first ring. She felt a spike of panic. Why wasn't she answering?

Thyra forced herself to take a deep breath and let it out slowly. Her mom was probably busy in a meeting or something. She would call her back as soon as she was able to. Until then, Thyra needed to do her best to handle things on her own. Her mom had raised her to be strong and capable. Hiding in a bathroom stall didn't seem like something Sharon Ariksen would do.

"It's over, Thyra," she said to herself. "You're okay."

Repeating those words to herself, she managed to calm herself down. It had been scary, but she was unharmed, and Coach Jones had been there to handle Fenton Ririe. No doubt he would take the necessary steps to report what happened. It was over, and nothing was going to happen between now and when she could talk to her mom about it later.

She felt her phone buzz against her leg and looked down at it. She saw Anna's name followed by; *saw you go by the door. You ok?*

Thyra's fingers hovered over the screen as she debated telling Anna about what happened with the recruiter. She desperately wanted to tell someone, and with her mom not answering her phone, Anna was the next best thing.

But the next best thing wasn't enough for something like this. Anna was a friend, but Thyra needed her mom. Thyra typed a quick message and slipped her phone back into her pocket. She stood up and left the stall, pausing in front of the mirror to make sure she looked half composed.

"It's over," she repeated to herself in the mirror. "It's all over."

Chapter 3

Gunnar Olafsson stood in front of the full-length windows of his office and looked out over New York City. Occupying the ninety-ninth floor of the Muspel Building, his office afforded him a view that very few would ever get to enjoy.

As President and CEO of the Muspel Corporation, a multinational telecommunications and energy conglomerate, he was one of the most powerful men in the city, if not the country, and he made sure that he played the part. His office was built from the most precious materials, his suits crafted by the finest tailors in the world, and he had a table reserved for him at all of the swankiest restaurants. To the outside world, he was a forty-something, handsome bachelor that had more money than he knew what to do with.

It was the image he chose to project to the world, a skin he wore as needed. He did everything possible to maintain that image in order to keep it in place.

Because the truth about who he was and what his company truly profited from was something altogether different.

The sun was just beginning to rise over the cityscape when he heard a knock on his door. He felt a flash of anger rise up. He had left strict instructions with his personal assistant that he wasn't to be disturbed before the opening of the financial markets. Unless his assistant was planning on finding a new job, there were only two people brave enough to ignore his instructions and intrude on his solitude—one worked for him and the other seemed to think more and more that Gunnar worked for him.

He turned around and touched a button on his desk. The lock on the door clicked open, allowing a giant of a man to enter. Built like an oak, Ivan Kuznetzov stood over six and a half feet tall and weighed close to three hundred pounds of solid muscle. A simple glance at his Instagram account would reveal videos of him lifting massive amounts of weight, all while bellowing in his native Russian.

"Sir," Ivan said in a reverent tone.

His accent was not as strong as it had been when Gunnar had first brought him into his employ, but it still was audible when he spoke quickly or was angry. While most in Gunnar's employ were Americans, the big Russian was a pleasant reminder of the old world and the characteristics Gunnar felt were disappearing in the modern age—unquestioning loyalty being the foremost. The Russian had proven his loyalty time and time again, which was why Gunnar felt no reservations about taking Ivan into his confidence.

That, and the Russian's formidable skill set as a bodyguard and hitman. Like all young men in Russia, Ivan had served his obligatory time in the Russian Military. During his time there he caught the eye of the Russian Special Forces. A few years spent learning the art of dealing death had made him into an impressive tool waiting for the right hand to put him to work.

Gunnar had found him, tested him, and when he was sure that Ivan was someone he could trust, divulged his secrets one by one. The Russian hadn't even blinked when he found out what his boss actually engaged in and what Gunnar expected from him. The big Russian dove into the work Gunnar gave him with zeal that bordered on obsessive.

"What do you have for me?" Gunnar asked, getting right to business.

Ivan crossed the room and placed a tablet on the desk. "Four new sightings."

Gunnar flipped through the pictures that were pulled up—all in high definition, courtesy of the dozen satellites the Muspel Corporation had circling the earth. He studied the faces in the pictures, committing them to memory.

"Any of them potential dangers?" Gunnar asked.

Ivan shook his head. "No. They will be no problem."

"Good," Gunnar said. "See to them."

"The same orders?" Ivan asked.

"The same as always," Gunnar said. "Alive, if possible, dead if not. Any magical items brought back here."

Ivan nodded. "It will be done."

This was the true purpose of the Muspel Corporation—eliminating magic and magic users from the world. He had fought against magic his entire life, locked in a war that had been fought hundreds of times since the beginning of man. It was an endless struggle between those that possessed magic and those that didn't. The fight between men who considered themselves gods and those they forced to worship them.

Telecommunications and energy were the front for Gunnar's fight against magic, but that was because it was the best means to Gunnar's end. On any given day, the Muspel Corporation had access to every text, phone call, email, and location of well over five hundred million people. When social media was taken into consideration, that reach grew exponentially until information on almost seven billion people could be accessed in one form or another.

Once the information was gathered and a target was found, the rest fell on men like Ivan. The big Russian's official title was Chief Inspector of Infrastructure and Field Operations—an absolute waste of breath that did nothing to describe what he actually did at the

Muspel Corporation. While his role at the company was ambiguous, all that mattered was that he had direct access to the CEO at any time, and that anything he or his men asked for was readily given to them.

Ivan and his men currently operated under something called 'The Odin Initiative', an energy program that was so secretive that not even the high-level executives had access to anything more than a vague description of what it hoped to achieve. It was a clean energy project Gunnar insisted would change the world. To this point, The Odin Initiative had yet to produce revenue while sucking millions of dollars from the balance sheet every year. That might have been a problem for any other company, but the Muspel Corporation was flush with cash, and no one batted an eye when a few million dollars was funneled away to some pipe dream project of the CEO.

The Russian reached towards the tablet and opened the internet browser. "There was one more that came across our radar over the weekend. One that I think you will be interested in."

"Over the weekend?" Gunnar asked, arching an eyebrow. "Why did you wait so long to bring it to my attention?"

Ivan shrugged. "It wasn't someone we'd been watching, so our satellites didn't pick it up. We may not have seen it if not for one of our agents spending time watching videos during his free time."

And there was the failure of his plan. No matter how much technology advanced, no matter how strong the lens or recording device, it was impossible to watch every living person. Even with the capabilities of a telecommunications conglomerate at his fingertips, Gunnar was handcuffed by the fact that he had a finite number of hours in a day and a limited number of eyes available to scan through the raw data gathered. It wasn't easy to find people that not only possessed the necessary skills to operate the complicated system without being caught but were also willing to break numerous laws by invading the privacy of average people.

"So, how did we find out about this?" Gunnar asked.

"It came up on social media," Ivan answered. He pulled up a video and pressed play. "Our tech department did some magic to slow it down and enhance it."

The video was of a girls' high school lacrosse match. Gunnar watched it with only passing interest as a blond girl with a thick braid steamrolled another girl with a brutal hit. The video suddenly slowed and zoomed in on the girl's face just as her eyes flashed with a bluish light. Gunnar leaned forward and studied the still image on the screen.

"Where was this?"

"In Idaho," Ivan said.

"Idaho?" Gunnar looked up. "No wonder she wasn't being watched. Do we know her name?"

Ivan nodded. "Thyra Ariksen. Daughter of Sharon Ariksen, an insurance agent in the city of Boise."

Ivan brought up a picture of the mother and daughter. The similarities between the two were clear, but it was the girl's eyes that held Gunnar's attention.

"What do we know about her?"

"Very little," Ivan admitted. "She has no links to any past or existing magic users we've tracked."

"And the father?"

"A mystery," Ivan said.

"I know those eyes," Gunnar said. He'd seen eyes like those before. It felt like a lifetime ago, but no length of time would be enough for him to forget. The question was, how did young Thyra Ariksen come by them? "I would very much like to meet Thyra."

"I'll get a team dispatched," Ivan said.

"Make it your best men, and make sure they know that this one," Gunnar tapped the picture of Thyra Ariksen emphatically, "I want brought to me alive and unharmed."

Chapter 4

Thyra ducked under the bar and centered the weight on her shoulders. She straightened her legs, lifting the barbell off its rest, and took two steps backward. Inhaling, she held her breath and dropped into a deep squat, feeling the strain on her legs as she paused at the bottom of the motion and then pressed upward. She did it again, letting her mind go still as she focused solely on maintaining proper form on each repetition.

She found exercise to be her escape, especially lifting weights. It came natural to her, and she found that she could easily outlift most of the boys at her school, a fact that was a rub for many of the football players. In fact, the head football coach had asked if she had ever thought about playing football. Thyra got the impression that he meant it when he said he'd find a spot for her on the team in a heartbeat. She always said no, reminding him that she was a lacrosse player and had every intention of playing the sport at the collegiate level. She wasn't going to let anything stand in the way of that goal.

Thyra finished her set and rested the bar on the rack. She was bending over to grab her water bottle when she noticed Bradley Jimenez enter the gym. A known prankster, Bradley always seemed to be on the verge of laughing. That wasn't the case today. He wore a grave expression that made Thyra hesitate.

Bradley scanned the gym until his eyes fell on Thyra. He hurried in her direction, and his mouth was moving before he came to a stop.

"Did you hear about Coach Jones?"

Thyra shook her head. "No. What about him?"

Bradley looked around the gym as if he was nervous about being heard. "The teachers don't want any students to know, but my mom is a nurse up at the hospital. She said that the ambulance brought Coach Jones to the ER last night. She said he was unconscious and covered in blood. Scratches, cuts, and bruises everywhere."

"What happened to him?" Thyra asked.

Bradley shrugged. "Apparently, he was found behind the school by another teacher. My mom didn't say much more than that, but she said it looked like he had been attacked by a bear. Bite marks and all. She said he's stable, but he's still unconscious. She said they gave him like, a hundred stitches or something like that. It was brutal. Real gory stuff." His eyes went wide. "But, don't tell anyone I told you. I don't want my mom to get in trouble. HIPPO rules, or something like that."

News delivered, Bradley moved off toward a group of boys, probably to share the news with them as well.

Thyra tried to process what she'd been told. It didn't make sense. Who—or what, if Bradley was to be believed—would attack Coach Jones outside the school? They lived in the middle of the city, so it couldn't have been a bear, but where did the bitemarks come from then? Hearing about Coach Jones made her feel terrible. He didn't deserve any of it.

But there was nothing Thyra could do at this point. He was in the hospital and was stable, according to Bradley. The doctors would take care of him, and she was sure the police would find whoever—or whatever—did this to him.

Thyra ducked back under the barbell and centered the weight on her shoulders. Inhaling deeply, she did her best to focus on the exercise and not on the jumbled ball of thoughts and emotions inside her. It only took one squat to realize that there was no silencing them. She tried to continue, but her focus was broken. Not just broken—shattered. Grudgingly, Thyra racked the weight again and stepped away from the bar.

She closed her eyes and tried to refocus, but it was no use. She quickly gathered up her belongings and headed for the locker room. With her workout ruined, she figured she'd get a head start on her normal lunch routine and finish up the last of her math homework. She was halfway across the gym when she was intercepted by Coach Greene, the head football coach.

"Hey, Thyra," the burly man said. Thyra noticed he was lacking his usual quick smile—probably because he had heard about Eddie Jones as well. Coach Jones was also an assistant coach for the football team, and the two men were good friends. "Just got a call from the principal's office. They would like you to come down for a minute."

"What for?" Thyra asked cautiously.

Coach Greene shrugged. "I'm not sure. Just head down after you get changed back into your street clothes, okay?"

Thyra nodded. "Okay, Coach."

The football coach turned away and headed back towards his office, leaving Thyra with an uneasy feeling in the pit of her stomach. Getting called to the principal's office was ominous enough on its own, but she couldn't help but feel it was doubly so considering what had happened to Coach Jones. It was a stretch to think that the two were connected, but she couldn't shake the feeling for some reason.

She hurried into the locker room and quickly got changed. Since her workout had been short, she didn't feel the need to fuss with her hair or check the little makeup she wore. The result was that she was in and out of the locker room in less than five minutes and on her way to the office.

As she walked the pit in her stomach grew. The secretary glanced up at her with an almost unfriendly expression and pointed at the door to the principal's office without saying a word. Thyra. Taking the cue, Thyra quietly opened the principal's door and stepped inside.

"Ah, Ms. Ariksen," Principal Anderson said, looking up from some paperwork on his desk. His tie was loose and the button of his shirt was undone, betraying his fatigue. He gestured to two chairs on the other side of the desk. "Please, take a seat."

Thyra complied and waited for the principal to speak first.

"I assume you've heard about Eddie Jones," Principal Anderson said.

Thyra nodded. "I have."

"I won't ask who told you," the principal said. "I have enough on my plate without trying to round up students guilty of spreading rumors. It was bound to happen, no matter how hard we tried to keep it under wraps. What matters is that it looks like Eddie will make a full recovery and be back for the start of the school year."

"That's good to hear," Thyra said. "Is that what you wanted to talk to me about?"

"No, actually," Principal Anderson said. "You'll have to excuse me. I have a lot on my mind with the school year ending and then this horrible thing with Coach Jones. I'm not quite as on top of things today as I'd like to be."

He leaned back in his chair and steepled his fingers in front of him. "I had a visitor today that came looking for you. A man by the name of Fenton Ririe."

Thyra tensed at the sound of that name. "What did he want?"

"I take it that you know who he is then," Principal Anderson said. "I'm sure he wanted the same thing all recruiters want—to set up a meeting with a promising young athlete and their parents. In this case, you and your mother. Normally, this would run through Coach Jones, but in his absence, it falls on me."

"I don't want a meeting with him," Thyra said.

Principal Anderson looked surprised. "Why not? I thought you'd be thrilled to know that someone has taken notice of your talent. Lacrosse is still a growing sport in Idaho, so a recruiter—even one from a small institution—is a big deal."

Thyra shook her head. "I already spoke to him. Yesterday, during school. Coach Jones pulled me out of class and took me to his office. This recruiter, Fenton Ririe, was waiting. He was aggressive, and Coach Jones told him to leave."

"A recruiter? During school hours?" Principal Anderson's brow fell, and he shook his head. "Was your mother there?"

"No," Thyra said. In truth, she hadn't seen much of her mom since the night before. Thyra had told her mom about what happened over dinner, expecting to get a 'mother bear' reaction, but she'd been surprised by the complete lack of emotion Sharon showed. Sharon had told her daughter that she would handle it, and that she'd make sure Fenton Ririe didn't bother her anymore. That was it. No explanation, no phone call to the school—just a strange, almost dangerous calm that seemed to take over.

"And Coach Jones still set up a meeting?" Principal Anderson asked, drawing Thyra out of her thoughts.

Thyra nodded.

"I find that hard to believe," the principal said. "Coach Jones knows there are proper avenues for recruiters to speak with student athletes. He wouldn't have agreed to such a meeting."

"I could tell Coach Jones wasn't happy about it," Thyra said as calmly as she could muster. "The meeting started out fine, but the recruiter turned aggressive toward me and Coach Jones really fast. He even grabbed me by the wrist before Coach Jones stepped in and gave me time to leave."

"He touched you?" Principal Anderson asked. "That is a serious allegation. There is zero tolerance for that kind of behavior. You're sure that was what happened?"

Thyra nodded, but her confidence wavered suddenly. She began to fear she had made a mistake when Principal Anderson's expression softened.

"I'm sorry if it seems like I'm doubting you," Principal Anderson said. "I've heard of recruiters being more aggressive and pushing for unofficial meetings with student athletes. I'm sure such meetings have happened under my watch without me knowing, but I'd like to think that they don't and that my coaches all adhere to a higher code of conduct. Especially Eddie Jones." The principal sighed. "When was this meeting with the recruiter?"

"Yesterday, during third period," Thyra replied.

Principal Anderson frowned, his eyes growing distant for a moment. He blinked heavily and then his eyes refocused on Thyra. His expression hardened and he leaned forward, resting his elbows on his desk.

"You're putting me in a difficult position, Thyra," he said in a grim tone. "On the one hand, I have a story from a student saying that a recruiter physically assaulted her and the only other witness is currently in the hospital. On the other hand, I have a recruiter that I've never seen before today that came to my office in order to begin the process of requesting an official recruitment meeting with you. Normally, I would side with you without question since my duty is to protect my students. But I can't help but see the holes in your story."

Thyra was shocked by the sudden change. "Holes? I don't understand what you mean."

Principal Andersen took a deep breath. "Besides the fact that the only other person who can corroborate your story is not in any position to do so, there is also the evidence presented by Mr. Ririe himself that proves your story false."

"What do you mean?"

45

"For starters, I know for a fact that Mr. Ririe was across town on Meridian's campus yesterday during third period," the principal said. "He was there all day, actually, and then spent the evening on two official visits with players and their families."

"How can that be?" Thyra said. "He was here. I saw him here. He spoke with Coach Jones and I."

"No, he wasn't," Principal said. "I was ready to believe you, Thyra, but I'm afraid you are caught in a lie. You've embarrassed yourself with this story, and I find it startling that you would use Coach Jones' injuries as a means to embellish whatever fantasy you've concocted. I don't know what you have imagined, or why, but it needs to end now."

Thyra was blind-sided by the sudden change in tone of the conversation. She sat back in her chair and stared in shock across the desk at Principal Anderson.

"The weight of proof is on his side," the principal said. "I don't know what reason you have to lie about all of this, but I think you owe him an apology."

"An apology?"

"That's right," Principal Anderson said grimly. "He should be here soon. I had planned to meet with you first to gauge your interest before sharing your mother's contact information with him. I told him to return at the start of lunch with the expectation that you would be on board. Now, instead of recommending an official visit with you and your mother, I think I should recommend that you apologize to him and the two of you part ways amicably. Be glad your story went no further than this office, young lady. This kind of lie could have been enough to lessen your prospects of future recruiting visits. If you apologize to him face to face, I'm sure we can avoid this casting a shadow over your future."

"You want me to face him?" Thyra asked.

"I expect you to offer a sincere apology," Principal Anderson said sternly.

Thyra felt a flash of anger cut through her shock. She couldn't believe this was happening. It wasn't fair!

"And if I don't?"

"Then your punishment will be determined," Principal Anderson said. "But you can be sure that it will be extensive. You'd also have to hope that Mr. Ririe doesn't push for anything further."

Thyra couldn't believe this was happening, but she didn't see any way out of it. She had no alibi with Coach Jones in the hospital, and it was clear that Principal Anderson had his mind made up.

The phone on his desk beeped and Judy's voice spoke. "Fenton Ririe is here to see you."

"One moment, Judy," Principal Anderson said. He looked across the desk at Thyra. "Make your decision, Thyra. You can choose to run and hide, or you can choose to face him and do the right thing. Don't risk your future by being petty."

Thyra ground her teeth in frustration. "You don't make it seem like I have a choice."

"You always have a choice," Principal Anderson said. "But you should know that in this case there is a right one and a wrong one. It's up to you."

It didn't feel like it. Unable to see a way out of this, Thyra steeled her nerve in preparation for seeing Ririe again. She pushed herself to her feet and started for the door. She pulled it open and stepped back into the main office. Her eyes fell on Fenton Ririe and immediately she felt her skin begin to crawl. For a brief moment, she froze in place, unable to move in any direction.

"Thyra Ariksen, right?" Fenton Ririe said as he stood. He smiled at her. "I recognize you from the game the other night. It's good to meet you."

By sheer force of will, Thyra made her feet move. She stopped a few feet short of Fenton Ririe and looked up at him.

"It seems that we have a misunderstanding," Principal Anderson said as he moved around Thyra and took up a position next to Ririe. "You see, Ms. Ariksen is convinced you made a visit to the school yesterday and spoke with her and Coach Jones in an unofficial capacity."

"Oh?" Ririe's eyebrows shot up. "I can assure you that didn't happen. I was across town at Meridian High all day."

"Which is what I told her," Principal Anderson said. "She also made the allegation that you physically assaulted her."

Ririe's eyes went wide. "I can assure you that did not happen. I would never use force to coerce a student."

Principal Anderson was nodding his head enthusiastically. "Of course not. You seem like a professional person, so I know what this kind of allegation could do to you if it was spread around. Which is why I told Thyra that I think it is only fair if she apologizes to you in person." He turned and looked at her. "Thyra?"

"I'm sorry for telling Principal Anderson those things about you," Thyra said stiffly. "I should not have brought them to him in the first place."

The underlying meaning was not lost on Principal Anderson. Thyra heard him hiss her name, but Fenton Ririe waved the principal off. He gave Thyra a broad smile.

"I accept your apology. I'm sure the news about your lacrosse coach's hospitalization has frightened you. Sometimes, when we're scared the mind can play tricks on us. I'm sure that is what happened here."

"That may be, Mr. Ririe," Principal Anderson said from where he stood, "but I find it alarming that she would target you specifically. I am sorry for any distress these allegations may have caused you."

"Don't be," the recruiter said. "I was at the State Lacrosse Finals, and I'm sure she saw me there. My appearance is somewhat rough, I admit, and this wasn't the first time that I have inspired discomfort in

48

those I meet. Once people get to know me, though, I can assure you that discomfort fades and is quickly replaced by something else."

Thyra could think of several things that 'something' might be, and none of them were pleasant.

The recruiter turned back to Thyra and smiled. "I hope that will be the case with you as well, Ms. Ariksen. I was very impressed by your play the other night. I actually came here today to speak with Coach Jones about you, in hopes of setting up an official meeting with you and your parents. I was sad to hear about what happened to Coach Jones. But I hope that doesn't mean I'll miss out on recruiting such a talented student athlete to Folkhaven College."

"I don't think I am interested," Thyra said sharply.

"Well, I am sad to hear that," Fentron Ririe said, his smile never slipping. The recruiter held out his hand. "In that case, let me shake your hand at least and all this will be forgotten."

Thyra stared at the recruiter's hand like it was a poisonous snake. She remembered the feel on his hand on her wrist, and every part of her screamed out against feeling that touch again.

"Ms. Ariksen," Principal Anderson said in warning. "Shake his hand so that we can end this business."

Thyra felt helpless, and she didn't see a way around the situation. It wasn't right to require her to shake his hand in light of what she told Principal Anderson, but here she was, faced with doing exactly that. Seeing no other choice, she decided to make it as quick as possible. She began to reach out, but the door to the office suddenly flew open and Mr. Agi filled the doorway. For a brief moment, time seemed to freeze in place as the English teacher and Fenton Ririe locked gazes. Thyra couldn't explain it, but it was clear neither man was happy to see the other.

"Ah, Ms. Ariksen!" Mr. Agi said, turning his attention to Thyra as he crossed the office. "What a pleasant surprise to find you here. I've been looking for you. I knew you were in the gym this period, but when you weren't there I wondered if you had left school for the day. You left some of your books in my class, and I wanted to make sure they were returned to you."

Thyra eyed the English teacher in confusion. The weight of her backpack spoke to all of her books being present, and even if she had left some behind, why would he think to come to the office in order to find her? She was about to ask that very question, but something in Mr. Agi's eyes stopped her.

"We should get them back to you before next period begins," Mr. Agi said. "I'd hate for you to be without them for class. Or worse, be late to class. I know Alice Brown has no patience for tardiness. The rigors of sophomore biology wait for no one."

"Excuse us, Bruce," Principal Anderson said, "but you are interrupting something."

"Am I?" The English teacher looked around the office, his eyes taking in the scene. "From the looks of it, this recruiter is making an unofficial visit with Thyra in your office. A visit with no coaches present, and more importantly, without her mother in attendance."

"This was by coincidence only," Principal Anderson said.

"Then you wouldn't mind if I stole Ms. Ariksen to return her books to her," Mr. Agi said. "It was a coincidence that I found her here, after all."

"Our business is almost finished," Fenton Ririe said, his eyes focusing on Thyra again. "One handshake, and Ms. Ariksen can go."

"A handshake that Ms. Ariksen doesn't appear anxious to participate in," Mr. Agi said. He turned to Principal Anderson. "Is this what we've stooped to, Jerry? Forcing our students to have physical contact against their will? A handshake may seem benign, but if we force Thyra to do this, how long before we are allowing worse to happen?"

"That's taking it a bit far, Bruce," the principal said, but Thyra was relieved to see doubt in his eyes.

"Is it?" Mr. Agi asked. "Maybe we should call Ms. Ariksen's mother and ask her how she feels about you *forcing* her daughter to shake the hand of a stranger?"

Mr. Anderson fidgeted for a moment before shaking his head. "I don't think that is necessary. Thyra, you can go."

"What harm could a handshake do?" Fenton Ririe asked before Thyra could move. "She made a serious and offensive allegation against me. I made the decision to ignore it, and all I ask for in return is a simple handshake."

"With a *man* like you, a handshake is never what it seems," Mr. Agi said grimly. "Come, Thyra. I have your books in my classroom. Let's make sure you aren't late for any of your other classes."

Thyra, confused as she was by Mr. Agi's comment, was grateful for the opportunity to escape and left the office as quickly as she could without looking like she was fleeing. Mr. Agi was at her side in a flash. He motioned down the hall away from the office.

"Hurry, Thyra," the English teacher said. "Time is short."

Not understanding, Thyra looked up at the clock on the wall. "This period doesn't end for ten minutes."

"It isn't the end of the period I'm worried about," Mr. Agi said. "When we get to my classroom, I will explain."

"Explain what?" Thyra asked guardedly.

"Trust me," Mr. Agi said. "Fenton Ririe is not who he says he is."

Thyra agreed with that, and quickly fell in behind Mr. Agi. As they turned down the hall leading to Mr. Agi's classroom, Thyra risked taking a look back. A chill ran down her spine when she saw Fenton Ririe standing outside the office watching her.

Chapter 5

Mr. Agi closed the door to his classroom behind them and locked it. He mumbled something under his breath and tapped the four corners of the door frame.

"What's going on?" Thyra demanded.

"You're in danger," Mr. Agi muttered as he moved to his desk. He opened a drawer and began to rummage through it.

"From Fenton Ririe?" Thyra asked.

"He's the most obvious danger, yes," Mr. Agi said without looking up, "but he is only the tip of the iceberg, unfortunately. We thought we had more time."

"Who is 'we'?"

Mr. Agi looked up from the drawer. "Your mother and I."

"You know my mom?"

Mr. Agi nodded. "Yes, quite well, in fact. You could say I've known her for what feels like forever."

Something about the way he said that last word sent a shiver through Thyra. "Who are you?"

Mr. Agi left the question unanswered as he continued to rifle through the drawer. Thyra heard a click and was surprised when Mr. Agi tossed aside the drawer. He reached into his desk and muttered a few words in a language that Thyra didn't understand. The teacher pulled a small, black velvet bag out from under the desk and stood up.

"Time to go," he said.

"Go where?" Thyra asked cautiously.

"To your house to pick up your mother," Mr. Agi said. "I called her the moment I heard that Ririe was here. She should be nearly home by now. We need to collect her and then get away from here as quickly as possible."

He headed towards the door, pausing again to tap the four corners of the frame, uttering more words that Thyra didn't recognize.

"What are you doing?"

"Making sure Fenton Ririe doesn't follow too close on our heels," Mr. Agi said. He turned around and uttered another string of words in a strange language. He finished and grimaced. "It's been a long time since I've done this, but it will have to do. Hopefully, it buys us enough time to get a head start on him."

Thyra felt a strange sensation settle on her, almost like she was wearing an invisible second layer of skin.

"What was that?"

"I created a mirror image of us and did my best to make us invisible to anyone looking for us," Mr. Agi explained.

Thyra looked at him in confusion. "Wait, what are you talking about? What do you mean you created a mirror image of us and made us invisible?"

"I mean exactly what I said," Mr. Agi said without looking at her.

"Are you talking about," Thyra hesitated before finishing her question, "about magic?"

Mr. Agi nodded. "That's right."

Thyra shook her head. "But magic isn't real."

"Magic is very real, Thyra," Mr. Agi said. "I know this may come as a shock, but magic exists! There's an entire world of people like me who are trying their best to live everyday lives while keeping their true selves concealed."

"People like you?"

"You know me as Bruce Agi, English Literature teacher, but that isn't my real name," he said. "My real name is Bragi."

Thyra's eyebrows shot up. She knew that name, but it was impossible. "Bragi? As in the Norse god of poetry and storytelling?"

He nodded. "One and the same."

"That's impossible," Thyra said.

"It's possible," Mr. Agi said, "and I'll prove it to you."

He opened his mouth and stuck out his tongue, causing Thyra to step back in surprise. Her jaw dropped when small blue, glowing symbols appeared down the length of his tongue. Thyra had never seen runes before, but she immediately knew that was what they were.

"Those are the runes Odin put on my tongue himself almost a thousand years ago," Mr. Agi said. "I know it may be difficult to accept, but I am Bragi. Those stories we studied, about gods, magic, and monsters—it's all real, Thyra, and you are caught in the middle of it. Right now, we need to leave before one of those monsters finds us."

"What monster?" Thyra asked, forcing herself to speak through her shock.

"Fenton Ririe," Mr. Agi said as he opened the door. He checked the hall and then looked back over his shoulder at Thyra. "He is no recruiter—he's the shapeshifter, Fenrir!"

Thyra's eyes went wide. She had heard the stories of Fenrir many times. Said to be bigger than a grizzly bear and possessed of a strength even the gods feared, the stories about Fenrir, the giant wolf in service to Hela, had always scared Thyra as a little girl. Faced with the possibility that they could actually be true, Thyra realized that those fears still lived inside her.

As if to emphasize that realization, she felt a bitter chill begin to work itself through her.

"We head for the parking lot and then back to your house," Mr. Agi said, scanning the hallway again. "We have to move quickly."

Thyra stood frozen in place. She had felt this kind of chill before, but it had never progressed this fast before. She tried to shrug it off and whispered softly, "Not now."

Mr. Agi heard her and gave her a confused look over his shoulder. "What was that?"

Thyra ignored the question and forced herself to walk towards the door. "Is the coast clear?"

"It's clear," Mr. Agi said.

Thyra was past him and running for the parking lot before he even finished. Bragi hurried to follow, but she easily outpaced him even with a river of ice quickly spreading through her. She was through the doors and into the parking lot before she realized that she didn't even know what kind of car Mr. Agi drove. A blue SUV honked suddenly, and the doors unlocked, answering her question. She ran over to it and was already buckled in the passenger seat by the time Mr. Agi reached the vehicle.

"I don't think he's following us," Mr. Agi said as he started up the SUV and put it in gear.

"That's good, right?"

Mr. Agi didn't look convinced. "Maybe. It means my magic did what it was supposed to, or that he never tried to follow us in the first place."

"And that's bad?"

Mr. Agi nodded. "That means we might be walking into a trap."

"A trap?" Thyra asked.

The moment the words left her mouth, her chest tightened, and her entire body went stiff as the cold fully enveloped her.

Mr. Agi noticed, and concern flashed across his face. "Thyra, are you okay?"

The answer was no but admitting it would only make it worse. She had gone through this before—the feeling of not being able to get warm, body aches, and feverish thoughts—and she knew that there was only one person who could help her.

"Get me to my Mom," Thyra said, her teeth chattering.

Mr. Agi sped up, tearing out of the parking lot and out into the street. He glanced over at Thyra repeatedly, the concern on his face evident, but he didn't speak.

Cars whizzed by as Mr. Agi turned onto Apple Street and turned south. A quarter of a mile later, he hung a right onto a quiet street lined with green lawns and two-story homes.

By the time they reached the Ariksens' house, Thyra felt like she had been sitting in an ice bath in the middle of the Arctic. Her body ached and her muscles were pulled so tight that she was sure her bones would begin snapping one by one.

This was worse than it had ever been.

Bragi roared into the driveway and put the SUV into park. He jumped out of the vehicle and came around to the passenger side door. He hooked one of Thyra's arms over his shoulders and gently lifted her out of her seat.

They were almost to the door leading into the kitchen when Sharon opened it. She took one look at her daughter and her face paled.

"When did it start?"

"Just a few minutes ago," Mr. Agi said as he stepped by Sharon.

"Put her on the couch," Sharon instructed.

"What is happening to her?" Mr. Agi asked as he set her down on the couch.

"Exactly what you think," Sharon said. She knelt down next to Thyra and put a hand on her forehead. "This has happened before, but never like this. It always showed itself like she caught a fever."

"This is no fever," Mr. Agi said.

"Go up to her room," Sharon said. "There's a brown stuffed bear on her bed. Bring that to me."

"I don't think a teddy bear is what she needs," Mr. Agi said. "Fenrir was at the school, and where he goes, his mistress is sure to follow. We can't stay here."

"I know that, but Thyra can't be moved until we know she is through the worst of it," Sharon said. She looked up at Mr. Agi. "Trust me. Get the bear!"

Mr. Agi didn't look pleased, but he complied, leaving Sharon alone with Thyra.

"I'm so cold, Mom," Thyra said weakly.

"You're going to be okay, honey," Sharon said as she gently stroked Thyra's forehead.

Mr. Agi returned with the bear. Sharon took it and put it under the blankets against Thyra's chest. Immediately, Thyra felt a surge of warmth begin to combat the ice in her veins.

"That will help," Sharon said. "You're going to be okay."

She stood up and hurried into the kitchen. Mr. Agi followed close on her heels.

"We don't have time for this," he said, his voice just barely reaching Thyra's ears. "We must go before Fenrir comes."

"We can't leave until we know Thyra is improving," Sharon said. "You know as well as I what could happen if we try to force her to move too soon. Is that what you want? Do you want her to go through this while we're all in a metal box on wheels? You know how dangerous that could be, Bragi."

Thyra's thoughts were beginning to get muddled, but the sound of that name cut through the haze momentarily. Hearing her mom say it served as confirmation that her English teacher had been telling the truth.

"Of course not," Bragi said. "But I don't think laying on the couch cuddling a teddy bear is going to do her—or us!—any good!"

"I'm her mother, so trust me when I say this will help," Sharon said. "I knew this was coming. It always does after she has an incident."

"An incident?"

"At the lacrosse game," Sharon said. "She lost her temper and her eyes began to glow. Just for a second, but it was unmistakable."

"Her body is battling her true nature," Bragi said in a voice just above a whisper. "I know the awakening is different for everyone, but do you honestly believe that staying here is what we should be doing?"

"Neither one of us knows what to expect from her," Sharon said. "Her awakening might be a small flash of magic, or it might be something much worse. Do you want to risk the latter happening while you're driving?"

Thyra couldn't grasp what they were talking about. She tried to call out, but it came out as a weak groan. The warmth from the bear had helped, but it wasn't enough. She was still ice cold, and even laying still was painful. She tried to find a comfortable position but lacked the strength to move.

She tried one more time to call out to her mom, but her voice failed her, and the effort cost her. The haze over her thoughts grew to a thick, dark blanket that threatened to swallow her completely. She tried to fight it off, but she couldn't. Her resistance shattered and she fell into the black.

* * *

Thyra's eyes opened to a world of blue. She blinked against the strange color of the sky, but it didn't change anything. She looked around and was surprised to see that she wasn't on the couch in her house anymore. In fact, she got the sense that she was in a place altogether different than the one she knew.

She turned in a slow circle and stared out into the endless blue abyss surrounding her. She had almost completed her turn when she stopped cold. Where there had been nothing but empty, blue space, a dark tree now stood. It was the strangest looking tree she had ever seen. The trunk was dark, almost black, and reached up until it was lost among leaves that shone with light.

Welcome, Thyra.

Thyra spun around in surprise. "Who's there?"

I've been waiting for you, the voice said.

Thyra tried to find the source of the voice, but it was only her and the tree in the endless blue expanse. She looked at the tree and felt a strange sensation wash over her. She felt like she knew the tree.

"Was that you?" She asked. "Are you talking to me?"

The tree stood as quiet as any other tree. Cautiously, she approached the tree, extended her hand, and let her fingers brush the dark bark.

Do not be afraid, Thyra, voice said inside her head. *We are alone, and you are safe.*

Thyra jerked at the sound of the voice and almost pulled her hand away. "You're a talking tree. Am I dreaming?"

In a sense, the voice replied. *You are not physically with me, but neither are you dreaming. We're somewhere between your reality and mine. Very soon the day will come when you will stand at my feet and touch my bark, Thyra.*

"How do you know who I am?"

I knew you before you drew your first breath, came the chilling response. *You are a part of me just as much as I am a part of you.*

As much as the tree's response unnerved Thyra, she didn't remove her hand. "What are you?"

I am the source of magic in the world, but you would know me by the name I gave Odin—Yggdrasil, the voice said. *I am the World Tree, and my roots run through all realms and all of time. I know everyone that has walked this earth, including you.*

The answer both alarmed and excited Thyra. She was talking to the World Tree from her mom's stories! But how was that possible?

I am the source of magic, the life force of the earth, and what connects all things, the tree explained. *I am the power to create and destroy, give life and take it. You see me as the World Tree because that is the form you would accept, but this is not my true nature. I have taken many different forms, depending on the champion I choose.*

I have always existed, the tree continued, *but rarely been understood. Mankind has worshipped me and cursed me. Men have claimed dominion because of me, and others have sought to kill any that bear my gift. They do not understand that I cannot be destroyed, nor can I be controlled. I exist in all time, in all places, and in everything.*

Thyra felt her head swimming with what the tree had just told her. "You're the source of magic? I don't understand. What do you want with me?"

I've been waiting for you, the voice said, *but you have proven to be resilient to my calls. Your stubbornness has proven to be a strong barrier. But time was growing short, and I could wait no longer.*

"Why were you waiting for me?"

You are the daughter of gods, Thyra, came the reply. *Your true nature has been hidden from you, but the time for hiding is over. The world is changing, and you are needed. You must accept who you were meant to be. Your potential is immense, and I will not let that potential be wasted.*

Thyra recalled Fenton Ririe saying something very similar about her potential and it sent a shiver through her.

"What does that have to do with me?"

You are what the world needs, the tree replied. *You are a child of both the past and the present—of the world of magic and the world of men. A bridge between what was, and what is. You are the key to help my power grow again.*

"Your power? You mean magic?"

Yes.

60

"And I have magic?"

Powerful magic, Yggdrasil said. *It has revealed itself at times, but only when your resistance flickered briefly.*

Thyra shook her head. "I don't understand. I've never felt anything magical happen."

That is because the truth has been hidden from you, the tree said. *You have built up walls to resist my call to you. Tearing down those walls is what causes your body to suffer, as you are now. You resist me, even now.*

"I'm not trying to resist," Thyra said.

Yet, you are, the tree stated. *Even now I am reaching out to you but cannot touch you. You are closed off, unwilling to accept your true nature.*

She remembered what Bragi said about her body fighting her true nature. "The cold that swept over me—that was my body fighting against magic?"

Yes. This is not the first time I've called to you but you have always fought against answering my call.

"How do I stop fighting it?" Thyra asked. "What do I need to do?"

Accept the truth, Yggdrasil said. *You are the daughter of gods, Thyra, and are a vessel of my power.*

"I don't understand it," Thyra said. That was an understatement—all of this was a lot to take in—but Thyra found herself wanting to believe it was true. Her mother had always said that the difference between *wanting* to believe and *believing* was a choice made. Thyra made that choice now.

"I don't understand, but I believe you," Thyra said. "I am the daughter of gods and can use magic."

Thyra felt a rush of exhilaration coming from Yggdrasil.

Then receive my gift, Thyra Ariksen.

Thyra felt a surge of energy rush into her from the tree. It felt like a torrent of fire that threatened to rip her apart. She let out a scream of agony as it continued to rip into her.

And then it ended. She sagged to her knees, her lungs screaming for air.

You are now connected to me, the voice said in her head. *You are a child of the storm, a being of fury and destruction, a creature of lightning. The storms will do your bidding.*

Thyra stood slowly. Immediately, she felt the difference inside. Where there had previously been an emptiness, there was now a ball of violent energy. She saw a pulsing blue cord that protruded from her chest and ran to the roots of the tree. She reached out with one hand to touch it but recoiled when she saw blue, crackling tendrils dancing between her fingertips.

"What did you do to me?"

You are connected to my power, the tree said. *You now can use the power you were born with but were unable to touch.*

"Magic," Thyra said to herself. She held up her hand and stared at the blue-white tendrils. "Is this lightning?"

You control the power of the storms, the tree said.

"Amazing," Thyra said in an awestruck voice. She turned her hand over and watched the tendrils of lightning perform their dance.

The time has come for you to return to the world of men, Yggdrasil said.

"Wait! That's it?" Thyra shook her head. "That's all you're going to tell me?"

I will call you again when there is more time. A shudder ran through the tree. *They are coming! You must go or all will be lost.*

"Wait!" Thyra began to protest, but a blast of bright blue light filled her vision, and her words were lost.

* * *

Thyra jolted awake.

She no longer felt ice cold and the pain in her body was gone.

One thing that remained, though, was the ball of angry energy inside her.

She looked toward the kitchen and saw her mom and Bragi still standing there talking. She sat up, testing her strength, and then stood. Her sudden movement caught their attention, and her mom hurried over to her.

"Thyra?" Sharon said, wrapping her arms around Thyra. "Are you okay?"

Thyra nodded. "I think I am now."

Bragi approached much more cautiously. "Did something happen?"

Thyra nodded. "I had a dream. Of a black tree with glowing leaves."

"Yggdrasil!" Bragi gasped. "You saw the World Tree?"

Thyra nodded again. "I think so. She told me that I had magic, and she did something to make it so that I could use it."

"It's called awakening," Bragi said. "But I've never heard of someone seeing the World Tree during their awakening."

"Did the tree say anything to you?" Sharon asked, a hint of fear in her eyes. "About who you are?"

"It said I am a daughter of the gods," Thyra said. "That I am a child of the storm."

Bragi nodded. "That's no surprise."

Sharon shot him a sharp glare. Something passed between the two of them that Thyra didn't understand and Bragi cleared his throat nervously.

"Did the tree say anything else?" Sharon asked, her eyes searching Thyra's.

Thyra wasn't sure what her mom was asking, so she shook her head. A look of relief crossed Sharon's face. Relief with a twinge of guilt.

"Did you know?" Thyra asked her mom. "Did you know that I had magic?"

Sharon turned back to Thyra. "I knew. What I didn't know was when the magic would awaken inside of you. It's shown signs a few times over the years, but you've always fought it off."

"That's when I've gotten sick?" Thyra said.

Sharon nodded. "You've always fallen sick a few days after your magic has come to the surface. It isn't out of the ordinary for that to happen, but you've always been different."

"What is out of the ordinary is the length of time it took," Bragi said. "Your mom said this has been happening for years off and on."

"And I had it in hand," Sharon said sharply without looking at Bragi. "Until now."

"Did the tree say anything else?" Bragi asked. "About something other than you possessing magic?"

Thyra nodded. "It said that someone was coming."

"Who?" Bragi asked.

Thyra shrugged. "All it said was 'they are coming.' What does that mean?"

As if on cue, the doorbell rang.

Bragi put a finger to his lips and then tip-toed down the hall towards the front door. He looked through the peephole and then pulled back like he'd been burned. He rushed back to Thyra and her mom, his eyes wide.

"I think we just ran out of time."

Chapter 6

"We know you're in there, Bragi," a woman's voice called through the door. "Don't make this harder than it needs to be. Open the door."

Thyra looked between her mom and Bragi. She saw the dread on both of their faces.

"Who is it?" Sharon asked.

"Fenrir and Hela," Bragi said.

"Hela?" Thyra asked, her eyes going wide with fear.

Bragi nodded. "It seems the dog wasted no time calling to his mistress. She must have been close already to be here so soon."

"She always kept him on a short leash," Sharon said.

Thyra found that an odd thing to say—how would her mom know a thousand-year-old goddess?—but that question didn't seem important at the moment. Sharon knew Bragi, after all, even though Thyra still didn't understand how that came to be.

"You have five minutes," Hela's voice came through the door. "If you aren't out by then, I'm sending the wolf in. Your time starts now."

"We can't walk out there," Bragi said. "My magic is no match for hers, you have none, and Thyra has barely had her awakening. Even if she tried, there's no guarantee she could even use her magic, much less give Hela even the smallest challenge."

Thyra didn't appreciate having her abilities marginalized so readily, but deep down she knew Bragi was right. The ball of energy inside of her waited for her touch, but she found herself recoiling from it reflexively. Even if she wanted to try, she didn't know what to do or how to do it. She'd be no help.

"Don't forget that I am not defenseless," Sharon said grimly. While Thyra was sure her eyes were wide with fright, her mom had adopted a deathly calm demeanor.

"That may be," Bragi said, "but do you think you can hold your own against both Hela and her wolf?"

Sharon took a deep breath and then shook her head. "One, yes, but not both. There has to be another way."

"I'm open to suggestions," Bragi said. "But we had better come up with one quick."

Thyra looked between the two adults, waiting for a plan to develop, but with each passing second her confidence began to grow weaker. She closed her eyes and tried to think. What could they do against Hela, a goddess? Thyra could only guess at what kind of power she had. What did they have that they could fight back with?

That thought made her pause, and she looked up at Bragi. "You're a god, right?"

Bragi nodded. "Yes, but not the kind of god like Hela. I'm no warrior."

"Maybe not, but what can you do?"

"I'm a storyteller," Bragi said. "I talk and put images in the minds of my listeners."

"Can you do that to Hela?" Thyra asked. "Can you make her see an illusion?"

Sharon nodded. "Thyra's right. Do you think you can convince her that she is seeing all three of us?"

Bragi shook his head. "Not without great difficulty. This is Hela we're talking about. She can sense a person's heartbeat from a mile away. She will know if we're not all there."

"Then we'll all be there," Sharon said. "We'll all be there, but you must make it so that what she sees gives you and Thyra time to escape."

"No, I'm not leaving you," Thyra protested immediately.

"Yes, you are," Sharon said. "I can give you and Bragi time to get away."

"How?"

"Because," Sharon said, "I'm the last face she'll expect to see."

"What?" Thyra asked. "Why would she expect to see you at all?"

"We've met before," Sharon explained without actually answering the question. "She'll be distracted when she sees me and may not see through illusion until it is too late."

Bragi was already shaking his head. "Even if that were true, it would take all my concentration to create an illusion she wouldn't see through. I wouldn't be able to split my focus long enough to walk, much less drive away from here."

"Then Thyra will have to drive," Sharon said.

Bragi was shaking his head. "I don't like it."

"You don't have to like it," Sharon said. "Just do it. We don't have time to come up with a better plan. You create the illusion and keep it in place long enough for you and Thyra to get away. I'll serve as a distraction. If I can keep Hela's attention long enough, she may not notice the illusion until it is too late."

"It's a terrible plan," Bragi said.

"But it's the only one we have," Sharon said. "Just do your part, and I'll take care of the rest."

Bragi muttered something under his breath but didn't argue. He closed his eyes and began to mumble to himself softly.

Sharon turned to her daughter and put her hands on Thyra's shoulders. "You will have to guide Bragi to the car. You must be as quiet as possible. Any sound could be enough to tip them off and ruin Bragi's illusion."

Thyra shook her head. "I don't know if I can do this. I don't want to leave you."

"Don't worry about me," Sharon said. "I am not as defenseless as you might think. I've faced a god or two in my life. I'll be fine."

"What? What do you mean you've faced a god before?"

Sharon took a deep breath. "There are so many things I wish I could tell you, but there isn't enough time. Just trust me. Can you do that?"

Thyra nodded numbly.

"Thank you, sweetheart," Sharon said. She cupped Thyra's face with her hands. "You're strong, Thyra. Stronger than you know and much stronger than you believe."

Thyra tightened her grip on her mom's arms. "This is crazy. Is this all just a bad dream that I'm going to wake up from?"

"This is no dream," Sharon said. "This is the world you were born into. I tried to keep you away from it, but I always knew it would find us. Magic, gods, monsters—this is your reality now. You have to be strong and believe in yourself."

"Why?" Thyra asked. "Why didn't you tell me before?"

"I thought I was protecting you," Sharon said. "I thought maybe I could keep you from becoming like the others."

"What others?" Thyra asked. She saw the guilt in her mom's eyes return.

"I'm ready," Bragi said, interrupting Sharon's response. He reached out and touched Sharon and Thyra on the shoulder. Thyra felt a similar sensation as before, like a second skin settling on her. "We must go now. I can only hold it in place for so long."

"You know what you have to do," Sharon said to Thyra. "Whatever you see or hear, keep quiet and get away from here as quickly as you can."

"Where should I go?" Thyra asked.

"Bragi will know," Sharon replied. "Trust him to guide you until I find you."

"Okay," Thyra said.

Sharon put a hand on Thyra's cheek. "I love you, sweetheart."

"I love you too, Mom," Thyra said.

"We must go now," Bragi said in a strained tone. "It's in place, but... she's...she's so strong."

"Follow me out the door," Sharon said, the deathly calm back, "and get to the car as quick as you can. Remember, stay quiet no matter what you see or hear."

Thyra nodded her understanding. She took Bragi's arm and began leading him toward the door. Her mom led the way down the hall, pausing for just a moment to retrieve a bar of polished steel from above the row of family pictures in the hallway. Thyra had often wondered about the two-foot long bar of steel that her mom referred to as the 'family heritage,' an explanation that was usually followed with words like 'tradition', 'honor', and 'loyalty.' At the end of the day, the conclusion Thyra had come to was that it was just a piece of metal.

But, looking at the way Sharon Ariksen held it, Thyra began to wonder if that was the case.

Sharon pushed the front door open, flooding the entryway with light, and stepped through slowly. Thyra hesitated, fear gripping her briefly as she tried to imagine what was waiting outside, and then took a tentative step through the door.

"You?" A dark-haired woman said, her vibrant green eyes narrowed to slits.

There was no doubt in Thyra's mind that this was Hela, the goddess of death. Her features were a complicated mix of soft curves and hard angles. She was regal, beautiful, and frightening all wrapped into one. Thyra tried to put an age to her but couldn't. She was mature, but still vibrant with youth.

"Hello, Hela," Sharon said, her deathly calm not cracking one bit as she spoke.

"This is a surprise," the goddess of death said. "When Fenrir told me about the girl, I was curious to meet her. That curiosity only grew when I learned that the old man was somehow connected to her. Now, I find you here. I'm giddy with excitement."

Thyra glanced at the goddess and didn't see anything bordering giddy in her grim expression. Menacing and hard, yes, but Thyra got the impression that Hela wasn't capable of displaying anything close to giddiness.

"Why are you here?" Sharon asked.

"You know why I'm here," Hela said. Her eyes moved to Sharon's left, to an empty space. "Where is it, old man?"

Thyra froze in confusion. Who was Hela talking to? Then she remembered Bragi's magic and realized that Hela was seeing something other than the truth.

"Where is what?" Sharon asked.

"Was I talking to you?" Hela snapped. "The old man has something I want. Once he gives it to me, I will be on your way. This doesn't have to involve you. Although, now that I know you're alive, I can't help but think that our paths will be crossing again very, very soon."

"It involved me the moment you came to my house with your dog," Sharon said. She held out the hand holding the steel bar. In a flash of light, the bar elongated into a six-foot long spear.

Thyra almost yelped in surprise when the spear appeared in her mom's hand. Any sound she might have made was thankfully covered up by the growl of Fenton Ririe as he rushed to stand between the two women.

"Come now," Hela said, placing a hand on Ririe's shoulder. She gently pulled him back to her side, almost like a dog being commanded to heel. "We are survivors of a war we did not start. I have no quarrel with you, as long as you give me what I want. All I want is the shard."

Thyra listened to the conversation as she led Bragi over to the SUV. She positioned him just behind the passenger door and then began to open it as quietly as possible.

"The shard?" Sharon asked. "I don't know what you're talking about?"

"I think you do," Hela said. "If you're alive, I can only assume that he must be as well. He must have told you about it."

Thyra had the feeling that the 'he' she referred to was not Bragi for some reason but was so focused on opening the door quietly that she couldn't think about it. The door latch finally came free and she pulled the door open slowly, praying that the hinge wouldn't betray her by squealing in protest.

"I know the shard is here," Hela said. "I can feel it close."

"I don't know what you're talking about," Sharon said, "but I can tell you that if you think we have this 'shard', you're wrong."

"I'm not wrong," Hela said. "I know he brought it here. Clearly, he just didn't tell you. What a surprise."

He? Were they talking about Bragi, or someone else? Thyra wasn't sure, but she was so focused on staying quiet that she couldn't consider the question.

Thyra got the door open all the way and began to help Bragi into the passenger seat. The old man must have been able to divert some attention from maintaining his illusion because he slid into the seat without Thyra having to do much of anything.

"You didn't know him as well as you think you do," Sharon said.

"Didn't I?" Hela sounded amused. "Perhaps not, but that doesn't change our situation. The shard is here."

Thyra closed the passenger door without a sound and began to move around the SUV. She risked a look back at the confrontation between her mom and Hela. She was shocked to see a polished, circular shield resting on her mom's left forearm. She didn't know where that came from, but its fit Sharon and the deadly persona she had adopted.

"If he is dead, like you clearly what me to believe, how do you explain the girl?" Hela said, her eyes drifting to an empty space to Sharon's right. "This must be your daughter. She looks just like you. But, those eyes. She is her father's daughter. Have you told her about him?"

Hela's question broke Thyra's focus and she looked up mid-step. Distracted, she didn't see the loose cement as she set her foot down. The cement shifted underfoot, the sound of stone grinding cutting through the air like a gunshot. Thyra's brief hope that it went unnoticed was dashed when she saw Ririe turn and stare right at her, his eyes narrowing dangerously.

"Something's wrong," he growled. He inclined his head slightly and sniffed the air. He looked at the empty spaces on either side of Thyra's mom suspiciously. "I see them there, but I smell them," he pointed right at Thyra, "there."

Hela looked at Sharon, her expression darkening. "Very clever."

The world seemed to stand still for a split second and then everything burst into frenzied motion. Ririe dove for the SUV but came up short as Thyra's mom crossed the distance in a flash and took his legs out from under him with her spear. She slammed her shield down as he tried to rise to his feet, dropping him again. She planted one foot on his neck to hold him in place and adopted a defensive posture.

Their ruse ruined, Thyra rushed to the driver side door and tore it open. She swung herself in and quickly jammed the key into the ignition. She gave it a twist, the engine roaring to life, but she hesitated.

"I see them now," Hela said. She held up a hand and Thyra felt a strange sensation, almost like something was moving around under her skin. Everywhere it went, it left behind a revolting, oily-feeling residue. Suddenly, her body went rigid and refused to obey her. "I can feel her power. She is strong, both physically and in her magic. A true credit to her heritage."

"Leave her alone," Sharon said. "She has nothing to do with this."

Hela tsked. "Of course, she does. You may have hidden who and what she is from her, but that doesn't change the truth." She looked over Sharon's shoulder to where Thyra sat. "You have questions, I can see them in those blue eyes. You deserve to hear the answers. Before it's too late."

"Enough!" Sharon spat. "Do not threaten my daughter."

"I'm beginning to understand," Hela said. "I came here assuming it was Bragi that had kept the shard hidden for all these years. I was wrong. After all, he wouldn't have been stupid enough to touch it after all those years of keeping it safe. No, only someone truly desperate would be foolish enough to touch a shard and ignite its power. Someone trying to help soothe the pains of the awakening, perhaps?"

"We're leaving now, Hela," Sharon said. "Release Thyra, or your wolf gets a shave."

Hela's smile was dark as she spoke. "I don't believe you'll do it. There's too much of that cursed Valkyrie honor in you, Sif."

Sif? Thyra recognized the name, but she couldn't remember why or where she had heard it.

Sharon placed the tip of her spear between Ririe's shoulder blades and glared at Hela. "Make a move, and this spear goes into his heart."

Uncertainty flashed across Hela's face. "That won't be necessary. I didn't come here to spill blood. Only to take what I require."

"We're leaving," Sharon said as she removed her foot from the back of Ririe's neck. His body tensed, but he made no attempt to move. Sharon stepped over him and reached for the handle of the door, her eyes never leaving those of Hela. "You should forget about this shard."

Hela shook her head. "That isn't going to happen. A storm is coming. Our kind have been in the shadows for too long. I say the time has come for the proper order of things to return. The world of men needs to be reminded where the power truly lies, and I plan to stand at the top. The tide is turning, and I will be ready when it…"

She trailed off, her eyes going distant. "Someone is coming."

The roar of engines split the air just before three black SUVs squealed to a stop. The doors opened and men in tactical gear piled out, barking commands and raising military-style rifles.

"Not good," Bragi said, coming out of his trance. He took one look at the men and his face went pale. "Not good at all!"

Hela's hold on Thyra faded suddenly and she regained control of her body. She spun in her seat and looked at the men. "Who are they?"

"The Muspel Corporation," Bragi said.

"The who?"

"Put it in gear and get ready to drive," Bragi said. Thyra did as she was told but kept her foot on the brake.

Outside the vehicle, Ririe pushed himself to his feet, in direct defiance of the orders that were being yelled at him and moved slowly to stand beside Hela. From the way Hela and Sharon were watching the newcomers, it was clear that the new threat superseded their previous squabble.

Sharon gently pushed the SUV door shut and took a step away from it. She turned her head slightly, her eyes meeting Thyra's, and mouthed a single word, "Run!"

Before Thyra could protest, her mom charged forward. The sound of gunfire filled the air and Thyra reacted instinctively, releasing the brakes and slamming on the gas. The SUV surged forward towards the house, and Thyra barely managed to turn the wheel to avoid crashing into the garage. She drove across the grass along the side of the house and straight through the bushes she had helped her mom plant the year before.

Thyra turned the SUV onto the road and pressed her foot down on the gas. Behind her, the sounds of gunfire rang in her eyes, spurring her on.

It wasn't until she was about to make the turn onto Apple Road that panic set in. She slammed on the brakes.

"What are you doing?" Bragi demanded.

"I can't leave my mom!" Thyra said in a voice tight with fear. "They were shooting at her!"

"Going back won't do her or us any good, Thyra. There's nothing the two of us can do for her that she can't do for herself."

"But she could be—" Thyra couldn't bring herself to say the word she was thinking. She shook her head. "I can't leave her behind."

"Thyra, trust me," Bragi said. "I don't like leaving your mother behind any more than you do, but we have to go."

Tears began to fill Thyra's eyes. "What if she's hurt?"

"Look at me, Thyra," Bragi said, waiting until she looked into his eyes. "If anyone can survive what just happened, it's your mother. The best thing we can do for her is to honor her wish and get to safety."

"I can't leave her," Thyra said.

"Then get out of that seat, and I will," Bragi said sharply. He must have realized how harsh he sounded, because he immediately looked remorseful. "We have to do this, Thyra. No matter how much it hurts. And we don't have time to argue. So, if you can't drive away, I will do it for you."

Thyra hated herself for it, but she finally nodded in agreement. Bragi was out of the SUV in a flash and was racing around to the driver side. Rather than get out of the vehicle, Thyra climbed over the console and settled into the passenger seat.

She looked back towards her house, hoping that maybe she would see her mom running after them, but she knew that wasn't going to happen.

She closed her eyes in denial of what was happening as Bragi sped out onto Apple Road and drove away.

Chapter 7

Thyra watched the grass covered hills pass by through the window of the SUV. They were somewhere outside of the city, but Thyra had long since stopped trying to keep track of where. Bragi had made dozens of turns, backtracked at least ten times, and made five random stops before pulling the SUV back out into the flow of traffic. He finally settled on a direction as the sun was setting on the horizon, but it wasn't until they were outside Boise heading east that he seemed to relax.

"Where are we going?" Thyra asked.

"Somewhere safe," Bragi said.

"What do you mean by 'safe'?"

"Somewhere where no one expects us to be," he replied.

"You've got to stop giving me answers like that," Thyra said in frustration. "I just left my mom behind with a bunch of guys shooting at her on one side and the goddess of death on the other. You giving me non-answers is not helping me feel any better!"

"I understand your frustration," Bragi said, "but I'm still working on this. The plan your mother and I had worked out was thrown out the window and now I'm winging it."

"You're *winging* it?" Thyra couldn't believe it. "My mom could be hurt or worse, and you're *winging* it?"

"I'm doing my best," Bragi said gruffly.

Thyra knew she should give me some slack, but she couldn't. She was afraid for her mom, confused about what was happening, and clueless about what lay ahead.

"Turn the car around," Thyra said. "If you don't have a plan, then I do—we go back and find my mom."

"We can't do that," Bragi said.

"Why not?"

"Because there's nothing we can do for her!" Bragi snapped. "We are not equipped to handle those kinds of threats. I am an old man who tells stories and creates illusions with words—not a warrior! And your magic has yet to reveal itself, much less prove to be under your control. We'd have no chance against those men, much less Hela."

"And my mom does?"

"You saw her," Bragi said. "She is far from helpless, trust me. If anything, she is probably safer than we are. The Muspel Corporation has a long reach and they will be looking for us."

"The Muspel Corporation?"

"A company that deals in telecommunications and energy," Bragi said. "But that is just a front. The CEO is set on eliminating magic and people like us. His name is Gunnar Olafsson, and he is a dangerous man."

"Why did they come after us?"

"Besides the fact that we have magic?" Bragi grimaced. "There's a long history there. A painful one."

Thyra rested her head back against the seat and stared at the roof of the car. "A few days ago, my greatest worry was my math final. Now, there's guys shooting at us, I've come face to face with Hela and Fenrir, and there's some guy who wants to rid the world of magic. This is crazy."

"I wish I could say that was the worst of it," Bragi said, "but there are more things waiting in the shadows of our world. Things that might be even worse than Hela or Gunnar Olafsson."

"How's that even possible?" Thyra said. "Hela is literally the goddess of death! What could be worse than that?"

Bragi took a deep breath. "There are things I fear more than Hela."

Thyra considered asking what those things could be, but she had other questions that needed answering.

"Why did Hela and Fenrir come looking for us?"

"The answer to that is interwoven with the very reason of our existence," Bragi said. "I'll try to explain eight hundred years of history as quickly as I can." He took a deep breath. "I guess I should start at the very beginning with the fact that magic exists and has since the very beginning of time. It's a gift that few are born with. Over the course of human history, there were times when it was accepted, even sought after. During those times, magic users often found themselves elevated to god-like stations—like the Norse gods. We were a small group of magic users that rose to power after Odin sought out Yggdrasil and became its champion. We became gods and lived as such for hundreds of years.

"Of course, the same thing happened to us as happened to others. Our pride blinded us. The common man became jealous and began to hate the very gods they created. Magic users were often hunted down and slaughtered by the very people who worshipped them and offered sacrifices in their name only a short time before. Magic became more of a curse than a gift during those times."

"Okay, but what does that have to do with why Hela came looking for us?" Thyra said impatiently. "She acted like she thought you had something. A shard?"

Bragi tensed at the word. "I don't know why she said that. Why she would think that I have one escapes me."

"Why not? What was she talking about?"

Bragi shifted in his seat uncomfortably. "Do you remember the story of how Odin lost his eye?"

Thyra nodded. "Odin went to Yggdrasil seeking knowledge. He hung from its branches and finally was given what he wanted. But he lost an eye in the process."

"That's mostly true," Bragi said. "He didn't go seeking knowledge in the sense of 'how far away is Antarctica?' or 'what are the clouds made of?' He went seeking power. Yggdrasil granted his request, took his eye, but gave him something in return—the means to make his magic stronger. The tree gave him the Eye of Odin."

"The Eye of Odin?"

Bragi nodded. "A talisman. An orb shrouded in blue fire. It was the source of power for the Aesir—the name we gave ourselves. It could take a weak magic user and make them strong, a gifted user and make them a god."

"So, where is the Eye?" Thyra asked.

"Destroyed," Bragi said. "Almost a thousand years ago when Asgard was attacked by an army of those that had once worshipped us. They were led by a man called Surtur. He swore he would destroy the gods, and he succeeded. Some of us escaped, but we were forced to spend years in hiding, living in fear of Surtur's wrath."

"If the Eye was destroyed a thousand years ago, why would Hela think you have it?"

"Not all of it, a piece," Bragi corrected. "And as for why she would think I had a shard, I don't know. I haven't given it any thought for hundreds of years. It was destroyed, and that was all that mattered."

Thyra processed the best she could. Every answer led to a dozen new questions until her thoughts were a blur. Finally, she caught hold of one and held onto it.

"So, how are you still here?" Thyra asked. "You say all this happened a thousand years ago. You were a god. Does that mean you're immortal?"

"Yes and no," Bragi said. "I can live forever, but only as long as I am not killed."

"That doesn't sound like immortality," Thyra said.

"That's because it isn't, but we used the word anyways," Bragi said. "The secret to living forever was something wars were fought over, and it was one of the reasons why Odin sought out Yggdrasil. I could tell you everything about how our people came to obtain immortality, but it's a long story. What you need to know is that Odin claimed it and gave it to those he trusted. But he recognized the mistake that was made by those that possessed it before. Instead of keeping the power to himself, he chose another to control the gift of immortality. Her name was Iduun."

"Iduun?" Thyra repeated. "I know that story. She was in charge of a special garden."

Bragi nodded. "That's right. Her garden was where she hid the fruit that granted immortality. The location of her garden was in a place only she knew. Not even Odin was allowed to know. Instead, she gave summoning stones to nine of the most powerful Aesir. She would show herself only when summoned by at least three of the nine. Until summoned, she tended to her garden and kept the power of immortality safe. Utterly and completely alone."

Thyra sat back and tried to digest everything she'd been told. After what she'd seen and felt, there was no reason to doubt that Bragi was telling her the truth, but it was still a shock.

"Why did Surtur attack the gods?" Thyra asked after a long silence.

"Because he saw the truth of what we were," Bragi said. "There were some among our number who did not or would not adjust to the life of being a god. Odin warned us that we needed to remain aloof and to not meddle in the affairs of man unless it was absolutely necessary. There were many that struggled with adhering to that counsel. As a result, the truth was made evident."

"What truth?"

"That we were only men and women," Bragi said. "Yes, we possessed great power, but at the end of the day, deep down, we were no different than those that worshipped us. We were fallible and were weaker than we let on. That led to questions about how we became gods in the first place. By that time, Odin had let his pride overcome his caution and displayed the Eye for all to see. The dots weren't hard to connect. Once the common people realized the truth, our doom was inevitable. Surtur was upon us before we knew it."

Bragi took a deep breath. "For many years, I thought I was the only one that survived. Asgard was destroyed, the Eye of Odin destroyed, and I was certain that I was the only one left. There was no way to take back what had been taken from me, or to rebuild what we had. All I could do was wait for the day when Surtur came to end my life." Bragi shook his head. "Somehow, that day never came."

"I don't understand," Thyra said. "What did Surtur want?"

"What all men who realize they stand lower than another want," Bragi said grimly. "To be equal."

"He wanted to be a god?"

Bragi shook his head. "Not exactly. What he wanted was for everyone to be equal. Once he realized that we were just men and women, his love for us turned to jealousy and hate. He demanded that we share the gifts we had with everyone. When Odin refused, Surtur swore that if Odin would not share the Eye then no one should be allowed to possess it. He threatened to take what he wanted by force and tear down everything the Aesir had built. He called it 'Ragnarök.' Odin dismissed the threat as foolishness, never thinking that Surtur would try to deliver on it, much less succeed."

"So, Surtur was the cause of Ragnarök?" Thyra said.

"No, our pride was the cause," Bragi said. "Surtur was a side effect that festered into a sickness that spread into an uprising that tore down everything we had built. The same thing had happened before to others, but we thought we were different. That we couldn't be removed from our vaulted thrones. We were wrong, and we paid the price."

Bragi's eyes grew distant, and Thyra could tell from his expression that he didn't like whatever he was seeing.

"So, this Gunnar Olafsson guy, why does he want to destroy magic?"

Bragi shrugged. "Surtur's ideals didn't die with him. The war against magic has waged for centuries without pause. Gunnar Olafsson is just the latest one to continue it. The difference between him and some of the others is that he has the money and technology to elevate this war to new heights. He is a true heir to Surtur's hate for magic."

Silence took hold as they both fell into their own dark thoughts. Those dark thoughts led Thyra to questions about the Muspel Corporation. She pulled out her phone and did a search. The company's website was the first to show up and she clicked on it. The first thing she saw when the page loaded was the company's logo. She thought it looked like a headless stick figure running. It was dressed up, but it still had an odd, archaic look.

She saw a page about the company's leadership and clicked on it next. Front and center was a picture of Gunnar Olafsson. At first glance, there was nothing about him that said he was an evil manic trying to rid the world of magic. He had dark, short hair and a handsome face. But, then Thyra saw his eyes. A shiver ran down her spine as she looked at the picture. Something about his gray-blue eyes was unsettling, almost as if they were watching her through the screen.

She turned off her phone to escape the feeling and put it on her lap. She looked out the window again and watched the sagebrush covered hills pass by. This part of the state was dry and lacking in scenery. It was rural Idaho at its most expansive and devoid of life, and it did nothing to help alleviate her mood.

Bragi's phone went off suddenly and he reached for it reflexively. He gave it a brief glance and then put it in a cupholder in the center console.

"What is it?" Thyra asked.

"The good news is that your mother is alive," Bragi said.

Thyra felt a wave of relief wash over her. She closed her eyes and let out a sigh. She reveled in the thought that everything was going to be alright for a brief moment, but then she sensed that there was something Bragi wasn't telling her. She looked at the old man and saw the worry in his eyes.

"There's bad news, isn't there."

Bragi took a deep breath and let it out slowly. "Hela has her and is demanding we give her the shard in exchange for your mother."

Chapter 8

Bragi put on his blinker and exited the highway. They were about two hours east of Boise, caught between the small farming communities that lined the main thoroughfare.

Bragi drove for a mile or so and then pulled off to the side of the road. He put the SUV in park and Thyra couldn't help but give him a concerned glance.

"Why are we stopping here?"

"This is as good of a place as any," Bragi said.

Thyra knew what was expected of her—call Hela and discuss the goddess's demands—but even with an hour of coaching from Bragi she didn't feel prepared. She stared at the screen of her phone, her finger hovering over the green call icon.

"Just say exactly what we practiced," Bragi urged her on.

Thyra nodded, but she didn't feel very confident. Now that the moment had arrived, she felt her nerves take control.

"You're sure about this?" Thyra asked.

Bragi nodded. "It has to be you."

"I don't know if I can do this," Thyra said. "What if I say the wrong thing? I could make it all worse."

"Trust yourself," Bragi said without hesitation. "Call her."

Thyra nodded, but the pep talk hadn't changed anything. She was still scared stiff.

"Do it for your mom," Bragi said.

Thyra felt fresh courage swell within her.

"For my mom."

She pressed the call button and then quickly put it on speaker. Although Bragi said she needed to be the one who talked to Hela she felt more comfortable with Bragi being able to hear the conversation. The phone rang twice and then clicked.

"Hello, old man," Hela purred through the phone.

"Hello, Hela." Thyra tried to say the name in a strong tone, but it came out in a squeak. "It's Thyra Ariksen."

"Ah, my dear, Thyra," Hela said through the phone. "It's so good to hear your voice. I would have introduced myself long ago if I had only known of your existence."

Thyra could only imagine what kind of introduction she had in mind. "I want to talk to my mom."

"That isn't possible," Hela said.

"Why not? What did you do to her?"

"I did nothing to harm your mother," Hela said. "Quite the opposite, in fact. She was injured during the fight with Gunnar Olafsson's men. I healed her wounds, but she is sleeping. She fought bravely, but I wouldn't expect anything less from a Valkyrie."

"A Valkyrie?" Thyra asked in confusion. "What are you talking about?"

"So many secrets," Hela said with a mirthless chuckle. "She hid so much from you, and for what? Hiding the truth from you did not protect you from your fate. Just be glad it was me that found you, not the other two heirs."

Thyra saw Bragi tense and gave him a suspicious look. Her question was directed at him just as much as it was Hela. "What heirs?"

"I don't have the patience to explain your history, Thyra," Hela said. "Are we going to come to an agreement or not?"

"What do you want?" Thyra said as confidently as she could manage.

"I want the shard of the Eye of Odin," Hela replied.

"I don't know anything about a shard," Thyra said truthfully.

"But the old man does," Hela said, a hint of irritation entering her voice. "Put him on the phone."

"No," Thyra said, and then hesitated. She looked at Bragi and received an encouraging nod. "You have my mom. You talk to me."

"Very brave of you," Hela said. "I hope the old man has told you what the shard is."

"I know about the Eye of Odin," Thyra said.

"Good. Then you can guess why I want it."

Thyra actually couldn't. She looked at Bragi and shrugged, unsure of what to say.

"I hear him breathing," Hela said. "Can you hear me, Rune Tongue?"

"I hear you," Bragi said.

"You saw Gunnar's brazenness," Hela said. "He will know that we were involved. How long do you think it will be before he tries to finish what he started? He is not satisfied to eliminate the weak among us anymore. He will come for me and he will come for you. I have no intention of being powerless when he does."

"We don't have the shard," Bragi said, abandoning their plan to have Thyra do all the talking.

"Don't lie!" Hela snapped. "I felt its presence there, and I felt it leave with you."

Bragi's eyes narrowed. "I am telling you the truth. I don't have a shard of the Eye. I never have."

"Then the girl does," Hela said. "I thought you had used the Eye to ease her awakening, but perhaps it was with her the entire time."

Thyra's eyes went wide. "I didn't even know what the Eye was before today—why would I have the shard?"

"Just another secret you will have to uncover for yourself," Hela said.

"The shard is with you, whether you know it or not. Find it and give it to me if you want to see your mother again. If you don't, I will be forced to find a use for her. When I am through with her, she will be a shadow of the woman you call Sharon Ariksen."

Thyra swallowed hard. "And, what do I do if I find the shard? Where can I find you?"

"Monroe, Wisconsin," Hela said. "Go there and call this number. I will tell you where to meet me."

"Wisconsin?" Thyra shook her head. "Why there? Why can't you wait here in Idaho while I look?"

"Gunnar Olafsson and the Muspel Corporation know I am involved now," Hela said. "That means others will know soon as well, and they will come looking for me, for you, and for the shard. I will not be caught defenseless. What you have set in motion cannot be stopped now."

"Me? What did I do?"

"You had your awakening," Hela said grimly. "Bring the shard to me, Thyra Ariksen. I will give you three days. Do not disappoint me."

Hela hung up before Thyra could get another word in. She sat back against her seat and put her hands over her eyes with a groan. "What are we going to do, Bragi?"

"There isn't much we can do, other than give her what she wants," Bragi said.

Thyra took her hands away from her face and looked at him. "And how are we supposed to do that when we don't know where the shard is?"

"I think we might," Bragi said.

"What? What do you mean you think 'we might'?"

Bragi looked in the backseat and picked up Thyra's teddy bear from where she had haphazardly tossed it when she got in the SUV.

"Your mom said she gave this to you whenever you had one of your episodes."

Thyra didn't like his choice in words, but she swallowed down her annoyance. "Yeah, so what? I've had him for years. It was comforting."

"I think the shard is inside," Bragi said.

"Wait," Thyra turned in her seat to face him, "why would you think that?"

"Because holding this teddy bear helped you fight off the sickness that comes with the awakening of magic," Bragi said. He turned the bear and gave it a squeeze. "I don't feel anything inside."

"That's because it's a stuffed animal," Thyra said. "The only thing inside is stuffing."

Bragi shook his head. "No, I can feel it now. It's faint, but I feel it."

"Feel what?"

"The same feeling I felt over a thousand years ago when Odin first put the Eye in my hand," Bragi said. He looked up from the bear. "The shard is in here."

"Are you sure?"

Bragi nodded. "I'm positive."

He handed the bear over to Thyra and she took it gingerly. Now that she knew that a piece of some thousand-year-old talisman was inside, it was hard to look at the stuffed animal the same way.

She gave the teddy a brief search but didn't feel anything out of the ordinary. "So, where is the shard?"

Bragi shook his head. "I don't know, but I know someone who can tell us."

"Why can't we just give Hela the teddy bear?" Thyra asked. "Call her right now and say that we found it. We've got to be ahead of them, so we can just tell them where to meet us, she gets the shard, I get my mom back, and everything is settled."

"We can't do that," Bragi said. "Hela cannot have it."

"She can if it gets my mom back," Thyra insisted.

"I want to get your mother back just like you," Bragi began, "but until we know what Hela has in her possession, we cannot risk giving her the shard. If she were to unite enough pieces of the Eye, who knows what she might be capable of. We will face her in three days, but I want to be more prepared when we do."

"What about my mom?" Thyra said. "We can't leave her with the goddess of death and Fenrir!"

"You heard Hela," Bragi said. "She said your mother was wounded, and that Hela had healed her. You may not believe me when I say this, but if your mother is injured, the safest place she can be is with Hela."

"Safe? How can she be safe with her?"

"Hela was a gifted healer before she became the goddess of death," Bragi replied calmly. "If your mother is injured, Hela is the one who can help the most. I think that as long as Hela thinks we're going to deliver the shard she will have no incentive to hurt your mother."

"Are you sure?"

"No, but right now we can't control what she does," Bragi said. "We have to move forward and do what we can to find the shard. We can only hope she holds to her word."

"That's comforting," Thyra said. Unable to find a new argument, she turned away and looked out the window. Her mind went back to the conversation with Hela and something that had been said. "Hela said that something has been put into motion and that she didn't want to be powerless against it. What was she talking about?"

"I'm not sure," Bragi said. He put the SUV in gear. "But I know someone who may have an answer."

"You seem to know a lot of people," Thyra said. "Someone who can help us find the shard, someone who knows what Hela's talking about—unless these people all live next to each other, I don't know if we have enough time to go find them all."

"That's true, but we're in luck," Bragi said, pulling back out into the road. "In this case, it's the same person, and she doesn't live too far from here."

Chapter 9

It was dark when Bragi pulled off the road and parked the SUV in front of an old, battered aluminum potato cellar. If their first stop had seemed devoid of life, this place was ten times worse. The fields looked like they hadn't seen a plow for years, and the half dome potato cellar looked like it hadn't seen use in even longer.

Bragi got out of the vehicle and walked up to the door. Thyra opened her door and got out but stayed near the SUV. Bragi knocked on the door and waited. When there was no answer, he knocked again, but with similar results.

"What are we doing?"

"Putting an ear to the ground," Bragi said.

"Doing what?"

Bragi looked up at the light hanging overhead and grumbled something before walking back over to the SUV.

"Hela is preparing for something that has her scared," Bragi said. "We need to know what."

"And you thought we'd find the answer in an abandoned potato cellar?"

Bragi gave her an irritated look. "It isn't abandoned. At least, it wasn't the last time I stopped here."

"When was that?"

Bragi shrugged. "Six years ago."

Thyra snorted in derision. "Geez, that must feel like it was only yesterday."

"When you've lived as long as I have, six years passes in the blink of an eye," Bragi said defensively. "The woman who lives here would never leave. Not willingly, at least."

"Well, it doesn't look like she's here now," Thyra said. "We are wasting our time here when we should be helping my mom."

"This is helping your mom," Bragi said. "And this potato cellar isn't abandoned."

He pointed up above the door. It took a moment before Thyra saw what had caught his attention. A red light blinked on and off in the shadows.

"A camera?" Thyra asked.

Bragi nodded. "She's seen us by now. We just have to wait."

"For how long?"

Her question was answered by the sound of heavy locks being pulled back on the other side of the door. A moment later, it swung open and a bent, ancient-looking woman stepped into the light. Thyra couldn't help but stare. The woman couldn't have stood taller than four and a half feet tall, with stiff, straight gray hair that fell to her shoulders and leathery skin that was crisscrossed with scars.

"I thought I made it clear what I would do to you if you ever tried to come back here, Rune Tongue," the woman said in a voice that sounded like gravel being ground underfoot. "I told you I'd cut out your tongue and boil it with your eyeballs in a soup before feeding it to you while pouring molten metal over your body."

"Apparently, I have a short memory," Bragi said with a nervous smile.

"You're standing on my doorstep, so you must," the old woman snorted.

"I just couldn't stay away," Bragi said.

The old woman grimaced. "By the gods, you look old."

92

"And you're as beautiful as ever," Bragi said with a broad smile.

"Your flattery is wasted on me, Rune Tongue," the old woman barked. She looked at Thyra. "This one is too young for you. And too strong, by the look of her."

"We need your help, Asiri," Bragi said, ignoring the comment.

"You always do," the old woman snapped. "Did you ever think that maybe I'm tired of giving it? I came to this place to live in peace. You think I've had a moment of it? No! No sooner than I carved out a place to call my own, men like you started banging on my door."

"What can I say?" Bragi shrugged. "You're the best there is."

"I'm the only one there is!" Asiri looked at Thyra and her face softened slightly. If stone could soften. "No sense standing out here in the cold. Come in, girl." She looked at Bragi and grimaced. "You too, Rune Tongue. If you must."

With that, the old woman turned and disappeared back into the potato cellar. Bragi started to follow, but Thyra stayed rooted in place.

"Hold on," Thyra hissed. "Who is she?"

"Someone with her ear to the ground," Bragi said.

"And how is some old woman living in a potato cellar supposed to help us rescue my mom?"

"Come inside," Bragi said. "Not everything is what it seems. Believe me, it's better if you see for yourself."

Bragi ducked into the potato cellar and left Thyra standing alone outside. She hesitated, but the SUV honked suddenly as the doors locked, making her decision for her.

"She better not try to stick me in an oven or something," Thyra muttered to herself.

She grudgingly followed Bragi into the potato cellar. The door slammed behind her with a resounding bang that made her jump. Swallowing her heart back down where it belonged, she looked around the inside of the potato cellar. The long, domed building was empty and smelled of fertilizer and moist earth. Why anyone would want to live in such a place escaped Thyra.

"This way," Asiri barked. The bent old woman was walking toward a little office built along one wall. She opened the door and switched on a flickering light.

"I love what you've done with the place," Bragi muttered as he stepped into the office. "Warm and inviting."

"Quit flapping your tongue," Asiri snapped. She bent down and pulled up a panel of the floor, revealing a dimly lit set of stairs. "This way."

"You look like the years have treated you well," Bragi said as they followed her down a narrow flight of stairs.

"You mean, I haven't shriveled up and died," Asiri snorted. "I've been too busy to die. It seems like every practitioner left has suddenly been showing up at my door asking for me to forge something for them. My forge hasn't been quiet in almost a year."

"And you've probably profited greatly," Bragi commented.

Asiri gave him another angry glare but didn't respond.

"Excuse me," Thyra interjected. "But what are we talking about? Practitioners? Your forge?"

"'Practitioners' is another word for magic users," Bragi explained. "And as for Asiri's forge, she is the last of a dying breed."

"Not dying," Asiri corrected. "Dead. Extinct."

"Not entirely," Bragi said. "You're still alive."

"Only because I'm too stubborn to die," Asiri snapped. "I wish I would, believe me."

"I still don't understand," Thyra said. "Who are you?"

"The better question is 'what' is she," Bragi said. "Asiri is the last of the dwarf craftsmen. Her people were the ones who crafted all the great weapons of the Aesir."

"Not only the Aesir," Asiri hissed. "My people were impartial. We made weapons for anyone who could pay. Vanir, Frost Giant, dark elf—didn't matter who, as long as they had coin."

"Be that as it may," Bragi said, "the dwarves were an important part of Aesir history."

"Hold on for a second," Thyra said, eyeing Asiri closely. "You're a dwarf?"

Asiri stopped suddenly. "What of it girl? You have something against dwarves?"

Thyra shook her head. "No! I just thought...well, you'd look different."

"How so?" Asiri asked in a dangerous tone.

"You know," Thyra said slowly. "Maybe bearded. A Scottish accent and a mug of ale, or something like that."

She saw Bragi tense in the corner of her eye, but she refused to look away from Asiri. The old woman's icy gaze made Thyra feel like she was being stripped clean of her flesh, but she had a feeling that looking away now would only make things worse.

A deep sound, like gravel being ground across concrete, escaped Asiri's throat and the corners of her mouth twitched up. Her shoulders started to shake as the sound grew to a low rumble. It took a moment, but Thyra realized Asiri was laughing.

"I like this one!" Asiri said. "She's got nerve!"

"She does indeed," Bragi muttered. "More than she should at times."

Asiri waved them on. "Come!"

They descended another set of stairs before they came to a metal door that looked like it belonged on a bank vault rather than a potato cellar. Asiri opened a series of locks and then swung it open. A blast of heat hit Thyra in the face as she walked through the door behind Bragi. They entered a room lit by orange light and full of machinery.

"Follow me, but don't touch anything!" she said as she led Thyra further into the cavernous room. "Count yourself lucky, girl. There aren't many alive that have seen the inside of a dwarf forge."

Thyra couldn't help but marvel as she looked around the room. Hammers, tongs, and other smithing tools hung on the walls in perfect order. Two fires burned hungrily, fed by some fuel source that Thyra couldn't see.

Asiri continued. "These forge fires had been quiet for nearly two hundred years, and I had no intention of ever starting them again. But, for some reason, I agreed to light them again six years ago. Biggest mistake I've ever made."

"Why did you light them again?" Thyra asked.

Asiri let out a growl. "Foolish pride. And maybe a trick of the mind."

She turned and scowled at Bragi who put up his hands. "I only gave you a little nudge. You were already itching to forge again. It didn't take much to convince you."

"A nudge?" Asiri hissed. "I think it was a bit more than a nudge."

Bragi shrugged but didn't respond to the allegation.

"Come on, girl," Asiri said. "I've found it's better to keep an eye on Rune Tongue when he's close, and two when he isn't."

Asiri led Thyra to a table and nodded toward a series of designs drawn in dark lines. Pictures of swords, hammers, shields, and helmets were scattered on the table. As she scanned the drawings, Thyra was surprised to see two designs that looked more modern. One was a pair of high-top athletic shoes.

"You make shoes?"

"My fathers made some of the greatest weapons history has ever known," the dwarf commented, "and now Asiri, last of the dwarves, is being tasked with making footwear. Believe me, if they weren't more than they appear and for someone who will put them to good use, I never would have done it."

Thyra couldn't help but ask, "What's so special about them?"

"To start, only one person can wear them," Asiri said.

"Why's that?"

"Because I made them just for him, and like any good dwarf, I took precautions to make sure no one could steal them away," Asiri explained. "No one besides him can wear them, or even move them for that matter if he doesn't want them to."

"That's a weird thing to want," Thyra said.

"Comes in handy if you ever have to step on the jaw of a giant," Asiri said with a wink. She stepped back suddenly and looked Thyra up and down. "What about you girl? What kind of magic do you have?"

"I, uh, I'm still figuring that out," Thyra said.

Asiri's eyes narrowed. She reached for a small, chrome ball on her table and held it out towards Thyra. "Hold this."

Thyra took it from the dwarf and held it with one hand. It felt warm in her hand. "What is it?"

Asiri ignored the question. She snatched the ball away and muttered, "Interesting."

The dwarf quickly retrieved a foot-long metal rod and placed it in Thyra's hand. Immediately, blue-white tendrils of light cracked to life along its length. She dropped the rod onto the table and backed away. "What was that?"

"That was lightning," Asiri stated matter-of-factly. Her eyes narrowed and she looked at Bragi. "And not just a small spark. That was a definite, and powerful reaction. Who is this girl?"

"This is Thyra Ariksen," Bragi said.

"I guessed that already," Asiri said sharply. "But *who* is she?"

"She's one of my students," Bragi began, but Asiri didn't let him finish.

"Don't lie to me, Rune Tongue!"

"I didn't lie to you about who she is," Bragi said defensively.

"But you didn't tell me the whole truth!" Asiri insisted. "When you came to me six years ago, you said the girl could manipulate electricity, not that she could *command the storms!*"

"Is there a difference?" Bragi asked with a shrug.

Asiri's eyes went wide. "Is there a difference? Of course, there is! It makes all the difference when making a weapon to know who you're making it for. Now, tell me who she is, or I will deliver on my threat."

Bragi shifted his feet uncomfortably. "She is the daughter of Sif."

Thyra had heard that name again—she just couldn't place it! She'd heard it in some of the stories about the Norse gods, but only briefly and she couldn't remember in what context.

"Sif?" The dwarf's eyebrows shot up briefly, but her surprise was short. Her eyes narrowed dangerously again. "That can't be. She died during Ragnarök."

Bragi shook his head. "She survived. She was taken to safety before the battle began and was protected until recently."

"How is that possible?"

"The Vanir Sleep," Bragi said.

This time, Asiri's shock was clear. The dwarf slowly sat down on a stool. "For nearly eight hundred years?"

Bragi nodded. "It was the only way."

"Can we stop for a second," Thyra interrupted. "What is going on here? I'm tired of you two talking over my head like I'm not here. Will someone please tell me what you're talking about? You keep calling my mom Sif and Hela said she was a Valkyrie—why?"

Thyra looked between the dwarf and Bragi, waiting for one of them to speak. Asiri crossed her arms over her chest stubbornly, making it clear that she had no intention of being the one to answer Thyra's questions.

"Because, that is your mother's real name," Bragi said with a sigh. "She was the leader of the Valkyries long ago."

"Wait, you're trying to tell me that my mom is a thousand-year-old Valkyrie?"

"More like thirteen hundred years old," Bragi said, "but I'm sure even she's lost count."

Thyra almost laughed at the idea, but then she remembered seeing her mom standing there with a spear and shield in hand. Suddenly, the idea wasn't so farfetched. But there was something more about that name, she knew it. Something important.

"The daughter of Sif," Asiri said in a voice barely above a whisper. "And she is like the other two?"

Bragi nodded slightly. "She is."

"What other two?" Thyra asked.

"For now, all you need to know is that there are two others that share your unique gifts," Bragi said.

"Gifts?" Thyra asked. "You mean, what I just did with that bar? Lightning?"

"Yes," Bragi replied. "But you don't need to concern yourself with them right now. No one even knows if they're still alive."

"You're fooling yourself if you think they're dead," Asiri said. She looked at Thyra with an expression Thyra couldn't quite decipher. The dwarf looked back at Bragi and shook her head. "Why didn't I see it sooner? It all makes sense now."

"I may have helped you misunderstand," Bragi admitted.

"You used your magic on me again?" Asiri hissed. Her anger was surprisingly short-lived, though. She sat back and massaged her temples with her knuckles. "I was not prepared for this, Rune Tongue. Your trickery led me to create something unworthy of this girl. It's not adequate."

"What do you mean it isn't adequate?"

"I can't give what you asked for to someone like her," Asiri said. "It'd be like giving a child's toy to an adult and expecting them to make use of it. In fact, it is giving a child's toy! I won't do it."

"What child's toy?" Thyra demanded, looking between the two.

Again, Asiri made it clear that she was in no mood to do the talking.

"Fine," Bragi finally relented. "I told you I came here six years ago, but I didn't tell you why. I came here to have Asiri make something. I didn't give her all the details or tell her who it was for, but I asked her to craft a tool and hold onto it until I came for it."

"What kind of 'tool' did you ask her to make?" Thyra asked.

"Not a tool," Asiri snapped. "A weapon. I use tools. I don't make them!"

"Funny," Bragi said. "Just a second ago you were calling it a toy. Which is it, Asiri?"

The dwarf woman's eyes narrowed. "I make weapons, and I made one for her, even with bad information about who it was meant for."

"A weapon?" Thyra said. "For me?"

Asiri looked at Thyra and nodded. "Think of it more as a conduit for your magic. Something that magnifies what is already inside of you."

"And you've kept it here for six years?" Thyra waited for Asiri's nod before looking at Bragi. "I haven't known you for six years. Why would you have Asiri make something for me when I didn't even know you?"

"You may not have known me," Bragi said, "but I've known you since you were small. I've watched over you and your mother for years."

"That's only a little creepy," Thyra said. "Why did you have Asiri make me a weapon? Why would you think I would need one?"

"Because I knew this day would come," Bragi said. "Your mother tried to delay it, but it was a vain attempt."

"What day?"

"The day when you would be forced to meet your fate," Bragi said ambiguously.

"What fate?"

Bragi fell silent. He looked away from Thyra's intense stare and

100

studied the floor at his feet instead.

"Enough!" Asiri snapped. "I'll give it to her only so you'll quit dancing around the girl's questions."

Asiri stood up suddenly and stalked across the forge. She opened a cabinet and pulled out what looked like a lacrosse stick. Thyra was sure her eyes were tricking her, but as the dwarf came back over, she saw that it was in fact a lacrosse stick.

"Here," Asiri said, holding out the lacrosse stick towards Thyra. "Its name is Lynnedslag. It means 'lightning bolt' in the language of your fathers."

Thyra hesitated in taking it. "I'm confused. Why are you giving me a lacrosse stick?"

"It isn't just any lacrosse stick," Asiri snapped. "It's a dwarf-forged weapon, capable of magnifying the magic you have inside, and more."

"It's a lacrosse stick," Thyra said, still not understanding.

"I know," Asiri said in a tense voice. "I did the best I could with what I was asked to make. If you have issues with the end product, maybe you should take it up with the one who requested to have it made."

"We live in a different time," Bragi said. "She couldn't walk around with a battle-axe or a giant spear, could she? I knew she loved lacrosse and thought this would be a good way of disguising the weapon she'd need." He looked at Thyra. "Take it."

Thyra shook her head. "I don't want a weapon."

"You will take it," Asiri said in a tense voice, "or I will go throw it in the fire and use it to cover Rune Tongue in red hot metal!"

Thyra's resistance wavered under the fire in the dwarf's voice. She carefully reached out and took a hold of the lacrosse stick. The moment her hand closed around the shaft, a sharp pain raced up her arm, causing her to grimace.

"Ouch!" She looked at Asiri. "Why did it hurt me?"

"It was just getting to know you," Asiri said, the fire in her voice abated somewhat. "It's an old dwarf way of ensuring only the intended user can put a weapon to use. Now no one but you can use it."

"Almost no one," Bragi corrected.

"*Almost* no one," Asiri said, glaring at the old man. "Rune Tongue is right. It's a matter of blood. A close relative, a brother, sister, father, mother, perhaps even as far as an aunt or uncle, can use a dwarf weapon, but at a reduced level. As long as you live, though, it will only respond in its full power to you, and you only."

"Why's that?" Thyra couldn't help but ask.

"Call it a professional courtesy to overly concerned gods afraid their own weapons would be turned against them," Asiri said. Bragi began to say something, but she silenced him with a finger. "You've done enough talking, Rune Tongue! You have forced my hand and left me embarrassed. You at least should do me the courtesy of letting me see my creation put to use."

"I don't think we have time for this," Bragi said. "We came here for answers, not lessons."

"And I won't say another word until I know that this girl can use what I created!" Asiri's voice cracked like a whip. The dwarf turned back to Thyra. "The stick responds to you, but since you don't seem comfortable with your own magic yet, it will require a keyword to ignite its power. Say its name."

"Say its name?" Thyra raised an eyebrow. "What will happen?"

"Just do it, girl!" Asiri said. "Say, 'Lynnedslag.'"

"Okay," Thyra said. She looked down at the lacrosse stick. It looked like any other lacrosse stick she had used, but she knew for certain that wasn't the case. The only way to find out why was to do what Asiri said. Softly, she said the name, "Lynnedslag."

She felt the stick throb in her hands and then the strange sensation of something flowing out of her and into Lynnedslag. With a sharp crack that split the air, a blue-white ball of electricity sprang to life in the basket. Except, electricity wasn't the right name for what she saw.

"Lightning?" Thyra said in awe.

"Lightning!" Asiri said with a nod, a crooked smile creeping across her stony features. She looked up at Thyra. "The stick was created to magnify what you have inside you, and you're definitely a child of the storm." The dwarf's eyes danced with excitement. "Now use it."

Thyra looked at her in confusion. "Use it? How?"

"I don't know," Asiri said. She gestured with an odd movement. "Just use it."

"You don't know how it works?"

"I make weapons," Asiri said. "It isn't my job to teach the buyer how to use them." She looked at Bragi for help. "Your turn, old man. I made it, maybe you can help her figure out how to use it."

"It's a lacrosse stick," Bragi offered. He shrugged. "Use it like you would any other lacrosse stick. My knowledge of dwarf weapons is not extensive, but it's a place to start."

Thyra looked at him. "What do you mean?"

"Score a goal," Bragi said. He pointed at a pile of scrap metal. "Over there. Try to score a goal into the wall."

Thyra looked at the pile of metal. It was roughly the size of a goal.

"Score a goal," she repeated. She adjusted her grip on Lynnedslag and imagined a goal in place of the scrap metal. She let years of muscle memory take over and took a shot on goal. Instead of a lacrosse ball, it was a ball of lightning that shot through the air and struck the metal, tendrils shooting in every direction as it danced through the scraps. Then, the pile suddenly shot apart!

Thyra put up an arm to protect her face as scrap metal flew through the air in every direction. When she was sure that nothing was going to strike her, Thyra lowered her arm and looked at where the pile of scraps had been. Only the biggest pieces remained near where they had begun, but even they had been moved, revealing a burnt, smoking section of wall where they had been stacked.

Asiri whooped loudly. "I knew it would work!"

Thyra couldn't help but smile. She looked down at Lynnedslag. A new ball of lightning had formed in the basket, crackling with destructive energy waiting to be used. She looked up and smiled at Asiri. "That was awesome!"

"I knew I was good," Asiri said with a smile that seemed out of place on her, "but I have to admit I surprise even myself."

Thyra looked at Bragi with a big smile, but she was surprised to see his expression was less than enthusiastic. He smiled at her, but she could tell it was forced.

"That's wonderful, Thyra," Bragi said. "You did great."

Thyra's smile slipped. "Then why don't you look happy?"

Bragi let his smile go and his expression turned grave. "Because, with every step you make towards unlocking your potential, you are moving closer to a fate I can't protect you from."

"What fate?" Thyra asked. Bragi and Asiri shared a look, but neither one answered the question. "What aren't you telling me?"

"There are some things you aren't ready for," Bragi said. "Besides, it isn't my place to tell this secret."

"I don't care if you don't think it's your place," Thyra said. "If you know something else about me or what I'm facing, I think I deserve to know."

"Even if it causes you pain?" Bragi asked. "Even if knowing the truth does nothing but put you even more in danger's path?"

"Yes," Thyra said.

"Okay," Bragi said. "Ask your questions."

Thyra knew the one she needed answered, but she hesitated in asking it. There were so many clues that were pointing at an answer, but she needed to hear it from Bragi.

"Who is my father?"

Bragi exhaled slowly. "Somehow, I knew that would be the first question. Maybe we can start with something smaller. Warm up to that one."

"Tell her the truth, Rune Tongue," Asiri said. "She deserves to know. She's had the truth hidden from her for long enough. It's time she hears it."

"I think she's smart enough to already have guessed," Bragi said. He looked at Thyra. "Haven't you?"

Thyra had her guess, but even thinking it seemed impossible. In light of everything that she had learned, though, was there any other explanation?

"Yggdrasil said I was a daughter of gods and that I command the storms. You said my mother is Sif. At first, I didn't recognize that name, but now I think I do. She was a Valkyrie and a goddess, but there's something more. Something that I couldn't remember about that name at first. But now I remember. She was married to another god."

Bragi nodded slowly. "That's right. But, which one?"

Thyra licked her lips nervously. "*The* Norse god. She was married to Thor."

"Your memory serves you well," Bragi said. He took a deep breath and let it out slowly. "Thyra, you are Thor's daughter."

Chapter 10

Thyra sat on a chair in the corner of Asiri's forge and stared blankly ahead. Her body was numb, every bit of her energy devoted to sorting out the torrent of thoughts racing through her mind. She hadn't been surprised by what Bragi had told her—she had already begun to put the pieces together—but it was still a shock.

Thor was her father. She was the daughter of *the* Norse god.

Lynnedslag laid across her knees, looking like any other lacrosse stick now after Asiri had taught Thyra how to dismiss the lightning. To her surprise, she already felt a bond with Lynnedslag, and had the strange desire to never let it out of her sight.

Bragi and Asiri sat across from each other, the dwarf sipping carefully at a cup of tea. Thyra was aware of their conversation but was too busy with her own thoughts to take part. They seemed content to leave her alone with those thoughts.

"Something is coming," Bragi said. "Something that even had Hela worried. If she is worried, then we should be too. What do you know, Asiri?"

"I know my forge hasn't slept for months," Asiri muttered. "It seems every practitioner is trying to get their hands on one of my weapons."

"Why?" Bragi asked.

Asiri shrugged. "Don't know, don't care. As long as they have coin, I could care less."

"We both know that isn't true," Bragi said. "You're part of what is happening, whether you are willing to admit it or not. If there is trouble, it will come looking for you, too."

Asiri tried to hide the discomfort on her face by taking another sip of tea, but it was clear on her craggy features. She grimaced as she set her cup down. "Ask your questions."

"What have you heard, Asiri?" Bragi asked.

"Whispers," Asiri said. "No more."

"What kind of whispers?"

The old woman took a deep breath and then let it out in a rush. "There's a war coming, Rune Tongue. A war against people like me and you."

"There is always a war against people like us," Bragi said. "That's why our kind have been forced to hide for centuries."

"I'm not talking about hiding," Asiri said as she shook her head. "I'm talking about a real war. Not one fought in the shadows. A war fought for the entire world to see. Like the one that nearly ended us years ago, except this one will be shown on screens all around the world. There will be no more hiding until every last practitioner is either dead or under control."

Bragi shook his head. "Who would want to start that kind of war? Who knows enough about magic to want the world to know it still existed only to then snuff it out?"

"You know who," Asiri said. "Surtur is coming to finish what he started."

"Surtur?" Bragi shook his head. "That's not possible. He's been dead for almost a thousand years."

"You visited his grave?" Asiri cocked an eyebrow at Bragi. "Seen the body, have you?"

"Of course not," Bragi said. "But there is no way he could still be alive."

"No way?" Asiri tsked. "You of all people should know better than to say that. There is a way. You simply don't want to consider it."

"What are you talking about?"

Asiri raised an eyebrow. "You know what I mean. He found her."

"No," Bragi said sharply, shaking his head. "I know what you are suggesting, and it isn't possible. She disappeared during Ragnarök. For all we know, she was killed with the others."

"Did you see her body?" Asiri asked. Bragi sat back as if he had been slapped. "I didn't think so. That means you can't afford to discount the possibility."

This caught Thyra's attention and she looked between the two. "Who are you talking about?"

Bragi stood up and began to pace. Thyra looked to Asiri as the old woman took another long sip of her tea.

"You really think Surtur is still alive?" Bragi asked.

Asiri nodded. "Not only alive, but with enough resources to finish what he started. You heard of the Muspel Corporation?"

"We had a run in with them earlier," Bragi said grimly. "You think Surtur is involved with them?"

"Involved?" Asiri snorted. "He leads the company. Gunnar Olafsson and Surtur are the same man!"

"That's impossible," Bragi said. "I've seen his picture. They look nothing alike."

"For someone who has lived for a thousand years and reinvented himself dozens of times over the years, you're being very closeminded," Asiri said. "A man can change his appearance. You of all people should know that. Besides, you know as well as I that the Muspel Corporation carries on the war against magic. Doesn't it make sense that it's led by the man who tore down the Aesir?"

Bragi started pacing again. "I don't know how I didn't see that."

"You're saying the guy who killed the gods is still alive?" Thyra asked.

"How?"

"Iduun," Asiri replied.

"Surtur somehow summoned Iduun and ate the fruit," Bragi said. He stopped pacing and his shoulders sagged. "I should have known better than to think she had been killed."

"Yes, you should have," Asiri said grimly. "Idunn was far too valuable. She was the only one who knew the way to the fruit that granted immortality. Did you actually think Surtur would kill her?"

"I always hoped that she had escaped somehow or was just hiding away in her garden, waiting for the right moment to show herself again," Bragi said. "But, after years of searching and trying to reach her, I realized that she wouldn't come. Not even to me. Her death was better than the alternative."

"Why did you have to search so hard?" Thyra asked. "You had been there before, right? Why couldn't you find her garden again?"

"Iduun and her garden don't exist in one specific place," Asiri explained. "The easiest way to explain it is that her garden exists in a place that mirrors our realm."

"Like Yggdrasil?" Thyra asked.

"Right," Bragi said. "And like Yggdarsil, only Iduun can open the gate to her realm. Which is why the Aesir needed the summoning stones I told you about."

"Who had the keystones?" Thyra asked.

"Odin kept one for himself," Bragi said, holding up a finger for each name he listed off. "Freya, Thor, Tyr, Heimdall, and Njord each had one. There were two others, but they had their stones taken from them by Odin as a result of their misdeeds. As far as I know, when Surtur attacked those two stones were still in Odin's possession."

"Who were the two that lost their stones?" Thyra asked.

Bragi shook his head. "You don't need to know their names. They are gone, and their shame is not worth reliving."

"Okay, but that still only makes eight," Thyra said, counting her fingers again to be sure. "Who was the last one?"

"I was," Bragi said. "That's why I thought I could summon Iduun after Surtur attacked."

"Wait, you said there had to be three stones to summon Iduun," Thyra said. "Why did you think Idunn would show herself to you?"

Bragi took a deep breath and held it. When he spoke, his voice sounded haunted.

"Because, Idunn was my wife."

Thyra felt her heart break for Bragi. "I'm so sorry. I can't imagine."

"There's no time for wallowing in sorrow," Asiri stated. "Bragi has had centuries to do that. We need to be in the here and now. We have to believe that Iduun is alive and she gave Surtur some of the fruit. Or, she was alive long enough to give him some, at least. What matters is that his heart's still beating! Now, he wants to finish what he started with Ragnarök."

Bragi spun around, his eyes red. "What he started? He destroyed everything the Aesir had built and killed nearly all of us. He accomplished what he set out to do! He humbled us and tore us from our gilded halls. What more can he hope for?"

"The elimination of magic altogether," Thyra offered.

"That's surely part of it," Asiri said. "But I'm convinced there's something else he wants. Something the Aesir kept from him all those years ago. A power that was denied him by the girl's father."

"The Eye of Odin," Thyra said, catching on to what the dwarf was hinting at.

"That's right," Asiri said. "He wanted the Eye, but he didn't get it. He's had centuries to fume over that failure."

"But the Eye was destroyed," Thyra said. "Why do you think he's still trying to get his hands on it?"

"Take it from a dwarf," Asiri said, "what is broken can always be fixed. If he has enough pieces then it wouldn't be hard to do."

Thyra looked at Bragi and met his eyes. They were both thinking the same thing. "That gives another explanation for why Hela wanted the shard so badly."

"What shard?" Asiri said. Neither one answered, so she cast an angry look at Bragi. "What shard, Rune Tongue?"

"Hela found us, and when she did, she said that we had a shard from the Eye," Bragi said.

"If she's after a shard, does that mean that she has the pieces," Thyra offered, "or that she is trying to make sure someone else doesn't get them?"

"I think it's the latter, even though it wouldn't surprise me if she had managed to get her hands on parts of the Eye," Bragi said. "I'm not sure which one is worse—Hela or Surtur?"

"Both are bad," Asiri said. "But back to you and the girl. Do you have a shard?"

Bragi nodded slowly. He reached over and picked up Thyra's stuffed bear. "We think it is inside this bear."

"You think a piece of the Eye of Odin is inside that?" Asiri snorted. "Have you had your head checked recently?"

"This is not something to joke about," Bragi said. "Hela said she felt the shard with us. I didn't believe her, but I've come to think otherwise after looking at some of the evidence."

"Evidence?" Asiri snorted. "Like what? The bear is magically soft?"

"Like the fact that Sif gave the bear to Thyra to help her fight off the sickness of the awakening," Bragi said. "And that I can feel its power even now. It's faint, but it's there."

"Let me see that bear," Asiri said, holding out one hand.

Bragi handed it over and Asiri immediately moved to her worktable. She reached for the same metal rod she had given to Thyra and ran it over the bear. The rod stopped over the bear's head and Asiri's eyebrows shot up. Asiri put the rod down and then leaned in close. She reached for a small hammer and gently tapped against one of the bear's eyes. The hammer rebounded in Asiri's hand like she'd swung it with all her strength against a solid rubber ball.

"Interesting," Asiri said.

"What?" Bragi asked.

"There's definitely something there," the dwarf woman said. "I can't say if it's a shard of the Eye or not, but whatever it is, it's protected by a strong warding spell."

"Can you get by the ward?"

Asiri shook her head. "No. This magic is beyond me. I can't say for sure, but whoever put this spell here was incredibly strong. God-like strength." She looked at Thyra. "How long have you had this bear?"

Thyra shrugged. "As long as I can remember."

"And you sleep with it often?"

Thyra bristled a bit at the question. She didn't like the implication made. "I'm sixteen. I don't sleep with stuffed animals anymore."

"Don't get your britches in a twist," Asiri said. "Just answer the question—do you hold this bear often?"

Thyra shook her head. "No. Only when I have one of my episodes. The rest of the time it sits in the corner of my room."

"If the shard is inside the bear, it would have helped ease her the discomfort of the awakening," Bragi said. "Or even delayed it, as seems to be the case."

Asiri tapped the bear's eye and looked at Bragi. "Here's your answer. An ironic one, if I've ever seen one. A shard of the Eye, kept safe in the eye of a stuffed animal."

She handed the Eye back to Bragi, who asked, "You're sure you can't break the spell?"

"If I said I can't, then I can't," the dwarf said. "I have no magic, and even if I did, whoever put the warding spell there was very powerful.

Hela might be strong enough to undo the spell, but not very many others."

Bragi began pacing again as he fell back into his own thoughts. Asiri watched him with her dark eyes as she took another long sip of her tea.

"So, now we have to worry about who has the rest of the Eye," Bragi said grimly.

"You said Surtur wanted everyone to be equal," Thyra said. "That his reason for attacking the gods was because they wouldn't share their power. Why didn't he stop there? Why didn't he just get rid of the Aesir and be done? And why would he eat Idunn's fruit to gain immortality if he wanted everyone to be equal?"

Bragi's brow furrowed as he thought. "What are you getting at?"

"You told me that the Eye of Odin gave the Aesir their powers," Thyra said. "So, why would Surtur want it if not to use it himself?"

"But then he would become what he despised," Bragi said. "He marched on Asgard with the intention of taking the Eye and ridding the world of magic. He said that if magic couldn't be possessed by all, then no one should have it."

"Did he really want everyone to have it?" Thyra asked. "Or did he just want to replace the Aesir and claim power for himself."

"No, I don't think so," Bragi said. "That sounds too much like what Hela began talking about before Ragnarök. She wanted to create a new order of magic users and use the Eye to restore her vision of balance to the world. Magic—and power—would still be held by the few and they would rule without opposition. Surtur marched against us with the idea that everyone should be equal—possessing magic, or not."

"But, are you sure that's what he still wants?" Asiri asked. "I think the girl has a point. What if Surtur eliminated the Aesir not with the intent of ridding the world of magic, but of replacing the Aesir with a new power?"

"With Surtur at the head," Thyra added.

Bragi looked between the two of them. "You think he wants the Eye so that he can gain magic himself?"

Asiri nodded. "What other good would it do him?"

Bragi pondered this for a moment. "I guess that's possible. Eight hundred years is enough time for a man to change his motives. But, if that's true, it's a far scarier possibility."

"Why?" Thyra asked.

"Because there is no telling what he would do with it," Bragi said. "Or who he would give power to. At least with Hela the spread of magic would be more concentrated. With someone bent on creating equality the consequences would be catastrophic."

"How so?" Thyra asked.

"Because magic has been a closely guarded secret for centuries," Bragi said. "After our fall, most magic users were wise enough to keep quiet. The ones who didn't paid the price. But if Surtur were to succeed in his plan and give everyone a chance at having magic, the result would be unimaginable." Bragi shook his head. "That doesn't sound like him. He wanted to eliminate magic completely, and that's the war he has been waging ever since if we are to believe that Gunnar Olafsson and Surtur are the same."

"They are," Asiri said. "And what makes you think he's trying to eliminate magic?"

"Have you heard something to the contrary?" Bragi asked.

The dwarf nodded. "Whispers that wherever the Muspel Corporation goes, magic users disappear. But, from what I've heard, not all of them are being killed. More and more, those that don't offer resistance are being taken alive. More importantly, any weapons or tools of magic are being confiscated and taken back to Surtur."

"How do you know that?"

Asiri grimaced. "I've had more than a few of my own creations fall into the Muspel Corporation's clutches. Not something I'm very happy about."

Bragi considered this for a moment. "Whether he is trying to eliminate magic or possess it doesn't matter. Either way, we can't let him have the Eye. Which is easier said than done since we only have a piece of it and don't know who has the rest. I think the best we can hope for is to protect the shard and keep it from both Surtur and Hela. That may even be too much, all things considered."

"We have to get my mom back," Thyra said. "Hela wants the Eye in exchange for my mom. We have to figure out a way to get her back."

"You can't make that trade," Asiri said.

"We have to, or Hela made it clear that she will hurt my mom," Thyra said. "We don't have any other choice."

"You're definitely in a bad spot," Asiri agreed. She looked up at Bragi. "Sounds like you need help, Rune Tongue."

"Which is why we came to you," Bragi said.

Asiri snorted. "And what good can I be? I'm an old woman and have no power that would help you in this fight. You need a warrior. Someone strong. Someone even Surtur walked carefully around and Hela respected. Someone who can level the playing field. Maybe even turn it in your favor."

Bragi gave the old woman a confused look. "What are you talking about?"

"I'm talking about the gatekeeper of Asgard," Asiri said.

Bragi immediately began shaking his head. "No. We can't go to him."

"Why not?" Asiri demanded. "Give me one reason!"

Bragi continued to shake his head. "He's untrustworthy, for one, and two, he'd never listen to a word I said."

"Not you," Asiri said. She pointed at Thyra. "But maybe her. He might listen to the daughter of Thor and Sif."

"Who is she talking about?" Thyra asked.

Bragi looked at her. "Someone I want to avoid unless our situation is truly dire."

"Doesn't get any more dire, if you ask me," Asiri said. Bragi gave her a scathing look, but the dwarf returned his gaze with an equally intense stare of her own.

"Who is it?" Thyra asked.

"The one man who was physically stronger than Thor was," Bragi said. "And the one Odin held responsible for not putting a stop to Surtur before he could bring about Ragnarök. But," Bragi turned back to Asiri, "I don't know where he is. Even if I did, I would exhaust all my other options before going to him."

"You may not know where he is, but that doesn't mean I don't," Asiri said. She was tapping one of the designs on the table idly with one hand.

Bragi raised an eyebrow at the old woman. "You know where he is?"

Asiri nodded. "Most of the practitioners that contact me try to be discreet with their identity. They're wasting their effort, of course. I've found there is a lot you can tell about a person from what they ask me to make and what they want it to do. And then there is this human invention called the internet. It's surprising how much information can be gleaned just from a simple address."

Asiri slid the paper toward Bragi. Thyra craned her neck to see and was surprised to see the design for the high-top athletic shoes that had caught her eye earlier.

"How do you know it's him?" Bragi asked.

"My father always told me that this one always prided himself on the strength of his arm and hated using magic," Asiri said. "The dwarves of my grandfather's age tried to convince him to commission a dwarf-made weapon, but he refused time and time again in favor of relying on his own physical strength. From the looks of it, he still feels that way. I've made weapons capable of terrible things, and could have made one for him, too. One that would have made him a truly awesome force. But, no, he asks for a pair of shoes. Made from an impressive list of materials, mind you, but shoes all the same."

"He goes by the name Luke Vincent," Bragi said as he read the address. "And he owns a gym? Fitting. Hammer Forged Gym. A little conspicuous, but he wasn't known for being creative."

"And fortunately for you," Asiri said, "you're headed in the right direction already. Hudson, Wisconsin. Not directly on your path to Monroe, but not too far off of it."

Thyra cleared her throat. "Excuse me, but who are we talking about?"

"His name is Vidar," Asiri answered. He looked at Thyra. "He was the god of strength."

"Vidar?" Thyra shook her head. "I've never heard that name."

"That's because he wasn't very popular," Bragi said. "Or very god-like."

"Why?"

"He was Odin's hitman, to put it in terms you'd be familiar with," Asiri said. Bragi gave the dwarf woman a glare, but Asiri didn't seem bothered. "That's what he was, don't deny it."

"I don't deny it, I just don't like being reminded of that side of Odin," Bragi said. He turned to Thyra. "Although Odin used him for *other* purposes, Vidar's chief responsibility was protecting Asgard. The city had one main gate, and it was impenetrable when closed. Unfortunately, there was only one man physically strong enough to put the crossbar into place—Vidar."

"Seems like a design flaw, don't you think?" Asiri said off-handedly. "One man was both the key to the safety and downfall of Asgard. No wonder he went into hiding! He was both protector of Asgard and

Odin's personal killer—that would be enough responsibility to drive any man mad."

"And this Vidar can help us?" Thyra asked.

Bragi nodded somewhat reluctantly. "He's one of the last remaining Aesir. He might know more about the Eye's state in this age, he might not. Either way, he could prove to be of value to us. If he will talk to us."

"Which is a big 'if,'" Asiri said.

Thyra was about to ask what the old woman meant when she noticed a small red light blinking on the wall behind Asiri. She motioned with her chin.

"What's that light for?"

Chapter 11

Asiri turned around and hissed a strange word. Before Thyra could say anything else, Asiri was on her feet and running across the forge. She opened a side door, revealing a room with a series of monitors on the wall.

"More visitors," Asiri called over her shoulder. "You need to see this, Rune Tongue!"

Bragi and Thyra hurried to the room and looked over the old woman's shoulder. Asiri pointed to one of the monitors and Thyra was surprised to see a half dozen men in suits standing around Bragi's SUV while two more were standing at the door to the potato cellar.

"Is this live?" Bragi asked.

"What good would a surveillance system be if it wasn't live?" Asiri snapped.

"I'm guessing these aren't customers of yours, then," Bragi said.

Asiri shook her head. "I don't think they're here for me."

"Who are they?" Thyra asked.

"Trouble," Asiri said. She pressed a button and the camera zoomed in on the two men standing at the door. They must have heard the sound of the camera adjusting because they looked right at it. "I think the Muspel Corporation found you."

"How do you know?" Thyra said. "These guys don't look anything like the thugs that attacked us at my house."

"Different clothes, same apes," Asiri said. "Who else would come bothering me on the same night that you two show up?"

"How?" Bragi said. "We didn't have anyone tailing us. I made sure of it."

"They found you all the same, and you led them to me in the process," Asiri said.

"If they knew to come here, then they already knew about you," Bragi concluded. "It seems you weren't as careful as you thought."

Asiri grimaced, but she didn't argue the point. She zoomed the camera out again until Bragi's SUV was visible. "I don't think you're going to be able to use your vehicle anytime soon."

Thyra watched as the men surrounding the SUV stabbed the tires repeatedly before walking over to the door. They talked for a minute among themselves before two men split off in each direction.

One of the men still at the door looked up at the camera and spoke, "We know you're in there, dwarf. We know the old man and the girl are here, too. Hand them over and we'll leave you in peace."

Asiri bit her lip as she looked at the screen. "You've brought trouble to my door, Rune Tongue. I may have to deliver on my threat after I deal with these apes in suits."

"They knew where you were, Asiri. Do you really think they're going to leave you alone just because you hand us over?" Bragi asked.

"Might be worth a shot," Asiri grumbled.

"We don't have time for this," Bragi snapped. "We need to find a way out of this mess. Do you have a backdoor to this place?"

"Not one we can use now," Asiri said. She pointed to another monitor that showed the rear of the building. As if on cue, the four men appeared in the camera's view and took up position by a door.

"Last chance," came the man's voice through the speaker. He waited a few seconds before shaking his head. "You should have done it the easy way. Now we have to tear this place down around you."

He motioned with one hand to one of the other men who stepped back and gave the door a heavy kick. The echo reached them a moment later.

"They won't get through there like that," Asiri said, a note of pride in her voice. "I made that door. It'll take more than that to break down. We're safe in here."

Thyra watched as the men conversed at the door. It seemed they had come to the same conclusion about the door. One of them jogged out of the camera's view and then returned a moment later with what looked like a shotgun. He held it to his shoulder and pointed it at the door. Thyra flinched when the muzzle flashed, and the sound of a gunshot echoed down the stairs to the forge.

"Will your door hold up against that?" Bragi asked.

Asiri's face darkened. "It's dwarf-made. It will hold."

"I don't think that's an ordinary shotgun," Bragi said. He pointed to the monitor. "Look there."

Thyra looked closer and was surprised to see a strange glow emanating along the barrel. The glow grew more intense—even in the black and white video—and then was discharged in a flash of the muzzle.

"I don't think that's a gunpowder flash," Bragi muttered.

"What else could it be?" Asiri asked.

"You're the weapon maker," Bragi snapped. "You tell me."

Asiri's brow furrowed as she concentrated on the screen. They watched as the men tried the door again. It held, but they were determined. The gun was fired two more times in different spots on the door.

"Cursed fools!" Asiri hissed. "They're messing with things they don't understand! Harnessing power in that way—they're likely to blow themselves up!"

"What are you talking about?" Thyra asked.

Asiri nodded toward the screen. "They've found some idiot who thinks he can do what I do and make weapons. Only whoever they found is still limited by his human mind and stuck to simple designs they were comfortable with."

"It looks like it works to me," Bragi said.

Asiri cursed angrily. "When I find who is building these weapons, I'm going to nail him to the wall and use him as target practice!"

They watched as the strange shotgun was fired one more time, tearing a hole right through the thick metal. This time, when the goons kicked the door, it swung in with a resounding bang.

"We need to leave," Bragi said. "Tell me there is another way out."

Asiri was shaking her head with a grimace. "I'm not going to be run out of my home. Not without a fight."

"As long as that fight is happening while we are escaping," Bragi said. "You saw what that shotgun did to the door. We are in more danger than we can handle. We need to leave now!"

Asiri was still watching the monitors with a grim expression. "I'm not leaving."

"We are," Bragi said. "With or without you."

"Then it's without me," Asiri said stubbornly.

"What do you think they will do to you if they capture you?" Thyra said. "Shake your hand, apologize for shooting up your door, and then leave you alone? I may not know much about the world of magic, but these guys look like they mean business."

"Thyra is right," Bragi said. "If you stay, they will take you, and I don't think they will roll out the red carpet."

Asiri continued to watch the screens grimly. A growl escaped her lips as she watched the men enter the potato cellar and begin to fan out.

"Not without a fight," she grumbled. The dwarf reached over and flicked a switch on the wall. The monitors were lit up suddenly with a flash of light and then went dark again. "That will slow them down."

She flicked another switch and the sound of grinding gears filled the air. The old woman jumped up suddenly and stormed past Thyra. "This way, Thyra Thorsdottir."

"What's that sound?" Thyra asked as she hurried after the dwarf.

"A distraction," Asiri said over the tumult. "This way."

She led them to the far end of her forge and pushed open a door that Thyra would have missed at first glance. Asiri waved Thyra and Bragi through into a narrow room. A tarp was draped over something big at the center of the room.

Asiri pointed to it. "Get the tarp off of it while I make sure these lackwits don't get their hands on my forge."

Thyra and Bragi began pulling the tarp off while Asiri moved back to the door to her forge and began speaking softly to herself. Thyra and Bragi finished pulling the tarp off, revealing a jet-black Camaro SS.

At any other time, Thyra might have taken a few minutes to admire the car. She'd always loved muscle cars, especially classic ones from the mid-sixties to early seventies. Even though this one was a modern model, it still made her heart race just looking at it.

There was an audible pop from the doorway and then Asiri came hustling over.

"Don't stand there," the dwarf spat. "Get in, girl!"

"Where did you get this?" Thyra asked, pointing to the Camaro.

"Payment for services rendered," Asiri said as she popped the trunk and slid a metal briefcase in. She slammed the trunk shut and tossed the keys to Bragi. "You're driving."

Asiri opened the passenger side door and slid into the backseat. Thyra got in behind her just as Bragi started the car up. The engine growled to life with a deep rumble.

"Now what?"

Asiri pointed to a remote hanging on the visor. "Push the top button."

Bragi reached up and hit the button. The sound of heavy gears working preceded the wall in front of them sliding aside, revealing an angled driveway.

"Hold on," Bragi said. He shifted the Camaro into gear and gave it some gas. The car lurched forward, pushing Thyra back into her seat as it accelerated upward.

"Now, the bottom button!" Asiri said over the roar of the engine. Bragi reached up and quickly hit the remote a second time. Just ahead, something moved in the darkness and Thyra could see stars. The Camaro leapt out into the night and landed on the road just outside the potato cellar, its wheels squealing as they made contact with the asphalt.

They were about half a mile down the road when headlights suddenly appeared behind them.

"We've got company!" Bragi said.

Thyra watched in the side mirror as the headlights quickly grew bigger. "They're gaining on us!"

"Not for long," Asiri said. "Step on it, Rune Tongue!"

Bragi obliged and the Camaro's engine roared. It hesitated for a split second and then the power reached the wheels and it surged forward. Thyra glanced at the dash and watched the speedometer pass one hundred twenty miles per hour in a flash. The headlights began to fade into the distance behind them as the Camaro continued to gain speed. She wasn't sure if the engine topped out or if Bragi let up, but they finally leveled out at just over one hundred eighty miles per hour.

They continued at this speed until the headlights behind them were tiny specks of light in the distance.

"Ha!" Asiri said. "I knew they wouldn't be able to keep up! You didn't even give it everything it had."

Bragi's eyes were wide open. Thyra was sure she had the same expression on her face. She wasn't sure she wanted to test how much faster the Camaro could go.

"There's the freeway," Bragi said over the roar of the engine. He began to apply the brake. "I'm going to get on."

"Turn off your lights," Asiri said from the back seat.

"What?" Bragi gave her a frantic look in the rear-view mirror. "How will I be able to see?"

"Don't worry, Rune Tongue," Asiri said. "Do you think the engine is the only thing I've tinkered with?"

She leaned forward in her seat and reached toward the steering wheel. She pushed two buttons in quick succession and the headlights were suddenly extinguished. Thyra felt her heart jump into her throat as the lights went out but was surprised when a blueish light spread across the windshield. To Thyra's amazement, the road and terrain were visible in great detail.

"What is this?" Bragi asked.

"Something I've been working on," Asiri said proudly as she sat back in her seat. "I figured that if I ever needed to make my getaway, I'd first of all want to make sure nothing could keep up with me, but when I was away, I'd also want to be able to travel unseen and unheard. An electric engine met one need and this met the other. Check and check!"

"An electric engine?" Thyra asked. "In a muscle car?"

"A very powerful one," Asiri said with a hint of pride in her voice. "More powerful than anything the human mind has managed to dream up." She reached up and patted Bragi on the shoulder. "Relax, Rune Tongue. We're safe for now."

"What about this?" Thyra asked, gesturing towards the strange display on the windshield.

"Makes going out at night easier, don't you think?" Asiri asked in a self-satisfied voice.

"It's amazing," Bragi said in awe.

"You should be able to keep it around one twenty with no problem," Asiri said. "Don't worry about being seen or the police pulling you over. When the sun starts to come up, just push the button to return your view to normal."

"What are you going to do?" Bragi asked.

"Do you need to ask?" Asiri snapped. "Sleep!"

Bragi gave Thyra a wide-eyed look. "Wisconsin here we come."

Chapter 12

Gunnar Olafsson pushed aside the tablet and sat back in his chair. He had watched the entire attack on the dwarf's home via live feed. The failure of his men to capture Thyra Ariksen, the old man, or the dwarf was just another on a growing list of inexcusable shortcomings.

The debacle at the Ariksen home had been a colossal failure that resulted in the loss of five of his men. Luckily, the survivors had managed to sanitize the scene before the police arrived so that there would be no suspicion cast on his company.

The only positive that came from the day was that now he knew the goddess of death was in play. He had an entire team tasked with looking for any sign of where she'd holed up, but even with the capabilities afforded by modern technology Hela continued to be an enigma that consistently frustrated his attempts at logging her movements. Gunnar knew she would show up sooner or later, but could only guess what role she would play as the world changed. Now he had his answer.

"Your men have failed me twice today," Gunnar said to the hulking Ivan who stood nearby.

"There is no excuse," Ivan said. He quickly added. "But we are tracking them. They are headed east. Do you want me to send another team after them?"

Gunnar considered the question, finally shaking his head. "No. Let them run. It seems we are not equipped to take them even with the element of surprise, so we must adopt another tactic. We've tried going to them, now we must try waiting for them to come to us."

"Lay a trap?" Ivan asked.

Gunnar nodded. "Thyra and the old man led us to the dwarf. Perhaps they will lead us to others. We will watch and wait and move only when the time is right."

"I will alert our network to watch for them, but not to engage," Ivan said.

Gunnar nodded. "I am confident that we will have them in hand soon enough. Have your men gather anything of use from the dwarf's hiding place, and then destroy the building. We will not leave a hole for our prey to run back to."

Ivan nodded. "What of the goddess of death and her dog?"

"Don't forget Sharon Ariksen," Gunnar said. His temper flared at the mere thought of the woman. He had watched the assault on the Ariksen home as well, and he had been shocked by the appearance of a spear-wielding warrior in place of the insurance agent they had been expecting. "How did we know nothing of her existence before this?"

The Russian hesitated in answering. "She didn't appear to have magic, so there was no reason for her to be a person of interest."

The answer didn't please Gunnar. "Then your search has been too narrow. You saw the video. She may not have magic, but she was no ordinary suburban housewife."

Ivan didn't deny it. "It was a mistake that will not be repeated."

"Good," Gunnar said. "As for what to do about Hela and her wolf, we watch and wait. Now that we have a trace on the signal of Sharon Ariksen's phone we can finally learn where Hela's hole is. Perhaps she will prove useful."

Ivan nodded, but their exchange was interrupted by a condescending voice. "You are sticking your hand into a pit of vipers."

Gunnar closed his eyes and exhaled slowly. He had tried to forget that there was a third man in the room. He slowly opened his eyes and stared across the room at his 'silent' partner. Dark hair framed a face that was almost too perfect. Handsome was not a fitting word—no, he was strikingly beautiful. His features were so perfect that it was almost painful to look at him.

But it wasn't his perfect features that always held Gunnar's attention. It was his eyes. All it took was one look from those soulless, gray eyes to make someone forget the beauty of his face. One look revealed the black, swirling void inside. A void that swallowed all light and warmth and replaced them with darkness colder than anything imaginable. It was a drastic contradiction—perfect hate lurking just below a perfect surface.

His real name was a secret that only a few people knew—Gunnar included—but the name he had chosen to use was far worse in Gunnar's opinion. Asmodeus. Gunnar was well-versed enough to recognize the meaning behind that name as being 'prince of devils'. It was a fitting choice for a man who was the closest thing to a devil Gunnar had ever encountered.

"You don't agree with my plan for the goddess?" Gunnar asked.

Asmodeus's smile was cold. "Hela is dangerous. If anyone can spoil your plans, it will be her."

"I don't take her lightly," Gunnar said. "I know what she is and what kind of power she commands. That's why I haven't tried to take her before now."

"You haven't tried to take her before now because you didn't know where she was and because you're scared of her," Asmodeus corrected. "And you should be. She can boil the blood inside your veins and manage to keep you alive long enough to feel every excruciating moment of it. She can break every bone in your body with a thought and then heal them, only to break over and over again."

Gunnar sighed and gave Ivan an exasperated look. "You always have the most vivid stories, Asmodeus. You've told so many over the past year. It's been entertaining, for sure. But, the one thing you don't offer is *solutions*."

Asmodeus smiled grimly. "When a child makes a mess, you don't clean it up for them or else they will simply keep making the mess. Enabling the child's behavior only worsens the situation."

"Am I the child in this analogy?" Gunnar asked.

"When I came here, you were still obsessed with eradicating magic," Asmodeus said. "As if eight centuries of trying and failing hadn't been enough to teach you that you can't destroy magic. If it weren't for me, you'd still be chasing your own tail, trying to fight an endless and fruitless war."

"You give yourself too much credit," Gunnar said. "You've interfered more than you've helped."

"All I've done is stop you from destroying useful tools," Asmodeus said.

"You mean you've created a list of off-limits magic users that you've recruited into your service," Gunnar said.

Asmodeus shrugged. "Useful tools that you wanted to either enslave or destroy."

Gunnar had to look away to keep from losing his temper. The man was infuriating. A year ago, he had walked into Gunnar's office and demanded a meeting. Gunnar was just about to call security and have him escorted out of the building when the newcomer had uttered a name that Gunnar hadn't heard for centuries. Caught off guard, he made the mistake of letting Asmodeus into his office and into his confidence.

He'd been paying for the mistake ever since, no matter the benefits that Asmodeus said had come Gunnar's way.

"You've failed to capture the girl and the old man two times now,"

Asmodeus said. "Your men have looked like fools, and it won't be long before these mistakes catch up with you."

"I'm well aware of that," Gunnar snapped.

"Then, perhaps it's time for another approach," Asmodeus said.

Gunnar looked at Ivan. "Isn't that exactly what I just said?"

Asmodeus smiled wryly. He stood up and casually headed for the door.

"Where are you going?" Gunnar asked.

"To do what you couldn't—get the girl."

"And how do you propose to do that?" Gunnar asked. "They are in transit. They could change directions at any time, and there is no telling where they will go to ground."

"You said Hela is involved now," Asmodeus said. "She has the girl's mother. I think it's obvious where they will be going."

Gunnar looked away in frustration. That seemed obvious now, and it angered him that he didn't see it before. He glared at Ivan in an attempt to express his displeasure that the Russian didn't make the connection either. Ivan shrugged his heavy shoulders, adding fuel to Gunnar's temper.

"You can't just waltz in there," Gunnar said, turning back to Asmodeus. "Hela will recognize you, and you know it."

"There are ways around that," Asmodeus said.

"You mean *magic*," Gunnar scoffed.

"It amuses me," Asmodeus said, "how readily you scoff at the very thing that has brought you long life, wealth, and a vast empire." He chuckled to himself softly. "You should be more grateful."

Gunnar scowled at Asmodeus, but Asmodeus's smile only grew more brazen.

"Don't worry about my methods," Asmodeus said. "In a few days' time, you will have the girl, her mother, the old man, the dwarf, and Hela in hand."

"That's a tall order to fill," Gunnar said.

"But I will succeed," Asmodeus said. "I will succeed where you have failed. Repeatedly."

Gunnar bristled, but he didn't get a chance to offer a rebuttal. Asmodeus cast one more condescending smile in his direction and then left. Even after the door closed, the sound of his steps on the marble floor sounded echoed in Gunnar's ears.

He needed a plan. Gunnar couldn't allow Asmodeus to get to Thyra Ariksen or those with her before he did. The girl was important, more so than he could have imagined. He had formed a guess about her identity, but now he couldn't help but wonder if he had underestimated her value.

Then there was the unknown of who the girl's parents were. The video of her mom left him thinking that Sharon Ariksen was a shield-maiden at the very least, if not a Valkyrie. One important enough to have been given fruit from Iduun's garden. That would explain how she was still alive, but it also raised more questions. He knew some of the Valkyries were granted immortality, but it was never said which ones. He didn't recognize her face, which wasn't surprising. Valkyries had always worn masks in battle to hide their faces, and he couldn't remember a time the Valkyries weren't engaged in one battle or another.

The question of who the father was one Gunnar thought he had an answer to, but he also recognized the impossibility of the situation. He had made sure that god was dead, which meant the girl was either the spawn of another or was an anomaly. Gunnar didn't think the latter was plausible, but he had no proof to the contrary.

One thing was certain in Gunnar's mind. Hela's entrance into the mix only confirmed that Thyra Ariksen was no ordinary teenager. The goddess of death wouldn't step out into the open for just anyone. She was too crafty to risk showing her hand unless the reward outweighed the risk. The girl was important, and Gunnar needed to know why.

"We cannot afford to wait for Asmodeus to find them," Gunnar said. "Alert our network. Tell them that they are to do everything in their power to harry them into our trap without engaging them directly. We know that they are most likely headed to meet Hela. We will be waiting for them there."

"What do you think might be the reason for Hela's interest in the girl?" Ivan asked.

"I have a guess," Gunnar said, "and if I'm right, we have to ensure Asmodeus doesn't get to them first."

"It seems your partnership is not so healthy anymore," Ivan commented. "Maybe it needs to be dissolved. Do you want me to kill him?"

Gunnar looked up at Ivan, his eyes flashing. The big Russian wasn't bothered by the vitriol in his boss' eyes.

"I'll kill him if you want me to," Ivan said like he was discussing the weather, not murder.

Gunnar snorted. "And die trying."

The big Russian shrugged. "I've killed plenty of men in my life. Can Asmodeus be that different?"

"You can't kill him," Gunnar said, shaking his head. "No one can."

"All men can die," Ivan said.

"Not this one," Gunnar said grimly.

Chapter 13

Bragi pulled off the highway just as the sun was beginning to rise. Thyra opened her eyes and looked out the window as they pulled into the parking lot of a convenience store. She'd been awake for a while, but kept her eyes closed so she could be alone with her thoughts. Bragi put the Camaro into park and yawned.

Asiri woke with a snort as the car came to a stop. The dwarf sat up and looked out the window. "Where are we?"

"Montana," Bragi said. "Just outside of Billings."

"I came through here a while back," Asiri said. The old woman looked out the window and shook her head with a grimace. "I remember it being prettier."

Thyra looked out at the dry fields all around them with barely a tree in sight and found herself agreeing with Asiri. Summer had come early and hard here. There wasn't a blade of green in sight.

"At least we made good time," Asiri grumbled.

"That's true," Bragi said. "You were right about this car being fast. If we keep this pace, we should be in Hudson by the evening."

"Not a minute too soon," Asiri grumbled. "My backside is already sore."

"Let's get something to eat, and some fuel," Bragi said with a smirk. "Then we can get back on the road. You two coming?"

Asiri shook her head. "Not me. I'll stay right here. Just bring me something palatable."

"Didn't you just say your back is sore?" Thyra asked. "Don't you want to get out and stretch out?"

The old woman shook her head. "You may not believe this, but a bent old woman with a sharp tongue tends to draw attention. I'll stay here."

Thyra was about to argue but she saw Bragi give her an almost imperceptible shake of his head.

"We'll bring you something," Bragi said. "Come on, Thyra. Let's stretch our legs for a bit."

Thyra got out of the car and shut the door behind her before giving Bragi a confused look. The old man motioned for Thyra to walk with him. He led her down the sidewalk to a small grassy area off to the side of the convenience store.

"Asiri has reasons for being cautious about being seen," Bragi said.

"Like what?"

"Like not trusting humans," Bragi said. "Her people were some of the first to be killed off when the Aesir fell. She may not want to admit it, but the Aesir protected them from a world that was very distrusting of her kind. When Ragnarök happened, the dwarves were exposed. They were given no mercy. I can only imagine what her life has been like since her family was killed."

"Did Surtur kill her family?" Thyra asked.

"Not directly," Bragi said, "but the absence of the Aesir left creatures of magic vulnerable. There were many that shared Surtur's view of the world that were all too eager to snuff out anything they considered a threat. The way the dwarves created weapons was misunderstood, and mankind is not tolerant of what they don't understand."

"How was it misunderstood?"

"What the dwarves did looked like magic to a normal person, but it wasn't," Bragi said. "They were advanced and had talents that were extraordinary, but it wasn't magic. In many ways, they married science and magic together, but that didn't matter. The dwarves created weapons of immense power, and because of that they were hunted down and killed."

"Is she really the last of her kind?"

"I don't know," Bragi said with a sigh. "It's possible. She seems convinced it's true."

"That's so sad," Thyra said. "Were there more like the dwarves? Other kinds of people that were hunted and killed?"

Bragi nodded. "There were. Some were exterminated by men. Others simply couldn't adapt to the way the world was changing and died off on their own. The world of men has not been kind to creatures of magic."

Thyra let the words sink in. Finding out that she was the daughter of a Norse god and had magic should have filled her with excitement, but the more she learned about this world, the more she realized it was a world steeped in danger and painful history.

"There's something I've been meaning to ask you," Thyra said. "How did my mom, you, Asiri, even Surtur all come to be in the U.S.?"

"The promise of a new start enticed us," Bragi said. "The Old World was too dangerous. There were only so many places to hide, and for someone that could live forever without aging, it's only so long before your face is recognized. America was a clean slate, and an opportunity to escape the past."

"Doesn't look like that worked too well," Thyra said.

Bragi looked toward the rising sun and shook his head. "No, I guess not. I fear the only real escape from the past is dying."

The finality of that statement shook Thyra.

Bragi exhaled deeply. "Come on. Let's go get something to eat. I think my belly button is dangerously close to touching my spine."

They walked back to the front of the store and went in. Thyra wandered down the aisles while Bragi excused himself to the restroom. She lingered near a stand of fresh cinnamon rolls but decided against buying one. The last thing she wanted was a sugar spike and crash. Not that there were many health-friendly options. After walking the aisles, she decided the sticky treat was as good as anything else available, regardless of the crash it would likely give her.

She was heading back to the cinnamon roll stand when the bell over the door rang and a thick-limbed trucker sauntered in. He nodded to the clerk behind the desk and headed straight to the soda fountain. Thyra wouldn't have thought twice about seeing a trucker in a convenience store, but something about him set off warning bells in her head. She tried to ignore them as she opened the glass door and retrieved a cinnamon roll, but they refused to be silenced.

Putting her sticky treasure in a cardboard box, she moved toward the front of the store and began studying a rack of sunglasses. Putting on a pair of dark aviators, she turned the rack so that she could use the mirror to keep an eye on the trucker. To her surprise, he was watching her. Trying not to show her discomfort, she tried on another pair of glasses before slowly making her way down the aisle toward the restroom door.

She positioned a rack of postcards between her and the trucker and made a show of sifting through them. She glanced up twice and both times her eyes met those of the trucker. He was making no attempt at hiding his interest.

The door to the restroom opened and Bragi came out. He smiled at her, but the smile froze when he saw the look on her face.

"What's wrong?"

"Hold this for me, *Dad*," she said loud enough that she was certain the trucker heard. She handed the cinnamon roll to Bragi. "And I decided I don't want a fountain drink. Nothing good over there."

Bragi gave her a confused look. "Okay. Can I get you something

137

else?"

"Anything but a fountain drink," Thyra said. She motioned with her eyes and tried to put an emphasis on her words. *"Nothing good* is over there."

Bragi's eyes narrowed slightly before flicking toward the drink fountain. Thyra saw him tense and was certain he had seen the trucker.

"I'll just wait for you here," Bragi said, returning his attention to Thyra. "You can pick out something when you get out."

Thyra slid past him and closed the door to the restroom behind her. If she had needed to use the restroom before, that need was forgotten now. She waited long enough to make it appear like she was actually using it before flushing the toilet and then turning on the water at the sink.

Satisfied that she had spent enough time, she shut off the water and engaged the hand dryer. She let it run through its cycle and then reached for the door. She pulled it open but froze in her tracks when she saw the trucker standing just outside the door talking to Bragi.

"I hope ya don't mind me sayin' so, but that is a good lookin' Camaro," the trucker was saying to Bragi. "I've got an old '68 Camaro I've been trying to restore for years but seeing that one makes me wonder if I wouldn't be better off just gettin' me a new one."

"It's a lot of fun to drive," Bragi said with a smile, but Thyra could sense the tension in his voice. "But there is no beating the classics, right?"

"You've got a point there," the trucker said good naturedly. "I'm headin' east with a big load. Picked it up in Bend, and drivin' all the way to Detroit. Where ya'll headin'?"

"Still undecided," Bragi said.

The trucker looked past him to Thyra. "This your daughter?"

"Yes," Bragi said.

The trucker nodded, but something in his eyes said he didn't believe it. He looked back at Bragi and smiled.

"Well, I just had to say how jealous I was of your ride." He nodded to Bragi and then winked at Thyra. "Ya'll travel safe! Maybe I'll see ya'll on the road."

He turned and walked out of the store, turning once and giving them a small wave as he walked back to his truck.

"What was that all about?" Thyra asked.

"We need to get out of here," Bragi said quietly. "Get what you need and let's go."

"Why?"

"I'll tell you in the car," Bragi said.

Thyra sensed the urgency in his voice and hurried to do as she was told. She grabbed a bottle of chocolate milk, a Dr. Pepper, and a few energy bars and added them to what Bragi had quickly gathered up. Bragi produced a crisp bill and handed it to the clerk.

"Ya'll need some gas today?" The clerk asked.

"No, just the food and drinks today," Bragi said in a pleasant voice. The clerk handed over some loose change, which Bragi dropped into the change bowl next to the register. "Have a nice day!"

"Travel safe," the clerk said dismissively as they gathered up their items and headed for the car.

"We may have some trouble," Asiri said before they had even closed their doors.

"The trucker?" Bragi said as he started up the Camaro.

Asiri nodded. "He was a little too interested in my car. I don't think he could see me through the tint on the windows, but I saw him well enough. He was looking for someone, and from the look on his fat face when he came out, he found them."

"Us," Bragi said. He looked down at the dash and grimaced. "I should have filled up the tank first. We're low on gas."

"Too late for that," Asiri said as she looked out the back window.

"He's waiting over by the pumps."

"Can the electric engine get us the rest of the way?" Bragi asked.

"Not without a charge," Asiri said. She looked at one of the gauges. "Right now, I'd say we have a hundred miles left. A third of that if we have to drive more aggressively."

"I think we're going to have to," Bragi said. "Stopping to fill up isn't going to be in the cards. Not until we lose our tail."

"You think he'll follow us?" Thyra asked.

Bragi looked in the rear-view mirror and nodded. "He's sitting in his truck right now. I bet as soon as we pull out, he'll follow right behind us."

"This thing can outrun him," Thyra said. "You saw what it did last night. Just give it some gas and he'll be in our dust."

"I'm not worried about him keeping up with us," Bragi said. "I'm worried about who he told and what will be waiting for us down the road."

"You think he works for Surtur?" Thyra asked.

"I don't think, I know," Bragi said darkly. He put the Camaro in reverse and backed out. He shifted it into drive and rolled forward. "What do you see on the side of his truck?"

Thyra glanced over at the truck and felt her stomach sink. "Muspel Corporation" was written in big, block letters on the side of the trailer. She recognized the strange logo from the website.

"How did they find us?" Thyra asked.

Bragi shook his head. "I don't know. But, it's clear Surtur's reach is farther than we thought."

"What do we do?"

"We get ahead of him," Bragi said, giving the Camaro some gas and moving toward the freeway. "And then we hope that we can avoid whatever or whoever he told about us."

They hadn't even pulled out onto the road before the big truck began following them.

"When he's out of sight," Asiri said from the back seat, "get off the freeway."

"And do what?" Bragi glanced in the rear-view mirror. "If they found us this easily, they can find us wherever we go."

"Yes, but the main roads are the ones that they will be watching," Asiri said. "If we can get off of them, we might be able to avoid being seen."

"This ride won't last much longer if that's the case," Bragi said. He pulled onto the freeway and pushed down on the accelerator. The semi surprisingly matched their acceleration. "You said it yourself, we're low on both gas and battery power. Once they both go out, what then?"

"Just lose the truck and get off the freeway as quick as you can," Asiri said. Bragi began to argue, but she cut him off. "Just do what I say, Rune Tongue!"

Bragi grimaced but didn't say anything. Instead, he stepped on the gas even harder and the Camaro charged forward. The speedometer showed that they passed eighty miles per hour but Bragi kept his foot on the gas. Thyra glanced in the side mirror and was shocked to see the semi still keeping close.

"He's not falling behind," Thyra said.

"His trailer must be empty," Bragi said. "So much for hauling a big load."

"He'll fall back," Asiri said. "That engine was meant for hauling, not speed."

Thyra didn't know if she trusted the old woman's estimation. She kept glancing back as they drove, and each time the semi was still hanging in behind them.

They'd gone thirty miles without putting more than a hundred yards between them and the semi when a chime signaled that they were getting dangerously low on gas.

"We can't keep this up," Bragi said. "We need to lose him now or never."

"Then lose him!" Thyra said.

Bragi stepped on the gas and the Camaro surged forward. The speedometer climbed above one hundred ten miles per hour in a flash and still Bragi kept accelerating.

"I hope there aren't any police cruisers nearby," Bragi muttered as he continued to accelerate.

"If there are, just keep going," Asiri said. "They'll fall behind, too."

Thyra glanced in the side mirror. She swore she could hear the semi's engine roar behind them, but she was relieved to see it falling behind as the Camaro gained speed. It seemed Asiri's claim about the semi's engine not being able to keep up at high speeds would prove true after all.

It didn't take long before the semi shrank into the distance. A sign on the roadside said that there was an exit coming in a mile and a blue sign right below it stated that there weren't services for forty miles afterwards. She glanced at the dash and saw the gas gauge hovering over empty. The battery gauge wasn't any more comforting.

"Do we get off?" Thyra asked.

"No," Bragi said. "He's still within sight. If we exit now, he'll just follow us."

"Do we have enough to make it another forty miles on the charge?" Thyra asked.

"She'll make it," Asiri said, but Thyra sensed a hint of doubt in her voice.

The exit came and went in a flash. No one spoke as it faded into the distance behind them. Thyra found herself holding her breath every time they passed another mile marker, fully expecting the car to suddenly sputter and lose power.

"Thirty miles to go," Bragi muttered. He glanced at the battery gauge and shifted in his seat nervously.

"She'll make it," Asiri said firmly, but then added in a soft voice. "I think."

Thyra's eyes were glued to the blue battery gauge. She didn't dare look at the scenery or the freeway signs out of fear that the distance would somehow grow longer. It was irrational, but in the moment, rational thought was the last thing running through her mind.

The battery gauge grew steadily lower until it became only a sliver of blue. Suddenly, a chime sounded, and the blue sliver turned red. Bragi shifted in his seat and licked his lips nervously. Thyra couldn't watch any longer and closed her eyes. She sat in her seat, her hands clutching Lynnedslag in a white-knuckled grip and waited for the car to suddenly slow and die. Every bump in the road made her grip the lacrosse stick tighter.

The Camaro suddenly began to slow, and Thyra was sure that the moment had finally come. Then, she felt the car begin to climb slightly. She opened her eyes and was surprised to see them driving up the off ramp.

"We made it?" Thyra asked.

"By the skin of our teeth," Bragi said, but he still didn't look relieved.

"We still need to get far enough off the freeway that we won't be seen," Asiri said.

Thyra looked around. "I don't see a gas station."

"No," Bragi said. "I don't either."

"Uh, if there aren't any gas stations," Thyra said, "then there's no way there's going to be a charging station. Not in 'Middle-of-Nowhere,' Montana."

Bragi nodded. "I had the same thought."

"So, what are we going to do?"

Asiri leaned forward and pointed down a side road that curved up into a narrow and disappeared. "Quit your whimpering and get out of sight. Over there behind that hill."

Thyra looked up at the sign. "But, that's away from everything. The sign says there's a town eight miles the other way. Shouldn't we go there?"

"Do as I say, Rune Tongue!" Asiri said sharply. "Get out of sight."

Bragi looked ready to argue in favor of Thyra's point, but one look from the old dwarf was enough to convince him otherwise. He turned the Camaro and sped down the two-lane road. When they were a mile into the canyon Asiri nodded.

"Good enough. Pull over."

"Here?" Bragi asked. "If we stop, I don't know if we'll get the engine going again."

"You worry too much," the old woman snapped. "We'll get her going again, and she'll be chomping at the bit to go. Just do as I say, Rune Tongue."

Bragi reluctantly let off the gas and applied the brake.

"Out, girl!" Asiri snapped the moment the car came to a stop. "And bring that child's toy with you."

Thyra got out and stepped aside. Asiri scrambled out and hurried around to the back of the car and popped the trunk. She began fidgeting with something, grumbling to herself. Bragi joined her and watched what she was doing with a curious expression.

"Ah ha!" Asiri exclaimed suddenly. "Just takes a wee bit of creativity, Rune Tongue! That and no small amount of skill."

"And that helps us how?" Bragi asked.

"You'll see," Asiri said. She peeked her head around the car and looked at Thyra. "Come here, Sparks!"

Thyra walked over to join the other two. The old woman was holding a set of jumper cables that she had hooked to a foot-long metal rod. She clamped the other ends to the car's battery in the trunk and smiled.

"There!"

"I still don't see how that helps us with the car," Bragi said, shaking his head.

"How can't you see?" Asiri snapped. She pointed at Thyra. "We're standing here with the daughter of Thor, you blind, old man! We don't need to go to a charging station. We have one sitting in the passenger seat!"

Thyra's eyes widened in surprise. "What?"

Bragi raised an eyebrow. "You think she can charge the car with this?"

"Who's the dwarf here?" Asiri snapped. "Don't question me! I know what I'm doing."

"Wait," Thyra said. "What do you mean I'm going to charge the car?"

"You're going to use that little stick in your hands," Asiri said, "call forth some lightning, and I'm going to stand here safely holding onto the rubber of these cables until the car is charged."

Thyra looked at the dwarf woman like she had gone crazy. From the wild look in her eyes, Thyra was certain Asiri had.

Bragi nodded. "I see how that could work. You're sure that rod will split the power correctly?"

"Did you become a dwarf in the last minute?" Asiri said, casting Bragi a fiery glare.

Bragi shrugged and held up his hands. "I will leave you to it."

"Just get in the car and let me know when it's fully charged," Asiri said.

Bragi obeyed the command and slipped back into the driver's seat.

"Now, summon your magic, girl," Asiri said.

Thyra hesitated, but finally did as she was commanded. Lynnedslag pulsed in her hands and a ball of lightning cracked to life in the basket. She looked at Asiri and the dwarf woman nodded.

"Here it goes," Thyra said. She reached Lynnedslag toward the metal rod but was surprised when the dwarf woman pulled it back in a rush.

"Not like that!" Asiri shrieked. "You trying to kill me, girl?"

"What did I do?" Thyra squealed in surprise.

"Don't use the stick!" Asiri snapped. "You'd hit me with enough power to fry me and the car all at once."

"Why did you tell me to bring it then?" Thyra asked.

"Because unless you've mastered the connection to your magic in the last few hours, you still are reliant on the stick," Asiri said. "You will need to learn how to use your magic without the stick in your hands, but for now, you need it."

"So, what am I supposed to do?" Thyra asked.

"Not use the weapon!" Asiri said. She exhaled heavily and shook her head. "Use your hand, Sparks."

"My hand?"

The dwarf nodded. "Like I told you, your magic comes from you, not Lynnedslag. The stick just magnifies it to higher levels. There is no good way to regulate how much is used. But you should be able to control the flow if you do it by touch."

"What?" Thyra asked. "How?"

"Just do what I say girl!" Asiri said. "Since no one is here to teach you how to handle your magic, and Rune Tongue can't help with anything besides pretty pictures in your head, it falls on me to teach you."

"I heard that," Bragi called back.

Asiri ignored him. "I don't have magic, but I've helped enough of your kind to have an idea of how things work. So, do as I say, and maybe you'll learn a thing or two. Reach out your hand and take hold of the rod."

Thyra took one hand off of Lynnedslag and watched tendrils of electricity jump from finger to finger. She hadn't tried to summon her magic since Asiri gave her Lynnedslag, and she couldn't help but feel more comfortable with the thought that the magic came from the lacrosse stick instead of her. But she knew that wasn't the case. She had felt the well of power waiting patiently inside of her ever since her vision of Yggdrasil but hadn't tried to tap into it on her own. It still felt surreal to her, and part of her was afraid that if she tried to call up her magic on her own, she would fail. Lynnedslag was her crutch for now.

"Just grab the rod?" Thyra asked.

Asiri nodded. "And then control your magic so you don't fry me where I stand."

"How will I control it?"

"How would I know?" Asiri snapped. "Just do it!"

"That's easy for you to say," Thyra said in frustration.

The dwarf shrugged. "Never said I would hold your hand. Just learn quick so you don't make me into a dwarf kebob!"

"You're not helping," Thyra said.

"You're not helping, either," Asiri said sharply. "Get to it, Sparks!"

Thyra pressed her lips together to keep the angry comment that was forming from escaping. Gritting her teeth, she steeled her resolve and took hold of the steel rod. Immediately, she felt a rush of energy flow out of her into the metal. Sparks flew from the jumper cable and she almost let go, but Asiri motioned for her to keep going.

"Good!" The dwarf woman said, a wild smile on her face. "Now, focus and give it some more! Imagine you're pushing energy out of your body."

Thyra tried to do exactly that and was surprised to feel the flow of energy increase.

"Yes!" Asiri said. "You're doing it, girl! Keep going!"

Thyra did what she was told and tried to push more. What had begun as a small flow of energy quickly turned into what felt like a raging torrent. To her surprise, she saw the smile drop from Asiri's face and her eyes grow wide. Too late, Thyra saw the rubber on the cables melting and burning off.

"Too much!" Asiri said.

What happened next seemed to last forever to Thyra. Tendrils of blue-white electricity began to leap off of the exposed cable. Two of them arched up and then slashed back down toward Asiri's hands. The dwarf stood rooted in place for a split second and then suddenly shot backwards through the air. Thyra screamed in surprise and tried to stop the flow of power out of her, but her effort had the opposite effect and a bolt of lightning leapt through the air and struck the hillside.

Shocked, Thyra dropped Lynnedslag and the rod as a sharp peal of thunder filled the air. Then everything went deathly quiet. Tendrils of lightning still danced between her fingers, but she was too busy staring at what she had done to notice. A dozen feet away, Asiri was laying on her back, smoke rising from her motionless body.

Bragi appeared at Asiri's side. He put a hand to the old woman's neck to feel for a pulse. Thyra felt numb as she watched. A wave of guilt washed over her as she watched Bragi begin chest compressions.

"Did I kill her?" Thyra said weakly. "What have I done?"

Bragi checked her pulse again, and then began another round of chest compression.

"I killed her," Thyra repeated. "I, I, I didn't mean to. I don't know what happened. I didn't mean to!"

Bragi stopped to check for a pulse again, but his hand was suddenly slapped aside. Asiri coughed and rolled onto her side. "Stop that!"

Bragi jumped back in surprise. "You're alive?"

"Of course I am, no thanks to you!" Asiri said. She sat up and looked at Thyra. "And you, girl, stop your blubbering! I'm not dead!"

The dwarf woman stood up, her hair still sticking straight out and walked toward the car. Thyra watched in confused awe as the dwarf strode to the driver seat and peeked her head in.

"Ha!" Asiri called out hoarsely. "You did it, Sparks!"

The dwarf came around the side of the car with a broad smile splitting her features.

"Could have done without getting blasted by your lightning," she said, "but I guess that's as much my fault as yours. I told you to keep going."

Thyra's mouth moved, but her voice failed her. She finally managed to speak one word.

"How?"

"You really think a little lightning would be enough to kill me?" Asiri snorted. "Ha! I'm a dwarf, girl. We're made of tougher stuff than that."

"How are you alive?" Thyra asked, still confused. She looked closer at the old woman and was surprised to see her skin had changed color. "And why are you blue?"

Asiri looked down at her royal blue colored skin and let out a surprised grunt. "Looks like you hit me hard enough to ruin my Cloaker."

"Your what?"

"The device that makes me more acceptable to humans," Asiri said dismissively. "Don't worry. I'll fix it in the car."

Asiri turned to Bragi. "You gonna stand there all day, Rune Tongue?"

"A 'thank you' might be in order," Bragi said.

"For what?" Asiri snapped. "You trying to break my ribs? I was fine. We dwarves have more lives than cats."

"I'm starting to believe that," Bragi muttered.

"Let's get going," Asiri said. "That little demonstration won't go unnoticed. Thunder on a cloudless day? We shouldn't be here when someone decides to investigate."

The dwarf woman walked to the car, pausing long enough to look in the side mirror and grimace. She patted her wild, gray hair back down and then slid into the car.

"Come on, you two! We still have a long road ahead of us."

Bragi walked over to Thyra. "You okay?"

Thyra nodded. "Yeah, I think so. But, how is she okay?"

"Like she said, dwarves have more lives than cats," Bragi said. He motioned to Lynnedslag. "Don't forget Lynnedslag."

Thyra bent down and carefully picked up the lacrosse stick. She had a new respect for Lynnedslag after seeing what she had done to Asiri. She walked back to the car and slid into the passenger seat. Bragi started the Camaro and nodded in approval when he saw the battery gauge show a full charge. He turned the car around and began to head back toward the freeway.

"Do you think the semi-truck has passed us?" Thyra asked.

"If not, we'll outrun him again," Asiri said. "Besides, we're not going to take the freeway."

"The freeway gets us where we need to be the fastest," Bragi argued. "Isn't that what we want?"

"We'll get there plenty fast either way with this car," Asiri countered. "Just start driving, Rune Tongue."

Bragi reluctantly put the car into gear and spun it around. He avoided getting back on the freeway and began driving south.

Thyra settled into her seat and leaned back against the headrest as a wave of exhaustion hit her. She yawned and blinked heavily.

"Route 212 runs all the way to Minnesota, if I remember right," Asiri said, pointing to a sign on the side of the road.

"But how do we get there?" Bragi asked. "Route 212 is over fifty miles from here. Do you know which roads will get us there?"

"No, of course not," Asiri said, a hint of irritation in her voice. "But there are such things as maps and road signs..."

Thyra closed her eyes for a second. She thought about her mom and wondered where she was. Thyra hoped that she was safe, but nothing could be taken for granted.

Thyra opened her eyes and took a long, deep breath.

"…do you really trust those blasted directions?" Asiri was saying.

"They are reliable," Bragi said, holding up his phone. "We can see all the possible routes and it updates if we are forced to go a different way."

"If we can use them, doesn't that mean Surtur's men can too?" Asiri said.

"Yes, but they will expect us to…"

Thyra's eyes closed again and she didn't hear the rest of what Bragi said as the sweet oblivion of sleep washed over her.

Chapter 14

Sif woke up to an unnatural silence. She opened her eyes and was immediately assaulted by a blinding white light that hung overhead. She looked away and tried to blink away the image that was burned into her vision. When it finally faded, she saw that she was in some kind of hospital room. There were six other hospital beds in the room, all of them occupied by unmoving forms.

Sif tried to sit up, but her body screamed in protest from a dozen different places. She sagged back into the bed in pain.

"Good, you're finally awake," a female voice said.

Sif recognized the voice. She turned her head in time to see Hela step into view. The goddess crossed the room to stand beside Sif's bed.

"Where am I?" Sif asked, her voice shockingly weak.

"You are in my home," Hela said. "You're safe for now."

Sif didn't feel safe. Not with Hela nearby. "What did you do to me?"

"I healed you," Hela said. "The injuries you have are courtesy of the Muspel Corporation. Their weapons did a lot of damage, even to a Valkyrie."

Sif remembered the strange firearms the men from the Muspel Corporation carried. She had felt the fire of the strange projectiles they fired. She knew it wasn't something of the world of men. Magic was involved.

"It seems the Muspel Corporation has had a measure of success in turning magical weapons against us," Hela said, guessing at Sif's thoughts. "I don't know how they achieved it, but there's no denying what we saw."

"What happened?" Sif asked. "How did I get here?"

"You fought well," Hela answered, "but even a Valkyrie will succumb to the loss of blood. Luckily, I was nearby and was able to call you back from death's door. I did what I could in the moment, but time was short, and I was not able to tend to your wounds properly until we arrived back here."

"How long?" Sif asked.

"You've been asleep for a day," Hela said. "You're a true testament to the resilience of the Valkyries. Any other person would have slept for a week at the very least while recovering from wounds like yours."

"I suppose you think I should thank you," Sif said.

Hela shook her head. "No, I know better than to expect you to show any gratitude. You owe your life to me, but this isn't the first time that has been the case, is it? You never thanked me before, so why should this time be any different?"

"I remember you always exacted a price for your healing," Sif said grimly. "And it was rarely monetary. What kind of favor are you going to demand this time?"

Hela ignored Sif. "Considering all the hours I've spent patching up your body, healing your wounds, and making sure you lived to fight another day, I feel like I know you better than anyone."

Sif frowned. "Just because you've had your hands under my skin doesn't mean you know me."

"Doesn't it?" Hela raised one eyebrow. She put a finger on Sif's forehead and a wave of energy through Sif's body, making her arch her back. Hela removed her finger and Sif fell back to the bed, her chest heaving. "That should dull some of your discomfort, but I can't afford to heal you completely. I can't risk finding a Valkyrie's spear pressed against my spine."

Sif gritted her teeth against the pain. "I remember that hurting less."

"That's because we were on the same side back then," Hela said. "Until I know where you stand, you will feel every bit of the healing I do for you."

Sif looked around the room at the other beds. "Who are these people?"

Hela looked around the room. "The lost or forgotten. My patients are the refuse that mankind has thrown aside. They had no other place to go. Besides a morgue, but that is a waste of life."

"They don't look like they're living," Sif said.

"Call it what you will, but they are still drawing breath, and that's what matters, isn't it?" Hela stood up and moved to another bed. "Take this poor soul for example. When I found him, he had just swallowed an entire bottle of pills and chased it with a bottle of alcohol. Now, he's in excellent health, his addiction removed, and his emotional state normalized." She looked at the other beds. "The same goes for the others. They come here addicted to drugs, alcohol, and riddled with unhealthy appetites that decay their bodies. Some tried to take their own lives. I took them in and showed them mercy."

"And made them into what?" Sif asked. "Vegetables for you to experiment on?"

"Don't lecture me," Hela said. "It's a bit hypocritical coming from a Valkyrie. I'm a healer, and that is exactly what I'm doing here. I have saved these people from addiction, mind numbing depression, from early deaths due to the damage they've done to themselves or were going to do. I've cured them from the very vices that would've killed them. The world cast them aside. If not for me, they would be nothing but worm-food."

"It's shocking how someone who spent years saving lives can talk

154

so coldly about them," Sif said. "You're no saint, no matter what image you've concocted in your head. I know you better than that. I remember the monsters you created. Men and women cobbled together, in constant pain, and subservient to you because you alone could take it away."

"And I thought I knew you better than this," Hela snapped.

Sif's eyes narrowed. "What do you mean?"

"What were you thinking bringing a child into this world? You say I'm the monster, but from where I stand, you're the one who was foolish enough to think it was a good idea to have a child in a world that would be hostile to her if it knew what she was."

"My choices are none of your concern," Sif said.

Hela tsked. "I think they are. Your daughter's existence creates complications. The battle lines were drawn clearly, but her existence blurs all lines!"

Sif was surprised to see an unexpected expression on Hela's face—fear. Rather than speak, she decided to let Hela dictate the conversation.

"Surtur is alive," Hela said. "You don't look surprised by that, which tells me you already suspected that to be true. Did you also know that he has the Eye in his possession?"

Sif swallowed hard. "The Eye was destroyed."

"You only know what you've been told," Hela said. "Yes, Thor managed to strike it a devastating blow, and yes, he managed to shatter it into a thousand pieces. But, destroy it?" Hela shook her head. "No, not even he could manage that."

"What do you mean?"

"I mean that although he shattered it, it wasn't enough to destroy the Eye's power," Hela said. "That power survived and grows stronger with each shard Surtur recovers. Thor should have used the Eye to fight Surtur, but he made the fool's choice. Not only that, but then he had the gall to get himself killed and leave the shards of the Eye free for the taking."

"Thor died protecting it," Sif hissed, her emotions coming to the surface. "What more can you ask?"

Hela smiled. "I forgot. Your grief is still raw, isn't it? To you, those memories are still fresh. The death of Thor must still feel like an open wound."

Sif glared at the other woman, but she didn't acknowledge her statement. She was afraid if she did, she wouldn't be able to hide the truth of how she felt. She'd only been awake for seventeen years after spending eight centuries in the Vanir Sleep. Everything she had known was gone. She'd woken up in a world that was foreign to her and had been forced to spend the last seventeen years trying to make a life for herself and Thyra. She hadn't had the luxury of time to grieve.

"So, all of this," Sif said after a silence, "is just so you can keep a piece of the Eye from Surtur?"

"Yes," Hela said, but then there was a flash of fear on her face again. "And no. Much has changed while you've been in the Vanir Sleep. Surtur has waged his war without stopping, but something has changed in how he wages that war. He has been hoarding magical items since Ragnarök, but now he has begun trying to replicate them. With some success, as you were witness to."

"Why? He wants to destroy magic." Sif saw the uncertainty on Hela's face. "You don't think he's trying to destroy magic, do you?"

"I think he's attempting to harness it and create his own sick version of equality," Hela said. "He can't stop people from being born with magic, but he can level the playing field." Hela hesitated before continuing, "But his ambitions are not what scare me most."

"What does then?"

Hela sat down on the edge of the bed as if her legs had lost their strength. She looked down at her hands and exhaled slowly. "Baldur walks the earth again."

Sif experienced a storm of competing emotions—shock, fear, anger, and sorrow all took their turn washing over her as she considered what Hela's revelation meant. "Baldur is free?"

Hela nodded, her eyes struggling to meet Sif's. "Yes."

Sif's jaw went slack. This secret was enough to shake even the fiercest of the Valkyries.

"How?" Sif demanded. "You told Odin that he would never escape the prison you made for him."

"I was wrong," Hela said. "I underestimated him and the intensity of his rage. His hate for the Aesir was stronger than the magic I placed on him. He fought it, and finally clawed his way free."

"How?" Sif demanded. "You told us that he would never wake. You told us that your magic would keep him asleep until you broke the spell! You promised Odin you could keep him at bay."

"I never expected to be forced to keep him imprisoned for nearly a thousand years," Hela said in a tense tone. "That was too long to keep someone like him at bay. He found the cracks in his prison and he picked at them until there was nothing I could do to stop him."

Sif shook her head. "He was your monster, Hela! You created him, and you were supposed to be responsible for his fate."

"I didn't create him!" Hela snapped. "It was Odin and Freya that filled his mind with lies and demanded that I find a way to make sure he never felt pain. Yes, my magic changed him, but it wasn't me that betrayed him! You all loved him and treated him like he was above everyone. The Aesir made him into the monster he is! Not me!"

"You know that isn't true," Sif said.

"Isn't it?" Hela snorted in anger. "When he fell, when Loki learned of his one weakness, did any of you try to save him? No! You all left him to suffer and die. Once he saw the truth, once he saw that the rest of the Aesir had betrayed him, there was nothing I could do! I did my best to heal him, but there was nothing I could do to heal the betrayal he felt or the rage that built inside!"

"Don't lie," Sif said sharply. "You stoked his rage with your own! You fed it until it became too strong even for you to control."

"And I'd do it again!" Hela said sharply. She took a deep breath to calm herself. "I was betrayed just as much as he was. I was called a monster one moment and then was begged to use the very magic that the Aesir said was dangerous. Why? Because it was convenient, and they needed a monster. A monster they could use and then cast aside. That betrayal was made even clearer after I put Baldur to sleep. How long was it before Odin tried to strip me of my magic? A week! Baldur had barely fallen asleep before Odin moved against me."

"Because you were a threat to everything the Aesir stood for," Sif said. "What you were doing went against nature."

"Our existence goes against nature!" Hela hissed. "All of us are an insult to the natural course of things. We live for thousands of years, weave magic, and have the nerve to call ourselves gods! What I did was no worse than what Odin did by placing the Eye in each of our hands."

Sif's jaw set defiantly. "Baldur is your monster."

"He's everyone's monster now," Hela said. "Arguing about it won't change anything. Baldur is free, and he will be looking to exact revenge on any of us that remain. Including your daughter."

Sif tensed, sending waves of pain racing up from her torn muscles. "I told you, leave her out of this."

"Baldur won't leave her alone."

"But you will," Sif said in as menacing of a tone as she could.

"That might prove tricky," Hela said. "You see, she is coming closer as we speak."

"What?" Sif's face fell. "What have you done?"

"Ensured that I get what I want," Hela said. "I told you, my quarrel isn't with you or your daughter. If you would have handed over the shard, I would have left you in peace."

"I don't believe you," Sif said. "You wanted to replace Odin at the head of the Aesir. You wouldn't be able to stand not having all other magic users bend the knee to you."

"A lot has changed while you were asleep," Hela said. "I do not need you to bend the knee for me to stand at the top. The modern world presents opportunities that we never dreamed of when we were in power. I don't intend to remake what we had. I want to create something new."

The thought of what Hela would create was enough to send a shiver down Sif's back. This Hela was more dangerous, more calculating than she had been when Sif fell under the Vanir Sleep. Her ambitions had grown.

"You may not trust me," Hela continued. "You may even have reason to hate me, but your anger and suspicion are misplaced."

"You've dragged my daughter into his," Sif said sharply. "I have plenty of reason to be angry at you."

"She was part of it from the moment she drew breath," Hela said grimly. "Believe it or not, I don't want to hurt her. She will have a place of honor in the world I will create. Do you think the same is true about Surtur? What about Baldur?"

Sif didn't want to think about what either man might do to Thyra.

"So, Thyra gives you the shard and I go free?" Sif asked.

Hela nodded. "That's right. I have no use for you. Not without breaking your mind, at least, and that would be a waste in my opinion. No, I'd rather have you running free. Surtur and Baldur know about you now, and they will not rest until they find you. That means their focus will be split. You will buy me more time."

"More time for what?"

Hela shook her head. "I don't think so, Sif. I don't count you as my enemy in this fight, but you are not my ally. Once Thyra gives me what I want, our paths can diverge, and we never have to see each other again. As long as you stay out of my way."

Hela stood and walked towards the door at the end of the room. Sif watched her go silently. It wasn't until the woman was gone that Sif finally allowed herself to grimace in pain. She sagged back into the bed and closed her eyes. A single tear fell down her cheek as she thought about Thyra and wondered where she was.

One thing was certain—she hadn't done enough to prepare her daughter. She hadn't been careful enough, and now Thyra was the one that was paying the price.

Shaking her head, Sif whispered softly to the quiet room, "I'm sorry, Thyra."

* * *

Fenrir watched Hela with barely contained anxiety as she closed the door behind her. She locked the door and then crossed the room. As always, her presence was intoxicating for Fenrir. His love and commitment to Hela was what kept him going even after a thousand years and nearly as many painful waves of Hela's magic to keep the demands of time from claiming him. He was not immortal, but Hela's magic kept him as close to it as possible.

Fenrir waited until she was close before asking the question that had been plaguing him all night. "Did you find him?"

"I did," Hela said.

Fenrir felt his heart tighten. His mistress had made him stop and let her out in some small town on the Wisconsin border. He had tried to argue against leaving her, then tried to argue that the Valkyrie needed her healing touch, but his mistress had pushed aside his arguments without a second thought. She ordered him to leave, and he had no choice but to obey. He drove away grudgingly, his mood black.

He knew why she wanted to stop in that particular town. More specifically, he knew who she went to see.

"And his loyalty?"

"Is to himself," Hela said cryptically. "It seems eight hundred years haven't changed his feelings. Even with the threat of Surtur looming ever closer."

"He won't come?"

Hela shook her head. "I never could force him to do anything, not even when we were young. Nothing has changed."

"You told him what is at stake?" Fenrir asked.

Hela nodded. "I told him that something worse than me was walking the earth. He didn't seem to think that was possible."

"So, he won't come," Fenrir said grimly. He shook his head. "No matter. We don't need him. He has grown weak."

Hela's eyes flashed. "Don't forget who we're talking about. He is not someone we want standing across from us at the end."

"He's a disgrace," Fenrir said. "Always has been. He failed the Aesir and instead of facing that failure, he fled to the shadows. He's been in hiding ever since."

"You know why he failed," Hela said sharply. "He was betrayed."

"He was fooled," Fenrir snapped. "That's on him. He should have recognized the truth."

"You were always jealous of him," Hela chided. "Do not make that same mistake now."

Fenrir looked abashed for a split second, but then his jaw set, and his expression turned defiant. "I was jealous of the affection you paid him, but not of the power he wielded. He was too reluctant in how he used the gift Odin bestowed on him. He was a shadow of what he could have been."

"And that shadow was still the strongest warrior the Aesir ever knew," Hela said without hesitation. "Don't make the mistake of underestimating him. If you do, your hide might end up on his wall."

Fenrir's lips pulled back from his teeth and a growl escaped his lips. "I would tear him limb from limb!"

Hela's eyes narrowed and he knew he had made a mistake. "That would displease me greatly. Not because you would succeed, but because you'd prove I was wrong for keeping you around for so long."

She swept by him without another word, her wolf sufficiently rebuked. Fenrir stood in place, his chest rising and falling rapidly as he tried to contain his rage. How many times had his faithful devotion been cast aside in favor of the cursed fool? Each time felt like a hot poker being thrust into his side, and each time he swore it would be the last.

And every time, like the loyal dog he was, he came back for more.

Chapter 15

Thyra woke with a start. She had been dreaming, and not a single one of her dreams had been good. The worst one had been of a strange man who would have been strikingly handsome if it weren't for the anger and hate in his eyes. His skin was pale, almost pure white, like he hadn't seen the sun in years, and he was dressed in black, making the contrast all the more drastic. Thyra felt like she should recognize him, but she didn't.

In the dream, Thyra and the strange man stood facing each other, a glowing blue orb hanging in the air between them. Instinctively, Thyra recognized it as the Eye of Odin and knew that she needed to get it before the man did. She tried to reach it, but every time she took a step forward, he took one as well. Time and time again, they reached the Eye together, neither one being able to lay claim to it.

That dream had been troubling. It felt real, and even now she could feel the hate that emanated from him like an oily film on her skin.

The scenery outside had changed while she'd been asleep, but the situation in the car hadn't. Bragi was still behind the wheel and Asiri was busy working on what looked like a watch. The dwarf woman was holding a small screwdriver in one hand and was muttering under her breath as she worked.

"You're awake," Bragi said. "Did you sleep well?"

"I guess," Thyra said. She looked out the window. They were still on the freeway, but nothing around them looked familiar. The sky was gray overhead, and it looked like it was going to rain. "Where are we?"

"East side of North Dakota," Bragi said. "You've been asleep for almost eight hours."

"I don't feel like it," Thyra said groggily.

"That's normal when you first begin using your magic," Bragi said. "The first time I used my magic I slept for an entire day straight. I'm glad you're awake, though. We need to charge up the car again, and I'm having a hard time keeping my eyes open. Driving all night and into the day is catching up with me."

"What he means is that he's old," Asiri remarked snidely from the back seat.

"No argument there," Bragi said. "There is an exit coming up soon. Leads to some little town a few miles down the road. Probably a farming community, or something like that. Doesn't really matter. We'll pull off, you can do your thing, and then I am going to kick Asiri out of the back seat so I can sleep."

"No amount of sleep is going to help you, Rune Tongue," Asiri said.

Bragi glared at her in the rearview mirror, but Asiri didn't notice. Whatever she was working on had her full attention.

"So, is Asiri going to drive?" Thyra asked.

The dwarf woman let out a cackle that shook her entire body. Even Bragi cracked a smile.

"No, you will," Bragi said.

"Why me?" Thyra turned around and looked at the dwarf. "This is your car isn't it? Why don't you want to drive?"

Asiri looked up from her task and snorted. "Have you looked at me girl? I wouldn't even be able to see over the wheel! I can't drive this thing."

"You've never driven it?"

"No."

"Then why did you have it?" Thyra asked. "Why did you put all the work into it if you weren't going to drive it?"

Asiri shrugged. "If I had needed to, I would have."

"And if not?"

"I thought I might be able to make a nice profit off of it someday," Asiri said. "Plus, it gave me something to do when I was bored."

"When you were bored?"

"The human mind has always confused me," Asiri said thoughtfully. "They make such great advances, only to show how dim witted they are by putting limits on what they create. It took me two weeks just to sort through the mess they had made of the engine, and another two to rebuild it the right way. I could teach those lackwit, college-educated engineers a thing or two." She paused and her nose scrunched up. "But, drive one? No, I don't think so."

"This looks like as good of a place as any," Bragi said. He pointed to the right and a thick patch of trees. "Looks like we might be able to find some cover over there. Let's go get this car juiced up and then get back on the road. If we keep up this pace, we'll be in Wisconsin by nightfall."

"To find this Vidar guy, right?"

Bragi nodded. "That's the plan. Ill-advised as it is."

He pulled the car off onto a side road and drove to the stand of trees. He put it in park and got out with a yawn. Thyra got out, stretched her arms overhead, and moved around to the back of the car. Asiri was hot on her heels and quickly attached the cables to the battery in the trunk.

"I've made a few changes," the dwarf woman said as she worked. She held up the two ends and showed them to Thyra. Asiri had removed the clamps and replaced them with a series of magnets that were attached to either end of a metal rod.

"Where did those come from?" Thyra asked

"My dwarf bag of tricks," Asiri said. "This will make it easier to make a full circuit. The magnets are positioned so that one end is positive, the other negative. Hopefully, that means it will be more efficient with a lower amount of energy expended by you."

"Hopefully?" Thyra asked.

"There are no absolutes on a trial run," Asiri said with a shrug. She handed the rod to Thyra and then took a step backwards. "No offense, but I think I'll keep my distance this time."

"None taken," Thyra said. She realized she was missing something and looked back toward the passenger seat. "Let me get Lynnedslag."

"You don't need the stick," Asiri said sharply. "Your magic comes from you, not Lynnedslag. It's a tool, not a crutch, Sparks. Try to do it without your stick this time."

"Okay," Thyra said in an uncertain tone. She took a deep breath and tried to summon the lightning. Nothing happened. She tried again, searching deep for the well of power she had felt earlier, but she couldn't find it.

"I can't," Thyra said. "I can't find it."

Asiri's brow fell down. "What do you mean, you can't? Earlier today you were flashing and crackling like a sparkler!"

"I don't know why," Thyra said. "I can't find it. I need Lynnedslag."

"That's only because you tell yourself you do!" Asiri said sharply. "You need to learn to summon your magic on your own, girl, or you won't last long in this world!"

"I'm trying," Thyra said, her frustration building. "This is still new to me."

"New or not," Asiri said, "you don't have time to waste! Surtur is after you, and so is Hela. You should have been taught all of this long ago, and neither one is going to care if you haven't been! Do you think they're going to handle you with kid gloves? Maybe wipe your nose while you cry about how unfair all of this is? No! They will not take pity on you. Your only chance is to get stronger until no one will dare attack you. Right now, you're weak. I could take that stick away from you and you'd be nothing. Is that what you want?"

"I'm trying!" Thyra repeated through gritted teeth. She looked at Bragi stood near the front of the car. "I need Lynnedslag."

"With that attitude you do," Asiri grumbled.

"Go easy on her," Bragi said.

"We can't go *easy* on her," Asiri said.

"Tearing her down isn't going to do us any good either," Bragi retorted.

"Bah!" Asiri threw her hands up. "Fine. Time's growing about as short as I am, so go get your stick and let's be done with it! Go ahead and prove that you are too soft for this world."

That last comment pushed Thyra past her breaking point. Shaking her head, Thyra stayed put. "No, I don't want you to go easy on me. I'm not soft. You say I should be able to do it on my own, so I'm going to try."

"Thyra," Bragi said in a sympathetic tone, "there is no shame in needing to use Lynnedslag. Learning to use magic takes time, and you've only been at it for a day."

"No," Thyra said. "Asiri is right. I need to learn to do this on my own. I did it on my own in my vision of Yggdrasil, so I should be able to do it now, too."

"Don't worry, Thyra," Bragi said from where he stood. "You will learn with time. You've already made amazing progress. You should be happy about that. Here," he ducked into the car and when he stood back up, he held out Lynnedslag towards Thyra, "take Lynnedslag and charge up the car. We can work tapping into your magic another time."

"No!" Thyra said, her temper flashing to the surface. "I need to be able to protect myself. If I keep limiting myself, I am always going to

THE EYE OF ODIN

be reliant on someone else. You told me that we are vulnerable. Asiri has no magic, and you admitted that your magic won't be any help against Surtur's men. That leaves me, and I won't be the reason we fail. I'm going to do this on my own!"

Bragi didn't look pleased, but he made no attempt to stop her. He set Lynnedslag against the car within reach of Thyra and then stepped away. The temptation was there for Thyra to simply reach out and pick it up, but she forced herself to resist.

"Okay, Sparks," Asiri said. "Let's get this car charged up!"

Thyra turned her focus inward and began to search for the well of power inside of her. This time, she found it after a moment of concentration. Drawing on it, though, was another matter. She tried a dozen times to summon it but failed each time. Frustration crept in and was quickly turning to anger.

"I can't!"

"Fish guts, you can't!" Asiri snapped. "You say you want to do it, but you aren't even trying."

"I am trying!" Thyra said through gritted teeth.

"Not very hard," Asiri said. "You give up this easy when you play lacrosse? When someone beats you, do you let them do it again?"

"No," Thyra said. "I make sure it doesn't happen again, and then I beat them."

"Then, why are you letting yourself get beat by doubt and fear?" Asiri said harshly. "What are you afraid of, Sparks?"

Thyra shook her head. "I don't know."

"Yes, you do!" Asiri snapped. "Come on, say it! Say what you're afraid of!"

"I don't know," Thyra said in a tense whisper.

"No! That is unacceptable," Asiri said sharply. "Dig deep, girl, or you might as well quit and wait for Surtur to find you! Are you a quitter?"

"I'm no quitter!" Thyra said.

"Prove it!" Asiri said. "What are you afraid of?"

"Leave her be, Asiri," Bragi said.

"Be quiet, Rune Tongue!" Asiri snapped just before Thyra said, "Stop talking!"

Bragi threw his hands up in the air. "Fine. I just don't think we have time for this."

"The only way to overcome your fear, is to face it," Asiri said. "Now, face it."

Thyra took a deep breath and closed her eyes. There were a thousand reasons to be afraid as a result of what had over the past two days—her mom gone, Fenrir and Hela attacking her, her strange dreams, and her entire world being rocked by the truth of who and what she was. She could say any one of them and be telling the truth.

But she knew that wasn't good enough. Those things scared her, yes, but that wasn't what she was truly afraid of.

"I'm afraid," she began slowly, "of failing."

"Good," Asiri said. "What else?"

"I'm afraid that I can't live up to it all," Thyra said, her eyes still closed. "I'm afraid that I can't be what's expected of me or do what I have to do."

"Dig deeper girl," Asiri instructed.

Thyra inhaled deeply and tried to face the doubts and fears that lingered deep down inside—feelings that she tried to keep locked away. The deeper she pushed, the more she came to realize that one dark thought was at the root of all her fears.

"I'm afraid of letting go," Thyra said. "I'm afraid of stepping out into the unknown."

"Because you're afraid that you won't be enough?" Asiri asked.

Thyra shook her head. "No. I'm afraid that once I do, there will be no going back."

Saying those words out loud was like having a weight lifted off her shoulders. She hadn't realized it, but the fear of everything changing forever had festered inside her. If she fully accepted her magic, if she found the Eye, and if she became a part of this world she now knew existed, she knew there would be no going back. That fear had been holding her back without her even knowing it.

"Good," Asiri said. "Now make the choice to face that fear and conquer it."

Thyra hesitated. Did she want to conquer it? Did she want to take that step and finally accept that everything had changed and that there was no going back? What would happen if she decided not to move forward?

She knew the answer to that question—she would fail. Those two fears—the fear of failure and the fear of change—were complementary and opposite. If she didn't accept the changes, she would fail, and if she failed, the changes in her life could be catastrophic. Playing those two fears against each other, Thyra made her choice and confronted her fear.

Thyra found the well of power inside and tried to summon her magic, but it avoided her grasp again. Growing angrier, Thyra tried again, but this time she didn't summon her magic, she demanded that it come to her call. There was a brief resistance, then like a dam breaking inside of her, power flooded into her!

Thyra heard Asiri give a loud whoop and opened her eyes.

"Did I do it?"

The dwarf nodded. "Look at your hands, girl."

She held up her hands and saw tendrils of lightning dancing and crackling between her fingers.

"I did it!" Thyra said, a broad smile splitting her cheeks.

"Well done, Sparks!" Asiri said.

"Good job, Thyra," Bragi said, but his tone said otherwise. He ducked his head inside the car and then announced. "The car is charged."

"That fast?" Thyra asked in an exhilarated voice.

"You've tapped into your full power," Asiri said. "You're putting out enough power to light a city I'll bet! And with a few thoughtful modifications by yours truly, that kind of power didn't fry the battery."

"Well done, Thyra," Bragi said, "but we don't have time to celebrate. We must go."

He ducked into the backseat of the Camaro, leaving Thyra with a confused look on her face.

"Old grump," Asiri mumbled. She gave Thyra a crooked smile. "Needs his nap before he can be happy."

Thyra's smile returned. "I feel so alive!"

Asiri nodded. "I've heard that magic users feel a high while using their magic. I can understand to a degree. I get a similar high while working in my forge."

Thyra couldn't imagine it was anything close to what she felt, but she didn't say so. She picked up Lynnedslag and felt the lacrosse stick throb in anticipation. The stick seemed to sense her newfound power and was eager to join the rush of power flowing through her. She sensed the vast potential Lynnedslag possessed. She wondered what she would be capable of with that much power.

Thyra was about to get into the car when she felt an odd sensation in the air all around her. She paused and tried to figure out what she was experiencing. Every time she moved, she felt energy rise and fall. Curious, she reached outward instinctively. She quickly realized what she felt was electricity. It was muted in the ground and air, but she could feel raw, untapped power in the clouds overhead.

"Those clouds," Thyra said. "It's going to storm."

Asiri looked up and nodded. "Might."

"I am a child of the storm," Thyra said thoughtfully. That's what Yggdrasil had told her, and Asiri had echoed the sentiment. "Time to see if that's true."

171

Asiri gave her a confused look, but Thyra didn't offer an explanation. She began to walk away from the car, her eyes looking up at the clouds overhead. There was so much untapped power, just waiting to be directed somewhere by something. Or someone.

"Hey, Sparks!" Asiri called after her. "Where are you going?"

"There's lightning in those clouds," Thyra said.

She continued to follow her instincts and reached out to the lightning in the clouds, beckoning it to answer her call. She felt the energy begin to gather, but then it resisted. She tried again, but with a similar result. Her temper flared. This time, when she reached out, she didn't beckon, she demanded it answer her call. Just like before, her raw emotion obliterated whatever wall was in her way. The electricity in the clouds gathered into a crackling, destructive web that danced from cloud to cloud until it was directly over her.

Thyra raised Lynnedslag skyward and spoke, "Come to me."

Immediately, the world went blue-white and she felt an enormous flow of energy rush into her, filling her until she felt sure her skin was going to tear apart. Thunder cracked overhead loud enough that Thyra felt the ground shake beneath and then rolled away in every direction.

Thyra was amazed when she realized that all the energy that had been in the clouds had disappeared. Or, rather, had relocated. Into her!

She looked at her outstretched arm and was amazed to see thick ropes of lightning crackling up and down its length. In fact, thick tendrils of lightning snapped and cracked from every inch of her body. If she felt alive before, she was on a completely different level now.

"By Odin's beard," she heard Asiri gasp. "Did you just call down lightning?"

Thyra turned to the dwarf and was surprised to see her pushing herself to her feet.

172

"You did!" Asiri said. She looked Thyra up and down. "Where did it go?"

Thyra felt a smile spread across her face. "I think it's inside of me."

"Inside of you?" Asiri asked in awe.

Bragi came running over and stopped beside the dwarf. His eyes were wide with a mix of fear and shock.

"Thyra, what have you done?" he asked.

"I am a child of the storms," Thyra repeated. "I felt it in the clouds. I just had to touch it, to control it."

"What you're doing is dangerous," Bragi said. "You cannot hold it in like that."

Thyra didn't see a reason why not. She held up her hands, palms facing each other, and channeled some of the power coursing through her outward. An arm-thick bolt of lightning jumped to life, racing from one hand to the other.

"I control the storm," Thyra said. "It feels…it feels amazing!"

"Thyra," Bragi said, "listen to me! You must let it go. If you try to hold that much power you will grow tired, lose focus, and it will overpower you. You are putting us all at risk if you don't let it go."

"Let it go?" Thyra asked, not comprehending.

"You must send it somewhere," Bragi said. He took a tentative step closer. "Listen to me closely. You must send the lightning back to where it came from. You are not strong enough yet to hold this kind of power."

Thyra's temper flared briefly—how would an old storyteller know how strong she was!—but then the bolt of lightning between her hands went from a concentrated line to a jagged, crackling one that she had to focus to keep from shooting free.

"Okay, but how?" Thyra said, rational thought finally coming back to her.

"I don't know," Bragi said, "but you have to do it now, Thyra!"

Thyra looked up at the clouds again. She could feel where the energy that formed the lightning had been. It made sense that it could go back there again.

Following her instincts again, she sent the lightning back up into the clouds. Again, her world turned blue-white as bolts of lightning shot upward, forming a blinding web as it dispersed back into the clouds overhead.

She pushed the lightning upward until she exhausted the well inside of her completely. She let go of her magic and felt her knees buckle. Asiri and Bragi were at her side immediately, both hesitating briefly before offering her a supporting hand.

"That was foolish," Bragi chided her as they led her back to the car, but there wasn't any force behind it. His eyes were still wide, and she could see a hint of fear there as he looked at her.

"Foolish," Asiri said, "but amazing! I've never seen anything like it."

"Don't encourage her, dwarf," Bragi snapped.

"Don't discourage her, old man," Asiri snapped back. "You said we were vulnerable because we had no way to combat Hela or the Muspel Corporation. I don't think that's a concern now."

"Don't you see?" Bragi hissed. "Thyra just sent up a signal six miles high to anyone looking for us! Worse than that, people who weren't looking for her will be now. There are two more like her, and you can bet they will recognize what just happened for what it was."

"What do you mean?" Thyra asked. "What was this?"

"Grab your stick, and get in the car, Thyra," Bragi said, letting go of her arm and walking around the Camaro.

"No," Thyra said. "I want an answer. What do you think I just did?"

Bragi looked over the top of the car at her. "What you just did was make an announcement to the entire magical world that you exist!"

Thyra couldn't help but feel a little defiant, especially after what Asiri had said about her being strong enough that Hela and the Muspel

Corporation weren't a concern now. "What's so wrong with that?"

"Because," Bragi hissed, "now everyone will be looking for you, and I can't protect you when they find you."

"Maybe I don't need protection," Thyra said.

"You have proven that you are Thor's daughter with your power," Bragi said in a voice that cracked like a whip. "Don't make the mistake of proving it with your stubborn arrogance! It got him killed, and it will get you killed too!"

The rebuke stung and Thyra felt tears begin to form. She glared at the old man over the top of the car, but he met her stare with one of his own.

"I will not let you make the same mistakes he made," Bragi said. "Now, get in the car, both of you."

Thyra did as she was told, sliding into the passenger seat and quickly buckling her seatbelt. Bragi put the car in gear, his fatigue replaced by a different emotion that also gave him a lead foot. The Camaro spun out and back onto the road.

Thyra looked out her window to hide the tears running down her cheeks. They drove in silence for a long time before Bragi finally broke the silence.

"Thyra, I'm sorry," he said slowly. "I shouldn't have said that. Your father is dead, and speaking that way dishonored him."

Thyra ignored him. She was hurt, both by what he said about her, and by the fact that she had never known her father. She'd lived sixteen years without him but had yearned for a father figure every day. For the last day, she'd begun to see Bragi as sliding into that role. She had grown fond of him and found herself imagining her life with him as part of it.

Not anymore.

Chapter 16

Thyra stepped out of the bathroom after a long hot shower and sat down on the edge of the hotel bed. It felt good to be clean again after sitting in a car for a day and wearing the same clothes for even longer. For a brief time, it felt like the shower was washing away everything that had happened the past few days. It felt wonderful.

And then it ended. Reality came crashing back when she realized that she was still in a cheap hotel somewhere on the Wisconsin border with no clean clothes to wear. Reluctantly, she put on the same pair of jeans and lacrosse t-shirt she'd put on before going to school almost two days before.

Asiri was still sitting where she had been half an hour earlier on one other bed watching the TV with a frown.

"Hundreds of channels," Asiri grumbled, "and all of it is worthless junk. Whatever happened to good entertainment?"

Thyra didn't ask what the dwarf considered entertaining. With Asiri, the answer would probably be alarming. Asiri finally settled on a reality TV show following a group of scientists trying to monitor the movements of killer whales along the Alaskan Coast. Thyra watched idly as she re-braided her hair.

"You done being mad at Rune Tongue yet?" Asiri asked abruptly.

Thyra exhaled heavily and turned on the bed to face the dwarf. "No. Not yet."

Asiri shrugged. "Some things not even a hot shower can fix. He's definitely a pain in the backside."

Thyra smirked in spite of herself. "There's clearly some history between you two that I don't know about."

Asiri snorted. "You could say that. Rune Tongue has been a thorn in my side for a long time, whether he knew it or not. Just happens that the thorn became even bigger when he came to me six years ago. He didn't give me many details about what he wanted then, and I cursed his name for it. Now that I see what you're capable of and know who you are, I'm cursing his name even more."

Thyra smirked. She watched the TV for a few moments before turning back to the dwarf. "What about you?"

"What about me?"

"Well, I know nothing about dwarves," Thyra said, "and since you're the only one I know, you're the best person to teach me about them."

Asiri snorted. "Not much to tell. But, go ahead. Ask away."

"Okay. How about we start with an easy one. How old are you?"

Asiri snorted. "I quit counting the years a long time ago, but I guess I'm somewhere around seven hundred years old now. My father lived to eight hundred before he finally grew one step too slow. I don't know if I want to see that number."

"So, that means you were born after Ragnarök?"

Asiri nodded. "I was born in a hole where my parents were hiding from your kind. Humans, that is. My mother died giving birth, and my father died a hundred years later. I've been on my own since then."

"You've been alone that long?" Thyra felt a pang of sorrow for the dwarf.

"Ah, it wasn't so bad," Asiri said. "I was a loner from the start. All I've ever needed was my forge and the quiet. Don't feel bad for me, Sparks. I've lived a good life."

Thyra could tell that Asiri was being honest. She didn't pity herself or how her life had gone, so why should Thyra? It was a stark reminder that her own situation could be much worse.

Thyra had Asiri talking and it was nice to focus on something other than her anger at Bragi, so she asked another question. "How long were you in Idaho?"

Asiri thought about it for a moment. "Sixty years, give or take a few."

"And before that?"

"Too many places," Asiri said grimly. "Couldn't afford to stay in one place for long. People catch a whiff that a dwarf is close and before long it isn't safe."

"For you?"

"For everyone," Asiri said. "Idaho was good to me. It was quiet. People minded their own business. Plenty of space. I liked it there. Until Rune Tongue found me, that is. Then things started to turn sour again. I guess I'll have to find a new place when things settle down again."

"Do you think they will?"

"Can't say, girl," Asiri said. "I thought things had settled down. Now look at me. On the run from Surtur, Hela, and who knows who else with an old storyteller and the clueless daughter of Thor." Asiri paused for a second and grimaced. "No offense, girl."

"No, it's okay," Thyra said. "I feel the same way."

"And it's only going to get crazier for you, girl," Asiri said. "You've been sheltered from this world for a long time, and you've only seen the tip of the iceberg. Magic, dwarves, and lacrosse sticks that shoot lightning aren't even the beginning of what is hidden below the surface. So many secrets exist in the shadows. Believe it or not, I'm one of the more cheery ones."

"You're cheery?" Thyra asked with a wry smirk.

"Compared to a frost giant or a dark elf," Asiri said, "I'm as sweet as a meat pie!"

"That's comforting," Thyra said.

The researchers on the TV caught up to a pod of killer whales and the conversation died as both her and Asiri tuned in to what was happening on the screen.

Again, it was Asiri who broke the silence. "I know you're mad at Bragi, but you shouldn't hold it against him for too long. He is trying to protect you."

"I don't need protection," Thyra said. "You said it yourself. I'm not weak."

"No, but you also don't know what is waiting for you," Asiri said. "Bragi does. He's seen it all, and he knows what dangers are out there. I don't know everything about him, but I do know that he was there from the beginning. He was Odin's older brother, and he saw both the rise and fall of their power. If anyone can guide you, it's him."

Thyra knew Asiri was right, but she wasn't going to admit as much. Bragi's words had cut her shockingly deep, and she was going to hold onto her anger for a bit longer.

There was a knock on the door of their hotel room. Asiri got up and shuffled across the room, pausing just long enough to say, "He may be a real pain, but he's doing his best."

The dwarf opened the door and let Bragi in. The old man gave a tentative look towards Thyra but didn't say anything. No doubt handling the emotions of a teenage girl was foreign territory for him and he probably didn't know how to proceed.

"I hope you've been able to rest," was what he finally went with.

Thyra still wasn't in the mood for small talk, so she jumped right into the reason they had come here.

"We made it to Hudson," Thyra said. "What do we do next?"

"We make contact with Vidar," Bragi said.

"Okay. What do we know about him?"

Asiri was the first to answer. "His shoe size and his address."

"That's an in-depth profile," Thyra said sarcastically.

"I know more, but none of it from experience," Asiri said. "I was born after Ragnarök happened, and Vidar was rarely mentioned. He was a god, but he wasn't highly regarded."

"That's what you said before," Thyra said. "Why wasn't he liked?"

"He was the guardian of the Aesir," the dwarf replied. "Pretty much boiled down to keeping lesser magic users and the common folk in line by any means necessary. My father and grandfather spoke of him only once before they were killed. They said he hated being one of the Aesir and that the only reason he accepted the power the Eye gave him was because of a borderline obsession with being the strongest person alive."

"And was he?" Thyra asked.

Again, it was Asiri that answered. "Strong enough to crush stone with his bare hands and carry an entire Viking raiding ship on his back."

"That strong, huh?"

"That's only a story, and far from the truth," Bragi said, finally adding his voice to the conversation. "I was there when it happened. It was actually a ship with a full crew, and he didn't carry it on his back. He held it overhead."

"Sounds like Hercules," Thyra said, not sure she bought the story.

"That's an unfair comparison," Bragi said. "Hercules was soft. Spent too much time lounging near the ocean and drinking wine. He couldn't hold a candle to Vidar. He was smart to stay in Greece and away from the real warriors. Vidar would have shamed Hercules in short order."

Thyra looked at Bragi in surprise. "Wait, Hercules was real?"

"Real, yes," Bragi said. "But the stories about him were highly exaggerated. The Greeks had a knack for that."

"And the Norse didn't?" Asiri challenged.

"We embellished," Bragi admitted. "But trust me when I say that Vidar's strength made Hercules's pale in comparison. He was a force to be reckoned with before holding the Eye, and he was destruction incarnate after."

Thyra suddenly felt giddy and nervous all at once at the thought of such a person being real.

"We must be careful how we approach Vidar," Bragi said. "He is powerful, and may know things that could help us, but we don't know where he stands. We can't afford to give anything away about what we're doing until we're sure he will help us."

"Do you think he will stand in our way?" Asiri asked.

Bragi shook his head. "No, but his reaction to us—to me—might not be kind."

"Why not?" Thyra asked.

"Because I was a vocal critic of his," Bragi said. "There were times when I might have gone a little too far with that criticism, but that was only because I didn't think he could be trusted. He was dangerous, and I objected to his role. As a result, I was not one of his favorite people."

"How strong were your objections?" Asiri asked.

"Strong," Bragi said. "I never trusted him, and I must admit that I made his life difficult. He had few friends to begin with, and I made sure that he didn't find any others among our ranks. I was guilty of using magic to make the other gods view him as a cancer that needed to be cut away."

"No wonder he didn't like you," Asiri grumbled.

"Did my mom know him?" Thyra asked.

She could tell the question caught Bragi off-guard. He swallowed hard and then nodded. "Yes, she knew him."

"Did she trust him?" Thyra asked, her eyes locked onto Bragi's.

Bragi hesitated in answering. Finally, he nodded again. "Yes, she did

THE EYE OF ODIN

trust him. Probably too much."

Thyra shrugged. "Then I want to meet him. It's getting harder to know who to trust anymore, but if my mom trusted him then I'm sure we can count on him, too."

Bragi looked uncomfortable, but he relented. "Fine. We will give it a shot. But don't expect him to be happy to see me, or even give me a chance to talk."

Thyra had been expecting this and had already made a decision she knew Bragi wouldn't like. "Which is why you can't go. It has to be me."

Bragi started shaking his head before she finished. "No. I won't allow that. It's too dangerous."

"Then I'll take Asiri with me," Thyra said.

It was Asiri's turn to shake her head. "Not a chance, Sparks. It would be too suspicious if I showed up after he worked so hard to keep his identity a secret. He did his homework to find me, which means all it would take is one look at me and he'd be on the defensive."

"I'll do it alone, then," Thyra said.

"That isn't going to happen," Bragi said. "I will speak to him. Perhaps the years have taken the edge off of his feelings towards me."

Asiri snorted. "The years haven't dulled yours, so I'm pretty sure they haven't dimmed his. The girl is right. She needs to do it."

"We can't send Thyra in there alone," Bragi said. "She doesn't know him like I do. We don't know where he stands, and she doesn't have the experience to make a good judgement."

"I do it alone," Thyra said firmly. "You can come and wait outside, or across the street, but I am going in alone."

Asiri nodded, but Bragi still wasn't convinced. "I don't like this. I will come with you."

"I'm doing it alone," Thyra said, her mind made up. "Besides, I could use a good workout. I'll just wait for the right time to talk to him.

What could go wrong?"

"I don't think it will be that easy," Bragi said.

"Nothing about any of this has been easy," Thyra snapped. Seeing she was getting nowhere with Bragi, she turned to Asiri. "Do you think he'll listen to me?"

Asiri nodded. "If he'll listen to anyone, it will be you. Tell him who you are. Show him if you have to. Then tell him what is at stake. The Eye must not fall into the hands of Hela or Surtur. That should be all the argument you need."

"We can't tell him that we have the shard and that we need him to help protect it," Bragi said, shaking his head. "For all we know, he could be in Surtur's pocket. Or worse, in Hela's."

"Aren't you full of sunshine and optimism," Asiri said grimly. "You know he isn't aligned with Surtur, Rune Tongue. If anyone has a reason to hate Surtur, it's Vidar."

"And Hela?" Bragi snapped.

"We'll just have to take that risk," Asiri said. "I trust that Thyra can judge his intentions. You should, too."

Thyra was tired of the arguing. She stood up and put her hands on her hips. "I can do it. Even if you don't think I can, you'll just have to trust me. Okay, Rune Tongue?"

Bragi's brow furrowed. That was the first time Thyra had used the nickname, and she could tell he didn't take well to her using it. Thyra didn't care. At this point, he was her guide and she trusted his experience, but that was the end of her feelings.

Bragi finally nodded. "I trust you."

"Good," Thyra said. "But I see one problem with all of this."

"What might that be?" Bragi asked.

Thyra pointed at her clothes. "I can't go to the gym looking like this."

Bragi looked her up and down. "What do you mean? You look fine."

"I can't wear jeans to the gym," Thyra said. "And I don't want to wear the same shirt I've been wearing for two days straight during a workout. This thing smells bad enough as it is."

"Your point?" Bragi said, a hint of irritation in his voice.

"She's telling you that she needs to go shopping, you old goat," Asiri grumbled.

Thyra nodded. "That's right. Nothing wild and crazy, but if you want me to look like I belong in a gym owned by a thousand-year-old Norse god, then I need to have some different clothes."

"Fine," Bragi said, closing his eyes. "How much is this going to hurt?"

"Not too much," Thyra said. "A hundred bucks for clothes, and another hundred for shoes."

"What's wrong with your shoes?" Bragi asked.

"I can't wear my street shoes for lifting in," Thyra said matter-of-factly. "Make it two fifty so I have a little wiggle room, and still have enough left over to pay for a day pass at the gym."

He winced at the sound of the total. "You do know that I was living on a teacher's salary, right? Couldn't we spend thirty dollars at the thrift store?"

"You want him to trust me?" Thyra said. "If I walk into his gym looking like I bought my clothes at a thrift store I'll stick out like a sore thumb. Is that what we want? For me to set off his alarms?"

"I think you're shooting too high," Bragi said. "Two hundred fifty dollars is too much."

Thyra didn't budge. "It could be much worse. Trust me."

"I'd give the girl the money, Rune Tongue," Asiri said. "She's giving you a bargain."

Bragi sighed. "Fine. Let's get this over with."

* * *

An hour later, Thyra was standing outside Hammer Forged with a backpack full of her new gym clothes. The brick exterior of the gym was nondescript and looked like most of the buildings near the water. Built in view of the St. Croix River, it was beginning to show its age, but was doing everything it could to hide that fact. The red brick had been repainted recently, but it was a poor attempt at revitalizing the structure. There were several spots where the new paint was already beginning to chip off.

Thyra pushed the door open and was met with the sound of heavy weights and men grunting. The first thing that caught her eye was a whiteboard with a list of rules.

"Come to lift, not update your Instagram," Thyra read under her breath. "If you can't put the weight away, you shouldn't be lifting it. Work hard and respect the process. Maximum effort is encouraged—maximum egos are not. Mirrors are for checking form, not your hair."

Thyra couldn't help but smirk at the last one. She decided that she liked this place already.

"Can I help you, young lady?"

Thyra looked away from the whiteboard just as a sinewy man approached her. She took quick measure of him and guessed that he wasn't the one Bragi had sent her to find. From the amount of gray that was mixed in with his short black hair, she guessed he was in his late fifties to early sixties. He was fit, though, and it was clear that he was no stranger to the weight room.

"Yeah," Thyra said. "I'm visiting town and wanted to know if I could get in a workout. Do you take walk-ins?"

The man nodded. "We do. Ten dollars will get you a day pass."

Thyra reached into her pocket and pulled out a crisp ten-dollar bill. He took it and walked over to the desk he'd been sitting behind and retrieved a clipboard.

"Fill out this waiver, and you'll be set to go," the man said as he handed the clipboard to her. "Are you a minor?"

Thyra froze. She should have known he'd ask that question, but it had caught her off guard.

"Uh, no," Thyra said, doing her best to play off the hesitation as simply being distracted. "I'm eighteen."

He nodded. "Alright. Just need your name and signature at the bottom and you should be set."

Thyra filled out the rest of the information and handed the clipboard back. He eyed the sheet of paper and Thyra was certain he was checking her birth date. She had almost written her real birth date but caught herself just in time.

Finally, he looked up from the clipboard. He gave her a once-over and grimaced. "Forgive me for saying so, but you don't look ready to do any exercising. We don't do clothing rentals here."

Thyra motioned toward her backpack. "I brought my gym clothes with me."

The man nodded. "I should also mention that we don't have any treadmills or elliptical machines here, either."

Thyra felt a flash of irritation at the veiled assumption that she wasn't here to lift weights but she managed to force it down.

"That's fine by me," Thyra said. "I came to lift, and I heard this was the best place in Hudson to do it."

"You heard right," he said with a nod. "Right this way. I'll show you where you can change."

He turned and led Thyra around the corner.

"My name is Henry," said as he led Thyra around the corner.

"Thyra."

"Pretty name," Henry said, "So, how did you hear about my gym?"

"I've heard stories about someone that used to lift here," Thyra said. "I wanted to see if the stories were true."

"What stories were those?" Henry asked.

They turned the corner and into the gym itself. It was exactly what Thyra had expected. Racks of weights, machinery, and not a treadmill in sight. A half dozen men were busy lifting and paid them no attention as they wove through the room toward a pair of doors.

"An uncle of mine said that the strongest man he knew trained at the Hammer Forged Gym in Hudson, Wisconsin," Thyra said. "Stronger than anyone that had ever lived."

Henry glanced over his shoulder. "That's quite the tale. What was this man's name?"

Thyra shook her head. "He never gave me a name."

"Interesting story," Henry said. "Seen plenty of strong men come through these doors, but none that fit the description of being the strongest that ever lived. Just regular, strong men here."

Henry approached a door with "Ladies" painted on it.

"Here you go," Henry said. "We don't have a lot of women that come here, but I do my best to keep things clean and tidy. Feel free to use any of the equipment. If you need anything, I'm usually kicking around somewhere nearby."

"Thank you," Thyra said. She put her hand on the door but stopped short of pushing it open. "So, is this your gym?"

Henry nodded slowly. "I'm one of two owners. The other one is more of a silent partner."

"Silent?" Thyra asked.

"That's right," Henry said. "I handle the day to day operations. He prefers to stay busy in other ways."

"Does he come around very often?"

Henry's eyes narrowed briefly. "From time to time. Why?"

"Uh, just curious," Thyra said awkwardly. "I thought maybe he might know the man my dad talked about."

She felt a flush of embarrassment at how awkward that sounded.

Henry was still watching her warily, so she did the only thing she could think of to escape and pushed through the door into the locker room. Safe behind the door, she let out a heavy sigh.

"Smooth, Thyra. Real smooth."

The locker room was more of a glorified restroom with two full length lockers pushed into the corner. It was clean, though, and that more than made up for the lack of nicer accommodations. Thyra set her backpack on the floor and changed into her new gear. She never would have admitted it to Bragi, but she had used the opportunity to buy a pair of tights she had had her eye on for months. After what she had been through the past few days, she felt spending a little extra was justified.

She stepped out into the gym and took a moment to survey the room. Hammer Forged was a serious place and had the equipment to prove it. She saw an open rowing machine and decided to start there to get her blood pumping and her muscles loose. She sat down and let herself get lost in the rhythm.

When her muscles were warmed up, she stood up and stretched for a few minutes before walking over to an open squat rack. She loaded a bar with plates on each side and began to go through her routine. Her legs were stiff after a long day spent in the car, but by the second set of squats she was feeling back to normal.

She was in the process of adding more weight to the bar when she noticed a newcomer to the gym from the corner of her eye. Tall and broad through the shoulders, he stopped to talk to Henry for a moment while he scanned the gym. A few of the other gym rats waved to him and received a nod in return. Clearly, he was more than just a regular.

Thyra finished putting the weight on the bar and used the mirror to take measure of the new face. Thyra guessed that he was in his late twenties to early thirties. His brown hair was trimmed short and he had a full beard that covered his cheeks and jawline. He stood well over six feet tall—almost six and a half feet from the way he towered over Henry—and was broad through the shoulders. Thyra took a wild guess that he weighed somewhere around two hundred and fifty pounds. From the way his shirt stretched over his muscles it was clear that very little of that weight was fat.

He was dressed in athletic clothes, but it was his black, high top shoes that caught Thyra's eye. Even from a distance, she recognized them as the shoes from Asiri's design.

Thyra felt her heart beat faster. This was the man Bragi had sent her to find. It was Vidar!

She was so caught up in the realization that she didn't notice that he was looking in her direction. Henry said something to him, and he frowned in response. He said something in return and then turned and disappeared into an office with Henry close behind.

Unsure what to do next, Thyra went back to lifting. Rushing after him would probably only spook him. She would have to be patient. He had seen her, and she figured that sooner or later the opportunity to talk to him would present itself.

For the next hour she moved around the gym and worked up a sweat. She was busy doing a round of kettlebell swings when she realized that the room had grown surprisingly quiet. She put the weight down and looked around. To her surprise, all the other gym rats were gone.

The door to the office opened and Henry stepped out. He glanced briefly in Thyra's direction and then walked disappeared around the corner. A moment later, the man she felt certain was Vidar stepped out and crossed the gym in her direction. He had removed the hoodie he'd been wearing, opting to wear a shirt with the sleeves removed. One look at his arms was enough to set Thyra's pulse racing. All the words she had carefully crafted to say suddenly escaped her. She chided herself for being silly and focused on something other than his physique.

"The gym is closed," he announced in a deep, gravelly voice.

"Right now?" Thyra asked. "In the middle of the day?"

He didn't answer the question. Instead, he watched her with what looked like a mix of curiosity and trepidation. She didn't know what reason a six-foot six, two-hundred-and-fifty-pound behemoth would have to fear her, but it was unmistakable on his face.

"I've noticed that you keep looking toward the office," he said slowly. "Are you looking for someone?"

"I am," Thyra answered.

"And you think you'll find that person here?"

Thyra nodded. "That's right."

"Why's that?"

The question stumped Thyra. She ran through a list of answers, but each one sounded more ludicrous than the last. What could she say? That a thousand-year-old Norse god told her? That a blue-skinned dwarf woman said she made magical shoes for you? Or that her father was Thor, and that she was certain that he was Vidar, the Norse god of strength?

Seeing no good place to start from, she went back to the beginning of it all.

"My name is Thyra Ariksen, and my mom is Sharon Ariksen," she said. She waited for any degree of recognition to show on his face, but there wasn't any. Undeterred, she plowed ahead. "I know a man named Bruce Agi. He told me that the strongest man he ever knew trained here in this gym. I came to see if that is still true. You match the description."

"I'm flattered, but I can assure you that there are much bigger men out there than me. Turn on the World's Strongest Man competition and you'll see for yourself."

"I didn't say the biggest," Thyra said. "I said the strongest. I've been told that my dad was pretty well known for his strength. From what

I've heard, there was only one other man that was stronger."

"And you think that's me?"

Thyra licked her lips. *Here it goes.*

"I do," Thyra said with a nod. "I'm not the only one, either. I was brought here by a pair of mutual acquaintances of ours."

"I doubt that," he said. "I don't have many acquaintances."

"You have this one," Thyra said. She looked down at his shoes and pointed. "She made those."

"She makes shoes?" A wry smirk crossed his face. "Not sure I know any shoemakers."

"She's a unique person," Thyra said. "She makes a lot of stuff. Weapons, cars, shoes, she does it all."

"Interesting story but it sounds too fanciful to be true."

Time to pull out the big guns, she thought to herself. "I'm pretty sure you know my mom and my dad. He's been dead for a while, but he wasn't someone easily forgotten."

"I don't know a Sharon Ariksen, or any man by that last name," Vidar said, almost too quickly.

"You knew them by different names," Thyra said. "My mom's name is Sif, and you probably knew my dad as Thor."

Of all the possible reactions he could have had, the one he gave her was the last one she expected. He watched her for a second before holding out a ten-dollar bill. "Go home, Thyra Ariksen."

Thyra stared at the money in confusion. "I don't want my money back. I came here for help."

"This is me helping," he said coolly. "Take the money and go home."

Thyra shook her head. "I don't want the money."

"Then there is nothing left for us to discuss," he said. He returned the money to his pocket and began to walk away.

Thyra stood frozen in place, shocked by the sudden dismissal. She finally recovered and called after him.

"You knew him, didn't you?"

"Go home, Thyra," he said over his shoulder.

"I know who you are," Thyra said. "Vidar."

He stopped in his tracks at the sound of the name.

"You *are* Vidar," Thyra said.

He turned slightly and looked at her over his shoulder. "Where did you hear that name?"

"I'd never heard it until a few days ago," Thyra said. "Along with a lot of other names I thought were only stories. Thor, Hela, Fenrir, Surtur—I thought they were names from the stories my mom told me. Turns out, they aren't. They're real."

She expected some kind of reaction to what she said, but he didn't give one. He remained rooted in place, staring at her. Not wanting to give him time to escape, she kept talking.

"My mom was kidnapped, and I'm trying to get her back," Thyra said. "You'd know her as Sif."

He flinched at the mention of Thyra's mom, and although he tried to hide it, Thyra knew she had struck a chord.

"I don't know what you're talking about," he said, shaking his head. "My name is Luke Vincent. I'm sorry, but I am not this Vidar person."

"Yes, you are!" Thyra said. Any hesitation that she had felt was washed away as her temper flared. "You are Vidar. You were one of the Aesir, and you survived Ragnarök all those years ago. Admit it!"

"Ragnarök?" He shook his head. "I think you've been listening to too many stories."

Thyra's anger flared even hotter. She had one more card up her sleeve. She made sure the gym was empty one last time, and then stared straight into Vidar's eyes.

"I *am* the daughter of Thor," she said. She summoned her magic and let it fill her. Vidar flinched slightly as he looked into her eyes that now shone with bluish-white light. "Does this prove that I'm telling the truth?"

Vidar's shoulders sagged slightly, and he suddenly looked tired.

"Release your magic," he said. Thyra complied and he relaxed somewhat. "Why did you come here?"

"I told you that already," Thyra said. "I came here because I need your help."

"Help with what?"

"The Eye of Odin," Thyra said.

"The Eye of Odin?" Vidar asked. He didn't look surprised by the name. Instead, he looked annoyed. "That can't be. It was destroyed and the pieces lost."

"You're wrong," Thyra said. "It wasn't destroyed the way everyone thought it was. The pieces are being gathered, and they think I have a piece! I can prove it."

"I don't want you to prove it," Vidar said. "I left that life behind long ago, and I want nothing to do with being a god, magic, or anyone who does. I've done my best to forget it all. If you're smart, you'll do the same. Walk away, and never look back, Thyra."

"Don't you get it!" Thyra snapped. "I can't do that! My world has been flipped upside down. They came after me and my mom, and now she's been kidnapped. The only way to get her back is to give them a piece of the Eye of Odin, but I can't give it to them because I can't get to it and I don't know where the rest of it is. I came here because I was told you might be able to help me or at the very least point me in the right direction."

Thyra stopped and breathed heavily after getting that all out in one breath. Vidar stood with his hands on his hips, giving her an expressionless stare.

"So, can you?" Thyra asked. "Can you help me?"

"Who is 'they'?" he asked.

"There are lots of 'theys'," Thyra said. "Surtur, or Gunnar Olafsson,

Hela, Fenrir—they are all after me it feels like. All I know is that I need to get my mom back, and the Eye, or the shard, is what they want."

"Who has your mother?"

"Hela does," Thyra said.

His entire body went stiff. "I'm sorry, Thyra. I can't help you."

"You can't," Thyra said, "or you won't?"

"Does it matter?" Vidar shook his head again. "You may not be able to go home, but you can't stay here. I've spent lifetimes trying to forget what I am and what I did. Some girl claiming to be the daughter of Thor and asking for my help isn't going to change that."

Without another word, he walked back to his office and shut the door. Thyra watched him go in stunned silence. She saw Henry appear at the front of the room. He motioned toward the front door with his head. Thyra got the message. She gathered her gear, stuffed it roughly into her backpack, and headed for the doors.

Henry stepped to the side to let her by, but Thyra wasn't going to leave without a final word.

"You've got a great partner there," she said bitterly. "Do you know? Do you know who and what you're in bed with?"

"I know all I need to know," Henry said. "His past is his own, and it isn't up to you or me to make him face it."

Thyra had a hundred things she wanted to say, but what was the point?

She stormed past Henry and out the front doors. She walked to where Bragi was waiting for her in the Camaro. She got in the car and pulled the door shut roughly.

"Didn't go well, I take it?" Bragi asked.

"No go," Thyra said. "You were right about him. He won't help us."

Chapter 17

Henry locked the front door and pulled the blinds on the windows. The sun was setting over the La Croix, turning the surface of the river an eerie shade of orange. It matched the feeling he'd had ever since the girl arrived earlier that day. She had brought an eerie chill with her, one that seemed to chill Henry to the bone. He gave the wand on the blinds one final twist and blocked the outside world out.

He passed the open door to his office and walked into the gym. The man he knew as Luke was busy cleaning the gym and returning weight plates to the racks. Henry quietly joined him, and between them both they had things in order in half an hour.

Henry wanted to ask his partner about the girl, but he knew better than to force the conversation. He waited patiently and watched as Luke retrieved a black barbell from where it hung on the wall and walked over to one of the benches. He then proceeded to load both sides with plate after plate until there were eight fifty-five-pound plates on each side.

Luke laid down on the bench and reached up for the bar. He took a few breaths and then lifted the bar off the rest. The bar dropped to his chest and then rose with a sharp exhale from Luke. Back and forth it went nine more times before Luke re-racked it with a bang.

"You want some more on there?" Henry asked as Luke sat up.

Luke nodded. "Two more."

Henry nodded and walked over to the rack to retrieve two more fifty-five-pound plates. He slid them on to the barbell and replaced the weight collar. He figured there was still room for a few more if it went that far tonight.

Luke slid back under the weight and lifted it free of the rests. He pumped out twelve consecutive reps before putting the weight back down. He got up from the bench and signaled for two more to be put on. Henry added the weight and stepped back to watch. Twelve fifty-fives on each side of the specially made barbell was an obscene amount of weight. One thousand three hundred twenty pounds, and that was before adding in the weight of the bar itself.

The bar Luke used was almost as much of a mystery as its owner. In all the years of owning the gym with Luke, Henry had never tried to use the barbell or guess its weight. It was Luke's and no one else touched it. It hung on the wall like an unofficial mascot for the gym, and Henry was perfectly happy to treat it as such. All Henry knew was that it was heavy and made of tough enough stuff to handle the weight Luke put on it.

Luke pumped out eight solid reps, making them look effortless, before returning the bar to the rests. Henry heard the telltale sound of the bench pulling against the eight-inch bolts used to anchor it to the floor, but it didn't come free. That was good. He didn't know how much deeper they could go before they ran out of cement to anchor to.

Luke sat up and took a long, deep breath. The storm that had been in his eyes since the girl left was starting to break after the physical exertion. Henry guessed he was ready to talk.

"What're you going to do about the girl?"

Luke looked up and shook his head. "Nothing."

Henry nodded. "Probably a good choice. She was trouble."

Luke snorted. "You say that like she was some siren trying to steal my soul. She's just a girl."

"I'd prefer to see a grown woman sniffing around you," Henry said. "Like the one that came by the other night." He saw Luke flinch and knew he had touched a sensitive nerve. After years of knowing Luke, Henry knew better than to press that particular nerve too hard. "I'd at least know how to handle that. A pretty smile and flirty words aren't what concerns me. But this Thyra, she's dangerous to what we've built."

"How so?" Luke said as he stood and began removing plates.

"Because," Henry said, moving to help, "a beautiful woman has never been enough to break your focus and cause you to make a mistake. Plenty have tried, and they've all failed. Last night I felt you were the closest you'd ever been since I've known you, but you managed to rebuff her. This girl, though," Henry shook his head, "she's different. She may be enough."

"What are you talking about?" Luke said, his irritation clear on his face. "She's a teenage girl. I'm not that kind of guy."

"I'm not talking about romance," Henry said. "I'm talking about your sense of duty and of right and wrong. I saw your face when she left. A part of you wanted to tell her to stay and that you would help her with whatever problem she came to you with. I don't know if you'll be able to keep that feeling at bay if she asks again."

"Don't worry," Luke said. "We won't see her again."

Henry shrugged again. "If you say so."

Luke didn't look at him, but Henry could see the storm had returned to his face. Luke began peeling plates off the bar and Henry moved to help. When all the weights were back on the rack, Luke lifted the barbell and hung it up on the wall.

"Well, I think I'll call it a day," Henry said. "Doors are locked. Turn off the lights when you leave."

"Why do you think I'm staying?" Luke asked over his shoulder.

"After all these years, I know when you need some time to yourself," Henry said. He turned and headed for the front of the gym. He paused near the office and turned around. "Just be careful."

"Don't worry," Luke said sharply. "I can handle myself around the weights."

"That wasn't what I was talking about," Henry said. "You and I both know that girl will be back. Be careful when you go to help her."

Henry left his friend of nearly forty years with his thoughts. He slipped out the front door and began to walk back home without noticing the three black SUVs parked just down the street.

Chapter 18

Vidar put the weights down and wiped the sweat from his brow. Even after a thousand years, he still was amazed at the changes in his body. Although he possessed the strength of a god, somehow his body knew when he truly needed it and when he didn't. The result was that he could still get a good workout even with weights that should have felt like feathers in his hands.

Of course, the weights he used were still big enough that he was forced to lift when no one else was around. He couldn't lift the kind of weight he did in view of the gym rats that frequented his gym without raising alarm. At times, hiding in plain sight was a more difficult job than living as a god ever was.

The sound of the front door opening caught his attention and he turned around. He expected to see Henry coming back for something he had forgotten, but it wasn't his friend. Instead, six heavily muscled men in dark suits stepped into the gym. Alarms went off in his head, but he forced himself to stay calm as they crossed the room and surrounded him.

"Luke Vincent," a bald man with a belly as wide as his shoulders said. The result of extensive steroid use, he probably had a six pack of abs under his shirt, but you wouldn't believe it without seeing it. A quick glance at the other men told the same story. They were toughs sent to intimidate, and he was pretty sure he knew who sent them.

"The gym's closed," he announced.

"We're not here to lift," the bald man said with a smirk.

"Then what can I do for you gentlemen?"

The bald man smiled. "You can tell us about the girl who came to visit you earlier."

Vidar shook his head. "Not sure what girl you're talking about."

"Don't play dumb," the bald man said as he sat down on a bench and leaned forward, making sure to flex his arms as he did. "We know she came to see you, and we know that she wanted your help."

"If you know all of that," Vidar said, "why do you need me?"

"You know why," the bald man said. "Our employer wants to make sure you've kept to your end of the deal."

"Your employer?" Vidar asked. He wasn't going to play their game, and he wasn't going to be intimidated by a gang of juiced up thugs.

The bald man smiled. "Gunnar Olafsson."

"So, Gunnar has taken to hiring Mr. Olympia wannabes now, has he?" Vidar nodded. "An interesting move for an energy and infrastructure company. You guys have day jobs, or do you just juice and stare at yourselves in the mirror all day?"

The smile slipped off of the bald man's face and he looked around at his buddies. He stood up and took a deep breath.

"I don't think you're in a position to be giving out insults," he said slowly.

"No but taking it easy on the roids will help clear up some of that acne you boys are suffering from," Vidar said.

The bald man puffed his chest and jutted out his chin in response to the barb. "We were sent here to make sure you are sticking to the deal you made with our boss. It doesn't have to get ugly."

Vidar almost felt sorry for these guys. Gunnar clearly hadn't told them who they would be dealing with. Why would he? They were hired muscle, and disposable. They didn't need to know the important details.

But, as easy as it would be to knock them around, it would only do him harm. Gunnar Olafsson wouldn't take kindly to having his heavies getting abused and would retaliate. Which meant Vidar would have to find a new home. He knew deep down that would be a waste of time. There was no place he could hide from Olafsson.

"You can tell your boss that I've kept my end of the deal," Vidar said as calmly as possible. "I sent the girl away. I didn't help her."

The bald thug smiled. "See, was that so hard? You did a smart thing, Luke. You get to continue operating your gym in peace. Mostly, at least."

He looked at one of the other thugs and nodded. This one, a tall brute with a crooked nose, got a cocky smile on his face as he turned and looked at the row of mirrors on the wall. He bent down, grabbed a nearby bench, and flung it with a grunt. It slammed into the wall, shattering the mirror in the process. Vidar tensed, but didn't react. That was what they wanted, and he wasn't going to give it to them.

The bald thug shrugged. "For not being more cooperative. A little taste to remind you that if you step out of line, it will be much worse next time."

Vidar remained silent. Seeing that he wasn't going to fall for their game, the thugs quickly got bored.

"We'll let you get to cleaning up your mess," the bald thug said. "Just remember, we're watching you. We'll know if you try to help the girl."

He motioned to his buddies and they all began to head for the door. Vidar let them go. He waited until he was sure they were gone before walking to the front door and looking out. The street was vacant. He looked down at the lock and saw that it had been blown apart. He didn't know how they had done it so quietly, but he knew enough about the Muspel Corporation to know that it had deep pockets and access to the newest technology.

Seeing no other choice, he went back to the office and retrieved a chain and padlock. He quickly ran the chain through the doors and locked them together. He grabbed a sheet of paper from the front desk and scrawled out a hasty sign that they would be closed to hang on the door.

He retreated back into the main room and began to sweep up the broken glass, his temper roiling beneath the surface. He tried to think of how he was going to explain everything to Henry. The older man knew that there were dangers in his past, but they had never had anything like this happen before. Henry would be concerned, and he had every reason to be. This put him at risk as well.

Vidar had done everything possible to distance himself from his past and that world. He had been a recluse, avoided personal connections, and lived as quietly as possible. He had opened the gym only when he felt he had outrun the skeletons in his past. It had become his sanctuary, and he had done everything he could to keep it safe.

And yet, here he was, his past catching up to him and putting his peaceful existence at stake. He thought he had kept it at bay when he sent Hela away the night before, but then Thyra Ariksen showed up and it all came crashing back down. Things had spiraled out of his control before he realized he was even losing his grip.

He finished cleaning up the glass and carried it out to the dumpster in back. A black SUV was parked at the end of the alley in the darkness, but it wasn't hidden well enough to avoid his notice. It seemed that the thugs from earlier didn't trust his word. That or Gunnar Olafsson wasn't taking any chances. Either way, it ratcheted up the heat of his temper.

He retreated back to Henry's office and dialed his partner's cell. It was past midnight and he doubted Henry would answer so he took a moment to plan out what he was going to say in the message.

"Had some visitors at the gym," Vidar began after hearing the tone.

"A mirror was broken, and the front door will need a new lock. I cleaned up the best I could. I may need to take a day or two. Sorry for all of this."

He took a deep breath and let it out slowly. In that moment, he made the decision Henry had already known he would make.

"You should know that you were right, Henry," Vidar said. "I can't walk away from this one."

Vidar hung up the phone and scribbled a quick note to Henry. He grabbed a Hammer Forged Gym hoodie from a pile near the desk and dropped two twenty-dollar bills on the desk. He slipped it over his head and pulled the hood up. He turned off the lights and headed for the back door. Making sure the thugs in the SUV saw him, he stepped out into the dark of the night.

* * *

"Did you see his face when I broke that mirror?"

Dieter smiled and nodded. "He looked ready to cry! We left him shaking in his boots!"

Latrell snorted through his crooked nose. "I hope we get to go back again. I'd like to see him cry. After what he said, I think he could use another lesson."

Dieter laughed at the thought. He felt the same way. It felt good to put the small-town bumpkin in his place.

But, it hadn't been enough. Dieter felt like a harsher message needed to be sent.

He looked out the window to where Luke Vincent was walking. They had been following him with the SUV's lights off since he had left the gym, keeping far enough back that they went unnoticed. Vincent had stayed on a paved path close to the river that led north through Hudson. They were at the edge of town now, and the number of lights had steadily decreased.

Dieter recognized the opportunity and cast a devious look at Latrell. "Maybe we can still have a little fun."

Latrell's face was split by a wide smile and he nodded. "Let's do it!"

Dieter gave the SUV a healthy flow of gas and flicked on the lights. He was sure that the roar of the engine and the sudden flood of light would catch Vincent off-guard. He was disappointed. He slammed on the brakes and cursed. Vincent was gone!

"Where did he go?" Latrell asked.

"I don't know!" Dieter swore. "He was right there! You saw him."

"Yeah, but he's not there anymore," Latrell said. "He's gotta be around here somewhere."

"Get out and look for him then," Dieter said.

"Why me?" Latrell said.

"Because I'm the one driving," Dieter said. "What good is the SUV gonna be if no one is here to drive it?"

"Then let me drive," Latrell said.

"Don't be a wuss," Dieter snapped. "Get out and start looking."

Latrell grumbled something under his breath, but he unbuckled himself and opened his door. He grabbed a flashlight from the glove compartment and flicked it on.

"You're a real piece," Latrell said as he got out and slammed the door behind him.

Dieter watched as Latrell began searching the trees along the path. After a few moments, Latrell turned around and shrugged his shoulders. "I don't see him."

"He's got to be around here somewhere," Dieter said. "You keep walking and I'll drive alongside."

"Figures," Latrell grumbled. "You're a real team player, you know that?"

Dieter rolled his window up and turned on his brights. He began driving slowly, weaving back and forth so that he could shine his lights into the trees at regular intervals. There was no sign of Vincent.

He rolled down his window again and shouted to Latrell. "Anything?"

Latrell shook his head. "Where did he go?"

"He couldn't have just vanished," Dieter said. He shifted the SUV into park and leaned out the window. "I'm going to double back and-"

Something heavy struck the side of the SUV and spun it off the road violently. The vehicle finally came to a stop a dozen feet off the road. Dazed, Dieter expected to see that the SUV had been struck by another vehicle, but he didn't see one. The rear passenger side door was caved in, but there was no sign of what had caused the damage.

Latrell came running over and shined his light through the window. "You okay?!"

Dieter nodded his head. "Yeah. What was that?"

Latrell shook his head furiously, his eyes the size of saucers. "I don't know, man! One second you were on the road, and the next you weren't."

"What?" Dieter shook his head in confusion. "Something had to have hit me."

"I'm telling you, I didn't see anything," Latrell said. He shook his head, his eyes wide. "Man, something ain't right about this. We gotta get out of here!"

"Don't be a wuss," Dieter said. "Just help me get out of here."

He reached to open his door and had it halfway open when he saw a dark, hooded shape at the front of the SUV. The headlights lit up his features and Dieter recognized him immediately. It was Vincent!

Dieter stared in shock. He heard Latrell yell out, "Run him over!"

Acting from instinct, Dieter threw it into gear and stepped on the gas. The engine roared to life and lurched forward but stopped dead in its tracks almost immediately. The wheels squealed in protest as the SUV fought to move forward but couldn't.

Dieter looked to see what he had hit and was shocked to see Vincent standing there with one hand pressed against the hood of the SUV like he was holding it in place. It dawned on Dieter that that was exactly what Vincent was doing and his jaw began to work wordlessly. He watched as Vincent brought his other arm up over his head and swung it down viciously. Dieter flinched as the front of the SUV was creased in half and the roar of the engine went silent.

Latrell let out a terrified scream and bolted. Dieter felt like doing the same, but his throat was so tight with fear that he could barely get out a whimper. In a flash, Vincent was after Latrell, covering the distance with inhuman speed. Dieter heard Latrell shriek in fear and then saw Vincent dragging him back toward the SUV by his collar. Vincent slammed Latrell into the side of the SUV hard enough to shake the entire vehicle. Latrell fell to the grass with a groan and laid still.

Before he could react, Dieter's door was ripped off the hinges and was tossed unceremoniously out over the river like a Frisbee. Vincent reached in and pulled Dieter out of the vehicle.

"Where is the girl staying?" Vincent growled.

"What are you?" Dieter stammered.

Vincent slammed Dieter against the side of the SUV, stealing the air from his lungs.

"The girl," Vincent repeated. "Where is she staying?"

Dieter gasped for breath and shook his head. "What girl?"

Vincent slammed his fist down on the hood of the SUV, the sheer force of the blow snapping the undercarriage.

"Last chance before I do the same thing to you," Vincent said. "Where is she staying?"

Courage gone, Dieter blurted out the answer. "The Hudson Inn!"

"How many of your thugs are watching the hotel?" Vincent asked.

"Watching the hotel?" Dieter said. "No one is watching the hotel."

"You're lying," Vincent said, a murderous look in his eyes. He slammed Dieter against the SUV again, and this time Dieter felt at least one of his ribs pop. "Let's see if you're as dumb as you look. I'm going to start breaking your bones, one at a time until you tell me the truth. Where would you like me to start? A finger? Or should I make sure you never walk straight again?"

Dieter felt his bladder release. He decided the time for heroics was long past.

"Ten men!"

"What were you ordered to do?" Vincent demanded.

"A quick grab and go!" Dieter said in a hurry. "We were supposed to deliver her and the old man to our boss in New York."

Vincent's eyes narrowed. He grabbed the front of Dieter's suit and lifted all of his two hundred and sixty pounds off the ground with one hand.

"You made a mistake threatening me," Vincent said grimly. "Tell your boss that he should have left me in peace."

Before he could protest, Vincent threw Dieter against the side of the SUV. Dieter heard several loud pops and a searing pain ran through his body as more of his ribs snapped. Struggling for breath, he didn't even try to resist when Vincent pulled him away from the SUV's torn, metal husk and dropped him onto the ground next to Latrell. Then, Vincent did something impossible. He lifted the badly damaged SUV overhead and gave a mighty heave. The mangled vehicle flew overhead, cleared the row of trees that lined the river and landed in the dark waters of the La Croix with a splash.

Vincent came close and bent down next to Dieter. He reached out and lifted Dieter up so that his face was only a few inches away.

"My deal with your employer is over," Vincent said.

Dieter saw Vincent's fist go back and then flash toward his face. He felt his nose shatter beneath the blow but was unconscious before his brain had time to register the pain.

Chapter 19

Gunnar Olafsson stood up from his desk and began to pace. Ivan watched his boss silently, letting him digest the information he had just given him.

Gunnar stopped and looked at the big Russian. "You're sure that his cell signal puts him in the same city?"

Ivan nodded. "We've pinged his phone several times. He's definitely near the hotel where the girl and the old man are staying."

Gunnar clenched his teeth together to avoid cursing. He looked at the print-out on his desk detailing the activation of a small cell of Ivan's men.

"And you didn't authorize this?"

The Russian shook his head. "Of course not. I know your orders concerning Vincent, as do my men."

"Then why were they given an order to pay Vincent a visit?" Gunnar asked with barely contained anger.

"Somehow, Asmodeus gained access to our network," Ivan said. "That's the only possible explanation."

And the last one Gunnar wanted to hear. He had done everything in his power to keep Ivan and his small branch of the Muspel Corporation away from Asmodeus. Sure, the man knew about it, and Gunnar didn't try to hide anything his men did, but he did everything to keep his 'partner' from gaining any control over the program he had labeled the Odin Initiative. Somehow, he had failed, and now he was left wondering how much Asmodeus knew.

"This is inexcusable," Gunnar said. "Find the leak in the network and plug it. Then do a complete reset of our network—new codewords, access codes, everything!"

"That won't work," Ivan said.

"Why not?" Gunnar hissed.

"Because he's embedded far enough into the network that we can't be sure where the leak is, or how many there are," Ivan said.

"How?" Gunnar demanded. "How could he manage to do this? I thought I employed a whole team of tech heads to make sure the Odin Initiative was impregnable."

"You do, and it should have been."

"Then, how did he gain access to it?"

Ivan shifted his feet uncomfortably, and Gunnar could tell from the look on his face that he wasn't going to like the answer.

"He used your personal sign-on to access the network."

This time Gunnar did curse. He had underestimated Asmodeus. The man was turning into a colossal irritation.

"Give me the word," Ivan said, "and I'll kill him."

"You can't kill him!" Gunnar snapped, his voice cracking like a whip. He took a breath to regain control of his emotions then continued. "I told you once, he cannot be killed."

"How can a man not be killed?" Ivan asked. "All men can be killed, even the gods. There has to be a way to kill this one."

"Not Asmodeus," Gunnar hissed. "Forget it, Ivan. I will not waste your life on something so fruitless. He's our monster, and we have to learn how to live with him."

"What do you want me to do?"

Gunnar considered the question for a moment. Bit by bit, he created a plan for how to deal with his rogue business partner.

"Get him on the phone," he ordered the Russian. Ivan reached for his phone and quickly dialed a number. He set the phone on the desk and put it on speaker.

The line clicked and Asmodeus answered, "What a surprise to be hearing from you, Gunnar. How are you?"

"Let's skip the pleasantries," Gunnar said. "I know you're in Hudson, Wisconsin, and that you found a way to infiltrate the Odin Initiative."

"And scratched an itch that has been plaguing me for months," Asmodeus said. "You've been a bad boy, Gunnar. I knew that you were experimenting with replicating magical items, but this…this is ambitious, even for you."

"I don't appreciate you going behind my back," Gunnar said. "We are partners, aren't we?"

"Then why do you keep trying to go behind mine?"

"I've done nothing to undermine you," Gunnar said in exasperation.

"Haven't you?" Asmodeus asked. "The Odin Initiative—a misleading name for what you're trying to do, but it does have a nice ring to it. I'm sure the Board of Directors found it catchy. But, trying to harness the power of Mjolnir and Odin's spear, Gungnir? That is brazen."

A cold hand gripped Gunnar's chest. Asmodeus knew about the real purpose of the Odin Initiative, and there was no point denying it. Now, he had to wait and see if Asmodeus came to the right conclusion about what Gunnar hoped to do if he succeeded.

"You've been holding back important information," Asmodeus continued. "That is no way to conduct a partnership."

"The Odin Initiative has been my life's work," Gunnar said. "Not yours."

"Creating an endless supply of clean energy?" Asmodeus laughed. "I see through you, Gunnar. I've seen the plans, and I applaud you for creating such a believable lie, but I'm no fool. You want to replicate the two greatest weapons ever created, but not from some underlying altruism. You want their power for themselves."

Gunnar made no attempt to deny it. It would have been a mistake to try. Instead, he stayed silent and waited to see how far Asmodeus would take his reasoning.

"But that isn't the most alarming thing I found," Asmodeus said. "I have to admit, you had me fooled. I thought you had it. I truly did. I actually harbored a high degree of respect for you because I believed you had managed to keep your hands on the Eye for all these years. I felt certain that was why you never moved on Hela, that you were in a position of power. Imagine my disappointment when I learned that you only have a single shard in your possession. A large one, yes, but only one. Now I realize that you didn't move on her because you feared she might have more, and you didn't want to tip your hand."

Gunnar was truly afraid now, but he did his best to hide it behind a mask of rage. "This is an unforgivable breach of our partnership. You have crossed the line, Asmodeus. I demand that you—"

"Shhhh!"

Gunnar's mouth moved silently at the pure affront of being shushed.

"Say my name, Gunnar Olafsson. Say my real name, and I will say yours."

A chill ran down Gunnar's spine. He glanced up at Ivan who wore a confused expression. The big Russian didn't know the real name of Gunnar's partner. No one did. No one except for Gunnar.

"Say it!" Asmodeus demanded through the phone. "Say it, or I will make sure you never sit comfortably on your throne again!"

Gunnar knew that with what Asmodeus now knew he could deliver on his threat. Steeling himself, he spoke the name, "Baldur."

The sound of an exhilarated inhalation came through the phone.

"It feels good to hear it out loud," Baldur said. He let his breath out slowly. "It's been too long. Hearing you speak my true name fills me with power. Thank you, *Surtur*."

The line was silent for a moment as Gunnar tried to compose himself. Just hearing the name he had conquered Asgard under sent a shiver down his spine. He took no joy in hearing it again. He had used it until he outgrew its usefulness and had never used it since.

Thoroughly shaken, Gunnar tried to formulate what to do next. Finally, he asked the question weighing on his mind. "What will you do?"

"What you failed to do," Baldur hissed. "Wait for my call, Surtur, and don't do anything stupid until then. If you do, I will make sure to deliver on my threat. I know everything, and I will use what I know. Good-bye, Surtur."

The line went dead. Gunnar leaned forward and rested his fists on his desk. He stared at the phone, his anger raging inside.

"Get my jet fueled up," Gunnar said through clenched teeth. He looked up at Ivan. "I want to be in Wisconsin tonight."

* * *

Baldur hung up the phone and set it on the table next to him. He was always amazed by Gunnar Olafsson and his misdirected ambition. He had more wealth and power than any one man should have, and still Gunnar was unsatisfied. The fool thought his plans were foremost, that his precious Odin Initiative was the path to remaking the world.

Even worse, he thought it wise to act like he possessed the Eye of Odin! His bluff had worked to this point—he had even fooled Baldur—but for how long? And what would he do if he did manage to get his hands on the Eye? His lack of understanding of how the Eye worked was so deficient it was amusing. If Gunnar knew the truth about the Eye and the price it exacted, he wouldn't want any part of it. Baldur almost laughed at the irony of it all.

Pushing thoughts of his misguided partner from his mind, Baldur stood up and walked to the bathroom of the cheap hotel room. He turned on the light and stared in the mirror. His pale features were made all the more apparent by his black hair. Once, he had been called beautiful by everyone that laid eyes on him. Looking at himself in the orange glow of the hotel bathroom, he admitted that was the furthest thing from the truth now. The striking features were the same, but the man behind them had changed. The light that had once shown in his gray eyes was gone, replaced by an abyss of darkness. He doubted anyone would call him handsome now.

He heard footsteps in the hallway and his heart began to race in anticipation. The footsteps stopped outside the door and then came the telltale tap of the keycard against the magnetic lock on the door. Baldur watched as the door opened and the old man stepped into the room. He waited until the door was closed before stepping out into the room behind the old man. Like a wraith, he moved in and became the old man's shadow.

The old man finally sensed his presence and spun around, but it was too late. Baldur delivered a sharp jab to the old man's belly that stole his breath and a second to his throat that neutralized his voice. The old man crumpled to the ground with one hand on his throat. He looked up at Baldur, his blue eyes ringed in red. Slowly, recognition filled them. Then came the abject fear and disbelief.

"Hello, Uncle," Baldur said softly. "It's been a long, long time. You look surprised to see me."

Bragi struggled to speak, but it came out in a gurgle.

"I would have loved to hear you ask the questions I'm sure you have," Baldur said. "But they will have to wait. I couldn't have you calling out to the girl and dwarf or trying to use your magic on me. I need your help, and this was the only way to make sure you gave it to me."

Baldur reached into his pocket and pulled out a smooth black stone. An icy smile spread across his face as he turned it in the light. He made sure Bragi saw it too. The old man's eyes widened, and he shook his head frantically. Bragi tried to speak, but it came out in a hoarse cough.

"Don't fight it, Uncle," Baldur said. "It's almost painless if you don't fight it. Almost. If you fight it, though, it is extremely painful. Trust me, I know."

Bragi put up a hand in an attempt to stop what was coming, but it was a feeble gesture. Baldur extended his hand towards Bragi and triggered the stone. There was a flash of light and then the sensation of a vacuum that sucked in all the light in the room. Bragi stayed in place for a moment, and then he seemed to elongate as he was sucked into the stone. Baldur triggered the stone again, and the lights in the room flickered. Bragi was gone, taken to a prison somewhere between realms.

Baldur hurried to the bathroom and held the stone against his forehead. He spoke the words softly. Immediately, he felt a searing pain throughout his body, as his very makeup was changed by the spell. He dropped to one knee and gasped as the pain began to subside. He pushed himself to his feet and looked in the mirror. Instead of his pale, haunted features, he saw the face of an older man with a short beard and vibrant blue eyes. The face of Bragi.

He smiled, and the face in the mirror smiled back. "Revenge will be sweet."

Chapter 20

Thyra.

Her eyes opened to a world of blue. She recognized where she was immediately. She stood up and placed a hand against the dark trunk of Yggdrasil.

"I was wondering when you'd bring me here again," Thyra said.

You're changing the world already, Yggdrasil said. *Your power has grown.*

Thyra was in no mood for small talk. Her temper had been boiling ever since her conversation with Vidar, and she'd been unable to fall asleep for quite some time. Now that she had, she couldn't help but feel irritated that the tree was interrupting her sleep.

"Why did you bring me here?"

I've sensed a change, the tree said ambiguously.

"A change?" Thyra asked. "What kind of change? A change in me? That's an understatement. I feel like everything has changed in the last few days."

You have grown stronger and no longer deny your nature, the tree responded. *But that is not the change that I speak of.*

"What change are you talking about then?"

Where there was balance, you have created imbalance, Yggdrasil said. *Where there was imbalance, your presence moves things closer to equilibrium.*

"So, you brought me here because I'm disruptive?" Thyra asked. "Is

216

that good or bad?"

You force others to act in unexpected ways, the tree responded. *Vidar has acted, and now he is on his way to you.*

"Vidar?" Thyra was surprised. "He said he wouldn't help me. Why is he coming to me?"

I cannot judge his intentions, Yggdrasil said. *I can tell you that you must go with him. He will guide you to the Eye, even though he doesn't know it.*

I must give you a warning—be careful where you place your trust, the tree said. *You will hold the Eye of Odin in your hand, but for how long depends on whether you see through the lie to the truth behind it. They will seek to possess the Eye.*

"What?" Thyra asked. "Who are you talking about?"

One will ask you for it, Yggdrasil said without answering her question. *The other will try to force your hand. You must make a choice. The world will change further depending on what path you choose to walk.*

"What are you talking about?" Thyra demanded. "What choice will I have to make? Answer me!"

I cannot answer your questions because I cannot influence the result, the tree said.

"Cannot or will not?"

Down either path, my power in the world will grow, the tree said. *That is my purpose.*

"If you're not going to answer my questions, why did you bring me here?"

Because I would not lose you to this fight, if possible, the tree said. *You must survive.*

"Survive what?"

The tree didn't respond. Thyra felt a quiver rush through Yggdrasil and the branches shook overhead.

Do not trust blindly, Yggdrasil stated. *Awake, Thyra!*

* * *

Thyra was back in the hotel room, laying on the bed and staring up at the ceiling when she heard a knock at the door. Her head was still spinning from the vision of Yggdrasil. She hadn't noticed the first time because she'd already been weak, but the visions were physically taxing.

They were more taxing mentally, though. She was frustrated by the unanswered questions that plagued her and confused by the strange message the tree had delivered. Who was she talking about and what were the results from her actions Yggdrasil was talking about? Did she mean Vidar or someone else? Thyra didn't know but trying to figure it out was draining.

The knock came again and Thyra raised her head to look towards the door. Asiri grumbled something under her breath from where she sat on the other bed tinkering with her watch. From the look of concentration on her face, it was clear that she had no intention of getting up to answer the door.

"I'll get it," Thyra sighed as she got to her feet with a sigh. She looked through the peephole and saw Bragi standing there. She reached for the handle, but hesitated with her hand on the door, remembering her conversation with Yggdrasil.

"You going to open that?" Asiri asked from her bed.

"Working on it," Thyra said. She pulled it open and stepped aside so that Bragi could enter.

"You're awake," Bragi said as he came through the door. "Good."

"Hard to sleep with Asiri muttering to herself all night," Thyra said as she closed the door.

"I don't mutter," Asiri muttered without looking up.

Thyra gave Bragi a "see what I mean" look, but he swept past without noticing.

218

"We need to talk about what our next step is," Bragi said as he took a seat on the end of Asiri's bed. "Since Vidar was of no use to us, we need to come up with a new plan."

"Maybe we shouldn't be so quick to give up on Vidar," Thyra said.

Bragi gave her a surprised look. "What? A few hours ago, I thought we might have to lock you in the bathroom to stop you from going back to the gym and creating an electrical storm inside."

"I've cooled down since then." Thyra shrugged. "I just have a feeling. Maybe he just needed a little time to think about it."

Bragi shook his head. "Vidar won't help us. He's more stubborn than stone. We need to move on without him."

"And do what?" Thyra asked. "You said he could help us, and I still think he can."

"How?" Bragi snapped. "He made himself clear. Waiting for him to change his mind is not going to help us get any closer to finding the Eye."

A knock at the door interrupted the debate. Thyra looked at Bragi and Asiri, who shared a confused look. Bragi put a finger up to his lips and motioned her away from the door. The knock came again, and he moved to the door on cat's feet. Thyra watched him peek through the peephole. He backed away from the door suddenly and looked back at Thyra and Asiri with a strange expression on his face.

"Who is it?" Thyra whispered, although she already knew the answer.

The knock came a third time followed by a deep, gravelly voice. "Open up, Bragi. I know you're in there."

Thyra recognized the voice. The tree had been right!

"It's Vidar," Bragi said softly.

He slowly reached out and pulled the door open. It swung open to reveal Vidar's broad frame. He stepped into the room and waited for Bragi to close the door behind him. Bragi slid past and stood next to

Thyra, but his eyes never left Vidar's face. The opposite was true, as well.

"You're older," Vidar said in a grim tone. "Your eyes look less alive."

"Eight hundred years tends to do that," Bragi said. "Although, time doesn't look like it touched you. You look the same. Slabs of muscle and a chip on your shoulder. The only thing that's different is your hair."

"I kept what was important," Vidar said carefully. His eyes flicked to Thyra and he nodded to her. "Good to see you again, Thyra."

"The same," Thyra said. Even though the tree had told her he was coming, it was still a surprise to see Vidar after his quick dismissal of her earlier in the day. She had been cursing his name since leaving his gym, but now that he was standing in the hotel room Thyra felt some of her anger dissipate and be replaced by a cautious hope.

Vidar looked over her shoulder at Asiri. "You must be the dwarf."

Asiri nodded. "That's right. Shoes treating you well?"

"They're well made," Vidar said simply.

"What are you doing here?" Bragi said.

"Helping," Vidar said.

"You told me you wouldn't help," Thyra said. "Why the change of heart?"

"A deal was broken," Vidar replied flatly. "They interrupted my exile and threatened me. They pushed me over the edge and forced my hand."

"They?" Bragi asked.

"Gunnar Olafsson's thugs paid me a visit after Thyra left," Vidar said. "Wanted to deliver a message. I gave them one in return."

"What kind of message?" Bragi asked.

"One he won't like," Vidar said without a drop of emotion in his voice.

"So, you're here to help?" Thyra asked.

"My lot has fallen with yours for now," Vidar said with a nod.

"For now?" Thyra asked.

He nodded. "I make no promises beyond today."

"Comforting," Bragi grumbled. "With that kind of statement, why should we trust you at all?"

"Because, I have something to offer you," Vidar said. "This hotel is being watched by Olafsson's thugs."

"What?" Bragi looked up in shock. "How did they find us? We lost our tail back in Wyoming."

"Hard to lose a tail when you're driving a black Camaro SS," Vidar said. "Especially when you're going right where they want you to go."

"Why do you think we're going where they want us to go?" Bragi asked.

"What makes you think you aren't?" Vidar said. "They're setting a trap for you and you're walking right into the middle of it."

"What about my car?" Asiri asked. "Can we get to it?"

Vidar shook his head. "They have two SUVs parked near the Camaro right now. You won't even make it to the car, much less escape."

"You haven't seen that car run," Asiri said.

"It won't be running anywhere," Vidar said. "It's as good as Muspel Corporation property."

"I won't leave it behind," Asiri said stubbornly.

"You have to or else you'll never get out of here," Vidar said. "Your car is lost. You need to find another way."

"Do you have a better idea?" Bragi asked.

Vidar turned to him and hesitated. Thyra may have been imagining it, but he seemed bothered by something when he looked at Bragi.

"I'll clear the way," Vidar finally said. He reached into his pocket and held out a set of keys. "There's a vehicle waiting on the south side of the building. A blue truck. Take it but don't get on the freeway. I'll make sure no one follows and then catch up on the edge of town."

"You'll catch up?" Thyra asked. "How?"

"Blue truck, south side of the building," Vidar said without answering the question. "Stay on the frontage road leading east. Meet me on the edge of town. Be ready to move in five minutes. You'll know when to make a run for it."

"Hold on," Bragi said. "I'm not sure I feel comfortable with this. Do you really expect to waltz in here out of the blue and have us trust you?"

"You came here to get my help, didn't you?" Vidar shrugged. "This is me helping you."

"Why now?"

"I'm no fan of Gunnar Olafsson," Vidar stated.

"So, this about getting revenge, not helping us," Bragi said. "I don't trust someone motivated by revenge."

Thyra didn't know why Bragi was pressing the point, but there was no ignoring the fact that the air between the two men had turned to ice.

"Bragi, you brought us here because you said Vidar might know how to help us," Thyra said. The old man didn't say anything, so Thyra prompted him. "Right?"

Bragi reluctantly nodded. "But only because he was along our path. I wouldn't have sought him out on my own."

"And I would have been glad to be left alone," Vidar said. "Look at what one conversation with the girl has brought me. Trust me, old man, I'm no happier to see you than you are to see me."

Thyra jumped back in before either man could make another comment. "He told us about the men watching the hotel. That's worth something. I think we need to give him a chance to prove himself."

The two men continued to stare at each other for a tense moment before Bragi finally held out his hand.

"Blue truck?"

Vidar nodded and dropped the keys into Bragi's palm.

"Five minutes," Vidar said.

He turned and left the room without another word.

When she was sure Vidar was gone, she gave Bragi a questioning look. "What was that about?"

"What was what about?" Bragi asked, looking genuinely confused.

"Whatever that was with Vidar," Thyra said.

Bragi shrugged then shook his head. "I don't like this sudden change in his stance. I don't buy a visit from some goons as a good reason to suddenly decide to jump headfirst into the fight."

Thyra remembered her vision of the tree and the warning that Yggdrasil delivered about trusting 'him.' She wasn't sure if the tree was talking about Vidar, but then again, who else could it have been referring to?

"We don't have to trust him," Thyra said. "Not entirely."

"He told us about the trap," Asiri said. "And he seems sincere. I think he's here to help, and we'd be fools to turn him down. Let's just get out of here and then we can revisit whether we trust him or not."

"For now, we accept his help," Bragi agreed grimly. "You heard Vidar. We need to be ready to move in five minutes. Gather your things. I'll meet you downstairs at the back door."

He slipped out of the door, leaving Thyra staring after him. She heard a shuffling on the bed behind her as Asiri got down and began gathering her meager possessions.

"I can't leave that car behind," Asiri said. "My forge is in the trunk."

"Your what?"

"My forge!" Asiri said. "It's in a metal briefcase in the trunk. I can't leave without it."

"What?" Thyra couldn't believe what she was hearing. "How can your forge be in a metal briefcase?"

"Magic, girl," Asiri said. "I may not be a god, but I'm still a dwarf.

Where I go, my forge goes, too. I can't let those half-wits get their hands on it. You saw what they did with that shotgun at my home—imagine what they could do with a real dwarf forge? I can't let that happen."

Asiri continued to gather up her belongings without speaking, but she was clearly agitated. She latched her watch on her wrist and pressed a button. A moment later, her blue skin was replaced by a more normal shade.

"I can't let them have it!" Asiri said emphatically. "Gunnar Olafsson could do terrible things with it if it falls into his hands."

"Then, we won't let them have it," Thyra said as she retrieved Lynnedslag from the bed.

Asiri gave her a curious look. "What do you mean?"

"I don't understand it, but I saw what the weapons his thugs could do," Thyra said. "If keeping your forge out of his hands means that fewer weapons like those are made, then I'm in one hundred percent. You've helped me, so I'm going to help you. Is there any way we can get to your car without being seen?"

A small smile began to work its way across Asiri's face. She nodded. "Of course, there is."

"Okay. How do we get to the car?"

"We won't be going to the car," Asiri said. "The car will be coming to us. I'm sure the entrance will be watched, but if you can give me enough time, then I can get my forge."

"Then, let's go get it," Thyra said.

"Bragi won't like this," Asiri said cautiously.

"Like you said, we can't let Surtur's men have your forge," Thyra said. "I think it's better to ask for forgiveness than to wait for permission in this case."

A smile split Asiri's face. "I like you more and more, Sparks."

The dwarf gathered up the rest of her things and headed for the door.

Thyra put her backpack on and then followed the dwarf towards the stairs. Asiri hurried down the stairs and then burst through the doors into the front lobby. She gave a wink to the clerk behind the desk as she crossed the lobby to the front doors.

"Now, we wait," Asiri said as she pulled the Camaro's key fob out of her pocket and held it at the ready.

"What are we waiting for?"

"Vidar's distraction," Asiri said.

"We're supposed to be at the back door when that happens," Thyra reminded Asiri in a soft voice.

"We will be when it's time," Asiri said. "You just keep a close eye out."

The hotel clerk looked up at them and smiled, and Thyra returned the smile the best she could. She looked around the small lobby and realized that the clerk wasn't the only one who had taken notice of them. Two thick, suited men jerked to attention, and although they tried to hide their interest, Thyra felt their eyes on her.

"I don't think all of the thugs are outside," Thyra said carefully.

"Of course, they aren't," Asiri said without looking. "When things start happening, just be sure to give me enough time to grab my forge."

"It might help if you told me what your plan is," Thyra whispered.

"Simple," Asiri said. "Get my forge, stay away from the apes in suits, and get to Vidar's truck."

"I think there's a lot of details between all of that," Thyra muttered.

"Shhh!" Asiri said. "Get ready. I think this is it."

Thyra looked out the glass doors just in time to see a black SUV flip through the air and land on its hood. A moment later, a second one went sideways across the parking lot, brakes squealing, until it was forcibly wrapped around a light post. Thyra saw a dark shadow rip off one of the doors and throw a suited figure through the air like a ragdoll.

"Effective," Asiri said. She mashed on the key fob and Thyra heard the Camaro's engine roar to life. "See to our two friends and I'll grab my forge."

Asiri started for the doors as the Camaro rolled forward. Thyra spun around just as the two thugs got to their feet.

"Get the old woman!" One of them shouted.

Tasers appeared in their hands and they charged in unison. Thyra took a hesitant step back when she saw the weapons, the electricity snapping, but then she remembered something—she had a bigger one!

"Lynnedslag!"

Lightning sprang to life at the end of the lacrosse stick and both men stopped cold.

"What the—?"

A standoff ensued as the two thugs stared at her in shock and Thyra tried to decide what to do next. One of the thugs put up a hand, all the time eyeing the lightning crackling at the end of Lynnedslag. "Put the...the stick down girl."

"Get out of our way and you won't get hurt," Thyra said.

"That isn't going to happen," the thug said. "Do this the easy way and come quietly."

Thyra shook her head. "We're leaving."

"Will you just zap them and be done with it?" Asiri's voice called out.

Thyra looked over her shoulder and saw the dwarf hustling in her direction, metal briefcase in hand. When she turned back one of the thugs had taken advantage and was lunging for her. She reacted out of instinct and threw her arm out defensively. Her palm connected with his chest just before he wrapped his arms around her, and his body went rigid as her magic raced through him. She cut off the flow and he slumped to the ground.

"Frank!" The other thug shouted. He looked at Thyra, his eyes wide.

"What did you do to him?"

"Exactly what you were going to do to her," Asiri said. "Finish him off, Thyra, and let's get going."

The thug looked between them and then bolted suddenly towards the rear of the hotel. He was nearly out of view when Thyra recovered enough to realize she couldn't let him get away. She chased after him and turned down the hallway. Imagining she was on the lacrosse field, she brought Lynnedslag back and whipped it forward like she was scoring a goal. A bolt of lightning flashed through the air and flew true, connecting with the center of his back. The thug was launched off his feet onto his face and then spasmed on the ground briefly before lying still.

"Alright, Sparks," Asiri called down the hall. "Time to go!"

Thyra hurried back down the hall and followed Asiri toward the back of the hotel. They reached the backdoor, but Bragi was nowhere in sight. She scanned the parking lot, but there was no blue truck anywhere.

She was beginning to worry when she heard the squeal of tires and a blue truck tore around the side of the hotel. It came to a screeching stop in front of them and Bragi stuck his head out the window. "Get in!"

Thyra and Asiri hurried around to the passenger side and climbed in. Bragi stepped on the gas the moment the door was closed and peeled out of the parking lot.

"Where have you two been?" Bragi demanded, wide eyed.

Asiri held up her briefcase. "Getting my forge."

"Your forge?" Bragi's eyes went wide. "What do you mean 'your forge'?"

"You may not understand this, but no dwarf worth their salt would leave their forge behind without a fight," Asiri said. "All it took was a little distraction, and it was smooth sailing."

"What kind of distraction?" Bragi snapped.

"The kind Vidar provided," Asiri said. "Don't get yourself in a tizzy, Rune Tongue. It worked, I got my forge, and the girl took care of two thugs."

"I can't believe it!" Bragi said. "You risked everything to get your forge? How could you be so reckless?" He turned on Thyra. "And you! I can't believe you went along with it."

"I didn't go along with it," Thyra said defiantly. "It was my idea."

"What?" Bragi hissed. "How could you be so stupid?"

"We couldn't let Asiri's forge fall into their hands," Thyra said flatly.

"Yes, we could, if it meant getting away unseen!" Bragi bellowed.

"Oh, put a cork in it, Rune Tongue," Asiri said. "It worked out fine, and from what I can see, no one is following us. I'd say that was a successful escape. I don't like leaving my car behind, but it can take care of itself for now."

"Take care of itself?" Bragi said in confusion.

"I'd hate to be someone trying to steal it," Asiri let out a wicked cackle. "We're in the clear, Rune Tongue. That's all that matters."

Bragi didn't look convinced, but he didn't try to argue the point any further.

"So, how do we find Vidar?" Thyra asked after a tense silence. "Shouldn't we stay close so that he can catch up?"

"Don't worry girl," Asiri said. "I don't think this rust bucket can go fast enough for us to outrun him."

* * *

Vidar was five blocks away from the hotel when the first police car passed by, lights flashing and siren blaring. He could hear more sirens in the distance, but they were coming from behind him. It would be a long night trying to untangle the chaos in the hotel parking lot. Two flipped SUVs, another wrapped around a light post, and a half dozen apes in suits to question would keep them busy for some time.

The distraction he had created had been effective, but it had been made doubly so by something he hadn't expected. When the Camaro roared to life, he began to fear that the dwarf was more stubborn than he had thought. He had been surprised when the car rolled up to the doors, stopped briefly and then suddenly tore out of the parking lot. It had headed west, a fourth black SUV hot on its heels. The dwarf's ruse, however it was achieved, had proven deceptive enough to fool the driver and convince him to take up the chase even though no one was inside the car.

That removed two more of Gunnar's men from the equation, which left the two sitting in the lobby and the SUV parked on the backside of the building in addition to the four he had taken care of. He had guessed that as soon as there was action at the front of the hotel the SUV at the back would rush to help. He hadn't been disappointed. The SUV came roaring around the side and ran straight into him. It was going fast enough that all he had to do was lower his shoulder to send it flipping overhead.

Confident that the two men inside the vehicle were out of the fight, he had rushed into the lobby only to find both men already taken care of. He noticed singe marks on their suits but didn't take the time to study either one. He rushed to the back of the hotel and was relieved to see that his truck was gone.

Damage done, he ducked into the dark and hurried away from the hotel. He waited until he was sure no one was watching him, and then started running. Having the strength of a god meant more than just lifting vehicles overhead. It also meant that he could run at high speed and jump incredible distances. To the naked eye, he was little more than a fast-moving shadow in the dark. And thanks to the sneakers the dwarf had made for him, he was as silent as one, too.

His legs were a blur as he sped toward the edge of town. He kept one eye on the road in hopes of catching sight of his old blue truck, and finally was rewarded a few miles outside of town. He sped past and then stopped in the middle of the road under a streetlight. The truck slowed down and stopped short of where he stood, but he noticed that whoever was driving kept it in gear.

He walked up to the driver's side window and tapped on it. He wasn't surprised to see the old man behind the wheel. He waited for Bragi to roll the window down.

"No one is following," he stated.

"That's good," the old man said. He didn't make any move to put the truck into park.

"Are you going to let me get in?" Vidar asked.

"No one's stopping you," Bragi muttered.

"This is my truck," Vidar said. "I drive."

Bragi hesitated, but finally relented. He shifted the truck into park and got out.

"I'll ride shotgun, then," he said.

"No, you won't," Vidar said. "Thyra stays where she is. You can sit in the back with the dwarf."

Bragi's eyebrows dropped. He looked back at the tight quarters of the truck's cab and then back to Vidar. "Why?"

"Because it's my truck," Vidar said.

"I'll sit in the back," Thyra offered from the passenger seat. "Really, it's fine. Bragi can sit up here."

"No, Bragi is fine with sitting in the back," Vidar said. "I'm sure he'll appreciate the opportunity to rest after the excitement of the past few days."

Vidar knew he sounded harsh, but he didn't care. There was something in the old man's eyes that bothered him. He couldn't put his finger on it, but they seemed less alive than he remembered.

"Fine," Bragi said. "Thyra has longer legs. She's better suited to the front."

He moved around the truck and slid behind Thyra's seat. Vidar got into the driver's seat and put the truck into gear. He gave it some gas and continued out of the city.

"Where are we going?" Thyra asked.

"You said you think you had a piece of the Eye," Vidar said. "Where is it?"

Thyra held up her stuffed bear. "Right here."

Vidar gave her an incredulous look, but after a moment he could tell she was being serious. "I've seen crazier things, I guess. You're sure it's in there?"

Thyra nodded. "Asiri said it was protected by a strong spell."

"It's possible," Vidar said.

"Do you know how to break the spell?" Thyra asked hopefully.

"No," Vidar said.

"Then what are we supposed to do?" Thyra demanded.

Vidar had a sinking feeling in his stomach. He knew the answer, but he wasn't excited about the prospect of going *there*. He exhaled slowly. "I know where you need to go."

"Where do I need to go?" Thyra eyed him suspiciously.

"It's about two hours from here," Vidar said. "We will get there before the sun comes up, but we'll have to wait. It isn't a place you go in the dark of night."

"Why not?"

"It's haunted," Vidar said. "We'll need to stay off the highway. That's the first place they'll look for us. The frontage road will get us there just fine."

"Wait," Thyra said. "You can't just say 'it's haunted' and leave it there. What's it haunted by?"

Vidar's mind flashed back to a memory from several decades before.

He'd stumbled upon the place and its occupant by accident. He regretted it immediately, and he'd regretted it every day since.

"What's it haunted by?" Thyra asked again.

"A witch," Vidar answered. "The queen of all witches."

Chapter 21

Gunnar looked up from his tablet and the latest financial report as the wheels of his jet touched down in Madison, Wisconsin. It was dark outside still, a quick check of his watch showing that it was just past one in the morning.

Ivan jerked awake as the wheels squealed on the tarmac. The big Russian looked out the window and muttered something to himself in his native tongue. He stood up and headed for the mini bar at the back of the cabin and poured a cup of black coffee.

Unlike the big Russian, Gunnar hadn't slept during the flight from New York. His mind had been too occupied with grim thoughts. Not even the financial reports were enough to distract his mind. Things were spiraling wildly out of control. For someone who was used to being in complete command, the current situation was unacceptable. Between the failure to capture Thyra Ariksen and the concerns over what Baldur had planned, Gunnar felt more powerless than he had in centuries.

The news he had received mid-flight had only added to his frustrations. Four Muspel Corporation vehicles had been destroyed, and ten operatives sent to the hospital with serious injuries. There was no word on what had caused the destruction of the SUVs or the injuries to his men, but Gunnar had a guess. From the description of the damage, there was only one explanation—Luke Vincent, or Vidar, had finally broken their deal.

Gunnar shut the tablet and tossed it onto an unoccupied seat. Ivan sat down with his steaming cup of coffee and took a look sip.

"How did this all happen?" Gunnar asked out loud.

"You're sure it was Vincent that helped them escape?" Ivan asked.

Gunnar took a moment to think about how he wanted to answer. The Russian knew as much as anyone about the man known as Luke Vincent, but there were some things about the reclusive gym owner that Gunnar had kept from him. Ivan knew that Vidar had made a deal with Gunnar long ago, but the Russian didn't know the real reason why Gunnar had struck the deal. Gunnar had told Ivan that he allowed Vidar to live because he was not involved in the battle that claimed the lives of the gods, but the truth was something different. Gunnar knew that if Vidar had been there that day, his attack on the gods would have failed. Letting Vidar live in self-imposed exile was the only way Gunnar saw to keep him under control.

"It was him," Gunnar said. "The police may be confused, but there's no doubt in my mind what happened. SUVs flipped over, men thrown seventy feet through the air—there's no doubt Vidar was involved."

And his involvement angered Gunnar. He had honored his end of the bargain to this point by letting the former protector of the Aesir live in peace. Yes, he kept a close watch on him, but he had instructed his men to keep their distance. Gunnar wanted to keep tabs on him, the same way he had for nearly eight hundred years, but he had no desire to break the truce.

But Baldur had ruined it all by activating the operatives. Gunnar had spent the first half of the flight hoping that the damage could be contained, and that he could convince the disgraced god to still honor the deal. But when he learned about what happened at the hotel, he knew any chance of salvaging the deal was lost. Vidar had always been slow to anger, but once he reached his boiling point the only thing to be done was hope you weren't in his way. Baldur's actions had put Gunnar right in the middle of Vidar's path.

"What do we do now?" Ivan asked.

"We try to get ahead of Asmodeus," Gunnar said, shying away from using the man's true name. He couldn't shake the feeling that saying the name out loud somehow gave the man power.

"Do you have a plan?"

"Are you still tracking their movements?" Gunnar asked.

Ivan nodded. He reached into his suit coat pocket and pulled out his phone. "They are moving east. They are out in the middle of farmland. The signals go in and out of service, but they are still together."

Gunnar was glad at least one thing was working the way it was supposed to. Being the CEO of a massive corporation that maintained a massive telecom infrastructure had its benefits.

"Good," Gunnar said. "I have a feeling that they will work themselves to Hela. We will go to the town—Monroe? —and wait for them there."

"And, if they don't go to Monroe?"

Gunnar turned in his seat and looked back at the fifteen men wearing specialized tactical gear. They were the finest of Ivan's men, and were equipped with the finest weapons created thus far by the Odin Initiative. Weapons powerful enough to take down even a god.

"They will come to us," Gunnar said, "or we will track them down wherever they are and put an end to all of this."

Chapter 22

The sun was just beginning to rise when Vidar turned down a dirt road a dozen miles east of a place called Eau Claire. After spending the two-hour ride in silence, they had spent another three hours waiting in some dive with bad food and watered-down drinks. The poor fare only made the wait that much more unbearable and put Thyra on the verge of exploding. She was about to lose her cool when Vidar finally gave them the okay to get back in the truck and head to their destination.

"What are we going to find?" Thyra asked as they bounced along the road.

"That depends on what you're looking for," Vidar said.

Thyra rolled her eyes. "How do I know you're not just driving out into the woods and wasting our time?"

He shrugged his huge shoulders. "You don't."

"Bragi said that my mom trusted you," Thyra said. She saw Vidar flinch at the mention of Sif, which made her wonder again about the nature of their relationship all those years ago. That was a conversation for another time, though. "I want to trust you, too. But you're not giving me a whole lot to work off of."

Vidar shrugged again. "You wanted my help, and this is the only way I can think of to help. You'll just have to wait and decide for yourself if it's worth the time."

Thyra sighed. "You aren't very easy to talk to, you know that?"

"Then stop trying," Vidar grumbled.

He made a turn down a dirt road that was so overgrown Thyra never would have guessed it was there. Vidar drove at what felt like a crawl towards a thick grove of trees about a quarter mile ahead of them.

"I think I could walk faster than you're driving," she grumbled.

"You're welcome to get out anytime," Vidar replied in a similar tone.

"No one is getting out and walking," Bragi said. "We're almost there, Thyra. Don't lose patience now."

"I lost patience back at the diner," Thyra snapped.

Bragi ignored her. "You said a witch lives here. What's her name?"

Vidar shrugged. "Never asked. She made it clear that she wanted to be left alone."

"You said she was the queen of all witches," Bragi pressed. "What did you mean by that?"

"Exactly what I said," Vidar said. "She's powerful, and very temperamental."

"Do you have a guess as to who she truly is?" Bragi asked.

Vidar looked at him in the rear-view mirror. "All I know is that she wanted to be left alone almost as much as I did. We were both glad when she sent me on my way. If you're so interested in finding out who she is, then be my guest and spend the rest of the day wandering around in her woods. I have no intention of spending any more time in these trees than I have to."

Bragi looked like he wanted to push for a straight answer, but he relented with a sigh. Vidar returned his attention to the road, but his face spoke volumes. He drove on for a few more minutes before bringing the truck to a stop at the edge of the trees even though the road continued.

"Why are we stopping here?" Thyra asked.

"We go the rest of the way by foot," Vidar said, opening his door.

"The witch knows we're here. She'll find us if she thinks we're worth talking to."

"And if not?" Thyra asked.

"Then she'll send us on our way," Vidar said. He got out of the truck, but hesitated at the door and looked back in. "Bring the bear."

Thyra cast a suspicious look towards Bragi, who shrugged. She picked up the stuffed animal and then got out of the truck. She waited until Bragi and Asiri got out before moving to follow Vidar. He wove his way through the trees with no clear destination in mind. Every time Thyra felt she knew where they were heading, he would suddenly turn.

After several sudden changes in direction, Thyra couldn't keep silent. "Do you know where you're going?"

"I'm guessing you haven't dealt with many witches," Vidar said.

"I haven't had the pleasure," Thyra said, sarcasm dripping from her voice.

"I wouldn't call it a pleasure, meeting a witch," Vidar said. He stopped and looked up at the canopy overhead. "This forest is enchanted. It fools with the mind and shifts without reason."

"It *shifts*?"

Vidar nodded. He gestured towards the trees all around them. "Pick a destination, focus on it, and then try walking towards it."

"What?" Thyra didn't make a move. "Why?"

"Trust try it and see," Vidar said.

"I don't think that's a good idea," Bragi said. "Vidar is right about witch magic, and I won't risk Thyra getting lost in the forest."

"Then stay close," Vidar said, again giving Bragi an icy look. The two stared daggers at each other for a moment before Bragi relented. Vidar turned back to Thyra. "Consider this a learning experience. We'll follow you."

Thyra looked around. "Just pick a destination and start walking

238

towards it?"

"That's right."

"Fine," Thyra said. A dark, gnarled tree caught her eye and she figured it was as good of a destination as any. She started walking towards and the others fell in behind her. She was halfway there when she took her eyes off the tree for a split second to step over a fallen log. When she looked up again, the tree wasn't there. She stopped in her tracks and looked around. The tree she had set her mind on was nowhere to be seen.

"Where did it go?"

Vidar stopped next to her and offered a simple explanation. "Witch magic."

"How are we supposed to find anything then?" Thyra asked.

"We don't," Vidar said. "The witch will find us."

"We don't have time for this!" Thyra snapped. "We can't spend hours wandering in circles. My mom needs my help."

"Then stop trying to get somewhere," Vidar said.

"What?"

Bragi stepped up around Vidar. "I fear Vidar is right. There is no avoiding it. The witch will find us, we won't find her."

"Then, please, someone else lead!" Thyra said, her frustration rising with each heartbeat.

Vidar shook his head. "You're the one who has the greatest need. It's you the witch will respond to."

"My need?" Thyra said, receiving a nod from both men. Asiri shrugged her shoulders, offering no help. Thyra turned and looked at the forest. "Fine. I can't stay here, so what I *need* right now is to get somewhere. Any direction is better than standing here."

She set off in a huff, letting the other three decide if they would follow or not. At that moment, she didn't care if they all got lost as long as she got somewhere.

Thyra tried to do what Vidar and Bragi had told her, letting her need guide her. She walked with no real destination, picking her path at random. The other three stuck with her, but she noticed that with each change in direction they fell a little further behind. Vidar had forced himself in front of Bragi and seemed to be taking pleasure from being in the old man's way. Thyra didn't know why they both enjoyed needling each other so much, but their pettiness was getting old.

She had just made another change in direction when she felt a subtle change in the air. She was surprised to see a small cabin through the trees ahead of her. She turned around to say something to the others, but the words died before passing her teeth. They weren't behind her. She scanned the trees, sure she would see them coming along between the trees, but she didn't see any sign of them.

A chill ran down her spine. They were just behind her—where could they have gone?

"Your friends won't be joining us," a female voice said behind her.

Thyra spun around, calling up her magic out of instinct, and holding Lynnedslag out in front of her. She was shocked to see a middle-aged woman standing calmly a dozen feet away. Chestnut colored hair was pulled back from a face that was mature but still full of youth. Thyra remembered seeing the same ageless characteristic in Hela's face and guessed that this woman was none other than the witch Vidar had been talking about.

"I felt it best if we talked alone," the woman continued. "Don't worry, your friends are safe. They just took a wrong turn. I will take you back to them when we are finished."

"You're the witch," Thyra said.

The woman smiled ruefully. "That's true, although I've never found that term to be very endearing. Too many people were called that name and then met their deaths in very painful, barbaric ways."

Thyra stayed in a ready position, and her wariness didn't go

240

unnoticed.

"You can release your magic, Thyra Ariksen," the woman said. "I mean you no harm."

"You know my name," Thyra stated. Somehow, she knew that the witch would.

"I know more about you than that," the woman said.

"Which is why I think I'll hold onto my magic," Thyra said stubbornly. "You say you know me, but I know nothing about you. I'm at a disadvantage and letting go of my magic will only make my situation worse."

The witch smirked. "Fair enough. But, if not for my sake, release your magic for that poor bear's."

Thyra looked down at the bear and cursed when she saw that the brown fur was turning black around her hand. She quickly released her magic, but grimaced when she saw the damage that she'd done. As much as she hated to admit it, seeing what she had done to her old friend made her eyes well up with angry tears.

"That's better," the witch said. "I'm sure you have questions. Follow me to my home and you can ask them."

The witch turned and began walking towards the cabin. Thyra hesitated, giving the forest one last look in hopes of catching a glimpse of the other three, but true to the witch's word, they were still nowhere to be seen. She reluctantly followed the witch to her cabin.

The witch held the door open for Thyra with a smile. Thyra noticed for the first time the witch's clothing—a pair of jeans, a flannel shirt, and a pair of hiking boots. She even had a faint woodsy smell that completed her earthy look. She looked like she had stepped out of an outdoor magazine advertisement.

"Come in, and make yourself at home," the witch said, gesturing towards a small table with two steaming mugs of tea.

"I think I'll stand," Thyra said.

"You don't like tea?" The witch asked. She took a seat and swept a hand over the mug across from her. It shimmered briefly and then a cup of orange juice sat in its place. "Perhaps that will be more appealing. There are muffins on the counter. Help yourself."

Thyra stayed in place. "Who are you?"

"I'm the witch," the woman said with a coy smile. She took a sip of her tea and then set the mug back down. "I've been called by many names, but I won't waste our time together hiding behind any false names. My mother named me Frigg and that was the name my people knew me by, but you probably know me better by the name I was given by my husband after we married."

"What name would that be?"

"Freya," the witch replied.

Thyra's mouth went dry. That wasn't one of the names she had even considered possible.

"From the look on your face, you recognize my name," Freya said.

Thyra nodded. "You were Odin's wife."

"And the mother of Thor," Freya said. "Which, believe it or not, makes you my granddaughter."

Thyra was shocked by the revelation, but not enough to overcome her wariness. She wasn't going to fall to pieces at the unexpected reunion. She was beginning to see that her family ties were not traditional in any manner of speaking, and more often than not, involved dangerous dynamics.

"You don't look happy to hear that," Freya said.

"I'm learning to be cautious," Thyra said. "Maybe I should be running to give you a hug, but the last few days have left me feeling low on trust for people who show up out of the blue. Especially ones with magic."

"That's smart of you," Freya said. "Unfortunately, in our world, you can never be sure who is and who isn't on your side."

Thyra stood silent for a moment as she came to a decision on what to do next. Part of her was excited to meet her grandmother face to face, but it was drowned out by a voice that asked where Freya had been the last sixteen years of her life. Clearly, Freya wasn't all that interested in a strong family bond.

"If you're Freya," Thyra asked, "how are you still alive?"

"I'm sure you know about Iduun's fruit?" Freya said.

Thyra nodded. "I do, but I was told that Ragnarök claimed the lives of most of the gods. Yours included."

"It almost did, and I was content to let the world think it had," Freya said. "When our home fell, I wanted to stay and fight, but now I am glad I didn't. If I had, I would have died with the others. I had a reason to live, and so I ran from the fight. I've spent the long centuries hiding, no one knowing who I truly am."

"How did you come here?" Thyra asked.

Freya motioned to the chair across from her and Thyra grudgingly sat down. Freya took another sip from her tea and then answered the question. "Just like so many others, America promised a new start. A chance to escape the dangers of the old world." She met Thyra's eyes and held her gaze. "But, more importantly, I came here because of you and your mother."

"What about me and my mother?"

"Has Bragi told you that your mother slept for nearly a thousand years?"

Thyra nodded. "He called it the Vanir Sleep."

"That's right," Freya said. "It was a tool of my people—the Vanir. The magic of the Vanir was intimately attuned to nature, unlike Odin's tribe, the Aesir, whose magic was only used to wage war. Many of the Aesir called my people's magic witchcraft, but even the Allfather used the Vanir Sleep when the toll of the years became too much." Freya grimaced. "The Aesir got all the glory, but it was the magic of the Vanir that was the true power behind the gods. It was my people who made the crops grow, who blessed women during childbirth, and calmed the seas to ensure safe passage of boats. The Vanir manipulated nature for the benefit of man while the Aesir fought the wars."

Thyra shrugged. "You don't need to convince me."

"Don't I?" Freya asked, arching an eyebrow. "You take after them, Thyra. You are your father's daughter, which means you are a force of destruction. I wish that you were like me, in touch with the natural world that surrounds you, a bringer of peace, not death. But you are what you are. I cannot change your nature any more than you can change the nature that surrounds you."

"Lightning is a force of nature," Thyra said.

Freya nodded. "It is, but it only destroys. It is the rain and wind in the storm that create life."

Thyra was in no mood to argue with a thousand-year old witch. "What does all this have to do with me and my mom?"

"And you're impatient like your father," Freya commented. She took a sip of her tea and then answered. "Your father saw the end of the Aesir coming and asked me to find a way to protect your mother. The only way to do that was to put your mother to sleep. He asked me not to wake her until the time was right—when I was confident that she would be safe."

"And the time was right sixteen years ago?" Thyra asked.

"That's right," Freya said. "Although, it wasn't me that woke your mother. It was you."

"Me?"

Freya nodded. "I don't think your mother even knew she was carrying you until just before I put her to sleep. When I told them, your father made me promise to keep you both safe, no matter the cost. As painful as it was to see him fall to Surtur's men, I kept the promise I made to him." Freya paused and looked out the window.

Thyra could see the pain in Freya's eyes, and when she looked back, they glistened with unshed tears. "And now, you're here."

"So, you watched over my mom while she was in the Vanir Sleep?" Thyra asked. "For almost eight hundred years?"

Freya nodded. "I did. I kept her safe until you woke her again."

"How did I wake her?"

"You decided to enter the world," Freya said. "You grew slowly during the Vanir Sleep, but when you were ready, you came without warning. You knew when you would be needed."

"Needed for what?"

"To shape an age of man," Freya said. "The ages of men are circular Thyra. I've seen it many times in my life. Magic always plays a part in those cycles—waxing and waning in varying degrees. Every time, there is a hinge point where the cycle ends and begins anew. I feel that we're close to one such hinge point."

"What does that have to do with me?"

Freya looked at the teddy bear in Thyra's hand. Her eyes lingered on the stuffed animal long enough for Thyra to know it was no coincidence.

"The influence of magic is on a pendulum, swinging back and forth," Freya said, her gaze slowly coming back to Thyra's face. "Yggdrasil chose Odin to be its champion long ago, and for centuries, our magic—both Vanir and Aesir—grew stronger. But then the pendulum swung the other direction when Surtur attacked and began his war against magic. For too long, the pendulum has remained far to one side and the world has grown unbalanced. Mankind has grown powerful in magic's absence, but it has also grown jaded and drunk on that very power while the world of magic has remained in the shadows. I sense the pendulum is finally swinging back, and you are at the center of what is coming. You will force that pendulum to swing back towards balance."

"And become what?" Thyra asked. "A god?"

"If that is what is required of you," Freya said grimly.

Thyra shook her head. "No. I'm no god, and I don't want to be."

"Do you have a choice?" Freya asked. "You were born with magic, and now that you've learned to use it, you will never be able to stop." Freya sipped at her tea again, letting her words hang heavy in the air. "You have the power of a god. I can feel it raging inside of you. You may be able to keep it hidden for a time, but not forever. Even now, you bring change."

"What kind of change?"

"I heard word of a lightning storm west of here," Freya said. "Somewhere in North Dakota. All the news stations were talking about it. It even got the attention of the national news. Their explanation was a strange mix of atmospheric pressures that led to the storm. As for why it was so intense and concentrated, the only answer they gave, and I quote, 'a once in a lifetime phenomenon.'" Freya paused and watched Thyra's reaction. "Maybe you could offer a different one?"

Thyra grimaced. "Weather can be strange."

Freya nodded knowingly. "I didn't think so. What about what is being called a freak power surge in Wyoming? Small, but it left scorch marks alongside a rural road. A farmer heard what sounded like a transformer exploding, but there wasn't one anywhere nearby, and the electrical company said there was no damage to their infrastructure and no sign of a power surge in the area. What would you call that? Another freak occurrence?"

"I get it," Thyra said. "I've left some calling cards."

"You've done more than that," Freya said sharply. She shook her head. "There will be no hiding for you. Not now. You are forcing the world of magic into the light and I don't think there is anything you can do to stop, no matter how hard you try." Her gaze went to the bear in Thyra's hand. "Especially since you carry a shard of the Eye of

Odin."

Thyra gripped her bear tighter. "How did you know I had one?"

Freya looked up and met Thyra's eyes. "Because, I put it there."

"You put the shard in my bear?" Thyra gripped the stuffed animal harder. "Why?"

"To protect you," Freya said.

"Protect me? This shard is the reason everything bad has happened to me over the last few days," Thyra said. "If you were trying to protect me by putting the shard in my bear, you did a terrible job of it."

"Yet, it succeeded in holding off your awakening until you were ready," Freya said. "If your magic had awoken too soon you would have been in great danger. We knew the shard would attract trouble at some point, but we hoped that it would give you time to grow into your power before that trouble arrived. From what I can see, it did."

"Who is 'we'?" Thyra had a suspicion, but she wanted to hear it from Freya.

"Your mother and I," Freya said. "Sif knew the dangers you might face, and she asked me to do what I could to give her time to prepare you. The shard was the answer."

"And you just happened to have a shard of the Eye of Odin sitting around?" Thyra asked.

"Yes," Freya said. Her expression changed, and for a brief moment the ageless quality fell away. She looked tired and old. "That was the other reason I forced myself into hiding from the world. The Eye had to be protected."

"I was told that Thor destroyed the Eye."

Freya shook her head. "He thought he could, and he made a valiant but foolish effort. He lacked understanding of what the Eye was. You cannot destroy a talisman like the Eye. All he did was temporarily make it unusable. And he paid the price for it."

Freya's eyes grew distant for a moment. When she refocused, her jaw set firmly, and her eyes took on a hard edge. "I took the shard after your father tried to destroy the Eye. There was not enough time to gather all the pieces, but I knew that I had to keep as much away from Surtur as I could."

"Did you take more than just the one shard?" Thyra asked.

Freya hesitated, but finally nodded. "Yes."

Thyra gaped. "Where is the rest of it?"

"Safe," Freya said. Thyra began to speak but Freya cut her off. "I know what you're going to ask and why you would ask it of me, but first, I must know, what would you do with the Eye?"

"Hela has my mom," Thyra said. Freya's features tightened, but that was the extent of her reaction to the revelation. "She said that she would let my mom go in exchange for the shard."

"And you would simply give it to her, knowing what she might be capable of with it?" Freya asked.

"Honestly, I don't know what she'd be capable of because I don't even really know what it does," Thyra said. "But, to get my mom back, yes, I'd hand it over in a heartbeat."

Freya inhaled deeply. "Hela was always troublesome. If she gets enough of the Eye, she would become very dangerous."

"Do I have a choice?" Thyra said.

"You always have a choice."

Thyra shook her head. "Not when my mom's life is on the line."

Freya inhaled deeply. "So, you would give Hela the shard?"

Thyra nodded. "If you can help me remove it from my bear."

"I can," Freya said. "And I will. The shard is yours by right."

That made Thyra hesitate. "Why do you say that?"

"It was Odin's burden, and should have been Thor's but he refused to carry it," Freya said. "Since the rightful heir refused to take it up, the Eye falls would pass to his offspring. I sense Yggdrasil's touch on you, which means you are the one the tree has chosen. I can't say I'm surprised, considering how the others turned out."

"The others?"

Freya ignored the question. "Let me make this clear—once you have the Eye, I want nothing more to do with it or what you plan to do with it. I was the queen of the gods long ago, and that life nearly killed me. I have no ambition to be at the forefront of this war. Once the Eye is in your hand, I am done with it and you as long as you carry it."

"Fine," Thyra said. The finality of Freya's words stung, but not enough to cut her. She had only known Freya for a few minutes—moving on without the former queen of the gods wouldn't change anything on Thyra's part. "Help me get the shard, and then I'll be on my way."

Freya nodded. "Give me the bear."

Thyra handed it over and watched as Freya waved her hand over the bear's face, her lips moving silently. Freya's hand began to shimmer as her magic gathered and her eyes turned a milky white. Her lips stopped moving suddenly and she extended her hand towards Thyra.

"Hold out your hand, Thyra."

Thyra obeyed and watched as Freya began to mutter to herself again. Thyra felt a pulsing energy coming from Freya's outstretched hand that steadily grew in intensity until it began to be uncomfortable. She grimaced as the discomfort grew to an ache, and then suddenly a sharp pain. She pulled her hand back and brought it to her chest with a gasp.

Across from her, Freya sat back in her chair and sighed. Her eyes returned to their normal hazel color as her magic faded. "You have what you came for."

Thyra cast a confused look in her direction, but then she felt something hard inside her closed fist. She turned her hand over and slowly opened it. A jagged blue stone bathed in blue flames rested in her hand!

She gaped openly. "This was what was inside the bear all this time?"

"No, the shard inside the bear was only a small one," Freya said.

"That is all the pieces of the Eye I managed to recover before Surtur's men overran Odin's Hall. It's most of the Eye."

"Most of it?"

"I had to leave some pieces behind to occupy Surtur long enough for me to escape," Freya explained. "If I had tried to gather all the pieces, I never would have escaped Surtur."

Thyra looked up. "But, why is it on fire if it isn't whole? And why isn't it an orb?"

"Just because it isn't physically whole doesn't mean it's magic is lost," Freya said. "Magic like that can't be destroyed, something your father either didn't know or chose to ignore. It may not be complete, but the connection to Yggdrasil remains. As for its shape, the magic of the Eye determined how the shards came together, not me."

Thyra looked at the Eye in awe. "But, why are you giving it to me? All I asked for was a shard."

"It's yours by birth," Freya replied, but Thyra could tell was more to it.

"You were the queen of the gods and have protected it for centuries—why are you giving it to me? I know next to nothing about all of this. Wouldn't it be safer with you?"

"Because I cannot be its caretaker any longer," Freya said. She looked at the Eye with contempt. "That stone has been my curse ever since Odin found it, and it has brought me nothing but pain. Because of it, I was forced to leave my people, and live among a people who held little love for me. Then I was forced to watch as my husband used the Eye to wage countless wars. It changed him, blinded him, and it eventually caused the downfall of everything he had used it to build." Freya shook her head and met Thyra's gaze. "I want nothing to do with that cursed thing. I'm tired of feeling its presence, always lurking in the shadows of my mind, its whispers always sneaking into my thoughts. I kept it safe long enough. Now it's your burden."

"My burden?" Thyra's eyes went wide. "What am I supposed to do with it? I'm sixteen! Give it to someone else. Someone wiser, like Bragi, or even Vidar—not me!"

Freya was shaking her head before Thyra finished. "It's your burden now. You are the daughter of Thor, the granddaughter of Odin. It is both your birthright and your burden. Odin tried to hoard it and your father tried to destroy it. Maybe you will be different."

Thyra didn't like the sound of that statement, but she didn't voice her concerns.

"Whatever path you follow, the Eye is yours now," Freya said.

"Is that it then?" Thyra asked. She closed her hand around the Eye, feeling its jagged edges against her palm. "Give me the Eye and send me on my way?"

"I've kept it safe," Freya said, "but it was never meant for me."

"I don't know how to keep it safe," Thyra argued. "I can't walk around with it in my hand for the entire world to see!"

"No, that wouldn't be smart," Freya said.

Thyra waited for something more, but Freya didn't offer anything. "You aren't being very helpful."

"You have what you came for," Freya said. "You have the Eye. Now you can trade it for your mother's life or choose not to. Do what you will. It doesn't matter to me."

Thyra was stunned. "You're just going to send me away without giving me any advice on how to keep safe something you've spent eight hundred years protecting?"

"It's yours now," Freya said. "You will find a way. Or you won't."

Thyra gaped at the woman. She didn't understand why Freya was so cold. No, not cold—heartless!

"Is this how you thought it would go?" Freya asked suddenly.

Thyra didn't understand what Freya was referring to. "Getting the Eye?"

"No, I'm sure that part of our visit was beyond anything you expected," Freya conceded in a grim voice. She took a deep breath and let it out slowly. "I've waited sixteen years for the day you'd show up at my door, always hoping for one thing, but knowing that it may never be possible. Now that you're here, I feel that I am making a mess of all of this."

Thyra couldn't keep her frustration inside. "You think?"

Freya flinched and then sighed. "I can do nothing more for you. Please go. I'm sure Bragi is about to tear this forest apart looking for you. If I don't return you to them soon, he may just try."

Thyra rose to her feet, still feeling confused by everything that had just happened. The witch had turned out to be her grandmother, but Freya was not like any of the grandmothers Thyra had imagined up for herself over the years.

"Don't judge me too harshly," Freya said, her expression conflicted. "Perhaps all these years of being alone have turned me into the witch everyone says I am. If nothing else, I hope you understand what I went through during Ragnarök." She shook her head, her eyes haunted. "I would rather live the rest of my life alone than go through that again."

"Well, you're doing a great job of making sure that happens," Thyra said.

Freya flinched again, but her cold demeanor came back to the surface in an instant. She rose to her feet. "It's time you returned to your friends."

"I couldn't agree more," Thyra said, already heading for the door. She pushed through and out into the cool Wisconsin morning air. She walked a few feet and then stopped, realizing she didn't know what way to go. She turned and raised her eyebrows at Thyra. "You mind pointing me in the right direction?"

"Just start walking," Freya said.

"Fine," Thyra grumbled.   She gave the woman—her grandmother—one last reproving glare. "It was a real treat meeting you. I can't say I hope we cross paths again."

Thyra stormed off, her hands clenched tightly at her sides. The Eye dug into her hand painfully, but she was too angry to care. She passed a carefully stacked pile of wood and her temper boiled over. She called up her magic and extended her arm towards the stack, a bolt of lightning jumping from her fist. The pile of wood blew apart, sending pieces flying high into the air in every direction.

Satisfied with her display, no matter how petulant it was, Thyra continued walking. She reached the edge of the trees around Freya's cabin and stepped back into the forest. She felt something shift behind her, and she turned around. She wasn't surprised to see the cabin was no longer there. Freya had given her what she came for, and now she was done with her.

Shaking her head, Thyra started walking again. She heard the sound of Bragi arguing with Vidar ahead and headed towards it.

The sooner they got out of this cursed forest and away from the witch's domain, the better.

Chapter 23

"This is your fault!" Bragi was shouting into Vidar's face when Thyra came within eyesight.

Vidar looked down at Bragi with a neutral expression, but his fists were clenched at his sides. "I don't control the witch or her magic."

"No, but you lagged behind on purpose," Bragi said firmly. "You put Thyra at risk. We were here to protect her, and you intentionally allowed us to get separated."

"There is nothing in this forest that you can protect her from," Vidar said. "If the witch meant her harm, she would do it."

Bragi shook a finger under Vidar's nose, but his protest was cut short when he noticed Thyra step into the clearing.

"Thyra!" Bragi said. "What were you thinking running ahead like that? You should have waited for the rest of us."

"She isn't a child," Vidar said.

"But she is a child in her understanding of magic," Bragi countered.

"Not from what I've seen," Vidar said.

Bragi turned on him. "What would you know? The Eye didn't give you magic, it just changed your anatomy to make you stronger."

"A form of magic," Vidar said. "I may not waive my hands and shoot lightning, but I know enough to judge her strength. No matter what you think, she's not a child."

The two men might have argued all day with neither one giving an inch, but Thyra didn't have time to let them go at each other. She had the Eye and now she needed to free her mom.

"I'm fine, Bragi," she said. "Vidar was right. I needed to face the witch alone. She didn't want to hurt me. All she wanted was to talk."

Bragi took a deep breath and let it out slowly. "Well, I guess there's no changing what has happened. What did you find?"

"The witch gave me what I came for," Thyra said. "She gave me the shard. And more."

She raised her hand and opened it, bathing the clearing in the light from the blue flames ringing the Eye. Bragi's eyes went wide.

"That's more than a shard," Bragi gaped. "She gave you the entire Eye?"

"Not all of it," Thyra said. "But, enough to make it work, apparently."

"Give it to me," Bragi said, holding out his hand.

Thyra's eyes narrowed and she pulled her hand back. There was a hunger in Bragi's eyes that made the hairs on her arms stand on end. She remembered the warning Yggdrasil had given her, but she had thought the tree was referring to Vidar.

"If the witch wanted you to have it, she would have given it to you," Vidar said, moving into Bragi's way.

The hunger in Bragi's eyes disappeared and he shrugged. "I just want to help her keep it safe. She can't go around with it in her hand."

"If you know of a way, you can tell her," Vidar said. "You're a teacher, aren't you? Teach, don't show."

"That's not how it works," Bragi grumbled.

"Then find a way to make it work," Vidar said.

Bragi looked ready to argue, but he finally relented. He looked at Thyra. "Odin had a trick for hiding the Eye when he needed to. It's a simple magic, tied to the Eye itself. Hold out your hand, palm up, and say, *inn i skygenne*."

"*Inn i skygenne?*" Thyra repeated. The moment the words left her mouth she felt the Eye pulse in her hand. The flames around the Eye flared outward and then the Eye seemed to condense down into itself until it disappeared with a pop.

"Where did it go?" Thyra asked, panic coursing through her. She had just barely gotten it, and now it was gone!

Bragi shrugged. "I'm not entirely sure. Odin only said it was what Yggdrasil told him to do. He got the impression that the Eye was returned to the tree's keeping until he called for it again."

"How do I get it back?" Thyra asked.

"When you want to summon it say, *inn i lyset*," Bragi said.

Thyra repeated the words in a rush and was relieved when the Eye reappeared in her hand, blue flames snapping at the air. She let out the breath she had been holding.

"Had us worried there for a minute," Asiri grumbled, giving Bragi a reproving stare. "Next time, explain what's going to happen first so we don't think the girl sent the Eye on a direct trip to oblivion."

Bragi's eyes went wide. "Don't blame me. I was *showing* her how to keep it safe. Besides, if she has indeed been chosen to be the Eye's keeper, the keywords will only work for her. Do you really think I'd put all this at risk now?"

"You could have explained it before," Asiri said. "Maybe save us all a heart attack."

"It's safe for now," Thyra said, closing her fist around the Eye protectively. "We need to get on the road. I got what I came for. Now, I just want to get away from this place and the witch."

Thyra turned and began to work her way back to the truck. As she expected, it didn't take long before the edge of the trees and Vidar's truck came into sight. It seemed Freya was just as anxious to have them gone as Thyra was to leave.

She reached the truck first and waited for the others to catch up. From the stormy look on Bragi's face and the way Vidar was clenching his fists, it was clear that words had been exchanged on the walk out.

Thyra waited for Bragi and Asiri to get in and then climbed in herself. She set Lynnedslag across her lap as Vidar started up the truck and put it into gear.

"Do you know where you're going?" Thyra asked.

"Away from here," Vidar said. "Gunnar Olafsson, Hela, Fenrir—they will not stop looking for you now that you have the Eye. We need to go somewhere they wouldn't expect and wait things out. When it's safe, we make our move."

Thyra shook her head. "That isn't going to work. We can't afford to wait things out."

"Why not?"

"Because," Thyra said, "we need to go to a city called Monroe. And we have to go there now."

Vidar closed his eyes and let out a tense breath. "Why do we need to go to Monroe?"

"I have to deliver it to Fenrir and Hela," Thyra said. "Hela said that if I want to free my mom, I need to give her the Eye."

Vidar opened his eyes and looked at her. "How did they get Sif?"

"Hela and Fenrir came to our house," Thyra explained. "She wanted the shard, but before she could get it a bunch of men from the Muspel Corporation showed up. She told Bragi and I to run. I shouldn't have left her, but I did. She was hurt, and Hela took her. She said she'd let her go in return for the shard."

Vidar shook his head. "I can't let you give it to Hela. You'd be making a catastrophic mistake."

"What other choice do I have?" Thyra asked.

"How about not giving it to her?"

Thyra shook her head. "That isn't an option. I'm not going to abandon my mom. It's my fault she's in this mess, and I am going to get her back."

"By giving the eye to Hela?" Vidar asked.

"If that's what it takes," Thyra nodded, "then yes, I will."

"Even if that means you put her right back in danger?" Vidar asked grimly. "Because that is exactly what will happen. If Hela has the Eye—not just a shard—Sif won't be safe. None of us will be."

"I'll protect her," Thyra said firmly. "All that matters right now is that I save her. After that, I'll handle what comes when it comes."

Vidar snorted angrily and stared straight ahead. "You do know what she'll do with it, don't you?"

"Of course, we do," Bragi said. "She'll wield the Eye's immense power and continue what she started. She'll force her extremism onto the world and put herself at the top of the power hierarchy."

"Extremism," Vidar repeated ruefully. He looked at Bragi in the rearview mirror. "Since when does wanting to protect yourself and those like you count as extreme?"

"When it involves subjugating others in the process," Bragi said.

"You never complained when it was Odin doing it," Vidar said grimly.

"Odin never subjugated the people," Bragi said sharply.

"What do you call forcing them to offer sacrifices for hundreds of years?" Vidar said in a bitter voice. "What about all the people who died with his name on their lips, believing that they were going to a life in paradise? He extorted and murdered all so that he could keep power."

"And your hands were some of the bloodiest," Bragi retorted.

"Enough arguing!" Thyra said before Vidar could speak. "I know that Hela will be able to do terrible things with the Eye, but all I care about is getting my mom back."

Vidar took a deep breath and returned his focus to Thyra. "You need to know that if Hela gets the Eye, an army of magic wielders will flock to her."

"What do you mean?" Thyra asked.

"For centuries, our kind of been forced to live in fear," Vidar said. "Practitioners of magic have been called witches and burned at the stake. They've been hunted by Surtur and those that think like him for centuries, afraid to fight back. How long can that continue? How long before they've had enough? If Hela gets the Eye and decides to enforce her will, there will be many who will rush to stand with her. She won't need an army made up of people she's collected from death's door, like Odin always thought she would try to build. She'll have an army of magic users at her back, and if she has the Eye, that army will be almost unstoppable."

"And you think she's already begun to gather support?" Bragi asked, suddenly interested.

"She's not stupid," Vidar replied. "You know how charismatic she is. If Odin hadn't grown jealous of her, she would have supplanted him at the head of the Aesir without a fight. She had supporters then, and she has them now."

"You sound like you know her plan a little too well," Bragi said. "Is there something you aren't telling us?"

Vidar's jaw clenched so hard that Thyra was sure she heard his teeth crunching.

"She came to me the day before you three showed up," Vidar finally said. "She tried to gain my support. She seemed to think that it wouldn't take much to get it."

"Why would she think that?" Thyra asked.

Vidar exhaled slowly, clearly not wanting to answer the question. Unfortunately for him, Bragi was more than ready.

"Because Vidar and Hela were lovers."

"What?!" Thyra spun on her seat and looked at Vidar, who grimaced. "Is that true?"

Again, it was Bragi who answered for him. "It's true. In fact, she was the reason why Vidar agreed to accept the Eye in the first place."

"Wait," Thyra looked back at Bragi and Asiri, "I thought you said it was because he wanted to be stronger than my father. You said it was because he was jealous."

"How many times do I have to hear that?" Vidar growled. "Is a thousand years not long enough for that lie to finally die?"

"What are you talking about?" Thyra demanded.

"I didn't accept the Eye so that I could be stronger than Thor," Vidar said. "I never wanted to be a god! In fact, your father begged me to accept the power the Eye would grant me, and I refused. I wanted to live my life in peace. But they wouldn't let me! So, what did they do? They used the one person they knew could get to me and convince me to accept the cursed gift of the Eye!"

"And you benefited greatly from it," Bragi said in a surprisingly cold voice.

"How did I benefit?" Vidar growled. "I became Odin's enforcer and lost any chance of a normal life! Everywhere I went my name was cursed. And for what? While I was doing Odin's dirty work, the rest of you were living as gods in Asgard. I killed, and killed, and killed again in the name of the Aesir, and it was never enough. What did I receive in return?"

"You became a god," Bragi said.

"I was cursed!" Vidar hissed. "I became a weapon, no more. I became a weapon in Odin's hand that he could use but never have any of the blood on his own hands. I killed so many in Odin's name, I can't even remember them all. You're right that my hands were some of the bloodiest, and I hated myself for every last drop."

"Yet, you failed to kill the one man that needed killing!" Bragi's voice cracked like a whip. His blue eyes danced in anger, as he stared at Vidar in the rear-view mirror. "You should have killed Surtur, but you didn't. You should have been in Asgard to hold the gates against Surtur, but you weren't! Where were you, Vidar? Where was the protector of the Aesir when you were needed?"

Vidar gripped the steering wheel with both hands as if that was the only thing keeping him from diving into the backseat to pummel Bragi.

"Why don't you tell Thyra where you were?" Bragi said. "Why don't you let her know why you failed? Why weren't you there to put the crossbar on the gates of Asgard? Why don't you tell her how your deal with Surtur came to be?"

Vidar's spine went stiff in his seat and he eyed Bragi in the rear-view mirror.

"What's he talking about, Vidar?" Thyra asked.

He ignored the question and turned around to look at Bragi. "How do you know about that?"

"I may be old, but I'm not stupid," Bragi said. "How else could you be allowed to live in peace for so long?"

Vidar turned in his seat, his eyes suddenly dancing with a dangerous light. "How do you know about that, old man?"

"I've had my suspicions for a while," Bragi replied grimly.

"What deal with Surtur?" Thyra demanded.

Vidar looked at her, and she saw remorse briefly reflected in his eyes before the anger returned.

"It was a mistake, Thyra, but I believed I was the last one," Vidar said. "I promised to live quietly, to never try to regain my status as a god, and in return Surtur promised to leave me alone." He looked back at Bragi. "But I never said a word to anyone about it. Never. So how do you know about it?"

"Does it matter?" Bragi scoffed.

"It does to me," Vidar said grimly. "And it should matter to Thyra, too. I never told anyone. Not even Hela when she found me. Only Surtur knew. Him and those in his employ."

"I'm not at fault here," Bragi said sharply.

"No?" Vidar asked. "There's been something off about you. From the moment I saw you, I could feel it, but I didn't know what it was. You aren't the Bragi I remember. In fact, you're starting to remind me of someone else."

"I'd hoped you had changed," Bragi retorted, "but I see that you are still as weak as you ever were. You made a deal with the devil, and now you admit that Hela came to you. What other reasons can you give us to doubt your loyalty?"

"I made a choice to be here," Vidar said.

"Reluctantly," Bragi snapped. "How do we know we can trust your intentions? How do we know you aren't going to betray us and run to Hela?"

Thyra had had enough of the arguing. She was confused and didn't know what to think. Up to this point, she had counted Vidar as being on her side. Now, she couldn't help but doubt where he stood.

"Enough!" Thyra said before the two men could continue. "This needs to stop. I don't have time to waste listening to you two bicker. My mom doesn't have time!"

"Thyra, listen to me," Vidar said, but Thyra put a hand up to silence him.

"Please stop," Thyra said. "Tell me the truth. Where were you when Surtur attacked Asgard?"

Vidar's jaw set stubbornly. "I was with Hela. Odin betrayed her and left her weak. Then he told Surtur where to find her. When I found out what he had done I abandoned Asgard and the Aesir."

"You see!" Bragi said. "He was more loyal to Hela than he was to the Aesir. How can we be sure that isn't still true?"

"When did you become so heartless?" Vidar snapped. "If it was Idunn that had been in Hela's place, wouldn't you have gone to her?"

"No, I would have done my duty," Bragi said coldly. "My loyalty to the Aesir was more important than running to my lover's arms!"

Vidar's face hardened to stone. Before anyone could react, he was out of the truck and was stalking around the front. He came to the passenger side door and pulled it open.

"What are you doing?" Thyra demanded.

Vidar didn't answer. Instead, he reached into the backseat and pulled a struggling Bragi out of the truck. He lifted the older man off the ground and pinned him against the side of the truck amid protests from Bragi and Thyra.

"Put him down, Vidar!" Thyra said as she jumped out of the truck.

He shook his head without looking at Thyra. "This man is not Bragi!"

"What? What are you talking about?"

"I know for a fact that the real Bragi never would have left Idunn alone," Vidar said. "The *real* Bragi put nothing over Idunn, not even loyalty to Odin!"

"Put me down, you fool!" Bragi hissed, but Vidar just pressed harder.

"Use your magic, old man," Vidar said grimly. "Let me see the runes on your tongue!"

"You've lost your mind!" Bragi said through gritted teeth.

"Prove it!" Vidar bellowed. "Prove that you're Bragi! Show us the runes on your tongue!"

He pushed harder, and the cab of the truck began to bend as he exerted more force.

"Vidar, stop this!" Thyra said. "I've seen the runes. He showed them to me."

"When?"

"Two days ago," Thyra said. "Put him down, Vidar!"

Vidar shook his head. "Don't you see, Thyra? This man is not who he says he is!"

"Help me, Thyra!" Bragi said weakly.

"He isn't Bragi!" Vidar repeated emphatically. "Get out the Eye and make him touch it. It will reveal the truth."

"Stop, Vidar!" Thyra shouted. She called up her magic and let it race through her. "We need him. I need him!"

"I'm trying to protect you, Thyra!" Vidar said. He pressed harder, and Bragi's face went a deep shade of purple.

"Stop!" Before she even thought about what she was doing, she threw out a hand and a lightning bolt flashed from her fist. It struck Vidar in the side and sent him spinning away. Bragi slumped to the ground, his limbs shaking from the shock he had unfortunately absorbed. He gasped for air and then coughed as he rolled onto his side.

Thyra stalked over to where Vidar was trying to rise to his feet a dozen feet away. He looked up with red-rimmed eyes, his face a mask of pain.

"He's not who he says he is," Vidar said through gritted teeth.

"As far as I can tell, no one is," Thyra said grimly.

"You can't trust him," Vidar said. He stood up and held out his hand. "Give me the Eye, Thyra!"

Thyra took a step back and held out her hand again. "Don't make me hurt you again."

"Don't be a fool!" Vidar roared. He took a step towards her. "I will not let you endanger the Eye because you're too blind to see the truth."

He took another step but got no further. Thyra unleashed a wrist-thick bolt of lightning that struck him in the chest and threw him backwards again. This time he was much slower to begin moving. Thyra watched him try to get up but he collapsed to the ground again.

Thyra watched him struggle and felt her anger be replaced by an unexpected emotion—sadness. She exhaled heavily and shook her head.

"I wanted to trust you," Thyra said. "Why did you have to mess it all up?"

"You have to believe me," Vidar said hoarsely. "That isn't Bragi!"

"I don't believe you," Thyra said. She turned and began to walk back to the truck.

"Ask him to show you the runes," Vidar called after her. "The runes, Thyra!"

She hesitated briefly but didn't turn back. Inhaling deeply, she walked back to the truck and helped lift Bragi into the truck. She moved around the side of the vehicle and got into the driver's seat. She put it into gear and gave the truck some gas.

"Well," Asiri said softly, "that was exciting."

Thyra clamped her teeth together so hard her jaw hurt to keep from saying what was running through her mind. She had wanted to trust Vidar and being proven wrong about him felt horrible.

She tried not to, but as they drove away, she glanced in the rear-view mirror and saw Vidar standing in the road.

"You did well, Thyra," Bragi said weakly. "He couldn't be trusted."

Those words felt like having lemon poured on an open wound. She returned her attention to the road and did her best to put all thoughts of Vidar out of her mind.

When they got back to the main road, she slowed the truck to a stop and pulled out her cell phone. She opened her call list and found the number Hela had used.

"What are you doing?" Asiri asked.

"Saving my mom," Thyra said.

She tapped the call button and put the phone up to her ear. It rang three times before she heard the line click.

"Tick tock, Thyra Ariksen," Hela said.

"I have it," Thyra said. "I have the Eye."

Chapter 24

Gunnar was sitting in a small coffee shop when he felt the phone in his jacket pocket vibrate. He pushed the long-forgotten cup of coffee aside and set the cell phone on the table in front of him. Ivan looked up briefly from the screen of his own phone and then went back to furiously typing out messages to his network of operatives. The Russian's phone had been buzzing almost constantly as he tried to monitor the situation and coordinate with his men.

Gunnar's personal phone had been quiet, though. And for good reason. There were very few people who were allowed to have the number. Which made him cautious about opening the message.

There was no name attached to the text, but the first few words were all he needed to recognize the source. He had been tracking Asmodeus—no, Baldur's!—cell signal, and he knew that he was close to Thyra Ariksen, but now he knew that he was with her.

The shard of the Eye has been found. Vidar dealt with. En route to exchange with Hela in Monroe. Address and time to follow. Have your men in place.

Gunnar turned his phone face down while he considered how to respond to Baldur's message. It seemed that his silent partner was going to deliver on his promise. Or was it a threat? Either way, Gunnar was sure the result was going to be unpleasant for him.

His phone vibrated again, this time with an address. He spun it around so Ivan could see. The Russian quickly tapped out a message to his operatives with the address attached and instructions.

Gunnar took back his phone and reread the texts. He was surprised that Baldur was sharing details so willingly after the exchange they had a few days before. That made Gunnar think that his partner wasn't as confident as he had been. Which meant Gunnar had leverage.

He picked up his phone and tapped out a quick message. *My men will be ready. When it is over, I want the shard.* Gunnar hit send and set his phone down. It took only a moment for his phone to vibrate and a new message showed up on the screen.

When I get my revenge, you can have more than just the shard.

A smile split Gunnar's face when he read those words. He had come to Monroe feeling like events were spiraling out of his control. Now, it seemed that things were looking up.

He showed the message to Ivan. The Russian gave him a curious look. "What does that mean?"

"It means that my search for the rest of the Eye of Odin might be coming to an end," Gunnar said with a smile.

He slipped the phone back into his jacket pocket and got up from the table. Ivan quickly finished a message and then hurried after him. He opened the car door for Gunnar and then slid into the passenger seat.

"Where to, boss?" the driver asked.

"We're going to check out a piece of real estate I'm interested in," Gunnar said. He gave the driver the address and sat back. A few minutes later, they were driving past an old, rundown building with a gravel lot on the side. It was the perfect place for a shady exchange.

Or an ambush.

"You sure this is the place you were thinking of?" the driver asked skeptically. "Looks like a dump."

Gunnar nodded. "Yes, this is it. This will do just fine."

Chapter 25

Thyra looked around the abandoned building and wondered what had once been here. From what she saw, her guess was that it had been a mechanic's shop, but it hadn't been in working condition for a very long time. Anything useful had been removed years ago and replaced by loads of junk.

She was wondering why Hela had chosen this spot for their meeting when she heard the sound of tires on the gravel outside. She glanced to where Bragi and Asiri stood. They both gave her reassuring nods, but the gesture was hollow to Thyra. She just wanted to get her mom back and have this all be over.

The door opened and her heart leapt when she saw her mom walk through the door. Sif smiled wanly when she saw Thyra, relief clear on her face. Thyra resisted the urge to run to her.

Thyra's attention shifted away from her mom as Hela entered the room. The dark-haired woman looked just as regal and dangerous as she had a few days earlier. Her eyes met Thyra's and held her gaze with an intense stare that made Thyra feel small and exposed.

Fenrir was the last one through the door. He closed it behind him and fiddled with the handle for a second before looking at Thyra with a suspicious look.

"Taken up lockpicking, have you?" He looked at Asiri. "Or was that the dwarf's handiwork?"

Asiri shrugged her shoulders. "Just taking precautions. Wanted to make sure we weren't locked in here with you."

"Afraid I might eat you whole?" Fenrir toyed.

"You'd only hurt yourself," Asiri snapped. "I'm too tough even for you."

"Do you want to put that to the test?" Fenrir said. "I can't remember the last time I tasted dwarf."

"There's no need to antagonize her, Fenrir," Hela said. She gave Bragi a cursory glance, then turned her attention to Thyra. "My, you do have your mother's look, don't you? That braid, your build—it all screams of you being the daughter of the great, Sif. But, those eyes," she smiled grimly, "those are Thor's. It's good to finally meet you. The real you that is."

"I can't say the same thing," Thyra replied.

Hela's eyes touched the lacrosse stick. "An interesting thing to be carrying. Are you planning on going to practice later?"

Fenrir chuckled at the quip, and Thyra gave him a scathing look. They thought they could mock her, did they? Well, she wasn't going to allow them to think she was weak.

"Its name is Lynnedslag," Thyra said. The lacrosse stick responded to its name and lightning crackled to life in the basket. Her display had the effect she had hoped for when Fenrir shifted his weight and his smile wilted. At least partially. Hela looked unimpressed.

"There will be no need for that," Hela said calmly. "I did not come here to fight. You have something I want, and I have something you want. We make a simple trade, and we both walk away. There is no need for unpleasantries."

Thyra's eyes flicked to her mom. "Are you okay?"

Sif nodded. "I'm fine, sweetheart."

"And she will stay that way," Hela said, "as long as you give me the shard. Where is it?"

"I have it," Thyra said. "But I want you to let my mom go first."

Hela shook her head slowly. "That is not how a trade works. You think you hold the cards, but you don't. I'm confident that you value your mother's life much more than you value a shard from the Eye of Odin." Without looking away from Thyra, she raised a hand in Sif's direction. "Should we put that to the test?"

Sif tensed suddenly, a look of discomfort spreading across her face. Her expression turned pained, and she let out a groan.

"Stop!" Thyra said. "Don't hurt her!"

"Hand over the shard, and she goes free," Hela said.

"Will you let her go if I show you the shard?"

A mirthless smile crossed Hela's face and she shook her head. "You are trying my patience. The terms have been set. You give me the shard of the Eye, Sif goes free. There will be no more negotiations. Try to change the terms again, and Sif will pay the price."

"Fine," Thyra said. "I get it. Just give me a second, and I will give you what you want."

She held out her hand and said the words Bragi had taught her. The Eye appeared in her hand with a pop.

"Here it is," Thyra said. She looked up into the cold eyes of the goddess of death. Thyra could see the hunger in Hela's eyes, but the goddess made no move to take it from Thyra.

"You said you had a shard," Hela said. "That is more than a shard."

"I came across more of it," Thyra said.

Hela's eyes flicked up to her face, as if she was trying to read any sign of deceit on Thyra's features. "Where did you find it?"

Thyra looked over Hela's shoulder to her mom. She saw the realization on Sif's face before she even gave an answer to the question.

"I met a witch," Thyra said, returning her gaze to Hela. "She helped me free the shard and gave me the rest."

"A witch?" Hela nodded slowly. "It seems you are better connected than I thought."

Thyra didn't acknowledge the comment. She extended her hand towards Hela. "What are you going to do with it?"

"I'm going to return things to their rightful order," Hela said. She took a wary step forward. "I'm going to do what Odin was too foolish to do, and what your father was too weak to do—create a world where magic rules without question. Our kind will no longer be forced to live in the shadows."

"My father was not weak," Thyra said defensively. "He shattered the Eye."

"When he should have been using it to strengthen his own," Hela said. "The Eye was given to Odin in order to reinforce magic's influence, not to serve as a showpiece. The Allfather lost sight of what he had been commissioned to do. As for Thor, he was always too soft when it came to those without magic. He cared for them too much. As a result, he put his own kind at risk. I won't make the same mistake."

Thyra wanted to argue, to tell Hela she was wrong about her father, but she couldn't. She hadn't known him, and as much as she wanted to hold him on a pedestal, a part of her wondered if Hela was right. Maybe things should have been different.

But that was in the past, and Thyra couldn't change any of it.

"I brought you the Eye," Thyra said. "If you want it so badly, take it."

Hela took another step forward, her eyes locked on the Eye. She began to reach for the Eye but stopped when the door was suddenly thrown open and the last person Thyra had expected—and hoped to see—rushed into the room.

"Vidar?!" Thyra said at the same time Hela said the name. She pulled her hand back and took a step away from Hela.

"What are you doing here?" Hela said sharply.

Vidar looked between Thyra and Hela, his eyes taking in the flaming orb in Thyra's hand. He moved cautiously into the room but stopped when Fenrir rushed forward to stand between him and Hela.

"Down, boy," Vidar said. "I don't have any doggy treats with me today."

"I should kill you where you stand!" Fenrir growled.

Vidar looked past Fenrir to Hela. "Call off your hound, Hela. I have no need for a new pelt to hang on my wall."

Hela put a calming hand on Fenrir's arm and pulled him back. He grudgingly stepped back, but his eyes never left Vidar.

"What are you doing here, Vidar?" Hela asked.

"I came to stop this from happening," he said.

"How did you find us?" Thyra asked.

"Wasn't hard," he said.

"But how did you get here so fast?" Thyra asked.

"He's the god of strength, girl," Hela said in irritation. "Did you think that only meant he could lift heavy things?"

Thyra looked at her in surprise. She hadn't expected such a swift, forceful defense to come from Hela. But maybe she should have, considering what she had learned about their history together.

"I came to protect you, Thyra," Vidar said. He scanned the room, his eyes settling on Bragi. "From him."

"Protect *her*?" Hela asked in surprise. But then his words sunk in and her eyes narrowed. "From the old man? Why?"

"He isn't Bragi," Vidar said grimly.

"This again, Vidar," Bragi said. "This is neither the time nor place for your pettiness."

"Show us your runes then!" Vidar barked.

Bragi started to answer, but it was drowned out as everyone started yelling at once. Amid the raucous, Bragi began moving towards the door. His slow movements seemed to go unnoticed by everyone until he was the closest one to the door.

But that was as far as he got. Hela suddenly yelled, "Enough!" and thrust her hands out toward Bragi and Vidar. Both men froze in place and stayed unnaturally still. Hela twitched her hands and both men stood straight as a board. She looked at Thyra, her eyes wild.

"You are a thorn in my side, girl," Hela hissed. "Not only did you refuse to give me the Eye and let us resolve things peacefully, but you had the gall to drag *him* into this just to spite me." She glanced briefly at Vidar and grimaced. "It seems I don't know him as well as I thought. He spurns me but comes running the moment the daughter of Thor is in peril. The irony is almost amusing."

"What did you do to them?" Thyra asked.

Hela ignored the question. She looked at Bragi and her eyes narrowed. "As for this one, I don't know who he is, but he is not what he seems."

"Let Bragi go," Thyra said.

"Bragi?" Hela asked. She shook her head. "Girl, I don't know why you think this man is Bragi, but your knight in athletic shoes is right. This man is not him. I can feel the darkness in him, flowing through his veins with each beat of his heart."

"What?" Thyra asked.

"Let's see if Vidar is right about the runes," Hela said. She arched her finger at the old man. "Show me your tongue."

Bragi's jaw clenched tight, clearly fighting the command, but ever so slowly his mouth opened wide. Hela flicked a finger and his tongue jutted out—there were no runes!

"No runes," Hela said, curiosity clear in her voice. "So, who is under the mask? Let's find out, shall we?"

She motioned with her head toward the old man and Fenrir hurried over. He began patting the old man down.

"Look for anything a masking spell could be attached to," Hela instructed.

Fenrir continued his search until one of his hands stopped on Bragi's left hip pocket. He started to dig into the pocket when Bragi suddenly jerked and Hela let out a pained scream. She fell to her knees with her head held between her hands, her scream continuing.

Before Thyra could even think, everyone in the room burst into motion. Bragi slammed his elbow down into the back of Fenrir's head, dropping the much bigger man with a thud. Fenrir's body hadn't even hit the floor before the old man was charging across the room toward Hela.

Or, at least that was who Thyra assumed was his target. She quickly realized that the goddess was not Bragi's intended target—she was! She stood rooted in place as Bragi leaped towards her, his hands reaching. She turned her body at the last second and he crashed into her and carried her to the floor. He landed on top of her, his hands already wrenching at her as he searched for something. For the Eye!

Thyra fought to keep the Eye away from him, but one of his hands closed around her wrist and wrenched it back painfully. Just as he was about to pull the Eye away from her, his weight suddenly disappeared. Thyra looked up in time to see Vidar fling Bragi across the room. The old man smashed into the wall with a dull thud and slumped to the ground. Vidar turned to her and offered a hand.

"Come on!" Vidar said. "We need to—"

A black, furry mass suddenly struck him in the side and carried him to the floor. Thyra was shocked to see a giant, black wolf on top of Vidar, its jaws snapping a few inches from his face. Vidar punched out with one hand, his fist connecting with the side of the wolf's head with a bone-crunching sound. The wolf yelped in pain, and then went airborne as Vidar bunched his legs and kicked it in the chest. The wolf landed on its back a dozen feet away but was back on its feet immediately and charged Vidar again. The two met again and fell in a tangle of fur and flesh.

Thyra scrambled to her feet and watched in shock as the two

combatants continued to battle. Vidar gained his feet and lifted the giant wolf off the ground. He twisted and threw the wolf against the wall hard enough that the entire building shook. Vidar followed right behind and speared his shoulder into the wolf's belly. This time, the cinder block wall was no match for the weight of the blow and both combatants disappeared through a hole in the wall.

Across the room, Bragi stood up and shook his head groggily. A gaping cut ran down the side of his face, but amazingly it closed and was replaced by a perfect layer of skin. He looked at Thyra and a chill ran down her spine.

"Give me the Eye, Thyra," he said grimly, walking in her direction.

Hela screamed again and Thyra glanced at her. The woman was still holding her head in her hands and tears ran down her cheeks.

"What did you do to her?" Thyra asked.

Bragi glanced at her and smiled. "No more than she deserved. I turned her own magic back on her. A thousand years of living in a prison of her making gave me time to learn a few things. Like how to turn her magic against her. She'll never touch me again."

He kicked out with one foot as he passed, and Hela fell forward onto her face with a wail. She writhed on the floor, her screams piercing the air.

"Who are you?" Thyra asked.

"Someone you should fear," he said. He came closer and held out his hand. "Now, hand over the Eye."

Thyra shook her head and pulled the Eye close to her chest. "Never."

"Oh, you will," Bragi said.

Thyra heard a gravel-throated roar just before Asiri launched herself onto Bragi's back. The old man stumbled forward under the weight, and then bellowed in pain as the dwarf woman jammed a screwdriver into the base of his neck. Asiri pulled the tool free and thrust it in again as Bragi tried to reach for her.

"Run, Sparks!" Asiri yelled.

Thyra was too shocked to move. She watched in horror as Asiri reached with her free hand and slapped a metal disc against Bragi's neck. An audible pop followed, and their bodies shot apart in different directions. The dwarf woman landed on her back with a dull thud several feet away and laid still. Bragi crumpled to the ground and twitched.

"Asiri!" Thyra ran to where the dwarf woman laid on the ground and fell down to her knees. The dwarf's blue skin was ashen and cold. Thyra checked for a pulse but didn't feel one. "No, no, no, no! Wake up, Asiri!"

"Thyra!"

She looked up just as her mom came sliding to the ground beside her. Sif wrapped her in a hug, but she pulled back suddenly.

"We have to go, Thyra!" Sif said. "Come on!"

"Wait, what about Asiri?" Thyra protested.

"I don't know," Sif said, "but I need to get you somewhere safe."

"We can't just leave her," Thyra argued.

"I need you to be safe!" Sif snapped.

Thyra saw the fear in her mom's eyes and her resistance crumbled. She nodded weakly and let Sif pull her up to her feet. Her mom began to pull her toward the door, but the opposite wall erupted suddenly, and a ball of fur and flesh came flying back into the room. Vidar rolled to his feet and unleashed a wicked haymaker that caught the wolf on the jaw and sent it spinning across the room.

Vidar stood up straight, his face and arms covered in blood. His legs wobbled briefly, but he kept his feet and strode toward where the wolf was struggling to stand. The wolf snapped out with its massive jaws as he got close, but Vidar stomped down on its lower jaw with one foot and pinned it to the floor. The wolf struggled, but Vidar's foot held it in place.

"Eight hundred years," Vidar rasped, "and that's it? I expected more."

The wolf bit down on Vidar's foot, but it didn't seem to bother him. He threw a powerful jab to the side of the wolf's head and it slumped to the floor. The wolf stubbornly tried to fight against Vidar's hold, and it was punished with another sharp blow. This time, it fell to the ground and lay still. Vidar stepped off the wolf's jaw and stumbled backwards, his chest heaving.

"Is that what I think it is?" Thyra asked.

"Not what," Sif said. "Who. That's Fenrir!"

Vidar turned toward them, the wild look in his eyes making his blood-streaked appearance all the more terrifying. He nodded to them, but then he looked to where Hela laid on the ground and his visage fell. He rushed to her side and fell to his knees. He lifted Hela off the ground gently and cradled her in his arms.

"Come on," Sif said, again pulling Thyra towards the door.

Thyra watched Vidar tend to Hela while still allowing her mom to usher her toward the door. They were halfway across the room when she heard a rage-filled roar just before a weight barrelled into her and knocked her forward. She managed to keep her feet, but she dropped Lynnedslag in the process. She spun around to face whatever had just hit her but stopped cold. The dark-haired man from her dream stood with one arm around Sif, and the other holding Lynnedslag to her throat.

"Hello, Thyra," he said in a voice that would have been melodic if it weren't for the pure hate that dripped from it. "It's good to finally see you in my true form."

Thyra stared blankly at this newcomer. In the corner of her eye she saw Vidar gently lay Hela on the ground and stand up.

"I should have known it was you, Baldur," Vidar hissed.

Thyra looked at Vidar in confusion and then back at the dark-haired man. A devious smirk split his pale features.

"You should have listened to Vidar, Thyra," he said with a dark chuckle. "I worried that he was on to me in the hotel room, and even more so in the truck. But I never should have worried. All I had to do was stoke the flames of your distrust and you got rid of him on your own. How could you distrust the sage guide, Bragi?" Baldur laughed mirthlessly. "Just like your father, you let your emotions overrule your sense. Look where it got you."

"You haven't won yet," Vidar said dangerously. "I'm standing right here."

"And you know that you can't beat me," Baldur said derisively. "No matter how many times you strike me, no matter how strong your blows, you cannot hurt me. I feel nothing!" He held up Lynnedslag. "And, now that I hold this, I can hurt you!"

"You can't use it. That's Thyra's," Vidar said, but Thyra heard the uncertainty in his voice. Even worse, she saw the uncertainty on her mom's face.

"You're wrong," Baldur said grimly. He spoke the lacrosse stick's name and lightning cracked to life in the basket. Before anyone could react, he thrust it toward Vidar and a bolt of lightning leapt from the basket and struck the big man in the chest. Vidar was flung backwards into the wall, his head smacking hard against the cinder block with a sickening sound.

"Ah, this is power," Baldur said. "Even when it isn't at its full strength, this weapon still is formidable. Too bad the dwarf will never know how successful she was!"

Thyra looked at Vidar, hoping the big man would get to his feet, but he laid still. She turned back to Baldur and shook her head. "How are you using Lynnedslag?"

"Come now, you already know the answer," Baldur said. "The dwarf explained it to you. It's a matter of blood, remember?"

Thyra thought back to the conversation when Asiri had given

Lynnedslag to her. She shook her head. "But, Bragi wasn't a close enough relation."

"But I'm not Bragi, am I?" Baldur said. "Come now, Thyra. Don't be rude to your long-lost uncle."

His smile grew grim as Thyra began to shake her head. "I don't know who you are, but please, let my mom go."

"I don't think so," Baldur said harshly. He looked at Sif. "Tell her the truth. Tell her who I am."

Sif attempted to pull free, but Baldur clamped down around her neck and moved Lynnedslag closer to her neck. "Tell her!"

"He's telling the truth," Sif rasped. "He is your uncle!"

The revelation was too much for Thyra to process. She shook her head in confusion. "My uncle?"

"Your parents failed you, Thyra," Baldur hissed. "Your mother should have told you about who you were. She should have warned you that your father's *brother* might still be alive." He looked down at Sif. "You should have known I'd come for you!"

"You were imprisoned," Sif said.

"And you should have known that I'd find a way free," Baldur said. "You all should have known that I would come back to get my revenge."

Thyra still couldn't shake the shock she felt. "You're my uncle?"

"Ah, family reunions are truly heartwarming," Baldur said snidely. "Yes, I am Thor's brother!"

"Half-brother!" Sif hissed between her teeth.

"But we share blood all the same," Baldur said without missing a beat.

"How?" Sif said. "How did you escape your prison?"

"Eight hundred years is a long time," Baldur said, his voice quivering with rage. "I found the weaknesses in Hela's magic, and I picked at them for centuries without her noticing." He looked up at Thyra, a cruel smile on his face. "When I escaped my prison and learned that my brother had a child, I knew I had to meet you. I must admit, you are everything I expected in the daughter of my little brother. Not nearly as much of a disgrace as the other two were."

Thyra didn't miss the reference to 'the other two', but she didn't have time to consider it. "Let my mom go, Baldur."

He shook his head. "I hold the cards. You saw what I did to Vidar. Imagine what I can do to Sif?"

"Don't hurt her," Thyra said.

"Then hand over the Eye," Baldur said. He moved Lynnedslag closer to Sif so that the lightning almost touched her skin.

"Okay!" Thyra said. "Just don't hurt her."

She took a tentative step forward and held the flame-ringed orb out. Baldur shook his head.

"Not to me," Baldur said derisively. He nodded over Thyra's shoulder. "To him."

Thyra followed his gaze and was surprised to see a string of armed men flow into the room. At their head was a man Thyra had never met but recognized from the picture on the Muspel Corporation website.

Gunnar Olafsson smiled as his men fanned out, pointing rifles at everyone in the room. "This is more than I ever hoped for! Hela, Vidar, Sif, and Thor's daughter, all in one room. This is almost as exciting as the day I stormed Odin's Hall."

"Enough gloating!" Baldur said harshly. "I delivered on my promise. There's the Eye."

Gunnar's features tensed at the rebuke, but he let it go unchallenged. He slowly crossed the room and stopped several steps short of where Thyra stood. His eyes moved to Thyra's outstretched hand and he licked his lips.

"I get the Eye in exchange for what?" he asked, looking up at Baldur.

"Help me finish what I started," Baldur said grimly. "They're all weak. Finish the job and the Eye is yours."

"Kill them all," Gunnar said carefully, "and I get the Eye?"

Baldur nodded. "It's yours."

Gunnar's eyes narrowed slightly as he pondered the offer. "You don't want the Eye?"

"For the last time, no!" Baldur hissed. "It didn't do anything for me a thousand years ago and it won't do anything for me now. Take it and do as you please."

Gunnar hesitated, his eyes narrowing. Finally, he nodded. "I get the Eye and you get your revenge. We're both satisfied."

"The perfect deal," Baldur said snidely.

"One I can live with." Gunnar said. He held out his hand. "Give me the Eye, Thyra. Do what your father should have done all those years ago."

"So, you can use it to rid the world of magic?" Thyra asked. She brought the Eye back to her side. "Or use it yourself?"

"Don't play with me," Gunnar said. "Your mother's life hangs in the balance."

Thyra looked at her mom and saw the fear in her eyes. That shook her more than anything. She glanced toward Vidar, but he hadn't moved. Hela writhed on the floor, but her movements were growing weaker. With Asiri down, she was out of allies. Not that any of them could have helped her, anyways.

Seeing no other choice, Thyra took a slow step toward Gunnar. She lifted her hand and held the Eye of Odin. She could see the hunger in his eyes as his hand rose to take it from her. Thyra began to put the flaming orb into his hand when Sif screamed suddenly. "Thyra, don't!"

Before she could react, Baldur grimaced and pushed Lynnedslag against her neck. Sif's entire body went stiff as the magic coursed through her. Baldur released her, and Thyra watched in shock as her mom crumpled to the floor.

"Mom!"

Thyra tried to run to her mom, but a hand grabbed her roughly by the wrist and held her in place.

"Give me the Eye!" Gunnar yelled.

Gunnar tried to wrench the orb free from Thyra's hand, but she clamped down on it as hard as she could. Enraged by Baldur's attack on her mom, Thyra refused to let the Eye go. Gunnar stepped in and swung his elbow toward her face with a roar. She twisted away, but the blow still struck her in the side of the head. A mind-numbing pain overcame her senses, but she somehow managed to keep a grip on the Eye of Odin.

On instinct, she summoned her magic and felt it surge to life within her. She looked up and saw hesitation in Gunnar's eyes, the electric blue of her own eyes reflected in his. She balled her fist and delivered a punch that was backed by the full force of a lightning bolt. Gunnar took the punch on the chin and shot backwards. He rolled across the ground and lay still.

A searing pain raced up Thyra's arm and she looked down. She still held the Eye of Odin, but Gunnar's grip hadn't been broken easily. Deep scratches marked where his fingernails had clawed her in an attempt to pry the Eye free.

She looked just in time to see Lynnedslag streaking toward her face. She brought up her arms to block it, but the force of the blow still knocked her down and made her head spin as her entire body screamed out in pain.

"You should have handed the Eye over," Baldur said, wading in. He swung Lynnedslag again, this time connecting with Thyra's stomach and driving the air from her lungs. "You sealed not only your own, but now your mother's death. Say good-bye."

Thyra saw him raise Lynnedslag and point it towards her mom's prostrate form. She felt the magic in Lynnedslag build and she screamed out in protest, "No!"

Time seemed to slow as Thyra lunged for Baldur's legs to try and stop him. In that moment, she realized that she was too far away. She felt Lynnedslag begin to discharge the magic built up inside it, and then everything was bathed in a bluish-white light.

Chapter 26

Time is short.

Thyra opened her eyes and looked up at Yggdrasil. "What? Why am I here?"

You must stop Baldur, the tree said.

"That's what I was trying to do!" Thyra spat. The tree stood silent and her temper flared. She slammed a fist against the bark of the tree. "Is that all you brought me here to say?"

It is imperative that Baldur not succeed, the tree repeated. *I saw this branch of possibility, but it was one I had hoped to avoid. But your choices have led to this point, and there is no going back.*

"My choices?" Thyra asked. "What choices?"

Your distrust of Vidar caused you to walk a dangerous path, the tree said. *If you had trusted him instead of the imposter, things might have turned out very different.*

"You were the one who told me to be careful who I trusted," Thyra said. "You never said who I should be careful of trusting. You said that no matter what, your influence would increase."

I was short-sighted, the tree admitted. *Now I see that if Baldur succeeds there is no positive outcome.*

"Then send me back! He's going to kill my mom."

Which is why I brought you here, Yggdrasil said. *Your mother cannot be allowed to die. Every future I see where she is not in your life results in*

284

catastrophic changes where my influence in the world diminishes.

"Is that all you care about?" Thyra snapped. "Your *influence?*"

It isn't just your mother, the tree said in an irritatingly calm voice. *If Hela dies, the future is very dark.*

"Then let me go back!"

Not until I'm sure you are prepared to do what you must, the tree said with enough sharpness to make Thyra take a step back.

"Do what I must?" Thyra said, recovering quickly from the shock of the tree's sudden outburst. "You keep saying I have to make choices, but that you don't want to influence the result. Now, you tell me you want to help me so that your influence will grow in the future. That sounds self-serving to me."

Think what you will, but in this situation, there is no positive outcome for me, Yggdrasil communicated. *Or for you and those you care for. You must stop Baldur from killing your mother and Hela. Even if it means you have to take drastic action.*

"Drastic action?" Thyra shook her head. "What kind of drastic action?"

You must let Baldur strike your mother with Lynnedslag's magic, the tree said.

"What? You just said I can't let him kill my mom. Now you're telling me to let him do it?"

I will protect Sif with my power, Yggdrasil said. *But, in return, you must do something for me. You must become my champion in this age and pay the price required.*

Thyra wasn't surprised by what she heard. She'd been expecting that the tree would ask this of her sooner or later. "A price? What kind of price?"

Odin gave his eye and his youth, the tree explained. *There were others before him that made sacrifices to be my champion.*

"Your champion?" Thyra shook her head. "I don't even know what that means, but I'm already sure that I don't want to be it. I just want to protect my mom."

If you agree to be my champion—magic's champion on the earth—I will keep Sif safe and I will teach you how to defeat Bragi, Yggdrasil stated.

"But I have to sacrifice something? Pay some price?"

That is correct.

"What price?"

It wouldn't be a true sacrifice if you knew beforehand, the tree replied. *It will be something unique to you and what you hold dear.*

"Like what?"

Do you agree to be my champion?

Thyra hesitated. She didn't like not knowing what the tree was going to do. "Is this the only way I can save my mom?"

The one with the highest likelihood of succeeding. All other paths lead to darkness where either Sif or Hela die. Sometimes both.

Thyra hesitated as she considered the offer. She hated not knowing what price Yggdrasil would exact, but the thought of losing her mom was too much. The choice wasn't a hard one to make.

"If being your champion is what is required to keep my mom safe," Thyra said slowly, "then I accept."

You have made a good decision, the tree said. *I will keep my end of the bargain. I will protect Sif.*

"You said you'd tell me how to defeat Baldur," Thyra said. "What do I need to do?"

You must make the two of us one, Yggdrasil stated.

Thyra flinched. "You mean, you and me?"

No, Baldur and I.

"How do I do that?"

You must unite the Eye with his flesh.

"Do what?"

Strike him with the Eye, and make sure the Eye and his blood become one.

286

He must bleed, or it will not work.

Thyra shrank back from the tree and looked up at the branches overhead. "A bit morbid don't you think?"

If you want to stop him, then you must make him bleed, Yggdrasil said. *You must go. Use the Eye on Baldur. Succeed and there is a path forward for you. Fail, and the future is grim for both of us.*

"Fine. Make him bleed," Thyra repeated. She was about to move away from the tree, but hesitated. "Baldur said that the first time he held the Eye it didn't do anything for him. Why?"

That is a story for another time, Yggdrasil said.

"Why didn't it work for him?" Thyra insisted. "The Eye is what gave the gods their power, but he said it didn't work for him. If I am going to be your champion, I need to know why it didn't work for him?"

The tree was silent for what felt like an eternity. Finally, it answered. *I sensed the evil in his heart and foresaw what he would do if he received the power of a god. I refused to impart my gift to him. That slight festered and he grew bitter. His anger resulted in Freya demanding that Odin find a way to make Baldur equal with all the others. Freya was blinded by her love for her first-born son, and Odin was blinded by his love for her. Freya demanded that Baldur be made impervious to pain and injury. Odin was too weak to say no, and commanded Hela to find a way to make it so. The process was...unnatural, but Hela succeeded. Baldur became the monster you just witnessed, and Hela was both blamed for it, and seen as the one means to control him.*

"She didn't do a very good job," Thyra said.

Evil like his cannot be contained forever, Yggdrasil said. *I've kept you here too long. You must unite the Eye with Baldur's flesh. Remember, you are the storm. Go, my champion.*

Thyra began to protest, but it came too late. She felt a pull that she couldn't fight, and a flash of light blinded her.

* * *

Thyra's roar of rage filled her ears as she returned to reality. She was back in the building and was still diving toward Baldur in an attempt to stop him from hurting her mom. She saw the lightning bolt streaking through the air towards Sif.

As much as she wanted to stop the lightning, she remembered the pact she had made with Yggdrasil. Instead of reaching out and trying to stop the lightning, she trusted that the tree would protect Sif and focused on striking Baldur with the Eye. She swung her hand at his leg, letting the jagged edge of the Eye lead and connected with the side of his calf. She yanked it back and struck again in the same spot, and then pulled it back again when he stumbled forward.

Baldur spun around, his face a mask of pure rage. "You will pay for striking me, girl!"

Thyra pushed herself to her feet and summoned her magic. "Don't count on it."

Baldur hissed and brought Lynnedslag up. "You can't hurt me, girl. I feel nothing, and any harm you do to my body will heal."

The statement made Thyra hesitate. She'd seen how quickly the cut on his head had healed, and so far, nothing that had been done to him seemed to slow him down. She glanced down at the Eye and was dismayed to see the flames burning greedily with no sign of blood on the jagged edge. She had failed, but that only meant she needed to try harder.

"You see the truth," Baldur said in a victorious tone. "You cannot stop me!"

"I am the storm, Baldur," Thyra said. She focused on the ball of lightning crackling in Lynnedslag's basket and commanded it to obey her. It gave no resistance to her call and it leapt through the air to her outstretched hand. "You say you don't feel pain, but have you ever been in a lightning storm?"

She didn't give him the chance to answer. Thyra unleashed a torrent of lightning that struck him in the chest and sent him flying backwards against the wall. Lynnedslag fell from his hand and rolled across the floor towards Thyra and she quickly bent down to pick it up while keeping a close eye on Baldur. He laid still briefly, his torso smoking, but surprisingly didn't stay down for long.

"I felt nothing," Baldur said through gritted teeth, a devious smile on his face. Thyra thought she saw a hint of pain in his expression, though.

"Let me try again," Thyra said. She drew in as much of her magic as she could and then pulled through Lynnedslag. She unleashed it all in a wild explosion of lightning that encased Baldur and burned his image into Thyra's vision. She stopped the flow of magic and blinked away the afterimage. Baldur was crumpled on the ground again, his body scorched and black, but already healing.

Thyra saw her chance and charged at him. She saw a wound on his chest that was just beginning to heal and dove for him, swinging her fist with the Eye straight for it. The wound was quickly closing, and she thought she might be too slow, but her fist struck Baldur just before the wound closed.

Baldur screamed in a mix of pain and rage and reached for Thyra's hand. He ripped it free and held her hands out wide. Thyra realized too late what was coming just as his forehead struck her in the side of the nose. She fell back, seeing stars and struggling to keep from losing consciousness.

She crawled away and turned around in time to see Baldur reach up and pull the Eye free from his chest with a roar. He held the flaming Eye up in front of him and stared at it with pure hatred etched on his face. Thyra saw what held his attention so closely—a line of red blood ran along the jagged edge of the orb.

"You made me bleed," Baldur said, a hint of disbelief in his voice. He looked at Thyra. "Now I will make you suffer!"

He started for Thyra, but the Eye suddenly flared in his hand. The flames ran up his arm and burned greedily at his flesh with a hunger Thyra had never seen before. Baldur screamed in pain, his eyes going wide as his arm turned black. He threw the Eye aside and stumbled backwards, cradling his burnt arm.

Thyra stood up slowly, using Lynnedslag to help her balance. She summoned up her magic again and began to draw in as much as she could hold. After she had filled herself as much as she could, she reached outward like she had in North Dakota and pulled at the lightning in the clouds above. There wasn't as much as there had been that day, but there was still enough, and when she called, it readily answered her call.

The lightning crashed down into her and when she looked up at Baldur, she saw a new emotion on his face—fear.

"You will not hurt me or anyone I care about ever again," Thyra said grimly. "I am the storm!"

Thyra unleashed everything she had into Baldur. Her vision went white again, but she didn't let it stop her. She kept the lightning going until she felt her knees begin to wobble. Spent, she let her hands finally drop down to her sides as thunder rolled outside. She blinked against the afterimages in her vision, and when she finally could see clear enough, she saw a gaping, smoking hole where Baldur had been standing.

Thyra flinched at the sound of a burst of gunfire and spun to her left. Gunnar's men were firing at a stack of tires, riddling the rubber with everything they had. Thyra couldn't see what had their attention and was surprised when a spear flashed through the air and took one of the armed men in the chest. Her mom spun out from behind the tires and followed close behind her spear, her feet churning with inhuman speed. She ripped her spear free, and spun toward the next man, her weapon sweeping out wide to take his legs out from under him and then flash down towards his chest.

The air was filled with the sound of guns going off as Gunnar's men began firing on Sif. None of the bullets came close. Sif danced between them in a blur, spear flashing through the air, and blond braid swinging behind her. In a matter of seconds, all of Gunnar's men were down and the room was suddenly deathly quiet.

As relieved as she was to see her mom alive, Thyra forced herself to look for Baldur. She scanned the room to make sure he hadn't escaped her, but she couldn't see him anywhere. She hoped that meant he was blown all the way to Canada, but something told her that wasn't the case. As long as he was away from here, that's all she cared about for now.

Baldur was gone.

Chapter 27

Thyra's legs gave out suddenly, and she crumpled to the floor. The side of her right knee suddenly went aflame with pain, like someone was driving a hot nail into it. She put a hand to her knee and was surprised to feel her leg bent at an unnatural angle. She gasped as the pain intensified even more. She let out a wordless scream of agony.

Immediately, she felt a pair of arms wrap around her as her mom rushed to her side. Sif hugged her and then moved back when she saw the pained expression on Thyra's face. "What's wrong?"

"My knee," Thyra said. "It hurts!"

Sif looked down at Thyra's twisted leg and her eyes went wide. "What happened?"

Thyra shook her head. "I don't know! Oh, it hurts."

"Lie still," Sif said. She touched Thyra's knee gently, but even the soft touch was enough to make Thyra almost black out. Sif grimaced. "I don't know what's wrong. It could be broken, it could be something else, but it needs to be secured in place. Stay here and I'll go find something we can use for a splint."

"Let me take a look at it," a woman's voice said.

Thyra looked up and saw Hela standing over her. She defensively tried to summon her magic but was too tired and it escaped her grasp. Hela must have guessed at the attempt because she put up her hands.

"Relax, Thyra," Hela said. "You did me a favor by distracting Baldur.

I don't know how he managed it, but he somehow turned my magic against me." She shook her head, and her stare grew distant. "I've never felt such pain." Her eyes refocused and she looked at Thyra. "I can help you. If you let me."

"Help me?" Thyra asked through gritted teeth. "Why should I trust you?"

"Because I am the greatest healer that ever lived," Hela stated.

"You're also the one who abducted my mom and held her ransom," Thyra hissed.

"I healed your mom actually," Hela corrected.

"You were trying to take the Eye for yourself," Thyra said in a pant. "How do I know you won't try to steal it from me?"

"You don't," Hela admitted. Her eyes briefly flicked to where the Eye of Odin laid on the floor, but she made no move to retrieve it. "I only wanted to ensure that Gunnar Olafsson didn't get his hands on it."

"You wanted it for yourself," Thyra said.

Hela sighed. "Trust me or not, I'm the *only* one that can help you."

"It's okay, Thyra," Sif said. Thyra looked at her mom in confusion. "Hela can help you."

Another wave of pain washed over Thyra and she closed her eyes. She'd never felt anything like this before! It was worse than any injury she'd ever had. Finally, she nodded. "Do it!"

Hela bent down and put her hands on the sides of Thyra's knee. Just the touch of her hands was enough to make Thyra scream in pain, but Hela didn't let go. Thyra felt a cold wave of energy course into her and gasped. She felt her leg snap back into place, the pain intense enough to make her almost pass out.

She didn't know how long it lasted, but when Hela finished it felt like she had just run an entire marathon at a sprint. Her heart raced and sweat ran down her face.

Hela removed her hands from Thyra's leg and sat back, her expression one of consternation. "Your wounds are…improved."

"Improved?" Thyra asked. She didn't feel pain radiating up her leg anymore, and she could tell that her nose had been healed. She sat up and tried to test her leg. Immediately, she felt that something was wrong. She tried to bend her leg, but it was so stiff she could hardly manage to move it. "Why is my leg so stiff? I can't bend it."

Hela looked perplexed. "I couldn't heal everything."

"What do you mean?" Thyra demanded. "What couldn't you heal?"

Hela shook her head. "I did everything I could, but your knee refused to be whole. It was like something kept me from making it right. I'm afraid I…I can't heal it."

"Can't or won't?" Thyra demanded.

Hela gave Thyra a scathing look. "No one could fix this! This is something beyond me, or anyone else. There is something blocking my magic from healing your knee. Something more powerful than anything I've ever come across." She shook her head. "I've done all I can do for you, Thyra Ariksen."

Hela's proclamation filled Thyra with dread. How did this happen? Her leg was fine until…until she came back from her conversation with Yggdrasil. Her dread turned to disbelief—was this the price she was going to have to pay? To have her knee blown out?

"I believe this is where we part." Hela stood up. Her eyes went to the Eye of Odin again, but she made no move toward it. She turned on her heels and walked away, leaving Thyra and Sif alone.

"Help me stand," Thyra said, hoping that getting on her feet might help her to loosen the stiffness. Sif carefully pulled Thyra up, but then had to catch her when Thyra's knee gave out under her weight. "What's wrong with me?"

Sif shook her head. "You just need time to heal."

Thyra looked at her mom and saw the concern in her eyes. Something about that look told Thyra that Sif didn't believe her own words.

"Come on," Sif said. "We need to leave. Lean on me. We'll do it together."

She saw Vidar slowly begin to come in their direction. He met Hela in the middle of the room and hesitated. The pair shared a brief conversation that Thyra couldn't hear. Hela shook her head in disgust and walked away. Vidar stared after her and Thyra could tell there was more he wanted to say. His shoulders sagged like a heavy weight had just been placed on them.

Vidar turned to Thyra and Sif, the conflict he must have been feeling forced down. He looked determined. "Someone will have called the police by now. We don't want to be here when they arrive."

"Too many questions," a gruff, gravelly voice muttered. Asiri limped closer and gave Thyra a pained smile. "Did you think you could get rid of me that easily, Sparks?"

"Dwarves have more lives than a cat," Vidar commented.

"Ah, we're just made of tougher stuff than we look," Asiri said. She looked at something on the ground. "Don't forget that."

Thyra followed her eyes to where the Eye sat on the ground. She tried to let go of her mom and walk on her own to retrieve it, but she didn't make it far before her knee gave out again. She fell forward onto her hands and knees. Sif and Vidar both rushed to her side, but she waved them off. Instead of trying to rise, she forced herself to crawl the rest of the way to where the Eye was.

"What's wrong with her leg?" Vidar asked.

Thyra couldn't see her mom's face, but she could hear the concern in her voice when she answered. "She was hurt somehow. Hela said she couldn't heal Thyra's knee."

"What do you mean? Hela can heal anything with enough time. A knee should be a walk in the park for her."

"I don't know," Sif whispered. "She said something in Thyra's knee resisted being healed."

Thyra's hand closed around the Eye of Odin and she rolled to sit on her butt. She studied the damage all around her—the lifeless bodies, the holes in the walls, scorch marks from her lightning—and felt ashamed suddenly. She had been the cause of all of this. Her and the cursed Eye of Odin she held in her hand.

"We need to leave," Vidar repeated. "Someone will have called the police by now. They will be here soon."

Without asking, Vidar came over and carefully lifted Thyra in his arms.

"I can walk," Thyra protested.

Vidar ignored her and started for the door. Sif and Asiri fell in behind them, both limping slightly from their own injuries. Thyra tried to wiggle free of Vidar's grasp, but it was no use. He was too strong, and deep down Thyra knew that she couldn't walk on her own, so she stopped trying to fight it.

"What about Bragi?" Thyra asked suddenly. "Where is he?"

Vidar shook his head. "Baldur still has Bragi imprisoned."

"How can you be sure?"

"Because I've seen Baldur use this kind of magic before," Vidar said. "He used to trap people and take on their identity for a time. He found it amusing. It always took Odin ordering him to release them before he would. You can bet that Baldur won't release Bragi until he is finished with him. If ever."

Thyra closed her eyes and exhaled. Poor Bragi. The old man didn't deserve this fate, and Thyra couldn't help but blame herself. She was who Baldur had come for, and Bragi was just collateral damage.

Vidar stepped through the door with Thyra in his arms. Thyra was glad to escape from the building and the memories it held. A half dozen black SUVs surrounded the building, but no one was inside. There were a few bodies lying in the gravel, but she tried not to look at them.

"The Muspel Corporation," Sif commented grimly. "Gunnar Olafsson won't take the loss well."

"Was he one of the ones you…" Thyra's voice caught in her throat, and she couldn't finish the thought.

Sif shook her head. "No. He got away."

"Which means he'll be back?" Thyra said.

"He will," Vidar said. "And he'll bring more men next time."

"What about Baldur?"

Sif's eyes pinched at the corners and she shook her head. "I don't know."

"Is it true that he can't be killed?"

"Yes," Sif said flatly. "Hela made him impervious to pain by request of Freya and Odin. It was a mistake, and it created a monster."

"I think I hurt him," Thyra said. She held up the Eye. "With this."

Sif glanced at the Eye briefly, but she didn't look confident. "Baldur cannot be killed. He'll be back."

Vidar and Thyra reached the truck and the big man gently put Thyra into the passenger seat. He climbed into the driver's seat and started the truck up.

"What now?" Asiri asked.

"Is your car still in Hudson?" Vidar asked.

"Close enough," the dwarf replied.

"Then I will take you that far," Vidar said. "After that, I think it's best if we part ways."

"Is that it?" Thyra asked. "You drop us off and then disappear?"

Vidar didn't respond to the question. He put the vehicle in gear and tore out of the parking lot. They had driven about a mile down the road when they heard sirens up ahead. Two police cars whizzed by and a fire truck followed close behind. Thyra tensed, sure that they would stop them, but the police cars passed them without a second look.

Once the sound of the sirens faded behind them, she looked at Vidar again. "I think I deserve an answer. Are you just going to leave?"

"You made your feelings about me clear," Vidar said.

"I didn't know who to believe," Thyra said. "I'm sorry. I was confused."

Vidar still refused to meet her eyes.

"Thank you for coming back," Thyra said. "I'm glad you did."

After a long pause, he nodded slightly. "You're welcome."

The conversation died down as everyone inside fell into their own thoughts. Thyra spent most of the ride obsessing over her knee. She massaged it and tried everything she could think of to loosen it up, but to no avail. It was stiff as a board and was not getting any better.

She finally gave up and tried to sleep, but her thoughts wouldn't let her. She knew she should feel better—she had the Eye of Odin, had defeated Baldur, and had her mom back—but for every positive outcome from the past few days, she had a dozen negative ones. Baldur had escaped, she only had a portion of the Eye, and although her mom was back, were they really safe?

Then, there was her knee. She knew injuries took time to heal, but she had a feeling in the pit of her stomach that this was no ordinary injury. Was this the price Yggdrasil had exacted on her to save Sif and Thyra be her champion? If so, would it ever get back to normal? Would she ever be able to play lacrosse again?

Those dark thoughts plagued her all the way back to Hudson. They were just outside the city when Sif finally broke the silence.

"Where will you go, Vidar?"

Vidar looked at her through the rear-view mirror. "Does it matter?"

Sif nodded. "Of course, it does. I know you still blame yourself for what happened, but you shouldn't. The burden placed on you by Odin was unfair. No one man could have stopped Surtur." She took a deep breath. "You should know that you have a place with us. You always have. You are family after all."

Thyra looked between them in shock. "Family?"

Sif nodded. "Something very few knew."

"Not even Hela," Vidar added softly.

Thyra looked between them. "Knew what?"

"Thyra," Sif said, "I'd like you to meet my not-so-little brother."

Thyra looked at Vidar in surprise. He gave her a tight-lipped smile and then Thyra saw it. Vidar had the same eyes as her mother, but it was the smile that Thyra had seen Sif give her thousands of times that really solidified the similarities.

"You two are brother and sister?" Asiri said.

Sif nodded. "We were far enough apart in age that very few ever made the connection. People just assumed that we just looked similar. It wasn't that uncommon back then."

The dwarf snorted. "You Aesir always were a close-knit group. Too close."

"Why am I not surprised?" Thyra said. "I feel like I'm related to everyone lately. The good and the bad."

"I won't ask where I fit on that spectrum," Vidar commented.

"The good," Sif said without hesitation. "We've all made mistakes in life, Vidar."

"Not like me," Vidar said.

"You have a place with us regardless," Sif repeated. "If you want it."

Vidar kept silent, but Thyra could see the conflict going inside him. She could tell that part of him wanted to go with them, and she decided that she needed to help push him over the edge.

"Please," Thyra said. "Hudson won't be safe for you anymore, and our life will never be the same again. If we're together we can at least watch each other's backs. Besides, I'd like to get to have the chance to get to know a family member who isn't trying to kill me or abandon me to the literal wolves. And," Thyra paused and leaned forward to look him in the eyes, "I'd like the chance to earn your forgiveness for not trusting you."

Thyra thought for a moment he was close to accepting the offer, but he shook his head. "I can't. Not yet. I have too many loose ends that I need to take care of."

Thyra sat back with a sigh. She heard Asiri give Vidar directions, but she had already fallen back into her own dark thoughts. They pulled into a parking lot on the eastern edge of town and Vidar put his truck into park. Asiri fiddled with the watch on her wrist and a few minutes later her black Camaro turned into the parking lot and stopped next to them.

Thyra got out of the truck with Sif's help and then turned back to Vidar. "You're sure you won't come with us?"

"Not yet," he said, looking up at Thyra. "You've done your father proud. I know you never knew him, but I see a lot of him in you."

Thyra nodded. "Thank you."

"Luckily for you, you take after your mom in the looks department, though," Vidar said, a small smile making its way across his face. "I told you that my lot was with you. It still is."

Thyra smiled for the first time in what felt like days. "Then I'll be seeing you."

He nodded. "You will."

Vidar put his truck into gear and gave a final wave as he drove away.

"Well," Asiri said suddenly, "I can't say this hasn't been exciting, but I for one think it's time to get on our way back to some peace and quiet."

"It won't last," Sif said grimly. "Not while Baldur and Surtur are both on the loose."

"And Hela," Asiri said.

Sif nodded. She helped Thyra into the passenger seat and then walked around to the driver's side. "It's a long road home. It won't ever be the same for you now."

Thyra nodded. "I know."

Sif exhaled heavily. "Let's go home."

Epilogue

Fenrir grimaced as Hela's magic washed over him. No matter the number of times he had felt her healing touch, it never got easier. It was like being thrown headfirst into an icy river only to be pulled out, thrown into a snowbank, and then dunked in a pot of boiling water. There were times when the healing process hurt more than what had caused the wounds to begin with.

His mistress always said it was easier for the patient if they were asleep, but she had insisted he be awake this time. He had a suspicion that she was trying to punish him for his actions toward Vidar. She hadn't said anything to confirm his feelings, but he knew she was displeased that he had attacked Vidar instead of Baldur. He had put her at risk by servicing his vendetta, and there was no doubt in his mind that the consequences were only beginning.

She pulled her hands away, and the icy river that ran through him subsided.

"There," Hela said. "I healed most of your wounds."

It only took a moment for him to realize what she meant. He tried to stand, but a sharp pain radiated from his right knee and he groaned in pain.

"A small reminder of my displeasure," Hela said.

Fenrir flinched. "I thought he was going to harm you."

"No, you thought you could take advantage of the situation and eliminate Vidar while I was being assaulted with my own magic," Hela said. "Instead of trying to help me, you sought to settle a petty vendetta. I should have left you there for the police to take. Alone, and on death's doorstep."

Fenrir flinched again, surprised by the vitriol in his Mistress's voice. He looked away, unable to handle the shame he felt looking into her eyes.

"But, luckily for you, you failed," Hela said. She reached up and caressed his cheek. "My anger will fade, and you still hold a place in my heart. You will return to my good graces."

Fenrir felt his heart begin to race at the prospect that he might regain Hela's favor. And maybe, just maybe, this time she would see that he was more than just her loyal dog. Maybe this time she would see him for the man he was.

Hela removed her hand and turned away. "Come. I have guests, and you have a task to see to."

Grimacing, he got to his feet and followed his mistress, his injured leg causing him to have a pronounced limp. He descended the stairs slowly with one hand gripping the rail tightly. Hela easily outpaced him and was at the bottom of the stairs before he had even made it down the first three stairs.

As much as he hated showing weakness, it did give him more time to take stock of the half dozen men and women standing nervously in front of his mistress. They were the first to answer Hela's call. From the look of them, he doubted they were anything more than weaklings looking for the protection of someone in a position of strength. They would be more of a distraction than a help.

But they had come, and more would follow. With time, Hela would have her army, with or without the Eye of Odin.

He reached the bottom of the stairs just as his mistress pronounced in a loud voice, "I am Hela, the goddess of death."

He couldn't help but take grim satisfaction from the way their reactions. Even if they had known who had put out the call, actually hearing the name and seeing Hela face to face was still a shock.

Fenrir limped past them and pushed through a door into the back of the barn. He stepped into the mock hospital room and shut the door behind him. Seven men snapped to attention with military precision the moment he entered. Healed by his mistress, the men still wore the same clothes and body armor they had almost died in. Another nine men were lying in beds in a vegetative state. They would join these seven once they were healed and would prove to be a strong foundation to build Hela's army on. They were foot soldiers, but they were valuable ones. They would be the modern-day version of a Valkyrie when his mistress was done applying her magic to them.

"Yesterday," Fenrir growled," you died for the Muspel Corporation. Today, you live to fulfill the wishes of Hela, the goddess of death."

All seven men stared straight ahead, giving no reaction to Fenrir's words. He didn't expect one. They were as close to zombies as it came. Their bodies were healed, but their minds were under the control of Hela. They would do anything that was asked of them.

Including, tearing down the Muspel Corporation from the inside.

* * *

Gunnar Olafsson slipped into his office and shut the door behind him. Things had not gone according to plan in Wisconsin—he had barely escaped with his life!—and he had spent the entire flight back to New York trying to come up with a way to spin the disaster so that nothing reflected back on his company. He knew that if there was even a whiff of the Muspel Corporation's involvement he would have the police and the FBI sniffing around. Even if he managed to appease them, he would still have to deal with the company's Board of Directors.

His mind racing, he didn't notice that someone was sitting in his chair until he was about to sit down. He saw the slightest movement and jumped in surprise, his heart almost skipping a beat.

"Hello, Surtur," Baldur said with a wicked grin, clearly enjoying that he had gotten the drop on his business partner.

Gunnar did his best to put on a calm facade, but inside he had gone cold.

"What are you doing here?"

Baldur smiled. "I thought it was time we talked."

Gunnar's eyes narrowed. "Talk about what?"

"We've been hiding things from each other," Baldur said.

"Like how you were disguised as a high school English teacher?" Gunnar snapped.

"And how you've been creating new ways to tap into the power of those," Baldur said, pointing to the wall behind Gunnar. The wall that served as a mask for the secret room where Gunnar kept his most prized trophies. The room that held Odin's spear and Thor's hammer. "I've known that you've been planning something for a while, but I must admit that I underestimated you. Hacking into your network was eye-opening."

Gunnar kept his expression neutral. "You should know that the firewalls have been changed. You won't be able to get in a second time."

"I won't, but not because of your efforts," Baldur said. He grimaced suddenly and put a hand to his chest. It was brief, but Gunnar was sure he saw pain etched on the other man's face. Baldur regained his composure and his smile reappeared. "I don't want to hide things from you anymore. I failed in getting my revenge, and you failed in obtaining the Eye of Odin."

"Because you went behind my back," Gunnar said.

"My point exactly," Baldur said. "From now, I want our partnership

305

to be exactly that. And, as a peace offering, I wanted to lighten your worries."

"How do you propose to do that?"

Baldur toyed with a tablet lying on Gunnar's desk with one hand. "You'll be happy to know that there will be nothing linking our company to what happened in Monroe, Wisconsin."

Gunnar didn't like Baldur's use of 'our company', but his irritation was overcome by curiosity. Baldur slid the tablet over to Gunnar and sat back in the chair with a pleased smirk. Gunnar picked up the tablet and read the headline at the top of the page.

"'Electrical surge in abandoned mechanic's garage.'" He glanced at Baldur who motioned for Gunnar to keep reading. "'Police and emergency vehicles were called to an abandoned mechanic's shop outside of Monroe last night when neighbors reportedly heard gunfire. Upon arrival, officers found the building empty but severely damaged. The cause is still undetermined, but authorities have suggested that the building's outdated electrical may have led to an electrical surge that started several small fires, including one that came in contact with a pair of propane tanks that exploded, blowing holes in the side of the building. The combination of all events also resulted in what authorities are calling an arc discharge that resembled lightning neighbors reported seeing. No injuries were reported.'"

Gunnar tossed the tablet onto the desk and looked at Baldur. "An electrical surge? Small fires? Do people actually believe this?"

Baldur shrugged. "All that matters is that there will be no suspicion placed on me, you, or the Muspel Corporation."

"I don't understand," Gunnar said. "When I escaped there were at least twelve of my men down, and vehicles registered to my company sitting in the lot. Where did they go?"

"Our company," Baldur corrected. "And, the answer to that question is what should worry you. Hela was never one for leaving behind one she thought could be healed. Even if they were already dead."

"You're saying that you think Hela took the bodies with her?"

Baldur nodded. "Which creates a very interesting logistical issue for our company."

Gunnar found himself nodding. He saw the danger as well. Twelve well-trained Muspel operatives, each one possessing technology sourced from Gunnar's experiments on the weapons he took from the Aesir and other magic users, could become a major threat. If Hela did have them under her control, she could use them to infiltrate Gunnar's company, and possibly get close to him. If he put out a warning to the other operatives, he risked questions being asked, and people sticking their noses where they didn't belong.

"What do you suggest we do?"

Baldur smiled. "Prepare for war."

Gunnar nodded. "War it is."

"I will begin preparations," Baldur said.

He stood up and began to walk towards the door. Gunnar was surprised to see another brief grimace on Baldur's face as he came around the desk, and his hand again went to his chest. Baldur played it off by adjusting the buttons of his shirt, but he wasn't a good enough actor to hide it from Gunnar.

Gunnar waited until Baldur was gone before taking a seat behind his desk. He steepled his fingers as he tried to piece together what he had just seen. Was it pain he saw on Baldur's face? If so, did that mean Baldur was no longer invulnerable to harm?

A smile began to play at the corners of Gunnar's mouth as he considered the notion. If true, it was something Gunnar could use in the future to make sure this partnership went in the right direction.

Or, perhaps to end it once and for all.

* * *

Modi swirled his drink slowly as he watched the fight in the ring. The combatants had taken the fight to the mat, the smaller man surprisingly finding his way on top and unleashing a series of devastating elbows to the bigger man's face. Unlike the rest of the onlookers in the bar, Modi wasn't cheering to see blood spilled. In fact, he was bored with it.

He took a sip just as the smaller man's elbow found a way through his opponent's guard with bone crunching effect. The blow elicited a loud reaction from the crowd. That kind of hit usually spelled the end of the fight, and the fifty or so onlookers were already beginning to call for bets to be settled.

They were wrong to think the fight over. Modi knew better.

With an enraged roar, the bigger man threw his opponent off of him and scrambled to his feet. Blood ran down his face and into a beard that had a hint of red in it. As always, Magni had waited for a taste of his own blood before his temper flared. Now that he was on his feet, the fight wouldn't last long.

Modi felt bad for the smaller man. He was skilled and Modi applauded his brazenness in taking on an opponent that easily outweighed him by eighty pounds. But, like all the others who dared face Magni in the cage, the man was going to be beaten within an inch of his life when all was said and done.

Magni struck his chest with a fist repeatedly and roared in rage. The smaller man backed up and began to circle around, his bravado diminishing some in the face of the sudden change in Modi's hulking brother.

Magni stayed in the center of the cage and let his opponent dance around him. The smaller man snuck in and delivered a quick set of strikes that did little more than anger Magni more. It happened two more times and still Magni made no move to block or retaliate. If this had been a sanctioned fight it would have been stopped due to

Magni's refusal to defend himself. But in the underground fight circle there was no referee and the fight only ended when someone either tapped out or got knocked out.

Modi watched his brother take another series of blows and rolled his eyes. Magni was playing with the smaller man!

"Finish it!" Modi yelled out.

Magni must have heard him over the rest of the crowd because he suddenly sprang forward and delivered a wicked left hand that sent the smaller man staggering.

"Finally," Modi mumbled. He took another sip of his drink and watched his brother ruthlessly dismantle the smaller man. In the matter of a few seconds, Magni was standing over his bruised, bloodied, and motionless opponent. The crowd had gone silent, shocked by the sudden and violent end to the fight. Even the most bloodthirsty of them was stunned by what they had just witnessed.

All except for Modi.

He rose from his seat with a sigh and slowly made his way over to the bar to collect his winnings. As always, he had put a bet on Magni. It was an easy way to make sure he always had enough money in his pocket to keep gas in the car they shared and drinks in Modi's hand. He ignored the glare he got from the bookie and walked took a seat further down the bar to wait for his brother.

He was nursing another drink when he heard a news report on the TV. At first, he only heard snippets, but something caught his attention and he looked up.

Modi got the barkeeper's attention and pointed to the TV. "Hey, can you turn this up?"

The barkeeper retrieved the remote from behind the bar and obliged. Modi watched in silence as a set of images flashed across the screen and a brunette reporter laid out a series of strange events that had occurred over the past few days. Unexplained electrical phenomena

THE EYE OF ODIN

in a farmer's field in Montana, a massive lightning storm in North Dakota, and an old mechanic's shop destroyed by an arc discharge and two propane tanks exploding. With each passing unexplained event Modi's hair began to stand on end and put a sinking feeling in his gut.

Modi watched as the story continued, a series of grainy pictures taken with cell phones crossing the screen. Most were just of the storms or were long distance shots lacking in any detail.

"We also continue to follow the situation in Hudson, Wisconsin, that left several men in the hospital and resulted in significant damages to both a hotel's property and that of the Muspel Corporation, a telecommunications company based out of New York City," the reporter said. *"While the identity of those involved has not been shared, a picture from the event has been released. Here we see a picture that the submitter says shows a girl glowing with what he said was lightning. All efforts to track down the identity of this young woman have been inconclusive. Police have given no indication if they believe these events are linked."*

A picture of a girl running with her back to the camera filled the screen. Modi jumped over the bar and snatched the remote from the startled barkeeper. He quickly paused the newscast on the image and replaced the remote in his hand with a bottle of whiskey.

By the time Magni found him, Modi was on his fifth shot. Magni took one look at the shot glasses lined up and sneered at his younger brother. "What's with you? I won."

He tossed an envelope bursting with bills onto the bar, but Modi ignored it. He downed another shot and steeled his will.

"We have a problem," he said.

"Yeah, you drink too much," Magni said, taking a seat on the stool next to Modi. One look from Modi was enough to wipe away his cocky expression. "What kind of problem?"

"The *little sister* kind of problem," Modi said.

Magni gave him a confused look, and Modi pointed to the TV and the image frozen on the screen. Magni's eyes narrowed as he read the words on the screen and studied the picture. The picture was grainy, but there was no doubting what it showed—a blond-haired, teenage girl with lightning striking her. Or *shooting out* of her.

"Impossible," Magni said.

"You have a better explanation?" Modi snapped, his eyes flashing with magic. He took a deep breath to get himself back under control and looked back up at the screen. He shook his head. "It seems dad was busier than we thought."

Magni clamped his jaw shut and began to breathe heavily through his nose. Modi already knew what his brother was thinking before he said it out loud, because he was thinking the exact same thing.

"It looks like we need to pay our little sister a visit."

The Lightning Goddess continues the fight!

Enjoy an excerpt from the next adventure in the Lightning Goddess story,
***The Garden of Iduun*!**

Chapter 1

It felt like waking from a long, dreamless sleep.

When his gray-blue eyes opened, he couldn't help but feel confused when he saw the blue of the sky through gently swaying tree branches. Somehow, it felt wrong, but he couldn't put his finger on why.

Sitting up slowly, he looked around at his surroundings. He was on a soft bed near a lush garden ringed by mature trees. The moment his eyes touched the garden, an overwhelming sense of peace flooded into him and washed away the confusion he felt. He knew that he belonged and was safe as long as he was in this garden.

Rising to his feet, he took an awkward step forward. A sharp pain lanced up his left leg and he sucked in through his teeth. He reached down and rubbed at this thigh. To his surprise, he felt a half healed wound beneath the soft, woven pants he wore. He couldn't remember where it came from. In fact, he couldn't remember anything that had happened before he woke up. As hard as he tried, everything before a few moments ago was a blank.

He walked carefully into the garden and slowly wove his way between the lush bushes and trees. He looked for some sign that he wasn't alone, but didn't any. He knew instinctively that a garden like this didn't just spring up on it's own, which meant there had to be a caretaker somewhere nearby. With no direction in mind, he wandered aimlessly, breathing in the smells of the garden and enjoying a ripe, red apple he took from one of the trees.

He had just finished with the fruit when he noticed a woman in a flowing white dress watching him from the edge of the trees. Shocked by her sudden appearance, he stopped in place and stared at her. She returned his stare without making any attempt to speak to him.

Finally, she turned and began to stride away deeper into the garden. Even though she had given him no sign, he felt confident that she wanted him to follow her. Still cautious, he matched her pace in order to keep some distance between them. He didn't know where he was or who she was, and he felt caution was better exercised and not needed than the contrary.

It wasn't long before the sound of people talking was carried on the breeze to his ears. They emerged into a clearing where a dozen other men and women dressed in a similar fashion to him were milling around. He could tell from their expressions that they were just as confused about what was happening as he was.

The woman he'd followed walked to the center of the clearing and turned to face him. He stopped a few steps shy of where she stood and waited for her to speak, taking the moment to get a better look at her. Her brown hair was swept over one shoulder and framed a face that he couldn't put an age to. Her vibrant green eyes sparkled with youthful exuberance, but she carried a maturity that made him think she was older than she appeared.

"You must have questions," she finally said. Her voice was melodic, and he had a sudden urge to ask to hear her sing.

Brushing aside the strange feeling, he asked the most obvious of his questions. "Who are you? Where am I?"

"You are in my garden," the woman replied.

"How did I get here?" He asked.

"I brought you here," the woman said. "You've been asleep for a long time. You were the last one to wake. The others have been waiting."

"We were all asleep?" he asked, scanning the faces around him.

She nodded. "My garden is a place of rest for those who need it.

314

You, of all people, were in need of rest."

"Rest from what?"

"Life," came the cryptic response.

He shook his head slightly. "That doesn't make sense."

"No," she said slowly. "I suppose it doesn't. Suffice it to say, you were very near death when I brought you here to heal."

His eyes narrowed. "Heal from what?"

Her eyes drifted to his left leg. "You walk with a limp. I was never a gifted healer, and your leg was the least of my concerns. Time does mend wounds, though." Her eyes rose to meet his. "Perhaps with time, your leg will regain its strength."

"I don't understand," he said. "How was I wounded?"

"In battle," she said. "Not just any battle. *The* battle—Ragnarok."

The sound of the name tugged at something deep inside, but it slipped through his fingers before he could grasp it.

"I don't remember a battle," he said.

"It was the only way to heal you," she explained. "I had to shield your mind from the trauma of your body or risk the passage of time claiming you."

"How long have I been asleep?"

"Almost a thousand years."

The response made the hairs on his neck stand on end. How was that possible? He looked around the clearing at the faces gathered. The unease he felt was reflected on their expressions as well.

Turning back to the woman, he asked his first question again. "Who are you?"

She smiled. "My name is Iduun."

Again, the name tugged at something buried deep down, but he couldn't penetrate the fog that covered his mind. Grasping onto a sliver of hope, he asked the question he hoped would help push the fog away.

"Do you know who I am?"

Iduun nodded, a curious expression on her face. "You look different with both of your eyes."

"Both of my eyes?" he asked in surprise. "Was I missing one before?"

Iduun nodded slowly. "It was taken from you. It seems that it's been returned. I wonder what that means for you. Perhaps another has been chosen."

"What do you mean?" he asked. "How could it be missing and then be returned?"

She ignored his question and continued to study him. "Your time here has changed you. It's changed all of you."

"If you know something about me," he said, a twinge of impatience entering his voice, "please tell me."

"Are you sure you want to know?" Iduun asked. "The answer may be a burden."

"How could knowing who I am be a burden?"

"Knowledge always requires a sacrifice," she replied cryptically.

"Only because the sacrifice makes the knowledge all the more precious." While it was his voice that spoke, they didn't feel like his words. Taking a moment to gather himself, he continued. "I want to know who I am. Please tell me."

"What if you aren't the same as you were?" Iduun asked. "What if you can't be the man you were before? Would you still want to know, even if there was a chance that what was in the past might never be again?"

He nodded. "I want to know."

"Very well," Iduun said. She drew herself up, the underlying nobility in her bearing coming fully to the surface.

"You are Odin, and you've been dead for almost a thousand years."

That name—his name—sent a bolt of energy through him. Odin, the Allfather, leader of the Norse Gods! Some of the fog that covered his mind retreated and he remembered sitting in a gilded throne with a strange orb ringed in blue flame hovering above a pedestal at his side. It wasn't much, but he clung to the memory with everything he had.

"I did in Ragnarok, didn't I?"

"Yes," Iduun said, "and no. When I found you, there was still a small spark of life left in you. It was enough for me to fan back into a flame. It took centuries, but the passage of time means nothing here."

"Why?" Odin asked. "Why did you save me?"

"Because," Iduun replied, "I knew the day would come when you would be needed." She looked around at the faces gathered. "When all of you would be needed?"

"Needed for what?"

Iduun's eyes turned sad and she took a deep breath. "To fight the real battle of Ragnarok."

About the Author

The author lives in Idaho. When he's not writing, he enjoys taking risks, making mistakes, and getting his hands dirty alongside his vivacious wife and three young daughters.

www.ingramcontent.com/pod-product-compliance
Lightning Source LLC
Chambersburg PA
CBHW071532110726
47908CB00007B/1847